LOVING IVY

KAT RYAN

LOVING IVY

Developmental editing by Sue Brown-Moore, SueBrownMoore.com

Proofreading by Victory Editing

Cover Design by Elle Maxwell of Elle Maxwell Designs

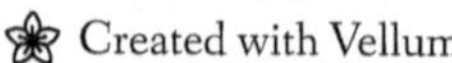 Created with Vellum

HOT CHOCOLATE AND MELLOWS

Ivy

The windshield wipers swept back and forth yet still couldn't keep up with the snow coming down. Our little town of Highland Falls looked like a snow globe come to life. I took a deep breath as I worked to relax my white-knuckled grip on the steering wheel. Saying a silent prayer of thanks for the four-wheel drive on my Jeep, I glanced in the rearview mirror.

Addie.

My four-, almost five-year-old was staring out at the swirling flakes with naked joy clear on her face. Maybe I needed to take more cues from her. I chastised myself for not seeing the beauty in what Mother Nature had seen fit to send us today.

"Whatcha thinking, babe?" I called back to her, smothering a yawn as I did so.

"Beautiful, Momma. So beautiful."

That's my girl. She recognized beauty. I prayed to the goddess that would always be the case.

I turned my focus back to the road. Who would have

predicted a freak snowstorm in early November in Illinois? Thankfully, owning my bookstore in the downtown area of our town allowed me the freedom to close up shop when Addie's preschool dismissed early because of the storm. I'd rushed out to pick Addie up but gone back to get everything officially shut down for the day. Now I was kicking myself for the lost time when I could have gone home with relatively clear streets. I was just praying that I could get us both home before it got much worse or before I dissolved into a puddle of exhaustion.

"Ads? What are you thinking we should have for snack today?" I called back.

"Oooohhhhh, Momma. Hot chocolate and mellows, 'kay?" she sang to me.

Sounded perfect.

The road showed no tire tracks, just a blanket of powdery white. It had been coming down for a few hours, and I'd hazard a guess we had three inches so far. Not as much as a January storm might bring, but for the first storm of the year, it was nothing to dismiss. Judging by the empty streets, the folks of Highland had decided it was a good afternoon to hibernate at home. Not far now, only a few blocks to go.

I turned onto Main, and my tires locked, sliding us around the corner and right up onto the curb. Son of a biscuit. My heart was hammering out a new rhythm as I looked back at Addie. She was grinning.

"Momma, what was that?" she asked with wide eyes. Well, at least she seemed to be having fun.

Deep breaths. I closed my eyes and focused on centering myself in peace and stillness, just like in my daily yoga practice. When I trusted myself to be calm, I called back. "Wasn't that fun, baby? Like a ride, right? Momma has to check it out, okay?"

"'Kay, Momma."

I wrapped a scarf around my neck, my mind already racing ahead to how in Hades I'd get us out of this one. I pulled on my gloves and then started at a knock at my window. The handsome face outside spiked my heart right back up to dangerous levels.

Jake Spencer.

When Addie and I moved to Highland Falls last spring, Jake Spencer was one of the first guys I met. To be fair, the first time we "met," he wasn't aware of me. I'd been practicing yoga on the screened-in porch of our home in the early hours before Addie woke up, and Jake had run by with his dog. And no shirt. Dang. First, my eyes found the adorable chocolate Lab. Even with the gloriousness that is, unfortunately, Jake Spencer, I will always check out a dog first. Upon setting my sights on said dog, I noted that the pup's leash was wrapped around their owner's waist. When my eyes traveled there, I saw an honest-to-goodness in-the-flesh V of muscles.

You know those two lines of muscles in the lower ab region? I thought they were fictional, but here was real-life proof. The sweat rolling down his abs pulled my eyes up his chest, and I literally fell out of tree pose. The gratitude I felt for his headphones knows no bounds. I would have been mortified if he'd seen me. That memory was still vibrant even seven months later. So you can imagine my excitement when I ran into him at the brewery he ran with Cole Sullivan called the Homestead shortly after I opened my bookstore. Unfortunately, it was then that I learned, while beautiful, he was a bit of an ass. And quite possibly a misogynist. So that's that.

Since then, for whatever reason, the two of us seemed incapable of being in the same space and not needling each other. I knew I was just as guilty as he was. I'd meditated on the struggle repeatedly. I'd never had someone bring out my desire to be *right* like Jake did. It just wasn't in my nature. I'd find the peace within, pledge to be civil the next time I saw him, and then immediately resort to childish name-calling or teasing within minutes of being in his presence. At this point, I was willing to give up and just say that it was what it was. We didn't need to be friends.

Even if I did want to run my tongue along his abs. Just a little bit.

"Ivy, open up, for Christ's sake," he said as he pounded on my door.

"Who's that, Momma?" my girl piped up from the back.

"Sully's friend, baby. I'm going to see if he can help us." I would be civil to this man in front of her. Part of being a parent was acting like a grown-up. I'd figure out how to do that if it killed me.

"Scoot back," I called as I pushed my door open and slid out. My feet disappeared into the snow. Dang. I was grateful I was in some boots today.

Jake scanned me up and down before using his hand to gesture from my head to my toes, then back. "What is this?"

I looked down at myself, then back at Jake. "What do you mean?"

"Your clothes, babe. I mean, what's going on with the flowy bathrobe?"

I swallowed back the comment that begged to come out. "It's a kimono, Jake."

"Where's your jacket?"

I fought the eye roll, but it might have slipped. "I didn't have one."

"Sweet Lord, babe. You need a jacket in a snowstorm."

"Realize that, *babe*. I didn't pay attention to the weather this morning. Luckily I had a scarf and gloves in the car. We're almost home anyway."

"You've got about five more blocks until home, *Ivy*. And you aren't going there without a jacket or in a Jeep with a busted tire."

"Busted?" I trudged around to look at the front tire on the passenger side. *Crapola.* I had no idea how I'd done it, but the tire was moving toward flat.

"Snickerdoodle," I swore.

"Snickerdoodle?" Jake was standing far too close for comfort.

"Can we get it off the curb and change the tire so I can get us home?"

Jake looked over the tire situation, then at my back seat. Addie waved at him. His face softened, and he tapped the window at her and waved back. My heart fluttered. Apparently today was the day for it to malfunction.

"Hate to say it, Ivy. But I think you and your daughter need to wait out the storm in my house. You shouldn't be driving on a donut in this. I'll get it off the curb and into my driveway. Then after the storm lets up, I'll change your tire."

Stay in Jake's house? The tug-of-war between brain and heart began. I mean, it was Jake's house. That wasn't a hardship. Or it wasn't as long as we didn't dissolve into three-year-olds fighting over the last cookie.

Be the adult, I told myself.

Taking a deep breath, I looked at him. Large snowflakes clung to his jet-black hair. He had a day's worth of stubble on his face. For all the grief he'd given me over my attire, he stood before me in a Henley and an unbuttoned flannel as well as a pair of jeans that were so worn I wondered if they'd split when he changed my tire. Small prayers. In short, he looked amazing.

"Thanks, Jake. We'd love to crash with you for a bit if you're sure." Let's hope he'd been too distracted to notice I was checking him out. Gracious. I needed to get myself under control.

"Great. Grab your stuff. I'm the white house right here. Will your kid mind if I carry her?" He walked around the Jeep to Addie's door, boots sinking into the snow with each step.

I was torn between swooning over him wanting to carry Addie and wanting to volunteer as tribute to take her place. *Deep breaths*, Ivy. I needed to grab some lavender oil out of my bag.

Jake met my eyes as he reached her door. "Ivy?"

Shaking my head, I found the ability to speak again. "No, Addie will likely love to be 'up high,' or that's what she says when Max or Sully pick her up."

He nodded and opened her door.

I made my way around as I heard him say, "Hey Addie, I'm Jake. Your mom said I can carry you into my house. Is that okay with you?"

I wanted to congratulate him on asking for her consent but figured that might have us devolve into one of our arguments. This sure didn't seem to be the same guy whom I'd gone rounds with repeatedly since summer about the feminist movement.

"Hiya, Jake. Our Jeep is up high," Addie said, doing her own version of jazz hands.

Jake laughed. "Yep, it sure is. I'll fix your car in a bit." He leaned over to unbuckle her harness. I watched as he made sure she was zipped up, mittens on, scarf wound around, and hat pulled down. My little grinchy heart began to melt.

"Jake?" Addie looked up at him from under her hat. It was riding a bit low. I waited with a grin. She was using her sweet voice that she brought out when she wanted something.

"Yeah, peanut?" he replied. Yep, the old heart was melting a bit more. *peanut?*

"Do you have hot chocolate and mellows?" she asked as she reached out for him to pick her up.

"Mellows are—" I began.

"Marshmallows. Got it, Steinem. I've got nieces."

Lordy. A few words and I longed to grab some snow and pelt the man in the face. "Not an insult, Jake. I'll gladly be compared to Gloria Steinem until the end of time."

Jake shook his head at me and turned toward his house as he shut the Jeep's door. Wrapping his arms around Addie, he murmured, "Yeah, peanut. I've got hot chocolate and mellows. Want some?"

Addie squealed and wrapped her tiny arms around his neck. I opened the door to lean in and grab my purse as I worked on convincing myself that this would all work out fine.

I know. I didn't believe me either.

2

DANCE PARTIES

Jake

As I set Addie down in the foyer, I tried to adjust my jeans surreptitiously. Jesus. What Ivy did to me. Every. Damn. Time. It didn't matter that each time we'd run into each other, I'd resolve to be the better person. Each conversation devolved into teasing, her insistence that her stance was always right. She was no better than my siblings. Somehow, she simply got under my skin. Seven months in, I was beginning to think she was dug in and not coming out.

Frankly, I wasn't sure I wanted her to.

There was a gentle tug on my sleeve, and I looked down into the most gorgeous pair of blue-green eyes I'd ever seen. Well, unless I caught Ivy's gaze; then it was a tie. While I'd seen Ivy and Addie around town since they arrived this summer, this was my first chance to actually meet Ivy's daughter.

Addie peered up at me from under her hat. "Mel-lows?" she whispered in a singsong voice.

Thank God for my nieces. I was prepared for this pint-sized visitor. "You bet, peanut. Let's get your layers off first though."

Woof.

Chief was voicing his displeasure from the kitchen where I had him gated in. Patience, dude. It had only been twenty minutes or so since I pushed him in there after seeing Ivy's Jeep jump the curb. What I hadn't divulged to Ivy was the small fact that most likely it wasn't her fault. There was a large pothole right before the spot where her Jeep now rested. In the blanket of snow, it was likely covered. I had a feeling she'd hit it before popping up on the curb. While the woman could be maddening, I was grateful she and Addie were completely unscathed after that bit of excitement.

A gust of wind blew in as Ivy rushed through the door, slamming it behind her. I looked up from unzipping her daughter's jacket to see the pink tint on her cheeks, shivering lips, and curves. Oh holy hell, those curves. She drove me to the brink, but I couldn't deny my attraction to her. If I tried, the tightness down below would proclaim me a liar. However, I'd learned my lesson long ago and worked to school my reaction.

"You know, you wouldn't be so cold if you had a coat."

"Sure know how to welcome someone into your house, Spencer," she said as she looked at me with what I assumed was likely an unintentional eye roll.

Ivy stomped snow off some, I had to admit, kick-ass brown-and-turquoise cowboy boots. Gloves and scarf tossed on my hallway table, she worked to tug off her boots as she hopped around on one foot, making faces at Addie. Her breasts swaying as she moved did nothing to help my condition.

Woof!

"Give me a minute, Chief," I called, finally getting Addie's jacket off her as she squirmed around.

"Where's your puppy?" She peered around the front half of the first floor. The living room fed into the dining room. The kitchen led to the back half with the den and bathroom. Addie plopped down on the lowest stair where the staircase started in the foyer to the upstairs and looked at me with her pleading big-eyed gaze. Damn, I'd be a sucker for anything she'd ask for.

"In the kitchen. Do you like dogs?" I was now actively ignoring Ivy. Seemed like a good self-preservation technique. Then we wouldn't argue, and I wouldn't want to explode before tackling the woman to the ground. Win-win.

"Yessssss!" she hopped up, raised her little hands, and spun in a circle. Damn. The kid was cute.

"Ads," Ivy called. "You need to get those shoes off before you walk around Mr. Jake's house."

"'Kay, Momma." She plopped down right where she was and began tugging at her shoes, sticking her tongue out in concentration. With a huff of defeat, she plopped onto her back and stuck a foot in the air in my direction. "Mr. Jake, help?"

I smiled at her scrunched-up face. "Just Jake, peanut." I took a step toward her and grabbed the foot to unlace her shoe.

"Addie." Ivy used a mom tone that shouldn't be attractive, but whatever. "What do you say?"

"Sorry. Please help, Mr. Jake."

"Gotcha, Addie, but just Jake. I'm no mister." I tossed one shoe to the side and grabbed her other foot.

"I'll say," I heard Ivy mutter under her breath.

"'Kay, Just Jake. Where's the puppy?"

I shook my head again; this kid was killing me. "Chief's

gated in the kitchen, but you can let him out. He won't bite, but he might lick you. Just be gentle."

"Got it." Addie looked up. "Want to see me run? I'm so fast I'm invisible."

I looked over her determined face. Her blond waves were tumbling over her shoulders and down her back. She was a miniature Ivy but sweet. She had on striped leggings and some dress on top that had a mind-numbing pattern with planets and stars. While she only came up to my waist, she seemed to have a huge personality in such a tiny package.

"How will I see you if you're invisible?"

Ivy laughed as she moved out of the foyer and to the living room couch to the side. She dropped onto the leather sectional, then curled up in the corner, watching us. As she met my eyes, she raised a brow in a pseudo challenge. I noted that there were shadows under her eyes, like she hadn't had enough sleep.

Got this, I tried to telegraph to her. She smirked, so who knows what message came through. My eyes ran over her fitted jeans, white shirt that clung just right, and that flowy thing that she called a kimono. While I knew she and Addie shared similar hairstyles of long wavy blond hair, today hers was up in some type of knot on her head, with a scarf wrapped around the base of the knot. She could be in an old photo from Woodstock and wouldn't look a bit out of place.

Addie began to run in a circle around me, her arms pumping furiously. "See, Just Jake? I'm so fast I'm a blur."

Laughing, I leaned down and grabbed her around the waist as she attempted to take another lap around. She giggled as she swung on my arm by her belly. "Enough running, peanut. How about some hot chocolate and mellows while we go meet Chief?"

"Yes!" Addie put her arms out like she was flying. "Does Chief like to dance?"

I propped her waist against my hip as I held her out so she could fly. My nieces used to beg me to do this for hours. Damn if I didn't miss them. Chicago wasn't far, but just far enough. Pausing our journey to the kitchen, I looked down. "Why would a dog dance?"

Addie let out a sigh that seemed to be old beyond her years. Apparently, that was a ridiculous question. "Just Jake, we *have* to have a dance party when we make the hot chocolate and mellows."

"A dance party?"

"Yes, we need to dance." She squirmed a bit in my grasp. "Fly please."

I shook my head as I headed for the kitchen. How had this pint-sized dynamo taken charge of my whole house already? As we moved to the back of the house, I heard a bit of laughter coming from Ivy.

"I heard that!" I called.

"Bet you did, Just Jake," she called back.

Good Lord. My relaxing Friday afternoon seemed to have taken a turn.

Addie and Chief were immediate best friends. Chief was a chocolate Lab just a bit older than she was. He'd be six next summer. And while my nieces weren't over daily, or even weekly, he'd grown up with kids around. When we came into the kitchen, Addie immediately requested to be put down. Once I complied, she marched over to Chief with all the assuredness of someone much older and, it must be said, bigger.

"Chief, sit."

The darn dog sat. I mean, he was trained and all, but this was not a trick he performed for my nieces. Come to think of it, who knows if they'd ever asked him?

Addie had put her hand out. Looking him in the eyes, she said, "Shake."

Chief raised his paw and put it in her tiny hand.

She shook with him. "My name is Adaline Marie James, but you can call me Addie. It's nice to meet you."

And with that, she dropped his paw and wrapped her arms around his neck. Two seconds later, she popped up and shrieked, "Dance party." I briefly wondered if one could spike one's hot chocolate when drinking with a four-year-old or if that'd be frowned upon.

My phone was on the kitchen counter. I grabbed it so I could do Addie's bidding. I mean, I could tell her no, but what fun would that be? "Do you know any bands, Addie?"

She began to bounce on her toes. "Yessssss. My favorite band is Fleeing Max. Do you have their music?"

Fleeing Max? I ran the name around my mind for a minute before hitting upon a possibility. "Do you mean Fleetwood Mac?"

She spun until her dress billowed up around her. "That's what I said, silly. My favorite song is 'Dreams.' Do you dream, Just Jake?"

I was exhausted simply trying to follow this conversation. The most unsurprising part of it would be that Ivy's daughter would love Fleetwood Mac. I mean, Ivy could be Stevie Nicks's love child, or at least they could share a wardrobe. I clicked Play on the greatest hits.

"Yeah, peanut, I dream. You ready to make some hot chocolate?"

"And mellows!"

"Heck yeah, can't forget those mellows." I moved to my cabinets and grabbed some hot chocolate mix that Sully had given me. Seems his grandma used to make it all the time. I'd been using it in my coffee for what Sully called a redneck mocha. Damn good stuff. I grabbed the marshmallows—sorry, *mellows*—the electric teakettle, and three mugs. I filled up the kettle and switched it on. I looked to Addie and worked to school my smile. She was swaying around Chief, who just sat still, looking at me, seeming a bit overwhelmed.

I see you, Chief. *I see you.*

"Addie, do you want to dance or sit up here to help?"

"Help, help!" she said, bouncing on her little feet.

"Can I pick you up?"

"Yep!" she said as she spun again. I wondered if Ivy had the kid in dance. Seemed like a natural fit. Thinking back to Ivy, I glanced up, wondering if she'd followed us in here. Nope. Maybe she was snooping around the house. Wouldn't shock me.

Giving Addie a spoon, I directed her to put a spoonful in each cup as I waited for the water to heat. Watching her, I guessed that these beverages would be extra chocolatey. Worked for me. I turned off the kettle before it heated all the way up. If Addie was like my nieces, she wouldn't want it too hot. Pouring it in, I then set the kettle down and helped her stir the mixture. We grabbed a few mellows for each one.

"Mine isn't all the way to the tippy top, Just Jake," Addie pointed out.

"We can make more, peanut. This way it won't spill so easy," I said, sliding her to the floor and hooking the three mugs on my fingers to carry them into the living room.

"Good idea. I spill sometimes," Addie said quietly.

"We all do, kiddo. No biggie. Want to go give some hot chocolate to your mom?" I nodded toward the living room.

"And mellows!" Addie said as she started running toward the living room.

Following her, I heard Chief behind me. We got about three steps out of the kitchen before Addie came flying back toward me.

"Shhhhhhh, Just Jake and Chief. Momma's asleep!"

Wow, that was fast. "Okay," I whispered. "Let me check on her."

We moved like a little train with me in the front, Addie in the middle, and Chief bringing up the rear. Addie grabbed my leg around my quad and whispered, "See?"

Sure enough, Ivy was curled up on the couch, and damn it all, she was a vision. She'd let her hair down; blond curls flowed over the pillow. I took a deep breath, noting that my heart was thudding. Yeah, I could get used to seeing this woman napping on my couch, her kid entertaining me in the kitchen. But I wasn't going there, not with her, not with anyone, right? Still, she still looked cold. I put the mugs down on the coffee table with a glance to Chief that had his butt hitting the floor. I grabbed a throw from under the coffee table and put it over her, tucking it in around her arms. Turning back to Addie and Chief, I grabbed our mugs.

"Addie, how do you feel about cartoons?"

Her little jazz hands shot to the sky.

3

———————————————

SURPRISE SLEEPOVERS

Ivy

I woke up in a fog. Dang, that was a hard nap. Glancing around, I had a moment of confusion until I saw a glimpse of Addie's purple coat on the hall bench by the front door. That's right, Jake's house. Tossing the blanket to the side, I paused. I didn't remember a blanket, just a feeling of sheer exhaustion from the work of opening a small business seven months ago, keeping up with a four-year-old, and dealing with a freak November snowstorm. Being a single mom was hard but worth it.

Speaking of being a mom, I went off to look for my kid.

First, I hit the kitchen. I saw signs that Addie had been here, namely a dusting of hot chocolate mix on the counter, open bag of marshmallows, and a teakettle. Seems like they'd had their hot chocolate celebration. I wondered if Addie convinced Jake to have a dance party? I chuckled. Surely Jake needed me to relieve him. Most thirtysome-thing-year-old guys didn't want to spend their afternoons with a four-year-old.

Before continuing my journey, I glanced out the

window. It appeared the snow had stopped. That was good, at least. I saw my Jeep was in Jake's drive. Hmm. How'd he move it with Addie in tow?

Glancing around, I noted that there was a short hall that led away from the kitchen and living room. Heading that way, I followed the sound of a TV. A door on my left was cracked open. Pushing it open, I peeked in. With one look, I saw a place I wanted to disappear into. It was a den lined with bookshelves, Pinterest-level cozy. Books overflowed the shelves, as did photos and mementos. Who the heck would have pegged Jake as a reader?

Directly across from the door there was a fireplace with a TV above. And on the sectional across from that with his back to me sat Jake. I silently moved toward the couch. Jake sat there in the corner, his legs stretched out on the sectional. As I drew closer, I saw Addie curled up with her head on his lap. She had a blanket thrown over her, Jake's dog resting his face on her feet.

Jake's eyes came to meet mine. "She's out," I whispered.

"Takes after her mama," he whispered back.

"I need to wake her so we can head home." I tried to ignore the pounding of my heart. *This man is an asshat*, I told myself. Nope. No impact. The cuteness factor of my daughter sleeping on him was threatening to veto any claims of Jake's general asshole-ness that I brought up.

Whatever.

Jake slid out from under Addie and replaced his lap with a pillow. With a quiet "Stay" to his pup, he gestured for me to follow him.

I smoothed the blanket over Addie and then put a hand on the pup's head. "Good dog," I murmured. I looked up and saw Jake leaning against the doorframe, watching. His eyes met mine, and I could swear something was there.

Then he blinked and turned back toward the kitchen. Holy mixed signals, Batman.

I shook my head and headed after him but left the door open so Addie could find us when she awoke. As I reached the kitchen, I noted that the sun was beginning to set. Heck, what time was it? I didn't wear a watch, and my phone was likely somewhere back with my purse.

Jake came to rest at the island, leaning back against it to watch me. "Nice nap?"

I felt my face heat a bit and stamped down my irritation at my own body's reaction to this man. So what if I fell asleep? I bet he would too in my shoes. "Yes, it was. Thank you," I replied as I worked to remove any sarcasm from my voice. "I'm not sure what time it is, but I should probably get home. You're likely ready for a normal Friday night at the brewery. We'll just get out of your hair."

"Slow your roll, gypsy," he began.

"Gypsy?" I interrupted.

"Addie had us dance to Fleetwood Mac. Seems to fit you," he said, scanning my body.

"Stevie Nicks is a goddess," I replied automatically. Truth needed to be spoken. Always. "However, gypsy is considered to be an ethnic slur."

"I'm sorry, what?" His brows drew together as he studied me.

I took a breath, wondering if this would be another long conversation with Jake. "*Gypsy* is a term Europeans used to refer to the Romani people when they came to Europe from northwest India. They are the largest ethnic minority in Europe and have faced great persecution over the years, including having millions of their population murdered during the Holocaust. They have asked that the term gypsy not be used. It's reinforcing racist stereotypes and dehumanizes a group of people. And really, it's the least we can do."

"So you're just going to strike that Fleetwood Mac song from the history books?"

Sigh. "No, of course not. But as Maya Angelou said, 'When you know better, you do better.' Of course I will still listen to Fleetwood Mac, but I will work not to use a term that has been said to be hurtful. It's not a hard ask."

"Okay then. Well, babe…"

Jake glanced at me with an eyebrow raised. I rolled my eyes in response.

He ignored me. "As I was trying to get out before, you're not going anywhere."

"But—"

"Ivy, let me finish. I called Sully and Harp for help with your Jeep. They swung by because Sully was closing up at the brewery."

"Closing?" I glanced around and found a clock on his stove. It was four thirty. The brewery didn't close until midnight or later.

"Patience is not one of your virtues, huh? At any rate, Sully and Harp swung by. I didn't want to leave Addie in here while you were sleeping and no one to watch her…"

Dang it. Heart melting. I needed to get out of this place ASAP.

"…so I called them. They got your Jeep in the drive before heading home and share two bits of information. One, your tires are crap. It's no wonder that the pothole took one out."

"Pothole?"

"Two, the weather forecast has changed. We have some freezing rain coming, starting anytime and continuing for the next few hours. The snow will likely be gone, but a layer of ice will be left in its wake until the warm weather coming tomorrow swoops in and leaves us with a muddy mess. Got to love Illinois. If you don't like the weather, wait a few moments, and you'll get something new. And so we're back to my comment about you not going anywhere." Jake leaned back, crossing his arms and looking pretty pleased with himself.

I took a breath. Then another one. I didn't like the word hate, but I strongly disliked men that seemed to feel like they knew it all. Mansplaining, if you will. While Jake might be right, I really wanted to tell him to take his ones and twos, and shove them.

Come on, Ivy.

Another cleansing breath and I was in a better place. I could do this. "Jake, thanks for that information. And the guys are likely right, I do need new tires. It's just with getting the bookstore off the ground, things are tight—"

"Ivy, you can't drive on bald tires. That's not safe."

Damn, he actually looked concerned.

"You're right. I meant to get them changed last week. I actually had an appointment to take the Jeep to Brian's shop on the edge of town. But Addie got sick, and I moved it to Monday, never thinking we'd be hit with a winter storm so quickly. Anyway, it's not raining yet. I'll just carry her the few blocks home and come back tomorrow for my car."

The words had no sooner left my mouth than the sound of sleet filled the kitchen. I glanced out the windows and back to Jake, only to find him watching me.

"As I was saying, freezing rain starting anytime," Jake said, the corner of his mouth sliding up in a small smirk. "So can we just accept the fact that you two are my houseguests this evening and move on with the night?"

Jake and I in the same house all night long? I might

combust. I could kill him. Or I could leave the trail of drool in my wake anywhere I went. It was a toss-up.

None of these were good options.

"Okay, okay, okay, we're staying." Yep, my heart began a new rhythm. Nothing to worry about here. Carry on. "So, um, what time did Addie go down?"

Jake glanced at his watch. "A little after four, I'd say. We watched some crazy show called *Paw Patrol*."

I groaned. "Sorry. She can watch that one for hours."

He smiled, running a hand through his hair to push it back. Dang. "Anyway, after two episodes of it, she decided she wanted to dress up Chief and wrapped her scarf around his neck."

"Lordy," I whispered.

"Then we danced some more before she asked me to make up stories. Second story in and she was sawing logs. Not sure what that says about my storytelling abilities."

"No, she often still naps around three each afternoon. I was thrilled when I saw her preschool got out at two here and they try not to have them nap at school. I guess a lot of parents don't want their four-year-old to nap, but I'm all about it. Addie is a night owl if I let her. She naturally likes to stay up until nine but sleeps until nine. School days are, of course, a bit earlier."

Jake's face registered some surprise. "Twelve hours typically?"

I laughed. "Yeah, her naps are usually short, just enough for her to get all that energy wound up again. She goes to a day care after preschool each day. Teri lets her take a little catnap when she arrives, then she's raring to go when the big kids come from elementary school to hang out until the parents arrive. I'll have to wake her up soon, though. This is later and longer than her usual siesta, and I don't want her to struggle to go to sleep tonight."

Jake nodded, then moved to his fridge, opening it to peer in. "I don't have a ton of food, but there are some staples in here for sure. What does Addie like?"

I moved behind him, carefully leaving a space between us, though the clean woodsy smell of Jake made me want to take a deep inhale. It was calming somehow.

Jake looked over his shoulder at me, waiting.

"What was that?" I asked.

Jake's grin was a bit much, like he knew what I'd been thinking. "I said what does Addie like to eat."

I shook my head and focused, looking around him at his fridge. "I can make her a grilled cheese and cut up some fruit."

He looked thoughtful as he nodded, then glanced back in his fridge. "Hmm, how about some chili and cornbread for us?"

"Sounds good." I leaned around him to grab the butter and cheese. As I did, his scent washed over me again. I wobbled a bit, only to find my balance when Jake placed his hand on my lower back.

"Easy, babe." His voice reverberated through me. I didn't know if I had the willpower to be around this man for the next fourteen hours or so. Didn't anyone in town own a sleigh they could get us home in?

I moved away from him, placing my ingredients near the stove. "Bread?" I'd just pretend that he wasn't making my entire body tremble. Denial was my friend, after all.

Jake pointed to a cabinet near his fridge. While I located the bread, he got a skillet out for me, dropped some strawberries on the counter near a cutting board, and started moving around to gather everything to make the chili.

"Want something to drink?"

I considered his question. I mean, on the one hand, a beer sounded like perfection. On the other hand, did I really need anything lowering my inhibitions right now? Oh Goddess, I could use some guidance. Hmm, going with the gut seemed like the right call. "Sure. Beer, if you've got it."

"Own a brewery, babe. What's your pleasure?"

"We're back to babe?"

"What do you prefer?"

"Or, I don't know, my actual name?"

"I like a nickname, Ivy. You have a good point with gypsy, so I landed on babe. What else? At the brewery this spring you shared that you identify as a green witch, whatever that means. I could go with that. Or should I search for something else?"

"Good memory," I murmured. "What was it Addie was calling you? Just Jake? Be careful, she does love to give out nicknames too."

"So, *Ivy*, I have an IPA, a stout, and a Belgium Wheat."

I considered his list. "Are you putting any beer in the chili?"

His eyes widened in surprise. I bit back my irritation. I mean, I can cook. Jake looked in his fridge and grabbed several items before turning to me. "Yeah, I think I'll use the stout. We started this last fall, and it has gotten better with each batch. It has hints of coffee and chocolate, which would work. Barn Owl Stout. Do you want that to drink too?"

Sounded good.

I nodded, and we began to work in silence until Jake leaned over and put his phone near mine on the counter.

"Do you have dance parties like Addie?"

I gave him a small grin. "Who do you think taught her?"

He tilted his head toward his phone. "It's hooked to the speakers. Maybe start playing some music, and the sleepy-head will join us?"

I placed the assembled sandwich in the skillet to begin to brown before wiping my hands on a towel and grabbing his phone. I opened his music app and looked over the selections. "Thoughts on Van Morrison?"

"'Moondance' is amazing."

"Agreed." I hit Play and let the music flow through me.

I was a pretty happy person generally, but our dance parties had started because since Addie was little, I helped her find joy in music. While I was never the girl at the party that people watched because she knew how to dance, I'd wager a bet that people watched because I let the music fill me up. Not every artist had that impact on me, but so many did. When those songs began, my eyes would close, my body would sway, and I'd be overcome with a feeling I couldn't describe. It would bubble right through me. Pure magic.

"Dance party, Momma!" Addie came running out of the den with the dog right at her heels. Whelp, she was up. Addie ran right at Jake and wrapped her arms around his thighs.

Jake grinned as he bent to scoop her up. Addie let loose a peal of laughter. My heart clenched at the ease of the two of them together. Nope. Not happening.

"Chief is dancing too," Addie called out as the pup spun in circles, chasing his tail.

I watched this man who drove me batty spin with my daughter, and my eyes began to fill up. To give myself a moment, I turned to the stove and flipped her grilled cheese.

As my phone began to vibrate, I grabbed it without looking at who was calling.

"Hello?"

A pause, then a woman's voice. "Hello? Is this Jake's phone?"

Sugar cookie. I glanced down at the counter. My phone was still sitting there. Oops.

I took a breath before looking at Jake, who was obliviously dancing with Addie.

"Yes, it is. Would you like to speak to him?" Great, I was probably talking to one of his hookups.

There was a longer pause, then she spoke again with amusement lacing her voice. "No, I'd actually love to know who's answering my son's phone, if you'd like to share."

Oh holy Moses. This was out of my league.

I held the phone out to Jake. "Jake?" He looked over at me and stopped spinning. "Your mom is on the phone."

His resigned expression was priceless.

4

THE BLESSINGS OF FAMILY

Jake

Taking the phone from Ivy, I made quick tracks to the living room. I'd need all my wits about me for this conversation. Margot didn't play.

"Hey, Mom. What's up?" I asked, coming to a stop in front of my sectional and staring off into the rapidly darkening night. The sound of sleet surrounded me.

"No, what's up from you, son? Spill. Who was that lovely voice, and what are you hiding?"

Damn. I felt an intense desire to have my brother Drew here. Drew was much better at deflecting Mom from conversations he didn't want to have. Namely, since we hit our midtwenties, when were we going to settle down and make her and Dad grandparents over and over again? Never mind that our sister had two daughters. Never mind that neither of us had been in a serious relationship in some time. Never mind that I had spent the past decade actively avoiding anything serious. Margot wanted more. I couldn't get too mad; our parents were the best. Mom could just be a bit much at times.

"Easy, Margot."

"Don't you Margot me, young man. Start talking."

It was dark enough that my reflection now stared back at me in the window. The look I gave myself was one of knowing. I was sunk.

"A friend, Mom. Her Jeep got stranded, and I helped them into the house—"

"Who is them?"

Crap. "Um, well, Ivy has a four-year-old daughter, Addie."

I could almost feel my mom vibrating with excitement over the phone. She called out, "Sam, *Sam*! Jake has a young lady friend over, and she has a four-year-old daughter named Addie."

Sweet Lord. My dad's muffled response was in the background. For such a chill guy, I wondered how he'd made it all these years with my mom. "Mom. Yo, Mom! Stop the wedding plans. I'm just helping her out..." My voice trailed off. It was no good. She was in a full conversation with my dad. Might have to wait this one out.

"So, wedding plans?"

I spun around to be met with Ivy's mischievous smirk. Good Lord. I did a nice thing today, and the shit just kept hitting the fan at every turn.

"Is that her?" Super, Mom was back. Some kind of sixth sense at work here. Clearly.

"Yes, Mom. We're getting ready to have dinner. Can I get back to you before you reserve the hall?"

"Now, Jacob, hush. I hope you're taking care of this girl. Make sure you've got dinner set up for her daughter. And for goodness' sake, do not start flirting with her when she's at your house and had a rough day..."

"Mom! I've got it. Now, I really need to get going." I

looked away from Ivy, praying she couldn't hear my mom's side of this conversation.

"Okay. I was just calling to remind you that your dad and I'd be staying at your place next weekend for the celebration. Is that okay, or will your lady friend still be there?"

Jesus. I could use some backup here. Looking at Ivy, no help was coming from there. She watched me with an expression bordering on delight.

Addie chose that moment to make her presence known as she tore down the hall from the kitchen with Chief. "Juuuuuussstttt Jaaakkkkke!" she screeched, running at me at full tilt. Bless her and her trusting nature, she leaped at me, and I immediately snagged her midjump, even while my phone was propped between my shoulder and my ear. "Who ya talkin' to? Do they want to have a dance party?"

"Dance party?" My mom's voice now sounded like she was trying to hold back some laughter. "And *Just Jake?* Sounds like you have your hands full, son."

I tried to do some damage control. "Ivy and Addie live down the block, Mom. The guest room is yours next weekend."

"Down the block? Then I look forward to meeting them when we're in town. Now, I'll let you get back to your guests. Love you."

Click.

I let Addie slide down as I looked at my phone. Damn, she really had hung up on me. My eyes found Ivy's, and I noticed her amusement had only increased in the past few minutes.

"Nope, don't say a word," I growled out as I looked over at Addie, who was dancing with Chief. I made a mental note to head to the butcher shop tomorrow and get Chief a bone. He was doing more than his fair share at the moment.

Ivy jerked her head toward the kitchen in a clear indication that I should follow her. For whatever reason, I found myself doing exactly that. Following her swaying hips down my hall was no hardship, that was for certain. The movement almost hypnotized me, but then I realized she was talking.

"I'm sorry, what did you say?"

Ivy spun to look at me from her spot by my island. Her smirk increased in wattage by at least double. "I said, *Just Jake*, that I was looking forward to meeting your mom next weekend."

"What? No, no way, no how."

"Whyever not?"

I was momentarily distracted by Addie racing around the island with her little hands dancing in the air. Chief was following her like the champ he was. Addie skidded to a halt in front of me, spun around, and said, "Want to see my shimmy, Just Jake?"

Looking at Ivy in confusion, I looked back at Addie. "What's a shimmy?"

Addie immediately began to dance while shaking her body back and forth. Lord help us all. After about thirty seconds, she called, "Momma, music." She took back off toward the living room.

"Do you care if I connect to your Wi-Fi to play some more music?" Ivy asked while scrolling.

"What?" I shook my head, trying to clear it from all that was whirling around. "No, that's fine." She handed me her phone, and I put in the info and then handed it back. My phone vibrated in my pocket. Who was calling now? My luck it would be Lou Williams. She and her husband, Verdell, ran around with the grandparents in town, and she was the queen of all gossip for Highland Falls. The way my luck was running tonight, she was calling for an exclusive for the town's social media page.

Sliding my phone out, I was relieved to see a text instead of a call. Even better, it was the group text I always had going with my siblings. Moving over to the window to get out of Ivy's way as she was plating Addie's food, I opened the message.

"I'm going to finish browning the meat for the chili," Ivy called over, doing her own shimmy to Fleetwood Mac as she moved. Watching her, I was hit again with how right it was to see her in my house, cooking in my kitchen.

Pull your shit together, I told myself. My phone vibrated again. I looked down and wished I hadn't.

Steph: *Who's Ivy?*

Drew: *This is fun, sis. Are we doing a guessing game?*

I groaned. Getting to our sister, Steph, was an unfair move by Mom. I wouldn't be hearing the end of this for a while.

Me: *No one. She's just a neighbor who needed some help, and because Mom's timing is impeccable, she called when Ivy was here.*

Drew: *Wait a second. Is this Bookstore Ivy?*

Steph: *Bookstore Ivy? Tell me more.*

Fuck my life.

Drew: *Seriously? Jake hasn't told you about Ivy? That's all I've heard about for the past six months or so. She drives him crazy, but I think he protests too much.*

Steph: *Interesting. What else do you know about her?*

Drew: *She has a kid, somewhere in the range of one to six-years-old.*

Steph: *Good Lord, Drew. That is not a range. That's half of childhood.*

Drew: *Can we go back to focusing on the fact that Jake has the hots for a woman with a kid?*

Me: *Am I needed for this conversation? And Drew, go to hell.*

I moved back to the island and jerked open a drawer. Dropping my phone in it, I slammed it as the vibrations continued.

"Well, aren't we in a mood?" Ivy said.

"My siblings have turned into nosy busybodies," I growled. I moved around to stand next to her. Grabbing the can opener, I opened the beans and tomatoes, dumping them in the pot of beef and onions that Ivy had browned. She grabbed some seasonings and starting adding them in, no measuring spoon in sight. I debated pulling one out for her, but this was chili. It would likely be good no matter what.

The growler of stout from the brewery was still on the counter. I poured a bit into the pot, then filled up our glasses. While I could still hear the vibrations from my phone, the music, beer, and smell of great food were all doing the work of relaxing me.

Ivy gave the chili another stir. She leaned over the pot to take a deep inhale. "That smells amazing. Just needs to simmer for a bit."

I nodded, trying not to make it obvious that I was staring. But Ivy, steam, beer, some chili simmering—it was a lost cause. "Yup. Longer the better."

She tilted her head as she looked at me. The notes from "Gypsy" began to flow out over the kitchen, and she raised an eyebrow. "So, *Just Jake*, do you feel like having a dance party?"

Just like that, my relaxed mood vanished.

I cleared my throat. "What are you asking, Ivy?"

She raised a brow as she came toward me, that kimono/robe thing billowing around her. Coming to a stop in front of me, she said, "Hmm, we've progressed to my name again?"

She slid her hands up to my shoulders. My arms found their way around her lower back without a conscious decision on my part. She began to sway with my body following suit like she was in charge. Or maybe she was. What in the ever-loving hell was happening? My heart was hammering out a new beat. Dang.

"I just love dancing, Jake. Thought you seemed a bit tense. That's all."

Closing my eyes, I decided to stop questioning what in the hell my life had become tonight and just go with it. I pulled Ivy closer until her body was flush with mine, her breasts pressed into my chest. We moved by the window, and I watched our reflections. Ivy's eyes were closed, her gorgeous hair cascading over her back. I couldn't see my hands—they were under this kimono thing—but I had a strong desire to let them move south and rest them on her ass. What was my life?

The notes of Fleetwood Mac continued to surround us. I could hear Addie talking to Chief in the living room. The vibrations sounded from the drawer again.

Ivy chuckled. "You think that's still your siblings?"

She started to pull away, but I tugged her back against me. "Probably."

Her head rested on my chest. I wished like hell that we were skin-to-skin. Damn. I couldn't think that right now or Ivy was going to be feeling more than the beat of the music.

"Why are they bugging you?"

Where to even begin? "Well, tonight it seems my mom called my sister to tell her you were here."

This time Ivy did pull back so she could meet my eyes. "And that's newsworthy?"

I felt my brows draw together. "What do you mean?"

"Well, I can't be the first women your mom found out is at your house. Why the five-alarm fire via text?"

"I don't have women here."

Now Ivy pulled back completely. I hoped she never tried to play poker, her face was not made for it. She appeared completely confused. "What do you mean, 'I don't have women here'?"

I controlled the eye roll that wanted to spring out and moved to stir the chili. "What I said. Women don't come here."

"So are you a monk?"

I laughed. "Hardly."

"So you hook up, but no one comes here." Ivy didn't look too broken up by that. I had to admit I wish she had, at least a little. What was up with that? "What about your family? Do they ever meet anyone you are dating?"

"Nope."

My phone called out from the drawer again.

Ivy looked from it, back to me, then outside. Her quiet expression made me a bit nervous.

"Ivy? What?"

Turning to face me, she grinned as she pulled my phone out and handed it to me. "Just thinking this visit with your family is going to be a lot of fun."

My heart beat ramped up again. "Um, no. *We're* not visiting with my family. I am."

Ivy shook her head at me as she moved to bring Addie's dinner to the chairs at the island. "Addie, dinner," she called. Looking back at me, she smiled. "Your parents are coming for the brewery's anniversary party, right?"

"Yeah." I had no idea where this was going.

"Well, I already told Emma I'd be there that night. I have a sitter and everything. And I can't wait to meet your mom. She sounds like a hoot."

Addie came running in then with Chief. She scaled the bar stool to begin devouring her grilled cheese and strawberries. My mind whirled while I set out Chief's dinner.

Glancing down at my cell, my day went from strange to a disaster. Or, at least a large headache.

Steph: *So it's settled, right?*

Drew: *Yep. Meeting you all at Jake's this weekend for the party. Clear off the couch and the basement, bro. We'll be there with bells on.*

What in the hell? Drew was coming back? Now? Steph and her family lived up in the suburbs near my parents. It wouldn't be as surprising as Drew coming in from Colorado.

Me: *WTF. I don't have time to scroll back through the novel you two have left on here. You guys are coming this weekend?*

Drew: *Wouldn't miss it for the world.*

My mom was going to meet Ivy in a week. My siblings were coming into town. This could only end in disaster.

5

PANCAKES AND STORIES

Ivy

I woke up gradually, stretching and letting the day ahead roll over me. Saturdays meant an afternoon at the bookstore, small crafts for Addie to keep her entertained. Tonight I'd go over the numbers for the week and prepare to do the whole thing again come tomorrow.

Rolling to my side, I quickly took in my surroundings. Memories of yesterday came flooding back. Jake's. If you had asked me yesterday morning how my day would go, I'd never have guessed correctly in a million years. It had actually been a nice night, which was just bizarre. Addie had eaten while the chili simmered. Then we poured some in mugs so we could eat while sitting on the couch with her and watching a Peanuts movie. Jake had *It's the Great Pumpkin, Charlie Brown*. Addie had gotten a kick out of it, and I smiled, remembering when I had watched the same one when I was her age. Parenting was fascinating. It was both the longest days combined with the quickest years. Sometimes it took my breath away.

Looking around Jake's guest room, I realized that Miss Addie must've already woken up. I wasn't too concerned. She really was a good kid. I'd put money on her waking early because she wanted to see Chief. Rolling out of bed, I moved to tug on my jeans. Jake had given me an old brewery T-shirt to wear to bed. I wondered what he'd think if it went home with me. In all honesty, it was incredibly soft and smelled like him. It would be criminal not to take it.

As I left the guest room, I took a quick glance down the hall. The door to Jake's room stood open. Shoot. I hoped he hadn't been woken by Addie. I mean, the guy could be annoying, but he'd already given up his Friday afternoon and evening. He should've been able to sleep in today.

Reaching the bottom of the staircase, I heard Jake's voice coming from the kitchen along with Addie's sleepy one. Peering around the doorway, I saw her tousled blond head sitting on the island next to Jake as he mixed what appeared to be pancake batter.

"'Nother one, Jake. Please?"

"You sure, peanut? You aren't all storied out?"

I chuckled and leaned against the doorway, watching them. Poor Jake. Addie didn't get storied out. I had resorted to limits—one book, one made-up story a night. Otherwise she was never satisfied.

"Story please!" Addie rocked happily in place.

Jake stopped mixing as he let out a breath and looked at the ceiling. I took the moment to appreciate all that was Jake Spencer. I mean morning scruff, tousled black hair, gray sweatpants—thank the goddess I was here for that— waffle T-shirt, and black-framed glasses. I had no idea he wore them, but holy sexiness, I was a fan. Jake moved around the kitchen, keeping his eyes on Addie as he gathered plates and syrup. His T-shirt stretched across his broad shoulders. The gray sweatpants, while loose, hugged his ass tight. Now if he'd just turn around... I mean, the man was a runner. He wasn't as bulky as Max and Sully, but he was solid, lean muscle. This was not a view I minded. Nope, not one bit.

"Okay, here goes. One night Princess Addie lay down in her bed, trying to go to sleep. Suddenly, she heard a noise. Da-da-dum-dum-dum. Da-da-dum-dum-dum. Looking around, she got out of her bed. She followed the noise to the window that looked out on her garden, and guess what? Addie was bug-eyed! Do you know what she saw?"

"The Little People!" Addie squealed, arms thrown high with, not shocking, jazz hands.

Jake grinned and turned to grab a griddle. He started preheating it for the pancakes, I guessed, as he continued. "That's right, babe. It was the Little People. A line of people only six inches tall or so were marching through her garden, around the apple tree, right up to her house. There was a band, which is where the music was coming from. Addie counted, and do you know how many little people she saw?"

"Forty-two!"

Jake laughed as he placed a hand on her head, giving it a rub. "Sure, peanut, forty-two sounds perfect. Do you want me to keep going?"

Addie cheered, I melted. I mean, what in the world was happening right now?

Jake grabbed a scoop, pancake flipper, and some plates. As he did, he continued, "So Princess Addie watched as the Little People marched in their band right up to her house. The line slowed down, but Addie didn't stop observing as the first people in line stood together and placed their hands against the third brick from the ground. Slowly, it slid into her house, creating an opening. Quickly, quietly, as the band stopped playing, the parade of Little People came into her basement…"

"Momma!" Addie squealed upon seeing me. I watched as Jake's cheeks heated up. Damn, the man could blush. That was new.

Moving across the kitchen, I pressed a kiss to Addie's head. "Morning, pumpkin. Did you wake Jake up?"

Addie immediately looked away, a sure sign she thought she might be in trouble. "Um…"

Jake had apparently recovered, because he let out a laugh at Addie's reluctant admission. "It might not be entirely Addie's doing," he said as he continued working on the pancakes. "I woke up to both her eyes and Chief's watching me from the side of my bed. My guess was that she woke up, Chief found her, and then she followed him as he worked to be allowed to go outside."

"That must have been an interesting way to wake up." I grinned.

Jake laughed. "Sure. I first heard a sweet little voice saying, 'Chief, quiet.' At that point, I rolled over and saw four beautiful eyes, two blue-green, two brown, peering up at me from the edge of my bed. It was a little creepy, to be honest, but not unusual for Chief."

"Mine were the blue-green ones!" Addie cried.

Jake rubbed her head. "That they were, Miss Addie. Chief's are brown."

I glanced around. "Where is he?"

Jake nodded toward the windows that looked out on his backyard. "It's fenced in, so he's running a few laps and letting the neighborhood dogs know he's up."

I glanced out, and sure enough, Chief was running around the yard, letting out a bark every so often, seemingly in his element. The joy of dogs did something to me. I wondered if it was time to buy one for my tiny family of two. Addie would love it, but with the hours I put in at the bookstore to get it off the ground in the first year, I felt like it would be unfair to the pup.

Coming back to the present, I looked around the grass and past Jake's fence to the street. It seemed to be ice-free. "Looks like the warm-up came as forecasted." Turning to look at Jake, I saw a look pass fleetingly on his face before he nodded and put a few more finished pancakes on a plate. I wondered what that was about.

"Yup, you guys are good to go home after you eat." He cocked his head toward the pancakes. Like I would turn that down.

I moved toward the island right as my cell began to vibrate. Teri's name popped up, Addie's day care provider. Looking at Jake and Addie digging into the pancakes, I held my phone up. "I need to take this." Jake nodded, and I moved back to the windows.

"Hey, Teri," I murmured, watching Chief now digging in the back corner of the yard. Crazy pup.

"Ivy, I'm so glad I caught you. Sorry to call so early on a Saturday." Teri sounded frazzled, and the woman watched anywhere from eight to fifteen kids a day. Nothing frazzled her. I straightened.

"You okay?" I looked over at Addie and Jake as he turned and caught my eyes. I reluctantly turned away from his heated gaze and focused my attention on Teri once again.

She sighed. "I will be. I just got off the phone with my

mom. She lives down by St. Louis and fell last night on the ice. She'll be okay, but they thought she broke her hip. Fortunately, the X-rays are saying she's okay, but I need to go be with her this week, make sure she takes it easy. Since my dad passed, she's on her own—"

"Say no more. I totally understand. Do you need me to call any of the families?" I thought about my schedule for the week and wanted to groan and crawl back in bed. With the holidays coming up, I had several items on my agenda that were going to be beyond boring for a four-year-old to sit through. However, it could be worse. At least I had the luxury of bringing her to the store. I had to be there. After our initial opening, the summer had had a dip in sales. We were just starting to build back. And beyond all that, Teri was amazing. We were so lucky to have her. I'm sure she was overwhelmed, and I wanted to ease any burden I could.

"No, no, I'm fine." Teri's sigh of relief was audible. "Thanks so much for being understanding. I'm so lucky with the families of the kids of my day care."

I laughed even while my mind raced. "Teri, we're all lucky to have you. Focus your attention on your mom. We'll make it until you can get back. And I'll send you a payment for this week through our payment app as soon as we hang up."

"No, that's too much." Teri sounded choked up.

"Nonsense. Remember, I'm a small business owner too. We need to look out for each other. Now, message me tonight and let me know how your mom is. Take all the time you need."

Teri was clearly crying quietly. "Thanks, Iv. You're the best."

"Back at you, babe. Take care." I tapped to hang up and quickly opened our payment app to send her the funds for the week. As I did, I thought about my freezer. I had a few casseroles in there for quick meals. I dashed off a text to Teri to ask if she wanted to swing by and grab one in a half hour or so before she hit the road. That way, their dinner for tonight would be taken care of.

"Momma, was that Miss Teri?"

I looked over at Addie and immediately felt like I needed to go back to bed. Being a single parent was fabulous at times, but when all the decisions rested on your shoulders, it was exhausting as well. I longed for a partner, just to have someone to lean on. Well, and the sex would be an added bonus.

Pasting on a big—read, fake—smile, I spoke to her. "Yes. Miss Teri was calling because her momma fell. Isn't that terrible?"

Addie gasped and put her hand over her mouth, overly dramatic as always.

"It's okay, pumpkin. Miss Teri just needs to head down to be with her momma for the week. Just like when you're sick and you want me around, sometimes mommas feel that way about their little girls."

"Poor Miss Teri's momma!" Addie said, then her lips turned into a frown. "Wait a minute. What will I do after school?"

Brace yourself, Ivy. Smile wattage turned up, I tried to muster as much joy as possible. "Babe, you'll come to the bookstore. It will be fun."

Addie dropped to the floor, boneless, as she wailed. "But Momma, the bookstore is so boring. I don't wanna go there every day."

I looked over her prone figure, then met Jake's amused expression. Over her wails, I moved toward him and sat down in front of my pancakes. Jake got up and moved across the island across from me as he began to gather up the dishes. One corner of his mouth went up in a small smirk. "Just so I'm on the same page, is our plan to ignore her?"

"Yep, I don't give any attention to dramatics. With Addie, she needs to get it out, and then it will pass quickly, unless she gets attention for that behavior. Then it is repeated, often."

"Noted. Do you mind if I give you a suggestion?"

I bit back a bristling remark that wanted to spring forth. Was Jake going to really suggest how I parent my daughter? I worked on centering myself. "Sure."

"How about I hang out with Addie this week after preschool, before the store closes?"

I grabbed onto the counter, concerned I might fall over in shock. I glanced down at my pancakes—delicious, I should add—and then back to this insane man. "I'm sorry. Are these pancakes spiked, or did you say you wanted to hang out with a four-year-old for three hours a day?"

Jake shrugged as he put the dishes in the sink and began running some hot water. "Sure, why not? You said she sleeps about an hour around three p.m., right? I could grab her, we'd have snack each day, she can nap and I'll get some paperwork done for the brewery, and then you could pick her up and I'll head in to work. No biggie."

I shook my head. Sure, no biggie. It was big. Huge. I had a moment of longing for my nana. What would life have been like if she was still here? If she could offer to help me out like this? She would have loved it. But then my mind flashed back to the phone call last night. "Jake, your family is coming into town this weekend. The brewery has the anniversary party. You have a ton on your plate."

Jake tossed a towel over his shoulder as he continued washing dishes, stacking them to the side of the sink to dry.

"Ivy, it's three hours a day. Truly, this is nothing. It will keep my mind off my family coming into town. And, quite frankly, you'd be doing me a favor. Sully and I hired a manager for the brewery last spring. This fall we've increased his duties, especially with Sully and Maggie's baby coming. Finn—that's our manager—is amazing and all, but I don't have as much to do anymore."

I let that roll over in my brain for a moment. "So what you're saying is that I'm actually doing you a favor here, right?"

Jake let out a bark of laughter. "Sure, let's go with that. Please let me hang with Addie this week so she doesn't have to go to the dreaded bookstore."

On that note, Addie popped up from the ground. "What? I can be with Just Jake after school?" She clasped her little hands together, holding them below her chin. "Please, Momma. Can I be here with Just Jake and Chief?"

I laughed. If this man really wanted to spend time with my daughter each day, who was I to stop him? I knew that my friends loved him. He was, by all that I could see, a natural with kids. He loved driving me crazy, but all signs were pointing to a decent guy underneath. I knew he had nieces around Ivy's age, so he was used to the dramatics of a four-year-old. And, quite frankly, this would be a huge help to me. I looked from her pleading eyes to Jake's laughing ones and threw up my hands. "Why not?"

Addie tossed her hands in the air again and began dancing around. "Jake, can I let Chief in?"

"Sure, peanut."

Addie went over to the door and opened it as Chief sprinted in the house, coming back to skid to a halt in front of her. "Chief," she shouted in his face. "I'm spending every afternoon this week with you!" On that note, Addie threw her arms around the patient dog's neck.

Looking back from her to Jake, who was now finishing up the dishes, I tilted my head to the side to observe him. "So, Mr. Spencer, tell me about these Little People."

Jake groaned and looked up at the ceiling.

6

———————

UNEXPECTED ARRIVALS

Jake

I glanced around the Homestead Brewery with a feeling of pride. Cole Sullivan and I had dreamed up this place years ago. Many late nights with a few beers under our belts, we'd talk about the type of place we'd want to open, if we ever did. Not sure I thought we'd end up in Cole's, or Sully as he was known to his friends, hometown. However, when this old barn showed up in a foreclosure, it was too good of a deal to pass by.

Sully and I met while he was in college and I was working construction. We both worked at a brewery in a nearby college town. During the day while he was getting his business degree, I was building houses and doing remodels. Eventually he moved up to manager at the brewery, and we spent our spare time starting to create our own beers. Sometimes we'd bullshit after a long shift, dreaming and planning about creating our own place, but it seemed like a pipe dream. Looking around, it truly was a dream come true.

The former barn had lots of cool features. There was

barn wood lining the walls of the bar. We had a mixture of low tables, couches, armchairs, and high-tops in small grouped sections throughout the space. It helped to make the big open space feel smaller, inviting. Off the entry to the right was a small hall that led to the restrooms, kitchen, and our tank room. In there we had more high-tops for tastings, and a few large windows that looked out over the restaurant.

This afternoon the place was quiet, the Sunday brunch rush was over, and we still had a couple of hours until the dinner crowd began filtering in. There were a few people gathered near the bar watching the Bears game, but mostly the staff was gearing up for the evening shift. I wiped down the bar, filling in for our bartender Daryl, who was on break. As I heard a throat clear behind me, I turned to see the smirks on two faces I'd rather not face this afternoon—Cole Sullivan and Maxwell Harp. Terrific.

"Beer?" I asked. Might as well face this head-on.

"Hmm, I'm not sure. Sully, what are you all brewing that's good right now?" Max rubbed his bearded chin like he was contemplating the problems of our age.

Sully's shit-eating grin was a sure sign that I wouldn't be enjoying this as much as they would. "Well, Harp, we have a lot of good beers. What are you in the mood for?"

"How about something chocolaty? And with a hit of mellows?" Max replied.

Sully laughed. "And then we can sit around and tell stories about the Little People? Sounds perfect."

"Fuck you both," I growled as they bent over laughing, slapping each other on the back. They were pretty damn proud of themselves. "How?" I really didn't need to say any more than that.

Sully faked that he wiped tears from his eyes. "Waited a

long time for a woman to capture your heart, Spencer. Didn't realize she'd be four."

"Screw off, Sullivan. Do you want a beer or not?"

Sully moved around the bar to grab his own glasses, pouring an Evolution IPA for himself and Max. "Stout?" he asked as he tipped his head toward the tap with Barn Owl on it. I nodded. Placing the beer in front of me, he clapped me on the back. "We're screwing with you, man. Maggie had a shift yesterday at the bookstore to help Ivy plan out some holiday orders. Seems like our bookstore owner was rather impressed with your natural ability to deal with her daughter."

Dammit, I didn't want to like the fact that Ivy was talking about me as much as I did. However, I knew I couldn't let these two know that I was feeling anything. Taking a sip of, if I might say, a damn fine stout, I tried to subtly ask, "Ivy was impressed?"

Max sank down into a bar stool across from us and chuckled. "Man, you're going to have to work on your poker face. I thought you couldn't stand this girl."

"I can't. I mean, she's fine, but she's a lot." I wasn't sure how to explain all that had been the interactions between Ivy and me over the past seven months or so. "She's just always pushing, always trying to get me to talk about big issues. She has a lot of strong beliefs, and God forbid if you don't fall in line with her way of thinking..." I trailed off, thinking of some of the conversations we'd had about politics since she'd arrived in town. And climate change. I mean, I knew it was a big issue, but Jesus.

I looked over the bar to where Sully now sat on the stool next to Max so they could apparently give me shit for the next hour or so. Great. "The first time Ivy came in here, she ordered a beer and then immediately began to question me about our sustainable practices and how we were planning to deal with the increasing temperature of the planet. She went on for quite a bit about how that will impact the ingredients in our beer."

Max nodded while Sully looked thoughtful. "How is climate change impacting our ingredients?" he asked.

I thought back to that late April day where Ivy had come in, hair up in some crazy knot, in a flowing skirt and tank top. She hadn't worn a bra, and I don't think I even heard half of what she said at first. Then she snapped her fingers in my face and started in on the climate. "Honestly? I can't remember it all. Something about how droughts will impact hop production and how we also needed to find ways to conserve water."

Sully sat there for a moment, then spoke. "Maybe we need to look into it. As a brewery, if we could find ways to help improve the environment while making the beer we love, that could be win-win." And then he grinned at Max before looking back at me. "And I sure don't want to piss off Ivy. The first time I met her was here back in April or May. Remember? She'd came in here to tell us about the bookstore. Then, somehow, she began to share the benefits of moon water, crystals, and something about my sign. Maybe she's a witch?"

"A green witch," Max murmured while taking a drink.

"I'm sorry, what?" Sully asked with a laugh.

Max raised an eyebrow. "That's what Emma said, that Ivy considered herself a green witch."

"What the fuck does that mean?" Sully asked.

"Hmm, maybe she's going to curse our boy's junk? Better watch out," Max said as he lifted his beer in a mock toast.

I dropped my head. These two.

"Not sure," Max replied. "Emma said it was something to do with plants. And maybe her essential oils? Not sure. So"—he glanced at me—"I think your junk is likely okay."

"But it might smell like flowers if she has anything to say about it," Sully finished.

I looked up at the ceiling. Lord, give me strength. Looking back at these two that I considered my closest friends, I dove in. "I have bigger problems than Ivy being a green witch or whatever."

The two fools looked at each other, then back at me.

"Do share," Max said.

"Margot is coming, and she talked to Ivy on the phone on Friday night," I said, my heart rate deciding that just that sentence alone meant it needed to speed up.

Sully had, unfortunately, been taking a drink of beer which he promptly sprayed over the bar. "Holy shit," he got out.

Max looked puzzled. "Margot, as in your mom? Why is that a big deal? She's amazing."

Sully was working to catch his breath. "Does she"—he gasped for some more air—"know about Ivy?"

"What's to know?" Max asked. "I mean she stayed at your house with her daughter, but you all didn't do any horizontal dancing, did you?"

"Hell no," I said, pissed. "Addie was there, and that's not happening anyway." My cock gave a twitch in my jeans to inform me he was fine with it.

"So, I'll reiterate. What's the big deal with your mom coming? Are you worried about the green witch putting a spell on her?"

Sully wiped the beer off his face before speaking. "Margot is going to be all over our boy, here. She's been waiting for ages for him to settle down. And Ivy comes with a premade grandchild. Oh, Spencer, you're in for it now. Margot and the green witch are going to be the best of friends." I was pissed to hear the joy laced through every word Sully spewed out.

A familiar voice came from the opening to our right, loud and clear. "Boys, you are so right. Margot is up in arms. And what's this about a witch?"

I looked over to see a familiar face that I'd missed for far too long. "Drew?"

Drew moved across the bar toward us, reaching Sully and Max first. There were backslapping hugs as I moved around the bar to greet my brother. Drew was younger by three years, but I'd been looking up to him—height wise—since he hit his senior year. He had two inches on my six two frame, but easily twenty pounds of muscle, if not more. After college he went and joined the US Forest Service's Hotshot crew. He'd been out West for the past seven years. I know my parents alternated between being proud and worried about him. With that career, I looked up to him in more ways than height.

I finally made it around the bar to these three and grabbed Drew by the back of his arm, tugging him out of the group so I could get my own greeting. Immediately he pulled me in for what felt a bit like being hugged by a bear. "Missed you, big bro," he said as he gave me a few slaps on the back.

I laughed, pulling back to look him over. "Missed me so much that you came almost a week early?"

A ghost of a look passed quickly over his face which made me refocus. Before I could ask, the relaxed Drew was back and he grinned. "Had to see this Bookstore Ivy in the flesh. Want to elaborate on her witchy nature for me?"

I watched him for a beat or two before asking the question that was making my gut clench. "You okay?" He looked fine, but that didn't mean anything.

Drew paused, then nodded. "All good, just ready to be around family for a bit."

Yeah, something was definitely up. Maybe the two of us could share a bottle of Irish whiskey tonight and figure out why he was really here early.

"Been a while since I've seen you guys," Drew said to Max and Sully.

"Too long," Sully said.

I moved back around the bar as I glanced at my watch. Daryl would be back in here in about twenty minutes. Grabbing a tablet, I looked over at these three fools whom I called friends. "Food?"

"Hell yeah," Max said. "We can order as we fill Drew in with how you've begun to associate with someone who likely is in a coven."

I shook my head as I pulled up our point-of-sale software. "Nachos?"

Drew looked from Max to me. "Do you all still have those fancy steak nachos you told me about?"

I considered that for a minute. "You mean the ones with filet for the meat?"

"Of course."

"Yup. Anything else?" I asked.

Sully requested wings with Thai sweet garlic chili. Max put in for a burger, which Drew quickly echoed. I got it all down, as well as my order, and then leaned on the bar so I could hear their conversation.

"...so apparently the woman likes oils and herbs, thus is considered a green witch," Max summed up.

Drew nodded, then tilted his head to the side just like he had as a kid when he was working through something. "I wonder if that's all the criteria. If so, half the population in Boulder would fall into that group."

I smiled, remembering my visit out to see Drew last summer. We'd spent a lot of time in Boulder, even though he lived west of the city. It was a pretty incredible place. Really, the whole state was. Drew had always been into outdoor adventures, and those were everywhere you looked in Colorado.

"So, you're here to check out Ivy. You sticking around for the anniversary party this weekend?" Sully asked, slapping Drew on the back.

"Absolutely," Drew said. "Also figured I could check out my investment. How's canning going?"

Drew had come on as an investor a few months back. Sully and I had planned on taking out a loan, but with his bun in Maggie's oven, so to speak, he was leery of taking on more debt and had bailed on our earlier loan opportunity. Fortunately, Drew had been looking for something to invest in, so we pulled him in as a partner for our canning operation. It had only been a few months but was already a great additional stream of revenue for us.

I grinned, pulling a four-pack from under the bar to sit on the counter. "Going great. We're canning our top sellers. Of course we still have growlers people can fill at the brewery, but the cans are available here and in a lot of stores in the area."

Drew nodded. "Plan on trying several when I'm here."

I put the four-pack away. "Sounds good. What do you want to start with tonight?"

Drew scanned the taps. "Barn Owl is your stout, right?"

I nodded, grabbing a glass and heading to the taps. "Yep. Notes of chocolate and coffee." I filled his glass while thinking of dancing in my kitchen with Ivy only two nights ago. Damn, it had only been a little over twenty-four hours, and I missed the woman.

"Shit!" I looked down to see the stout overflowing the cup and running down my hand. I quickly mopped it up while Drew, Max, and Sully laughed their asses off. I turned to set Drew's stout down as I saw him quickly put his phone away.

"Were you taking my picture?"

Drew shrugged, taking a sip of his stout to hid his smirk while my own phone vibrated.

Yanking it out, I saw a text in our sibling group chat. Pushing down my annoyance, I opened the app to see his message. There was a photo of me with beer spilling over the cup and a text from Drew.

Drew: *Bro is in serious crushing territory here. Spilling beer while he is apparently thinking about his girl. Sacrilege.*

Drew: *PS Steph—apparently Bookstore Ivy is also a green witch.*

Good Lord.

"Fuck off," I growled at him, moving to put my phone down. Before I could, it vibrated again.

Steph: *You do good work, little bro. And a green witch? Is she also into acupressure? Because my stress headaches could certainly use some help. Or does she do oils? Maybe you should just share her cell, Jake. I'll talk to her.*

Like hell I would. Good Lord.

Me: *Fuck, no. And I'm working. You two blue-hairs can continue your gossip session without me.*

Steph: *Ah, look, Drew. Jake's taking his ball and going home.*

Drew: *Nothing new here. Can't take the heat. That's why I'm the firefighter.*

Steph: *Nothing new with you either, baby bro. Your ego is as healthy as ever.*

Drew: *Not ego, I speak the truth.*

Me: *Jesus H. Christ, both of you, shut it.*

Steph: *Waiting for that number, Jake. Or Drew can stop by the bookstore and get it for me when he goes in this week. Ivy and I are going to be the best of friends, I just know it.*

Laughter pulled me away from my phone. I looked up to see Max and Sully both reading the conversation on Drew's phone while they all grinned at me.

"I really like your sister," Sully said. "She's no bullshit."

I shook my head. Steph was at that.

"Yeah, she's easy to like when she's not busting your balls," I shared.

"Amen," Drew concurred.

Lauren, our hostess, came over with plates and silverware in her hands. "Food's up in a minute, gentlemen. Where do you want it?"

Sully headed over to a high-top as Finn came over to me. "Go eat with the guys, I've got the bar until Daryl gets up here in a few," he said.

"Thanks, man."

I headed over to join the guys but pulled Drew back just before we reached the table. Placing my hand on his neck, I pulled his head toward mine. "All bullshit aside, glad you're here."

Drew put his hand on my shoulder as well. "No place I'd rather be."

I slid onto a stool at the four-top and looked around. There were still some guys at the bar watching the game, though it looked like the good guys were going to lose this one. A few tables had begun to fill up for the night. There was a handful of people standing at the counter by the door, some purchasing cans to go. A low murmur filled the place, people kicking back and relaxing. I glanced at Sully, and he caught my eye with a grin.

"We did it," I said.

Sully raised his glass up. "Fuck yeah we did."

Max, Drew, and I raised ours to meet Sully's. Clicking the glasses together, Max said, "Five years, guys. Nicely done."

Drew took a swig and looked around. "Proud of you two. You've built something pretty amazing here."

I nodded, sitting back and soaking it all in. "Yeah, we really have." Looking back at the guys, I said, "Saturday night is going to be a hell of a celebration."

Max grinned. "Hell yeah it is. I can't wait to see what Margot thinks of the green witch."

Drew chuckled. "I'll drink to that."

"She will have the wedding plans begun before the night is through," Sully stated.

Shit. It would be a hell of a celebration. If Mom had anything to say about it.

"Don't worry, man. I'm sure Sam will have Margot under control," Max said, grinning. Yeah, my dad was an amazing man. But he loved my mother and wouldn't dream of stepping in or giving her any suggestions. No, my mom and Steph would be running the show this weekend.

Sully laughed at my expression. Drew picked up his glass and held it out to me. "Good luck," he said.

"Thanks," I replied, tapping his glass with mine.

His eyes looked full of laughter as he took a sip. Setting his glass down, he raised an eyebrow at me and whispered, "You're so going to need it."

7

FAMILY INTRODUCTIONS

Ivy

I walked into the local coffee shop, the Sanctuary, that was housed in a former church. Emma and Maggie were meeting here tonight for yoga and had invited me to join them. I met these girls only seven months ago, but we were already fast friends. Emma was a librarian at the Ryan Library, the public library only blocks from my bookstore. We worked on several projects together. Maggie was a seventh grade language arts teacher in town, and we collaborated on a few projects through her work with middle school kids. Maggie and Emma had been friends since childhood and were both crazy gorgeous. Emma was absolutely the girl next door, my height, with wavy dark brown hair. Maggie was taller, an extrovert to Emma's quiet nature, with a riot of strawberry blonde hair, and she was rather pregnant, which made tonight's invite a bit of a surprise to me. Lately, Maggie had become more and more of a homebody.

Typically, a yoga class at five thirty p.m. on a weeknight would be a no go for me, unless I got a sitter. And frankly, that was just too much work. However, today was the first day that Jake was picking up Addie from school. He'd messaged me this afternoon, asking if I'd mind if he kept her for dinner. Seems he was having dinner with Cole Sullivan and his parents. Addie knew them from time that we'd hung out with this crew over the summer. That being said, a night to myself? Absolutely unheard of. So I'd greedily accepted the yoga invite. Goddess knows I could use some time to re-center myself.

"Ivy, Ivy, over here."

I looked across the room and saw Emma and Maggie toward the back of the room. Emma was engaged to Max Harp. Maggie had married Emma's brother, Sully, this fall. Their baby was due in two months. I grinned. Maggie didn't look that comfortable in her spot on the floor with the beach ball that had replaced her stomach.

"Thanks for saving me a spot," I said as I rolled out my mat and kicked off my shoes. I dropped onto the floor by the girls and looked over to Maggie. Leaning over, I squeezed her knee. "Looking good, chickie."

Maggie groaned and placed her hands on her beautiful belly. "Sure, sure. I feel like I might explode. We're definitely out of room in here. I told Emma I'll never get back off the floor, so you all are on duty. But my hips have been killing me lately, so I decided to come."

I nodded, remembering what it felt like to be nearing the end of my pregnancy with Addie. "This is absolutely good for you. You'll just have to modify some poses."

Maggie nodded. "Yeah, I talked to Kristine when we arrived. She said she'd give me a heads-up on how to modify or any poses to skip."

"When I was pregnant with Addie, yoga saved me. So did swimming, so you could try that too."

"Great idea, but I'm not sure if I'd even want to see myself in a swimming suit right now. Beyond the fact that I hate leaving the Y after swimming when it's cold out. Blah." Maggie shook her head. "Ignore me. I'm a grump right now."

Emma leaned over and squeezed Maggie's hand. "Babe, you're growing my niece. You bitch all you want."

I laughed as I began to stretch a bit, tilting one shoulder forward, pulling back with the other. So much tension in my upper back. Looking over the books and planning out how much inventory to have for the holidays did not make for a relaxing afternoon.

Glancing over at Maggie, I asked, "How are the seventh graders? Ready for the holidays?"

Maggie rolled her eyes. "Middle school children are a bit stir crazy midyear. Love them all to pieces, but I am absolutely fine having the third quarter off to stay home with this peanut. Luckily, it's a great class. My sub should do fine."

"Well, I certainly love having you at the bookstore on Sundays. We're going to miss you when this beautiful babe makes her way into the world. And just a reminder, you promised to put up some recommendations sometime soon." Maggie had worked in my store part-time this summer and continued with a shift on Sundays this fall. It was a huge help, letting me give Addie some time to sleep in this summer and a person to bounce ideas off of all fall. We'd found that when Maggie left book recommendations, many of her former students gravitated toward them. I knew she wouldn't be working for me again, or at least not for some time, once the baby came. Her life was about to get a whole lot busier.

"You bet. I've read a few great young adult books lately. I'd be glad to recommend them."

Emma had a bit of a twinkle in her eye when she spoke. "So, how was Jake's afternoon with Addie?"

I had filled Maggie in on Friday's festivities yesterday. "I'm assuming Maggie already told you what went down this weekend."

"Heck yeah she did. I'm floored that Jake's house is still standing."

I reached overhead, then dropped a hand to the side and leaned into it. "I have no idea what you're talking about."

Maggie hooted. "Sure, sure. You and Jake are super calm and rational around each other all the time."

I shook my head as I switched sides. "Come on. I'm a pretty calm person."

Emma nodded as she began some light stretches as well. "Yeah, you absolutely are except when you are around Jake Spencer. So, how the heck did the two of you survive the night?"

I let a small smile slip out. "I know you're right. I have no idea why we seem to argue so much."

Emma and Maggie looked at each other, then back at me. Emma laughed before speaking. "You read just as many romance books as we do, my friend. You know that super-hot chemistry is often covered by a whole lot of denial. And here, in this situation with Jake? The denial is strong in both parties. I, for one, can't wait to watch this all unfold."

"And I hear he has your daughter now at dinner with my in-laws." Maggie grinned at me. "I would have loved to have been there to see that, but I needed this more."

I shook my head at both of them as Kristine called everyone to focus and begin class. Chemistry. Sure. I mean, he was unbelievably gorgeous. I did often want to slide my hands through that tousled hair or over the scruff covering his face. And I might or might not have fantasized about Jake in those glasses and gray sweat pants a time or two since Saturday. Though that was completely normal, right?

Crap. I looked over to Emma and Maggie. We'd moved to child's pose, and Maggie was doing the best she could, but they were both watching me.

"I think I might be in some trouble here," I whispered.

Maggie raised a brow; Emma giggled.

"Ya think?" Maggie asked.

My head plopped down on the mat. I could resist this man, right?

An hour later, my body felt far more relaxed than when I'd began. "Let me give you a hand." I held a hand out to Maggie who was still down on the mat, looking like she was going to give up the ghost and just stay down for the next eight or nine weeks.

"Yeah, I think I'm going to need a boost from both of you." Maggie raised a hand to me, and Emma grabbed the other.

"Count of three," I said as we got it together and pulled her up. Emma reached over to roll up Maggie's mat for her. There was simply no way she was reaching that.

"Homestead?" Maggie asked, sliding the mat into the bag at her shoulder.

"Sure. Ivy?"

"Let me check and see if Jake's texted." I pulled my phone out of my purse and saw a few texts from Jake.

Jake: *Addie is a charmer. Sully's parents are more in love than they already were. Finishing up here, and I'll have* *her at your house by eight. Is that cool?*

Jake: *She now is making cookies with Anna, Sully's mom. She had a dance party to Van Morrison with Sully's dad. They might try to keep her, just a warning.*

I laughed. I'd enjoyed getting to know Anna and Lee since moving to town. Anna was a big reader and loved romance books as much as I did. She'd joined the romance book club that Emma and I ran as a joint effort from the public library and the bookstore. Sully and Emma's dad, Lee, read a lot of biographies. They were excellent customers and fast becoming friends.

Me: *They can have her if I can move in too. A win-win for everyone. They get a ready-made grandkid that they don't have to wait eight more weeks for, and I get someone to cook for me.*

Me: *And yes, eight is good. We're just finishing up at yoga and heading to the brewery for a bite to eat.*

I thought about what Emma and Maggie had said about Jake and me. I thought about the fact that he'd picked my kid up six hours ago and was hanging out with her just to help me out and because he said he enjoyed her. Jake had already logged more hours in Addie's presence than her dad had on a regular basis, not that I faulted him. I knew where we both stood. Even so...

Me: *In case I forget to tell you later, thanks for spending time with Addie today. I appreciate it.*

Jake:...

I quickly began to second-guess my decision to be genuine in a text. What was I thinking?

Jake: *No problem, babe. You have a cool kid. See you at eight.*

I rolled my eyes a bit at *babe* but had to admit the rest was nice.

Me: *Thanks, Just Jake.*

I looked up to see Emma and Maggie watching me. "Shoot, I'm sorry. I'm holding you guys up. We can go."

"Want to share with the class who the text exchange was with?" Emma asked, looking a bit smug.

I quickly moved to deflect. "It's nothing. Jake was just telling me when they'd be back, but I have time for dinner."

Emma looked at Maggie. "What do you think?" she asked her.

"Oh, it's for certain. The lady protests too much," Maggie replied. She linked her arm through mine and started moving us toward the door. "But we can discuss this later. I'm starving. You can't keep a pregnant lady from food for this long. It's criminal."

I laughed and let her lead me out the door. I'd needed this night more than I knew. And I was getting it, thanks to Jake Spencer. I shook my head. Who would have thought?

It was just a short walk to the Homestead; a few blocks and we were there. Even though it was November and we'd had a freak winter storm just a few days ago, tonight was mild. Illinois. The weather seemed unable to pick a season and stick with it.

We made our way through the doors of the brewery and headed to grab one of the four-tops near the bar. Maggie grabbed a stool as Emma and I bellied up, waiting for Daryl to come to our end. I soaked in the feeling of being out with these two ladies, what felt like some important friendships I could count on. My nana would have been thrilled. I smiled, thinking about her.

"I can grab drinks," Emma said, interrupting my

thoughts. "Seltzer water for Maggie. What do you want, Ivy?"

I scanned the taps, my attention coming back to the present. "I'll take the stout. It's named something that has to do with an owl."

"Barn Owl Stout," said a gorgeous bearded guy at the bar as he turned to face us. "You have good taste." He gave us a grin that was super familiar, but I couldn't place him.

Emma seemed to consider him for a moment, then broke out in a wide grin. "Drew?"

The guy looked at Emma for a beat, then smiled back at her. "Sully's sister, right? How've you been?" They moved toward each other and shared a hug.

Emma pulled back, laughing, then looked over from Maggie to me, I assumed to introduce us. But then her smile widened, and she looked back at Drew. "I think I have someone you're going to be happy to meet," she said as she turned him to face me.

Giving her a puzzled look, I simply decided to introduce myself. This was weird. "Hey, my name is Ivy."

Drew took my hand and his gorgeous smile widened. Wow, that was nice. "Oh, Ivy. Bookstore Ivy, right?" He looked to Emma, who nodded. "I'm so glad you're here. I think I should share my last name. I'm Drew, Drew Spencer."

I felt myself quickly take a breath. "Jake's brother?"

"One and the same, darling," he said with a bit of a laugh.

Oh boy.

8

BROTHERS ARE ALWAYS RIGHT

Jake

I pulled up at Ivy's house and glanced in the rearview mirror at Addie behind me. She was pretty mellow, much more than I would have assumed considering how late it was. My nieces tended to get wound up the closer it was to bedtime. But Addie's head rested on the high back of her booster as she stared out the window.

"You good, Miss Addie?" I asked as I turned off the car and prepared to head in.

Addie's eyes found mine in the rearview mirror. "Yep, just sweepy."

I grinned and slid out of my Silverado, heading for her door. In the past hour or so, Addie's *l*'s had become *w*'s. It was adorable.

Tugging open the door, I found that she'd already unbuckled and her arms were outstretched. I scooped her up along with her backpack, and we headed toward the house. The solid weight of her in my arms as she snuggled in took my breath away. Spending time with Addie today had been eye-opening. I'd always assumed I'd be a young dad. Hell, dating Rachel for years, planning our wedding, I'd figured I'd be there by now. However, as my sister liked to remind me, *man plans, God laughs.* Whatever. Rachel had done a number on me, and I'd avoided anything serious like the plague ever since, but somehow this pint-sized dynamo and her mom had me reconsidering that path.

Ivy's house was the perfect size for her and Addie. I'd moved in down the street years ago, long before Ivy and Addie moved to town, and often came by her place on my daily runs. It was a small cottage, navy siding with white trim. I knew the older couple who used to live there before retiring to Florida. They would have taken care of the place, which was great for Ivy.

Walking onto the screened-in porch, I briefly wondered if she had parents or siblings close. Was there anyone she could rely on to help her out? What if I hadn't been able to watch Addie? Who was her backup? What about Addie's dad? I'd assume this year had been stressful, what with starting a small business on her own. Sully and I had each other, along with his entire family, mine three hours away, and a town that didn't know how not to show their support as we started our business. Who did Ivy have?

Addie began to wiggle a bit as we neared the front door. "Down please," she said as we reached our destination. Leaning over, I placed her on the porch, and then she bolted for the door. It was open—I'd need to chat with Ivy about that—and she hauled ass inside.

"Mommmmmmmaaaaaaa!" she hollered, racing in.

What in the world? Had I thought she was mellow moments ago? Maybe it was all just an act, or she'd gotten her second wind.

I took a step into Ivy's house and looked around. Good Lord, it was like a greenhouse threw up in here. Her front door took you from her screened-in porch straight into her living room. I didn't know where to focus. Every surface had plants. I knew shit about plants, but there were ones on some built-in shelves that had leaves flowing down. Every flat surface had a small plant of some type. In front of the windows in giant pots sat larger plants with leaves the size of a dinner plate—some solid, some with holes in them. I'd never tried to have indoor plants. I was sure I'd never water them. I was impressed as much as I was overwhelmed.

Looking past all the green, I had to grin. Ivy's place screamed *Ivy*. Her couch was a bright blue, but I couldn't focus much on it. There were pillows, blankets, a crazy amount of patterns between pillows, blankets, and the rug underfoot. My sister would say there were lots of jewel tones, but basically it was a colorful space with a shit ton of plants. Everywhere.

It was a lot. And somehow, it was exactly right, exactly what I would have thought of for Ivy.

"We're coming, Just Jake!" Addie called from some place beyond the living room. I shook my head and dropped her backpack on the couch. Pounding footsteps headed my way as Addie tore around the corner and ran straight at me again. At least she wasn't quiet. There was plenty of warning about an incoming four-year-old. I bent down, scooped her up, and stood as Ivy came around the corner.

Damn. Not sure I was prepared for the sight of Ivy in fitted clothing. Her hair was in one of those knots she loved. But I could only assume the leggings she had on were for yoga. They hugged every inch of her, and I didn't know where to let my eyes rest. Her shirt was a light purple long-sleeved that seemed to match this living room but fitted because God must be happy with me. It had some weird-ass holes that her thumb poked through at the end, but I ignored that and just checked out the way it clung to her breasts.

Damn. It bears repeating. I wasn't sure I could form words. All the blood flow had left my head, or the top one at least. I needed to refocus on the fact that her daughter was in the room and the woman in front of me was not always my biggest fan.

My phone, of course, chose that moment to begin the vibration dance in my pocket. Sliding it out, I lowered Addie to the ground and gave Ivy what I hoped was an apologetic look. "Just a minute, sorry. Finn, Sully, and I are all out of the brewery tonight, so I just need to make sure Daryl doesn't need anything."

Ivy nodded as she moved to pick up Addie's bag. She sat down on the couch as Addie sat down beside her. I watched as Ivy pulled out a folder and they began looking through what appeared to be a million and two drawings. They all looked the same to me, but Addie seemed to have a story to go with each and every one.

My phone vibrated again. Looking down, I saw that it was Drew, not Daryl. Still, Ivy was talking to Addie. I moved over to the window to give them some space. I opened the text to see if Drew needed anything. He hadn't wanted to join Addie and me for dinner tonight, said he was exhausted. Maybe I should swing by the brewery to grab him some food before heading home.

Drew: *Met Bookstore Ivy tonight. You're in trouble.*

What? I glanced up from my phone to Ivy and Addie curled up on the couch with drawings scattered all over. They were studying one intently.

"You met my brother tonight?" I asked.

Ivy looked up, considered me for a moment, then a grin

spread across her face. "Drew? Oh yeah. We had dinner together."

For no reason at all, a wave of jealousy hit me square in the chest. What the hell? I know absolutely nothing would happen, but there it was and I wasn't going to deny it.

I looked from her, to my phone, debating. I'd known Drew longer; I'd deal with him first.

Me: *Fuck you.*

Drew: *Now, now, no need to be vulgar. I didn't tell her anything. Well, not much.*

Reconsidering, I decided the best course of action with him was simply to ignore. I'd deal with my baby brother after I was done here.

Ivy caught my eye as I slid my phone in my back pocket. She gave me a look that I couldn't read.

"What?"

She shook her head. "Nothing." Looking at Addie, who'd dug some crayons out of her backpack and was now doing some more coloring kneeling in front of the coffee table, Ivy looked back to me. "How did it go?"

I nodded at the end of her sectional. "Mind if I sit?"

Ivy leaned over, sweeping some of the drawings into a pile and placing them in a long bowl on the coffee table that was already filled up with other pieces of Addie's artwork. "Please."

I sank into the couch. While I was a bit mesmerized by the different colors and patterns of the pillows and blankets, the damn thing was unbelievably comfortable. "Let me see. Addie, what did we do after school?"

Addie looked up from her spot kneeling at the coffee table, tilted her head to the side, and seemed to ponder that. I held back my laughter. I wasn't sure if she was trying to be funny on purpose or she was really thinking. One thing I had learned over the course of our afternoon/evening together was that she was a bit of a ham.

"Um, Just Jake picked me up at school." She looked off in the distance. "Then Chief and I napped on the sofa. He was real tired, Momma."

Ivy grinned. "I bet he was. It was good of you to nap with him."

Addie nodded rather seriously. "I know." She went back to coloring as she talked. "Then we met Sulwe's momma and daddy."

Ivy nodded. "Was that fun?"

Addie nodded as she stuck her tongue out as she colored. She was cute. "Yeah. They wiv on a farm. His momma is a really good cook. We ate pasta, had a dance party, and made cookies."

"Sounds fun, baby." Ivy smoothed over Addie's hair as she watched her. "Where did your tutu come from?"

It was my turn to grin. Addie had been in plain leggings with a polka-dot shirt when I picked her up from school. When she and Chief had woken up from their nap and came in the kitchen, she'd been wearing a purple tutu. She told me it was her special outfit for dinner.

"My backpack, silly."

Ivy nodded like this all made a lot of sense. Who the hell knew? Maybe it did. "Of course, it's your party outfit," Ivy replied.

Addie was now completely engrossed in her drawing, which I could tell was a portrait of several people. Beyond that, no idea.

Ivy turned to face me, realizing—I'd assume—that Addie was now done with talking to the two of us. "So it went okay? Really?"

I studied her for a minute. She appeared a bit apprehensive. Thinking a bit more about the lack of support around her, I wondered if anyone had watched Addie for her before. "Of course it did. Addie's easy, and I love spending time with her." I watched as she visibly relaxed.

"Oh good. Thanks." She glanced around, as if she wasn't sure what we were doing here. "Um, do you want anything to drink?"

"Sure," I said, watching as her eyes widened in surprised. She hadn't expected me to want to stay. Oh, Ivy, I was absolutely finding out a bit more information about this maddening woman tonight, and a drink was a great way to start.

"Oh, um, I have a few different types of beers." She rose to head toward what I was assuming was the kitchen.

I stood as well. "I'll come with you."

She appeared flustered. "No, you can stay here. I'll bring you something."

I glanced at Addie, then back to Ivy. "Addie's fine here by herself, right?"

"Yep," Addie piped up from her coloring. "Momma, can I have a snack?"

Ivy looked over at the large wall clock and back to Addie. "It's almost bedtime. How about some cheese and crackers?"

Addie nodded and Ivy moved toward the corner she and Addie had come skidding through earlier. I followed her through a short hall, staircase opening to the second floor, and back to a large kitchen with a dining area attached. There was turquoise-blue tile covering the backsplash and counters, wood cabinets, and more plants. Of course. Ivy headed toward a cabinet and pulled out some crackers, then crossed to the fridge and took out the cheese.

As she began to assemble a plate for Addie, she nodded

toward the fridge. "You can grab a beer if you want one. Or there are glasses for water to the left of the sink."

I crossed to the fridge and looked in. "Should I be insulted that you have beer from another local brewery but not mine?"

I caught her smirk that she aimed at the counter. This woman.

"Sorry. I love their hazy IPA. And I typically have yours too. I'm just out."

She put the plate to the side, then called out, "Addie, your snack is ready."

Before I could even reply, the pounding of Addie's feet announced her impending arrival. She swooshed around the corner, tutu flying. Grabbing her plate, she called, "Thanks, Momma!" and took off toward the living room again.

"No crumbs on the floor!" Ivy called.

"'Kay!"

I shook my head as I looked in the fridge once again. "Okay, so I'll bring you some *Black Hole Sun* tomorrow. Do you want a beer now?"

Ivy didn't look over from her spot returning the crackers. "Nah, I'll grab some white wine in a minute."

I controlled the urge to roll my eyes at this woman. God forbid I actually get something for her. Instead, I grabbed my beer, her wine in the door of the fridge, and moved to the counter to look for glasses.

"Oh, um, thanks," she said as I handed her a glass moments later. "So it went okay?"

I nodded as I thought over the time I'd spent with Addie today. "Yep. Addie filled you in on most of it. Dinner with the Sullivans was great, as always. Anna loves to spoil me since my parents live a whole three hours away. I think she thinks that is simply a hardship no parent should have to face, so she asks me to come over often."

"And you don't say no," she pointed out, leaning back against the counter across from me and crossing her legs at the ankles.

"You clearly have never had Anna Sullivan's cooking if you'd even consider saying no. It's amazing."

"Well, they picked the perfect dinner for Addie. She loves pasta." Ivy looked at her wineglass, not meeting my eyes.

I studied her for a moment, then figured I'd just ask. "How about your parents? Do you see them much?"

Ivy looked out the windows to her backyard. "No, not much."

I watched her, waiting, hoping if I didn't say anything, maybe she'd fill the silence. Just as I was getting ready to break the spell, she looked back to me.

"My parents are pretty traditional. We don't have a lot in common."

I blinked, then grinned. "You mean you don't consider yourself traditional?"

She lightly kicked me, then returned to her spot. "No, not in the way of conservative bankers and country clubs."

Now that got my attention. "So how did all this gloriousness"—I motioned to all that was Ivy in front of me—"come from that?"

Her cheeks heated a bit, which was a total turn on. "My nana."

"Nana?"

Leaning to the side, she set her wine on the counter, then put her hands behind her to help as she hopped up. Grabbing her wine again, she took a sip. "My nana lived in Highland Falls when I was growing up."

My eyes widened. "Who?"

"Lorelai Bailey, my mom's mom."

Whoa. This all made so much sense as the memory of Mrs. Bailey came back to me. Super-kind soul. Died-in-the-wool hippie. "I remember Mrs. Bailey. She lived above your bookstore."

"Yup. She owned the building and left it to me when she passed."

I searched my memories, then asked gently, "Mrs. Bailey passed about five years ago, right?"

Ivy stared back into her wineglass. "Yes," she said softly. "I was only twenty-three, just out of college. I just had people in town manage the property for me until I was ready to move here."

"I'm so sorry, Ivy. She was a nice lady."

She met my eyes. "You knew her?"

I laughed. "We haven't talked about our pasts much, obviously."

Ivy grinned. "It's more fun to bicker with you about why we should have a woman president already."

"Oh yes. Or why I need to be out marching in the street for climate change."

Ivy pursed her lips. "Just trying to help you be the best you can be, Mr. Spencer."

This woman. Why did half our conversations feel like foreplay? And shouldn't I want to avoid that? "At any rate, I think you know Sully and I worked together in college and began dreaming up the brewery then. What you might not know is that's when we reconnected. My grandparents lived in Highland too. They moved down here when my grandpa retired from his job in Chicago. I came down for so many summers growing up, got to know Sully and Max a bit then. And as for your grandma, it's Highland. You know how it is. No one is really a stranger. But yeah, she was friends with Lou. She knew Max's grandma and mine."

"So we could have been here at the same time, in the same summers?" Ivy looked at her wine, a bit lost in thought. I watched as she sighed, then shook her head. What was she thinking about? "And I've met Lou but haven't mentioned who my grandmother was. Was Max's grandma like Lou? How about yours?"

I put my head back and let out a big laugh. Meeting her eyes, I shook my head and watched as she visibly relaxed. *That's better*, I thought. It was unreal how I wanted to take care of this woman. "No, not many people are like Lou, which is good for us all. Not sure what we'd do if they were."

Ivy was looking at her wineglass again but released an adorable snort. "Well, life would be a whole lot more interesting, that's for sure. Emma's told me stories about when she lived next door to her."

"The town is filled with stories about Ms. Lou. Her husband, Verdell, is a saint."

Ivy took a deep breath as she met my eyes. She looked pensive. "Jake, my house wasn't easy growing up. Or it certainly wasn't for someone like me. My parents and I are as different as you can get. But my nana? She got me. I came down here for a lot of summers and would stay with her, away from the disapproval of my parents, the expectations I couldn't measure up to. My biggest regret in life is that Nana didn't get to meet Addie. They would have been two peas in a pod."

I watched Ivy as a tear or two welled in her eyes, and my heart broke a bit. Fuck her parents. Before I could tell my feet to stop, I found myself taking the three steps to cross from my counter to hers. I placed my beer on the tile counter to her side, then took her wineglass and did the same. Everything in me screamed to kiss her, but it looked like she was almost vibrating with emotion. Her knees opened up, allowing me to step closer and lose myself in those gorgeous eyes. The need to hold her, to comfort her, was all-consuming and foreign as hell. There was a catch of her breath, but no words telling me to stop. We locked eyes, and I brushed a bit of her hair back, tucking it behind her ears.

"Ivy, if it's okay with you, I'm going to give you a hug. I think you might need one."

Slowly, she nodded as I pulled her flush with me. Her arms wrapped around to my back as she took a stuttering breath and buried her head into the nook of my neck. Her exhale was huge, and I wondered how much she was dealing with on her own.

My first thought was that I'd like to stand like this, holding her, every night in the foreseeable future.

My second thought was that my brother was right. I was in some major trouble here. And what surprised me more than anything? I wasn't sure I cared.

9

———

MATCHMAKER

Ivy

I took a breath and debated my next move. Sitting on the counter, my legs were currently spread beyond what my mother would consider was decent. Jake stood between them, his chest pressed against mine, my head tucked in his neck, and I was certain his glorious cream Henley might have a tear or two from me when I pulled back.

Yet I didn't want to pull back. Not. One. Bit. I wanted to sit here, on my counter, in my own kitchen, with his arms around me for at least the next hour. Or maybe twenty. Yeah, a large part of me just wanted to soak in this form of comfort from Jake. The other part of me wanted to show him I was strong enough on my own. To remind him that I didn't need him. Or maybe to remind me. The internal struggle left me paralyzed. I felt Jake's lips move on my neck and goose bumps rose up everywhere. Dang.

"You okay, Ivy?"

Okay. Let's define okay. I'm guessing the fact that my heart rate had increased by what was surely a minimum of twenty beats a minute wasn't okay. But he didn't need to know that. Right?

"Yeah," I whispered. Damn it, that sounded breathy, didn't it?

"You sure about that?" Hmm, he sounded a bit breathy too. What was that? I leaned forward and felt a certain hardness pressed against me that I had a feeling had nothing to do with the miles he ran. Well, that was interesting. Noted.

His hands tightened at my hips. My own hands began running up and down his back on their own accord. I mean, seriously, it was like my brain had waved the white flag and given up. My body was working on instinct, and that might be dangerous.

It took all the willpower I had in my entire body, along with some I called upon to rain down from the universe, and I pulled back to meet Jake's eyes. They were intense. My romance books would likely called them heated. My mouth watered because clearly I was no longer in control. I ran my tongue over my lower lip. Of course I did. What was this life? Jake's eyes watched, then he looked back at me. I bit my lip, not sure at all what we were going to do here.

"Babe." His voice was raspy. *My word.* That was nice.

"Just Jake?"

The corner of his mouth cocked up in a smirk. "Just Jake? Addie didn't use that as much today."

I let out a small laugh. "Beware. That might mean she's looking for a new name."

One of his hands left my hips, trailing up my side, over my shoulder, to come to rest under my chin. Meeting his eyes, I saw that he was studying me like he didn't know what this was either. Well, at least I wasn't alone here. That was good.

"Ivy," he whispered. "I want to kiss you—"

My breath caught. Wow. Yes. Now. All over, preferably. "I think I'm okay with that."

Jake smiled as he watched me, then pressed his lips against my forehead. He pulled back, then his eyes locked with mine. "As I was saying, Ivy, I want to kiss you. *However*, if I give in to that feeling right now, I think things will escalate quickly, and I have a feeling that we will be interrupted as soon as things begin to heat up. But..." He pressed his lips against my forehead again, then spoke with his lips moving against my skin. "I really, really, want to." He let out a groan which made the goose bumps spring back up, and everything began to throb. Wowza.

My eyes closed as I soaked all this in. Damn. And right as I was tempted to, I don't know, grab his face and kiss the crap out of him, I heard those thundering footsteps coming from the front of the house.

Jake pulled back to lean against the counter next to me, but I noticed he was facing the counter, not the door. I took a look from Addie swirling through the door to Jake and his now uncomfortably tight jeans and giggled like a middle school girl.

"Paybacks are hell, babe."

"Promises, promises," I whispered, delighted to see his eyes widen.

Hoping off the counter, I moved to scoop up my girl and prop her on my hip. "Tell Jake good night. He needs to get home, and you need to get to bed."

Jake held his fist out for fist bump from Addie. She complied as she dropped her head to my shoulder. "Night, Jakey."

"Jakey?" he asked, raising his brows.

I shrugged. "I need to get her to bed. Is everything set for tomorrow?"

Jake turned, pushing back from the counter, apparently under better control. "Yep, we're all set. I'll head out. Make sure you lock up after you get her down."

Eye roll contained, I nodded. "Seriously, thanks Jake." I paused, then decided to thrown caution to the wind. "For everything."

Jake nodded as he slid around me and to head out of the kitchen. "No thanks needed. I had fun today." He headed for the front door.

I had a feeling sleep would be a bit elusive tonight.

The bell over the door in the bookstore rang as a customer headed out. I glanced around the quiet space. For a Tuesday afternoon, we'd been surprisingly busy, which felt good. The space wasn't large, but it was perfection in my eyes. The bright yellow door was right at the front, along with large windows that looked out at downtown Highland. The store's name, Pages, was spelled out in large typewriter keys that faced the windows as well. Inside, the perimeter of the room was lined with tall shelves, books I'd agonized over and selected. The hardwood floors typically gleamed in the late-afternoon light, though not on this cloudy day. From my back spot at the register, I could see into all the spots around the store, other than our meeting room in the back that I'd set aside for book clubs.

With a sigh of contentment, I grabbed my phone to cue up some music. I debated as I scrolled. What was I in the mood for today? Looking out at the gray skies, I selected an album by a South African, Jeremy Loops. No matter the season, no matter the weather, the music flowed through and made me feel like it was a glorious and free summer day.

The lyrics to "Power" began to fill the store, and my body moved instinctively, dancing around as I closed my eyes and swayed to the music. I spun over by my diffuser, letting the scent of citrus surround me. What a glorious day. I thought about heading to the back to grab my watering can so I could take care of a few plants that I had scattered around the store, but the bell above the door grabbed my attention.

Looking toward the front, I saw Ms. Lou headed in, along with Emma and Maggie. I couldn't help the wide smile that broke out. This boded for a great visit, if not a few sales. Maggie seemed to buy more children's books each time she was visiting or working, even though her little bean still had weeks to percolate.

"Ladies, what do I owe for this blessing?"

Lou sniffed the air. "What's that smell?"

Shaking my head, I pointed to the diffuser on my counter. I couldn't wait to hear Lou's thoughts on this. It could go either way. Lou was my grandma's generation. Some embraced the holistic lifestyle, some just labeled it as kooky. I don't think Lou had decided where she landed yet. "We've gone over this, Ms. Lou. It's a diffuser for essential oils. Today I'm using some citrus blend. It's believed to boost moods and relieve some stress."

Lou gave me a skeptical look. "Not sure about that, but it smells pretty great. What's there for sexual energy? I might give some to Verdell so we can pretend we're in our forties again."

"Jesus," Maggie muttered.

I considered Lou's question for a moment. "Well, Lou,

from what you've said in the past, not sure if you two actually need any help in that department."

"Never turn down a bit of assistance, my dear. Life lessons."

Emma shook her head.

I decided to go with it. "But I think there's some research on lime scents to help increase libido, or some woody scents."

"Woody!" Lou cackled.

"Good grief, my middle school boys are more mature than you, Lou," Maggie said.

But I had to laugh. Lou was a trip. And the woman embraced life to the fullest, you had to give her that. "Woody as in sandalwood or patchouli, Lou. Just let me know if you'd like me to get some for you the next time I go to the store."

"I just might do that," Lou said with a wicked grin. "Now, let's get down to business. You know why we're here."

I looked at Emma and Maggie who watched me expectantly, then looked back to Lou. Clearly, I was in the dark here. "I'm sorry. I thought you all were just coming in to visit. Did we plan something and I forgot?" I was going to be really frustrated with myself if that was the case. Organization wasn't natural for me, but as a single mom and a business owner, I felt like I'd been getting there. Had I forgotten something?

Emma looked at Lou. "Good gracious, Louisa Williams. Be nice." Looking back at me, she continued, "Apologies on behalf of this one." She jerked a thumb at Lou. "She just gets excited when she thinks she's going to hear something juicy."

"Juicy?"

Emma nodded. "Lou had coffee with my mom this morning. Mom shared that Jake had Addie with him for dinner last night. She also shared that you guys arranged that when Jake had the two of you stay at his house overnight a few days back. So..."

Ahh, got it. Lou enjoyed being in the know, so she wanted the details. I finished for Emma. "So you all are here for the down-and-dirty information on one Jake Spencer and me?"

Lou clapped almost gleefully. "See, I knew there would be good dirt. Down and dirty, yes. We're here for this."

Wow. I wasn't even sure what to say about that. "Um, well, do we want to start with some tea?"

"Hell no," Lou said. "Start spilling."

Maggie pulled up a stool to prop herself on as she placed her hand below her belly. "Forgive her. She was on the front lines of Emma's relationship with Max and, to some extent, mine with Sully. She feels good when she's in the mix. But"—she raised a brow at Lou—"just so you know, she's no vault. The entire town will be hearing from her— either in person or on the town's social media pages shortly after we leave here."

Lou had the sense to look indignant. "I'm right here, Maggie. And watch yourself. I still have the video of you and Cole Sullivan making out at the auction this summer that I haven't shared in our social media group. I'm not afraid to use it." Lou looked offended.

Maggie gestured to her belly. "Not sure anyone is going to care, Lou. Clearly, we've done more than is in that video. And we're married now, so I think it has lost its punch."

Emma pulled the conversation back on track. "Anyway, Ivy, I'm speaking for Maggie and myself in that we would love to know more. Jake's brother interrupted our dinner last night, and you didn't get a chance to fill us in. While it was interesting to hear stories about Jake as a kid, that really did nothing to share where the two of you were at."

I nodded. Drew had shared silly stories of Jake growing up, having his voice crack well into high school, his poor coordination in sports in his first few years of his teens, and his lack of skills with the ladies. I had a feeling that many of his stories had been exaggerated for humor and embarrassment factor, but it still did the job of painting the image of a somewhat-insecure gawky teen that Jake could have been. I couldn't imagine that the self-assured, somewhat cocky man I knew now had ever been different, but who knows?

At any rate, I didn't feel like delving into everything I was feeling about Jake, even with my friends. "Jake was a huge help to me yesterday and is planning to be all week. Addie had a great time, and I'm beyond grateful."

Maggie eyed me suspiciously. "And that's it?"

I nodded. "What else would there be?"

"Some tonsil hockey, some horizontal mambo. I mean, have you *seen* that boy?" Lou seemed incredulous.

I could feel my cheeks heating. Damn. Deny, deny, deny. "Nope. Jake is just a friend, or as friendly as he and I can be. He and Addie have somehow hit it off, so I think he just likes to hang out with her. He says she reminds him of his nieces." I tried my best to look nonchalant.

Emma was studying me, which was a bit odd, but then her smile widened. "Oh, lady. Something happened last night, yes? This is good."

Oh Goddess. Well, I mean, it was all innocent. Nothing really happened, as much as I wanted it to. I'd go with that story. "No, nothing much. Jake was just a good friend and listened to me, which was unexpected, I suppose."

"And...," Maggie prompted, "because good friends listening don't make your cheeks light on fire."

I desperately looked for new customers on the street—I'd run out and welcome them in at this point—but of course nada. "Are you sure I can't get you all some tea?"

Lou started to speak, but Emma held up a hand to stop her. "I'm sorry, Ivy. You're relatively new here. We don't mean to be so nosy. I just realized this could be incredibly intrusive if you aren't used to us. It's just that we love Jake. He's ours. And you've become ours, so we'd be delighted if there was something there. But"—and she looked sternly at Lou, a bit less so at Maggie—"you don't have to tell us if there is something going on."

A pang of longing hit me. Between Jake, and now these three, it was nice to feel cared for. Ironically, it made me miss my nana more than I had for some time. Though I absolutely believed her spirit was all around me when I was at my shop. And I felt the nudge from her now and then, like she was giving advice. Right now? I felt her nudge to open up a bit. To trust. It was so hard—I felt like I'd been on my own forever—but maybe it was time.

"Well, maybe I wouldn't say there was nothing..." I trailed off, debating how much to share.

"Yes!" Maggie pumped a fist to the ceiling. "I knew it." Emma gave her a look, then Maggie continued much more subdued. "I mean, if you'd like to share."

So I spilled the story of last night. The conversation about my parents, grandma, the position we found ourselves in before he left. The forehead kiss. Hot damn, that kiss. Good Goddess, that kiss. If only more men knew how sexy a kiss on the forehead, the back of the neck, the side of the neck, was I bet it would happen so much more. I'd only relived it a time or twenty before bed last night. I shared with them my strong desire for a whole lot more than what we had. And bless their souls, no one interrupted. Lou simply took my hand in her wrinkled one when I shared who my nana had been and squeezed.

"And that's it." My face felt heated, which was silly, I supposed. "It's nothing really, just a moment. I'm sure I'm thinking about it far more than he is. I'm not sure why last night seemed important, but it did." I let my voice trail off as I thought about those minutes, because really, that's all it was. Minutes. But it was also a connection, and my life had seriously been lacking in connections before moving to Highland.

Lou cleared her throat, and I let my eyes meet hers. For once, she looked serious. "My girl, I should have made the connection between you and Lorelai when you came to town. Beyond the similar look, you share a beautiful spirit. There was just something about your grandmother that drew people to her."

I nodded. "I know what you mean. I loved being with her. She was soothing. I felt at peace simply by being around her."

Maggie smiled. "You're that way too, Ivy. I know I felt like spending time with you as soon as we met."

"Absolutely." Emma concurred. "I told Maggie that we were pulling you into our group when we met. You must take after your grandmother. I don't remember her well, but I know we met from time to time."

The warmth I felt at their words was indescribable. Nana had been the best person I'd known. If I was even a tenth of the person she was, I'd take it. But... "Well, if that's true, I sure don't relax Jake around me. We tend to bicker more than I do with anyone else."

Lou laughed. "Sweetheart, that's because you both are

strong. Like recognizes like. And my dear, you two are crazy similar to each other. You are nurturers—"

I sputtered. "Jake, a nurturer?"

Lou raised an eyebrow over her purple frames. "Need I remind you who has your child right now?"

"Sugar cookie," I swore. Clearly, she was correct.

"Ah, chickie, I think you mean shit," Lou said with a grin. "Addie isn't here right now. And as I was saying, here we have two nurturers who tend to have some strong beliefs. Of course you will disagree from time to time. So there's that, plus those disagreements just ratchet up the smokin'-hot chemistry that's already there."

Could that be it? Was Jake actually not a climate-change denier? Was he a proponent of women's rights? And bigger question, was I really so wrong about this guy? I mean, clearly I trusted him; he was watching my daughter. Thinking over our conversation last night, I realized how much I did like being around him. In five days, he'd become someone I relied on, that I considered a friend. But was that other stuff still there? What if it was? Was that okay?

"I think I need to slow down, think more about this."

"But," Lou began.

"We totally understand," Emma said, giving Lou a look. Lou rolled her eyes at Emma but then looked back at me, tilting her head.

"Do you have siblings, Ivy?" she asked.

"No," I said, trying to figure out how our conversation had completely turned.

"Hmm." Lou paused. "Cousins?"

I was quiet for a moment. Sometimes when I was here in Highland, surrounded by people who had roots, families, it was hard to acknowledge that I didn't have that. "No. My parents are both only children."

"I thought so," Lou said with a smile. "I was trying to figure out why Lorelai hadn't talked about you, but she did. You just had a nickname, didn't you?"

My smile spread wide. I hadn't thought about Nana's nickname for me in years. "Yes, she called me Pip."

Maggie looked at me. "Pip?"

I laughed. "Pipsqueak. I mean, I'm no giant now, but I was so small as a kid, short and superthin. Nana was a tall lady, around five foot nine or ten. You can imagine me as a seven-year-old, just an itty-bitty kid beside her."

Lou nodded. "Yes, Lorelai talked about you all the time, Ivy. She said she called you Pip, but that you had the roar of a lioness if you felt an injustice had occurred. She was so proud of you, my dear."

My eyes welled up. That was something I knew, but it was amazing to hear. "Thanks, Lou. I miss her so. Even more since coming back to Highland."

Lou patted my hand. "But she'd be so pleased that you were here."

"I hope so." My brain whirled, thinking of the bookstore and a phone call I'd had earlier in the day.

"What's going on?" Emma asked, her eyes narrowing.

I looked down at the pad of paper where I'd taken some notes, then back to the three faces that were watching me with nothing but concern. "It's just that being a business owner isn't easy."

"Tell me about it," Lou muttered.

I nodded, remembering that she used to own the coffee shop. "Well, Nana left me this building. She knew I dreamed of owning a bookstore. And I thought I had it all figured out, but the summer wasn't easy."

Emma's eyes widened. "Oh no. Did asking you to help fund the author series set you back?"

I grabbed her hand and squeezed. "No, no, it's fine. I budgeted for it. But when I first had Addie, things were tight. I've always sworn I won't let us get back to those times. So"—I shrugged—"I panicked a bit this summer. Sales have picked back up. And then today I had an unexpected call."

"Spill," Emma said, her eyes going from the notepad to me.

My heart thumped. I felt like if I said it, then it was real. And honestly, I wasn't sure if I wanted it to be or not. Inhaling and gathering some strength, I continued. "An indie bookstore in the Chicago area is looking to branch out. They offered to buy this place and have me manage it."

Maggie's mouth fell open. Emma looked surprised. Lou leaned over to squeeze my hand where Maggie had dropped it. "That relieves a lot of pressure from your shoulders. Is that what you want?"

I relished the solid feel of her as I closed my eyes and worked to find my center. What was it I wanted? Opening my eyes again, I looked at these women and spoke from my heart. "I don't know."

Lou patted my hand. "Then that's where you are. No decisions need to be made today, correct?"

I nodded. "No, not today." I felt some weight released just by sharing my struggle with them. I wasn't alone. "Thanks, Lou." I looked around the little group. "Thanks to you all. I haven't had anyone to confide in for years. It's nice."

"Besides Jake, you mean." Maggie grinned, lightening the mood.

I shrugged, ignoring the strong desire to pull out my cell and see if he'd texted lately. "I don't know what to think about Jake."

"I just want to put in my vote that I think you two could be good for each other," Emma said, following Maggie's lead.

The bell over the door sang out as we all turned as a group to see Jake walking in, holding Addie on his hip. Today she had on her red tutu with her rain boots that had bumblebees on them. Yes, she had dressed herself. Yes, I was completely fine with that. I mean, she was clothed. What else mattered?

And Jake? Well, my mouth might have begun to salivate just a bit. He was wearing worn Carhartts, work boots, a flannel opened over a fitted waffle T-shirt. His glasses were back, and I had no idea why they were so attractive, but they were. What on earth was happening to me?

Jake looked over our little group. "Well, hello ladies." He moved to Lou and leaned down to kiss her cheek. "Hello, Ms. Lou. Staying out of trouble?"

Lou looked absolutely delighted. "God knows I'm not. Where's the fun in that? I'm just singing your praises to Ivy here. We need to talk you up a bit so she'll bite."

"Lou!" I was a bit mortified.

Jake tipped his head to the side as he mouthed *You bite?* at me with a raised brow.

Gracious. And yum.

"Maggie, Emma, let's leave these two alone. Maybe they'll figure out what they need to be doing with their free time on their own."

Maggie and Emma grinned, leaning in to give me a hug before gathering their things.

Lou started heading for the door, but then she paused and spun to look at us. "Oh, Jake, I have to bow out of helping you organize the Reds of Christmas for the town next month."

Jake's head quickly followed Lou as he drew his brows together. "What? We only have a few weeks left, Lou. What came up?"

Lou laughed. "Oh nothing. Just some stuff with Verdell. It's only the final details that need ironing out anyway."

"I know, but that's typically the part you love," Jake replied. "We usually do that over dinners at the brewery. I can't believe you're ditching me. It won't be the same without you."

"Don't worry. I found someone to take my place," Lou said as she began moving again toward the door. "Right, Ivy? It will be great for you as a new business in town—if you decide not to sell, I mean. And you wouldn't mind a few dinners with Jake here and there, would you? Maggie and Emma can watch Addie. All right, toodles! Thanks for having us!" And she was out the door.

Maggie and Emma wrapped their arms around each other as they let out a laugh and followed Lou out and down the street.

What in the world just happened here? I turned back to Jake, who was watching me with Addie in his arms, still looking at the door, quite possibly wondering what tornado just left the shop.

"Reds of Christmas?" I asked what I felt was a good place to start.

Jake let Addie down as she began squirming in his arms. "Sell?" His gaze was intense.

My heart skipped as I took in Jake's expression. I had a strong desire to smooth his eyebrows down, maybe trace his lips?

"Ivy?"

I shook my head. "Um, I had a call today from an indie bookstore up north. They offered to buy Pages and have me manage it." My gut clenched at the thought of selling this place, even if I still got to be part of it. That was telling, I supposed. I looked over, seeing that Addie had moved to the kids' toys that I left out for little ones while their parents browsed.

Jake moved across the counter from me. "Can I help?"

"How could you help, Jake?"

"Well, I'm a business owner too. I'd be glad to let you bounce ideas off me, if that would help. Maybe while we figure out this event that Lou has just roped you into?"

"What is the Reds?"

"Technically, it's an event that the businesses in town participate in to increase sales around the holidays. In this case, I also think Lou is playing matchmaker once again. We should all be worried."

"Worried?"

Jake nodded slowly. "See, when Lou decides to play Cupid, it tends to work out in her favor."

"And we don't want that?"

Jake paused as he let his gaze roam over my face. "Well, I haven't before."

Interesting. "And now?"

He looked a bit frustrated as he raked a hand through his hair. "I don't know what I want anymore."

Me too, Jake Spencer. Me too.

10

SIBLING LOVE

Jake

With a glance at my watch, I dug in, my legs pumping to eat up the miles. Chief surged ahead, ears flying, brown coat gleaming, as we neared the end of our run. We'd been lucky this week. After that freak early-winter storm last Friday, we'd had mild temperatures. I'd been refreshingly busy with plans for the anniversary party on Saturday and time spent with Addie. I hadn't got in as many miles as I'd normally run. However, I had this morning set aside specifically for this. Sully had been at me for months, reminding me that we took Finn on to help make sure we had time for ourselves again, but it hadn't felt like a blessing until this week.

Turning at the corner, I began my last leg home. My legs burned with the effort to finish strong. I typically tried to get in about thirty miles a week, running five miles a day, six days a week. The cross-country team had been a haven for me from middle school onward. I wasn't always the most coordinated of kids, or the strongest, but something about the repeated pounding of my feet on the pavement had given me solace as a teen and still did.

As I was coming down the block, I looked over at Ivy's place. I'd taken a slow start this morning, waking a bit later than usual and doing some paperwork for the brewery over my eggs and coffee. I'd guess that Addie was already at preschool, Ivy at the bookstore. It seemed to be unreal that in just under a week, I felt like those two were woven into my life to some extent.

I'd picked Addie up for the past three days and each day learned a bit more about her. Yesterday she'd shared a bit about her classmates as we hung out at a local park. It seemed that Izzy in her class had the best 'magination; Addie liked to see what stories she'd create each day. Daniel in class made the best block towers. And Christian was her favorite artist.

The teachers had, apparently, brought in sidewalk chalk yesterday, and Addie had been all about it. Covered in the dust of her artwork, she'd told me all about the princess who fought to protect the knight that she'd drawn, slaying the evil dragon on her own. Clearly, Ivy's influence was apparent in her daughter. I couldn't wait to see how her day was today.

Chief and I turned in to my drive and headed for home. Pulling up, I stopped the timer on my watch and glanced at the distance and time. Not bad. Chief leaned against my legs as he panted.

"Good boy," I said as I gave his head a rub.

We headed in the backdoor, and Chief immediately went over to his water bowl, splashing the entire area with excess water before getting enough. I moved to the counter to see if I'd missed any calls, though I wasn't due into the brewery for an hour or so. Glancing at my phone, I held back a groan when I saw a group text from my siblings.

Steph: *How's my new best friend? Can I call her yet?*

Drew: *I only met her once. I think Jake might be ashamed of us. He doesn't want me unleashed.*

Steph: **gasp* Say it ain't so, Jacob Spencer. What could you possibly have to be ashamed of?*

Drew: *See, he's so ashamed he isn't speaking to us. Or letting me speak to Ivy, more to the point.*

Steph: *I mean, let's be honest, there is some room to be concerned with you...*

Drew: *I'm an angel and you're just jealous because Mom and Dad like me best.*

Steph: *Sacrilege. You take that back.*

Me: *Why do you two include me on these texts if you're just going to ramble on?*

Steph: *Look who finally showed up.*

Me: *Chief and I were running and just got home. My point stands.*

Drew: *Enough from you, doom and gloom. I'm coming into the brewery this afternoon. Clearly you need some Drew time to cheer you up.*

I had a strong desire to ignore the texts and walk away. No way was my admission of my afternoon plans going to be a small thing.

Me: *I have to watch Addie this afternoon. You can go in the brewery even if I'm not there.*

Steph: *Back the truck up, Jacob. Like hell we're glossing over this. Tell me about Addie. Are the adoption papers drawn up yet? When's the party?*

Me: *Smartass.*

Steph: *You know it. Seriously, can't wait to meet her.*

Me: *We're friends. There's nothing here.*

Drew: *Ignore him, I am. We know the truth.*

Placing my phone down on the counter, I headed up the stairs to my bedroom. No way was I going to sit around and continue the back-and-forth with my siblings. Damn, I loved them both, but they also were super annoying. However, as tiresome as our group text could be, I was also grateful for it.

The three of us had been super close growing up. With Drew moving out West and me moving three hours south, we didn't see each other as much as we once did. Our group text was full of us giving each other shit, which was absolutely perfect, honestly. And although I was a bit hesitant about the weekend, with Steph and my mom's unrealistic expectations about something going on with Ivy, I was fucking thrilled to hang out with my family.

Ivy. I leaned into the shower and turned it on, letting it warm up a bit. I walked back to my closet, then shucked my sweaty running clothes on the floor as visions of Ivy on the counter in her kitchen clouded my head. It was Thursday morning, but Monday evening might as well have been months ago at this point. I'd left Ivy's house, certain I was making the right call in not acting on the feelings that welled up in the moment, but damn it if I hadn't second-guessed myself daily since then.

Ivy and I were— Hell, what were we? Friends? Enemies? People who could annoy the shit out of each other? The honest answer, we were all that and more. Well, maybe not enemies; that seemed a bit strong. I wish I could figure out why she could push my buttons the way she did. The only person I'd known to do that before—scratch that— the only people I'd known to do that were my siblings. That didn't bode well, or did it? I certainly didn't see her in the same light as my siblings. There was a strong possibility of something more.

I headed into the shower, remembering her face as she sat on the counter. She'd been overcome, somewhat emotional. The fact that she'd opened up to me, told me about her parents, her grandmother, made me feel honored in a way. I'd tried to ignore the feelings that had filled me as she spoke, but they were there anyway. The desire to protect her, to take care of her, was overwhelming. However, I had a feeling if I'd told Ivy that, she might have kneed me in the balls. Maybe I was wrong, but I had a strong sense that Ivy wanted to take care of herself. I admired that and wanted to help at the same time.

Turning under the showerhead, I let the warmth soothe my exhausted muscles. I was spent. Placing my hands on the tiled wall in the shower, I let the water cascade over my back. My schedule for the day rolled through my mind, mentally rearranging things to clear time in the afternoon. As much as I hated to admit it, while seeing Addie was absolutely a highlight, the time spent with Ivy was what I looked forward to all day long. What the hell was that?

Tuesday I'd met Ivy at the bookstore with Addie. Monday and Wednesday, I'd brought her home. Standing around Ivy's kitchen, talking about our days, it was more comforting than I'd expected and made me want it in my daily life. It didn't hurt that Ivy seemed to favor yoga pants and fitted shirts at home. Yeah, that didn't hurt at all. Shaking my head, I slid my hand down to my rapidly hardening cock and gave in to the images of Ivy racing through my brain. I could analyze the shit out of this later. Right now I'd just enjoy it for what it was.

The day got away from me. Sully and I met to discuss can designs for our next batch of beer. Finn met with the two of us, looking over long-term projects for the month. We ironed out some staff schedules and finalized the plans for the celebration this weekend. I finally took the time to head over to the tank.

I looked up from my spot at the tanks at the sound of my name. Drew was making his way toward me. Checking my watch, I saw that it was just a bit after one. I still had a little under an hour until I needed to go get Addie from school.

"What are you doing here?" I asked.

"I said I'd be by this afternoon in our text thread," he replied.

Nodding, I grabbed a towel to wipe off my hands. "Have you eaten?"

Drew fell into step beside me as we headed toward the bar area of the brewery. "Yep, but I can sit with you if you need to eat still."

"I already ordered a burger a bit ago. It's likely almost up. Beer?"

He scanned the taps. "Evolution."

I moved behind the bar to pour his drink, then slid it across the space to him while grabbing one for myself. "Bar or table?" I covered my mouth as a yawn escaped. I wondered if I could convince Addie we both needed rest time today.

Drew looked from me to the customers scattered throughout the space, including the bar. "How about over there?" he asked, nodding toward a high-top in the corner.

I noted the privacy of that space and wondered if he was ready to share why he was suddenly in town. I kicked myself for not making more time for him over this past week. He hadn't crashed in my basement but in the Airbnb one of my neighbors had over their garage. While it was relatively cheap per night, my place was free, so we hadn't had the time to down some Irish whiskey and get to the bottom of his time here. I had a feeling he was working through some shit and wouldn't unload until he was ready.

Grabbing my drink, I followed Drew to the high-top. Our hostess, Lauren, appeared with my food as we slid onto our stools.

"Can I get you anything to eat?" she asked Drew.

He looked at my burger, then at a nearby table. "I didn't think so, but how about some nachos?" he said, glancing at a plate piled high with them nearby. "I'm sure this guy would be glad to help me with some of them."

"Absolutely," Lauren said, tapping her tablet before heading to check on a few other tables.

"So, to what do I owe the pleasure of your company for the past week?" I figured it was better to jump straight into it with Drew. He didn't tend to beat around the bush.

Drew took a long swig of the beer. "Damn, you guys make some fine hops." Pausing, he tilted the glass as he considered the beverage.

"Drew..."

He looked up, locking eyes with me. "Several reasons. One, I had time off I needed to take. My vacation days have been accruing for years. I just don't use them."

"You don't say." This had been a bone of contention between him and Steph and me for a while. While we'd been to see Drew for extended trips, he rarely came home for more than a weekend.

Drew smirked at me. "At any rate, I needed to take some time off. I also wanted to check on you.

"Me? Why?"

"Because I've been paying attention as you've talked for the past six months, big bro. Whether you realize it or not, you've been talking about Bookstore Ivy for some time. I wanted to get back here and make sure you didn't fuck this up."

I glanced around, noting the quiet hum of the restaurant, of satisfied customers, then looked back at Drew. "Clearly I'm not screwing up this place. In regard to Ivy, she's a friend. Sometimes. What is there to screw up?"

Drew looked serious as he pushed his beer aside and leaned in. His gray eyes were focused on me, and he looked more than a little pissed. "Are you going to make me say it, Jake? Steph and I have both been worried about you. You've not been in a relationship since Rachel and—"

My body got tense. "What does she have to do with this?"

Drew leaned back. "There it is. You need to let her go."

The need to get up, to leave, was overwhelming. I sat through it. "What the hell, man. Rachel and I have been ancient history for years. What do I need to let go?"

"Ancient history? When you're in a relationship for four years, think you're going to marry her, and she breaks an engagement weeks before the wedding, that might impact someone. It sure as hell has impacted you." Drew looked absolutely pissed. "And there is nothing wrong with feeling that way, man. Completely justified."

It had been years, ten years to be exact. Rachel and I got together our senior year in high school. She went to college, I joined a construction company in the college town she was in, and we made it work. So much so that we were going to get married as soon as she graduated. Well, until she told me there was someone else a month before the wedding. But I was over it. Had been for some time.

"Of course it impacted me, Drew. But that was a decade ago. Why would you think that would still be affecting me now?"

Drew gave me a skeptical look. "Not sure, man. Maybe because you've never been in another relationship. Hell with long-term shit, you haven't even had anything short-term."

"What the hell? Sure I have."

"Not sex, man, but a woman you date, go out with, spend time with, talk about. When has that happened last? And sex? That's not too frequent either, from what I can tell."

I held back the words that wanted to fly out. That it was none of his business, that it was my life, that I was doing just fine. Taking a deep breath, I took another one, and another. If I was being honest here, if the tables were turned, if I thought my siblings were struggling, I stuck my nose in their business too. I wanted to protect them, help them, be there for them. That's what we did.

"Here you go." Lauren popped up, sliding a plate of nachos in front of Drew. She dropped the plates and silverware on the table. "Anything else I can get you?"

We both shook our heads, and she left, telling us to enjoy our lunch. Straightening my back, I looked over at my baby brother. He wasn't so babyish anymore. Drew had been gone for so long sometimes I forgot he'd grown up on us. He was almost thirty, but I still remembered the ten-year-old following around his newly teenage brother. Nothing stopped him. He would take on the world if he could. And here he was, confronting me because he was worried. I'd do well to remember that. As annoying as he was, it came from a good place.

"Drew, I'm fine. No." I raised a hand to stop the onslaught of what I was certain was ready to come. "I get it. I really do. And you're right. After Rachel I didn't see the point in relationships anymore. Haven't for a while. Part of that's her and getting burned; part of that is being too damn busy. In that time, Sully and I began dreaming up this place. Then seven years ago, we started to make that dream a reality. For the past five years, I've poured myself into this place. It took us a lot of work to get to where we are right now, but I'm proud of it. Really, I am."

"You should be. This is fucking amazing. And now that you're canning, you guys have a new way to expand your business. But nobody? Really?" He raised a brow at me.

I shrugged. "Not sure. Just haven't met anyone that seems worth taking the risk for, even if I did have the time."

Now Drew leaned in. "Really? No one? Because I can think of someone."

I leaned back with a huff. "Ivy? We're just friends, and not even that at times. I drive her crazy and vice versa."

"Ever think that maybe all that tension was some shit-hot sexual chemistry you should explore?"

"No." I looked over at the bar.

"Ahh." Drew got quiet. "So you have thought of it. And maybe explored it? Spill, bro."

I closed my eyes, shaking my head. There was no point. "Nothing has happened. Truly." I took a breath, looking up at the ceiling before continuing. "It's just, well, there's been some chemistry."

"I'll say. That girl is smokin'."

I fought the bizarre urge to slug him with that comment. Jesus, I needed to get it together. "Anyway, she has a kid. You can't do anything casual there, and I don't know if I ever want anything serious again."

"Again? You're not a monk, dude. I mean, Jesus, Jake. I know you want a family one day, right? You're not going to be that surly old man sitting on the park bench, playing chess."

I picked up my burger and took another bite, thinking while I chewed. I mean, to be honest, I did see myself with a family one day, and time with Ivy and Addie had made that desire stronger. After Rachel, I stopped really dreaming about that for me. Like I thought it would probably happen, but didn't do the work to get there. If I was being honest, I had zero desire to let anyone get that close to me again.

"Earth to Jake," Drew said between bites as he inhaled his own lunch.

"You're a caveman. Slow down."

Drew continued eating. "Can't. These are unreal."

I glanced down at my watch. "I need to head soon. I'm picking Addie up and bringing her to Ivy's."

Drew wiped his hands on a napkin and stopped eating. Miracles do happen. "You're hanging at Bookstore Ivy's? Without Ivy?"

I gathered my silverware and napkin on my plate and slid it to the side. Thomas, one of our waiters, grabbed it, asking if we needed anything else. We both said we were good as everything was cleared away. Drew watched me expectantly, but I waited until we were alone.

As soon as Thomas left, Drew raised a brow and continued, "Well..."

I worked not to revert to my teenage self and tell him to shut the fuck up. "Yes, I'm waiting at Ivy's. This week I've had Addie at my place, the Sullivans', and around town. Today, I'm letting Addie show me her favorite toys." I stood up, preparing to grab my stuff to head out.

Drew stood up as well, pulling on his jacket as he took a step to follow me. I turned, looking at him in confusion. "What are you doing?"

Drew gave me a shit-eating grin. "Oh, I thought that was clear. I'm coming with you."

"I'm sorry, what?"

"Oh, big brother, we're not done with this conversation. And I want to meet this little girl that has you so wrapped around her finger. I'm hanging out with you and Addie today."

I briefly debated arguing with him about it, but honestly, what was the point? He'd likely just delay me getting to Addie, and I didn't want her wondering if I was coming.

"Fine, come on," I said as we headed for the door, knowing there was a damn good chance I would be regretting this.

11

BEAUTY SHOP

Ivy

As I headed in the back door of my house, I marveled at the quiet. I'd been able to get out of the store a bit early tonight. When Maggie had cut back on her part-time hours as the school year began, I had hired someone to take her place. Nic was amazing. Over the past few months, she'd taken on more responsibilities at the store, and I hadn't realized how freeing it was not to carry the entire load. I'd love to have her there full-time, but financially I couldn't swing it yet. Today Nic was closing up for the first time on her own, and I was beyond grateful. It had been a long day.

All week I'd contemplated the offer on the bookstore. In talking to their owner, today they'd submitted an official offer to me to look over with my lawyer, laying out the terms. I had a few weeks to look it over and let them know. Part of me wanted to say heck no, I had this on my own. The adult in me made me pause and consider it. They had the resources to grow Pages beyond what I'd been able to do on my own. And the notion of not having my finances wrapped up in a business that might fail felt like a huge weight I could lift. On the other hand, the fate of our store wouldn't be in my hands anymore. I wouldn't be my own boss.

Being an adult was for the birds.

I glanced around the landing area at the back door, listening for signs of life. Jake said he was bringing Addie here after school. I'd fully expected to come home and see toys strewn all over the house. I knew she was pumped about showing him her room and her dolls. Smiling to myself, I thought of Jake and the fact that Addie likely had him playing dolls with her all afternoon. I wondered if he would've balked at that or if it's something he did with his nieces already.

I moved through the kitchen and the hall before I came to the corner of the living room and stopped short. The sight in front of me was all kinds of beautiful. Jake sprawled out on one side of the sectional, his brother, Drew, on the other. Both men were sound asleep. I looked them over. Where they were admittedly both gorgeous specimens of man, I'd take Jake's dark hair, constant stubble, and grouchy attitude in a heartbeat. Yeah, I wasn't denying things in my mind anymore. Out loud? To anyone in the real world? That was another story, and the name of that story was denial. However, in my mind, I could fantasize all I wanted.

Today Jake was in an almost threadbare T-shirt advertising his brewery, an open flannel, and loose jeans that dipped down perfectly. Glorious. His T-shirt had ridden up to expose his abs with the dusting of hair disappearing into his jeans. Thank you, Goddess, for that view. What a gift. What a wonderful happy trail.

Glancing over at Drew, I saw that he was similarly dressed, with dark tousled hair that looked in desperate need of a cut, some Carhartts that had seen better days, and a Henley. His beard was well groomed but a bit longer than his chin in the front. He was taller and broader than Jake, who was in no way small. Now that he was asleep, I could see how exhausted Drew looked. Awake, his eyes were alight with mischief. Asleep, I noticed the shadow below them. I wondered if that was normal.

Finally, my eyes fell to Addie. She was kneeling at the coffee table between the two men. Clearly, she'd had a day full of movement. Even if I pulled her hair into a high pony-tail in the morning, her nonstop energy had her looking tousled with hair flying every which way by afternoon. Today she'd chosen leopard print leggings and a purple and pink polka-dot sweatshirt. I didn't see any socks on her feet, but she tended to shed those like a snakeskin once she walked in our house. Addie looked up at my entrance and smiled.

Putting her finger to her lips, she whispered, "Shh, Momma. They're sleeping."

Dang, she was cute. Sometimes it took my breath away to realize that I made her. I was so lucky.

I nodded at her, beckoning her toward me with the crook of my finger. We headed toward the kitchen, moving stealthily, not to wake the sleeping giants.

We got into the kitchen, and I picked her up to let her sit on the counter. Leaning forward, I laid a kiss on her nose. "How was your day, peanut?"

"So good, Momma. Jakey's brother is Drew. They both came to get me at school. We stopped by the park, then came here. I got out all my toys. We played dolls for hours." She paused as she thought for a moment. "But Chief couldn't come. He's resting at his house."

I smiled at her warped sense of time and her love of a dog she'd known for a week. Jake would've picked her up at school only a bit over two hours ago, but in the mind of a four-year-old, that was the equivalent of half a day or more.

"Did you take a nap too, or just the big boys?" I asked, grinning as I thought of how irritated Jake would be to hear me call him and Drew the big boys. I'd have to make sure I'd say it to his face later.

"I took a short one," Addie said. "The big boys"—I smiled hearing her pick up on that nickname—"said they'd lay down with me. When I woke up, they were sleeping. They must have been tired, Momma."

At first, her comment made me want to laugh, but then I considered her words. Jake had been helping me out all week. But he also had a full-time job, and he was getting ready for the anniversary party at the brewery on Saturday. Of course he was tired. To be honest, I felt a bit crappy that I hadn't thought of that before.

He'd jumped on helping me, but how had that impacted his already-full schedule? I mean, he'd said I was doing him a favor, but this had been a huge one for me. Was I ungrateful? This man drove me a bit batty on a regular basis, but who was he really? Why did I want to throttle him and then kiss the stuffing out of him? My mind flew back to that sliver of skin I saw above Jake's jeans as he slept on the couch. Phew. Was it warm in here?

"I'm glad you had fun with the big boys, Addie. You think it's time for a snack?"

Her eyes lit up. Addie loved to cook, to do anything in the kitchen. She was at the age where helping was a big deal. She desperately wanted to be independent, though she was still a ways from being able to do everything she wanted to.

"Can we cook, Momma?"

I bopped her on her nose. "You bet, babe. How about Chocolate Chocolate Chip Muffins?"

Addie raised her hands and shook them in the air as she did anytime she got excited. "Yes, Momma! Those are the best." Then she looked super serious. "But we can't give any to Chief. Chocolate is bad for dogs."

I looked at her, puzzled. Then I thought about the time she'd spent at Jake's this week. "Addie, have you tried to give Chief chocolate?"

She gave me her wide-eyed innocent look. "No, Momma. Just crackers. And cheese. And some turkey. But no chocolate. Jakey said that was bad."

I moved to grab the ingredients for the muffins as I nodded at her. "Okay, baby. But I also don't think you're supposed to feed dogs a whole lot of people food. Maybe check with Jakey on each item? He might prefer you give Chief a bone, and only once in a while."

"Okay, Momma. Music?"

"Absolutely, my girl." I tapped on my phone until one of Chris Stapleton's albums came up and turned the volume to low, letting it fill up the kitchen. Nodding my head, seeing that Addie was doing the same, I let the music fill me.

We moved with the ease born of many times cooking together. Addie was an expert stirrer—her words, not mine. She sat there, manning the mixer, while I added our ingredients. We whipped together the batch of muffins while the oven preheated. As the last bit of batter was placed in the muffin tin and I slid them in the oven, I heard a throat clear behind me.

Turning, I saw Jake in the doorway. He was leaning against one side of the doorframe, his legs crossed at the ankles, as he watched us. I wondered how long he'd been standing there. The look on his face was softer than I'd seen. I began to say something, but Addie beat me to it.

"Jakey!" she screeched, holding her arms out to him. Oh, my heart. He crossed to her, scooped her up off the counter, and swung her to his hip. Damn. Maybe it was good that we weren't doing anything romantic. That way she could have him in her life without having to worry about the two of us breaking up. Right? Right.

His voice was thick, likely from the hard nap. "Did you get some sleep, peanut?"

"I did, but you and Drew were still napping, so I colored."

He nodded, like he was considering what she said with the seriousness not everyone gave to a four-year-old. Damn if that didn't make me want to hug him. And maybe kiss him. Once or twice. Yeah, I know.

"What are you making with your momma?" he asked as he scanned the dishes scattered over the counter, then met my eyes. His smile was warm, and I wanted to melt into it.

"Chocolate Chocolate Chip muffins," I whispered.

"Momma, that was supposed to be a secret!" Addie spoke from her spot on his hip.

I looked at her in confusion. When did we decide that?

Drew spoke up from the door. "No worries, Addie. I'll take a muffin anywhere, anytime."

Jake shook his head. "Drew...," he cautioned.

"Not how I meant it, man. Not my fault your head is in the gutter." Drew moved toward the fridge. "Addie, do you mind if I have a beer?" He grinned at her, but then looked at me. I nodded permission.

"Drew, we don't need to stay. I'm sure these two have things they need to do," Jake said, moving to the counter near me to let Addie down.

"Momma," Addie began in a singsong voice. I knew where she'd be going with this. She loved having people over, and we didn't do it often enough for her. But that thought was derailed when I looked down at Jake's hand, wrapped around Addie as he lowered her to her previous spot on the counter.

Grabbing his hand, I turned it over in mine. "What's this?"

Drew immediately began to laugh.

I watched Jake's face in fascination as his cheeks got a bit red and he stammered, "Well, Addie asked, and I thought..."

Drew interrupted, "Addie wanted to play beauty shop." His voice was heavy with amusement.

"I painted the big boys' nails, Momma! Doesn't it look good?" Addie was positively giddy on the counter, doing her shimmy back and forth as well as she could when seated.

I raised an eyebrow at Jake as I gestured for him to give me both his hands. Yep, sure enough, ten fingers in a beautiful sparkly pink. "Absolutely looks beautiful, Ads." I said, knowing my shit-eating grin was on my face, but I was powerless to stop it.

"Don't leave my gorgeous hands out, Bookstore Ivy. They're pretty hot too, right?" Drew moved closer to me, showing me his hands as well, done up the same as Jake. "Can't dim my manly light, painted nails or not."

I laughed and started to reach for him so I could examine his as well, but Jake hip checked him and gave him a look that expressed his displeasure. "Watch it, Andrew." His voice was gruff, delicious.

That was interesting.

Drew's smile increased. "Oh, I can't wait to chat with Steph today," he said nonsensically.

"Sh— I mean knock it off," Jake growled.

The amount of testosterone in my kitchen was impressive. Time to take charge and balance it out.

I clapped my hands. "Okay, *boys*." I emphasized that word, and Jake made a face. "This is how it's going to go. If you'd like to stay for dinner, you're welcome to. We're having homemade pizza. Muffins will be ready shortly. Pizza in a few hours. There's beer in the fridge. Help yourself, then relax. You're guests in our house."

Drew nodded and immediately moved to the fridge, making himself at home. He opened the door, then glanced inside before looking at me. "Anything you want me to save for you?" he asked, gesturing.

I peered inside and saw that I was now stocked with Jake and Sully's beer. "When did you do this?" I looked to Jake.

He shrugged. "Can't have you drinking our competitors' beer, babe, when you could have ours."

"Babe? That's damn, I mean dang, adorable," Drew mumbled, earning an eye roll from Jake.

"To answer your question, Drew, you are welcome to anything in there. I think I know where I can get more if need be."

"I bet you do," he said with a smirk. "Now, if you two can excuse me, I think I need to message our dear older sister."

With that, Drew headed back toward the front of the house. Addie, ever the social butterfly, leaned over on the counter to roll onto her belly, then slid off the counter until her feet hit the floor. "I'm going with Drew, Momma," she called as her little feet pounded after him.

I shook my head, then looked at Jake. "I hope your

brother wasn't looking for any quiet time. That won't be happening here, or at least not until she goes to bed."

Jake moved to the fridge, taking a beer out himself. He held it out to me. I looked at the label, *Black Hole Sun*. Ah, he said he'd bring me their hazy IPA. Nodding, I took it and moved to a cabinet to grab a glass. "Want one?" I held mine up.

"Nah, I'm fine." Jake walked over to lean against the counter. Looking to his side, he picked up a Mason jar I had sitting on a window ledge above my sink. "What's this?"

I looked over as I grabbed a pot mitt to pull the muffins out with. "Oh, that's just moon water."

Now Jake looked more confused than ever. "I'm sorry, what?"

I grinned. I knew how this was going to go. And somehow knowing he was going to think I was off my rocker helped me feel like I was on a more even keel. "Moon water. I put out glass jars to collect rain water during a full moon."

Jake closed his eyes as he replaced the glass jar on the counter. Opening his eyes, he regarded me. "I know you've mentioned moon water before, and I know damn well I'm going to regret this, but why in the fuck would you do that?"

I pulled my muffins out of the oven and placed them on the top to cool. I let Jake wait as I took a sip of my beer. Putting the beer on the counter, I then hopped up to sit and took in Jake's expression. Yep, this was going to be great. "My nana taught me. Water from a rain during a full moon, or even a gibbous moon, has beautiful energy. The moon controls the tides, you know. Moon water is charged. I also have a rose crystal in the jar when I'm collecting it." I bit my lip, knowing Jake likely had so many things begging to burst from his gorgeous lips right now.

Jake watched me, and dang if his stare didn't seem a bit

heated. Interesting. "And what do you do with this water?" He moved closer, taking a hand and putting it on my knee, pulling it to the side. He slid between my legs, mirroring the position we were in just a few nights before. He put a hand on either side of my legs, but didn't move any closer.

Oh boy. Looking up at him, I whispered. "I use it to water my plants."

"You do have a lot of plants," he whispered back.

"I love them."

"Do you name them?" he asked, his gaze scanning my face, then trailing over my body to where we were practically pressed against each other.

"Yes. How'd you know?"

"Seems like something a green witch would do." He smoothed his hands over my legs. "Your yoga pants drive me crazy. I didn't know you wore them to work, I thought you just wore those long dresses."

I smiled inwardly. I knew those skirts and dresses drove him crazy. They screamed *hippie* to him. "Well, those are comfortable, but I also wear leggings and jeans just like everyone else."

Jake's hand skated up my arm, my neck, to grip my chin as he locked his gaze on mine. "You might be a lot of things, Ivy James, but you are definitely not like everyone else."

Wow. That was nice.

"Jake, what are we doing here?" I whispered.

He paused for a moment, as if he was debating his next move, giving me a chance to move back. Not happening. And then he said, "This." Leaning forward, he captured my mouth and pressed his lips to mine.

Holy hell.

Moving his lips ever so softly, his tongue traced over my lips, and they parted on a gasp. As his tongue met mine, it was on. My hands wrapped around his torso, pulling him against me as I let my hands roam up and down his back. One came to the front and slid under his shirt so I could touch that glorious chest.

His mouth continued to move, nibbling and sucking my lips. I moved against him, wanting the friction of his pelvis against my core. He tugged my hair, and I let my head fall back as he moved his lips to kiss down my neck. I moaned, wondering how I could keep this going all night long.

"Well, well, well." Drew's voice from the doorway pulled me out of the moment. Jake stopped moving, stuck his head in my neck and groaned as Drew said, "Big bro, I think you might want to revisit your earlier statements."

I peeked over at Drew, who stood in the doorway, looking very much like the cat that ate the canary. "Do you need something, Drew?" I croaked out.

Drew smiled at me, and I felt like there was more to that smile than an I-just-caught-my-brother-in-the-act grin, but I wasn't sure what that was. "Addie wanted hot chocolate and mellows. She said Jakey knew how to make it best. So I came back here to ask him. But then I saw all that." He gestured between the two of us. "So I had to take a picture and send it to Steph. Might want to find your phone, *Jakey*. I bet the messages are piling up."

"What the hell, man? Privacy mean anything to you?" Jake growled. I giggled. His head swung my way. "Ivy? You're laughing?"

I shrugged. "I don't have siblings. I like how you guys seem to tease each other."

Drew entered the kitchen, moving to the glass front cabinet with coffee mugs. "No seem about it, Bookstore Ivy. Teasing is part of the DNA of our relationship." Pulling out a mug, he put it on the counter, then looked at the Mason jar that Jake had put down. Running his finger over the tape I had on it listing the date from when I'd collected it, he looked at me. "What's this?"

Jake groaned again as he pivoted so that the counter was to his back and looked up at the ceiling. "Ivy, I beg you, don't tell him. You have no idea what you're getting into."

The laughter bubbled up inside me. My house felt cozier, more homelike somehow, with these two giant men squeezed into my small kitchen. I knew deep inside that my nana would love this, which made me love it all the more. I looked up at Drew standing on the other side of Jake and worked to school myself into my most serious voice. "It's moon water I collected during the last full moon when it rained," I said, then waited.

Drew looked at me for a beat, then Jake, and then broke out in a huge grin as he hooted with laughter. "Oh, Ivy, you are perfection," he said as he pulled my head toward him, kissed the top of it, then threw an arm over Jake's shoulders. Jake shook his head and then looked at me with a bit of a smile on his face.

Aw, man. This? This I could get used to real quick.

12

THE BOUNTY OF SIBLINGS

Jake

I leaned back, dropping my head to rest on the Adirondack I was sitting in, and looked up at the stars. My portable speaker filled the night air with the Stapleton album Ivy had been playing in her kitchen tonight. Apparently, I wanted to torture myself with memories of her as I sat out in the quiet night.

Chief ran a lap around my backyard, then another, and another. I debated heading in for more layers. It was that in-between temperature where a heavy flannel and long-sleeved thermal seemed to do the job, along with the firepit in front of me. I'd left Ivy's with some seriously conflicted emotions but was using the quiet of the evening to try to let it go. I went from wanting to figure out what this thing was between us to being certain it was nothing good and we should ignore it. I didn't want to put myself in a position to be hurt again, I didn't want to hurt Ivy, and I sure as hell didn't want to hurt Addie.

Damn, that little girl had me wrapped around her finger. I looked down, just able to get a glimpse of my pink nails in the glow of fire. Where does one buy nail polish remover? I remember my mom and Steph using it when I was a kid. I mean, I could have them bring it down when they arrived tomorrow night, but I'd rather have it already off and avoid any questions. Though Drew probably had photographic evidence of it.

Fire crackled in the background and I blew out a breath, watching the steam from my body evaporate into the air. Any time spent outside at night helped to remind me of how insignificant I really was in the scheme of life. Boy, did I need that right now. After Drew had interrupted us in the kitchen, we'd hung at Ivy and Addie's for several more hours. Addie and Drew had gotten along ridiculously well, but that was not surprising since he was basically a giant kid in an adult body. They colored, I made pizza with Ivy, and I let myself fantasize what it could be like if I had someone like that in my life for good. But no good could come from that.

Drew was right, though I'd never admit it to him. It took me far too long to get over Rachel. I'm not sure how someone lets go of having their dreams crushed in one fell swoop. As attracted as I was to Ivy, I wasn't sure if I wanted to chance it. Especially because of Addie. I mean, my heart was one thing. I didn't want to possibly hurt hers.

Chief tore by on another lap before skidding to a halt and letting out a bark as he looked over at the gate that opened to my backyard from the street. Looking over to see the gate opening, I had to say I wasn't surprised to see Drew enter. He raised up a bottle in greeting as he made his way over to me.

Plopping into the chair next to me, Drew set the bottle of Irish whiskey he'd brought on the arm of his chair. I glanced over. "Red Spot? Damn. You aren't screwing around this evening, bro."

"It's not every day you celebrate five years of a dream come true. Thought we should do it up right." He leaned back in his chair, his feet resting on the edge of the firepit. "And Steph chipped in with me." Chief came up and nudged Drew's arm until Drew put his hand on Chief's head, giving the spoiled dog exactly what he wanted.

"Steph did? Then maybe we shouldn't drink it without her."

"Give her a minute," Drew mumbled, eyes closed as he hummed along with Stapleton.

I sat there, soaking in the music until Drew's words registered. "I'm sorry, what?"

Just as I spoke, Chief gave a bark of warning and we had another visitor.

"You jackasses better not have started without me." Steph walked through the gate.

I stood up from my spot at the pit as she quickly made her way to us. Taking a few steps toward her, I wrapped her up in my arms. My siblings drove me crazy, but damn if it didn't feel amazing to have them both here right now.

I pulled back to look at her. "What the hell are you doing here? I thought you were coming down tomorrow night."

Steph grinned as she moved to hug Drew before turning to sit in one of the other chairs. "Well, Drew sent that smoking-hot picture this afternoon, and I decided I needed to get my ass down here before Mom and Dad so I could get the real scoop." She paused as she opened her giant-ass purse and pulled out three glasses wrapped up in some type of kitchen towel. Setting the glasses on the wide arm of the

Adirondack, she motioned to Drew and the bottle. "Gimme."

Drew shook his head as he laughed at her, but he passed that bottle.

Steph was the oldest of our trio. At thirty-five, she and Theo had been married for thirteen years. College sweethearts, they'd blazed the path that I thought I'd been on. Steph was in advertising, Theo in banking, and they'd settled in a suburb near the one we grew up in shortly after they married. Theo was the perfect complement to our outspoken sister. He somehow managed to smooth her path when she could have ruffled feathers, and they parented their two girls with ease. At least that's how it appeared on the outside.

"Where's Theo?" I asked, taking the offered glass.

Steph handed Drew one as well and settled back in her chair with her own. "We were going to bring Emily and Jennie down this weekend, but Emily has a soccer game on Saturday morning and Jennie has a friend's birthday party. He volunteered to stay home with them, and we'll all toast your success at Thanksgiving in a few weeks."

"Babysitting the girls for the weekend?" I asked while Drew spoke at the same time.

"He's a saint," Drew said.

"Shut it," Steph said, brow raised. "They're his kids too. I love those girls with everything in me, but I'm grateful every day that I married a man who understands that we are equally responsible for parenting, that it isn't babysitting if he stays home with them. You two are unbelievable at times."

Drew put his glass down, raising his hands in protest. "Hey, what the hell did I say?"

Steph shook her head as she stretched out her long legs

to reach the firepit. While we liked to tease her for being so much shorter than the two of us, her five-foot-ten frame was no slouch. "You two have praised the shit out of Theo since Emily was born. How *lucky* I am that he changed her diapers, that he got up in the night to bring her to me when I was nursing, et cetera. A year later, ditto with Jennie, or then it was how great it was that he entertained Emily while I was nursing. I mean, really."

Drew looked over at me. I shrugged. He bravely, or stupidly, continued the conversation. "So it's not great that he helped out?"

Steph growled under her breath as she looked at the sky. "You two are such idiots. It's not helping. They're his kids too. I mean, am I helping if I take care of them?"

Her words soaked in for a moment, then I murmured, more to myself than anyone else, "No, you're being a mom."

"Bingo." She pointed at me. "So why are dads seen as gods if they do what a mom already does all the time? It's thankless, I tell you."

Drew and I looked at each other, then back at Steph. "I'm taking it," I began, "that this means Theo sent you down here because he recognized you needed a break."

Steph looked at me, then sat back in her chair, her head nodding in beat to the music. "Yes. Work has been fucking insane. The girls' schedules are bonkers. Theo has been at the bank late every day for the past two weeks because of some closings he had to get ready. So he sent me, and I gladly took him up on it." Her head came up so she could regard me with a shrewd look. "Annnnd," she drew out, "he wants to know as much as I do what is up with Bookstore Ivy as well as"—she turned her look to Drew—"we want to know why baby brother is back for a whole week." She paused, picked up her glass. "But first, we should probably toast."

Drew and I picked up our glasses.

Steph stood up, so Drew and I did the same. "Jake, when you first told us about the plans you and Sully had for the brewery, Theo and I were nervous. Small businesses are a ton of work, but you all have succeeded beyond our wildest imaginations. We are so proud of you and can't wait to see how this place grows in the next five years."

We brought our glasses together, then took a small sip. This was good shit, not something you were going to down like you were still in college going out to crappy bars.

Steph's comment took me back to Ivy. Small businesses were a lot of work. Lou had made the offhand comment earlier in the week that Ivy could sell. When I asked, she'd shared the offer on the store. We talked about it more as we made pizza just a few hours ago. She'd gotten an official offer today. I could tell she was leery of selling, and honestly I thought she had something good going. But I knew how much work it was, and I'd had a partner. Hell, now a manager as well. My load was shared; hers was not.

Looking at Steph, I thought of how she and Theo shared the responsibilities that came with parenting. From what I could see, with parenting and with her business, everything rested on Ivy's shoulders. I was surprised with how much I wanted to help.

Drew cleared his throat, bringing my attention back to the yard and my siblings. "Steph said it all, really. We're proud of you guys, as much as I hate to admit it when you do good. But Jake, you've done good. Now if we can just get you to see the light with Bookstore Ivy, all will be well."

"To Bookstore Ivy," Steph crowed, raising her glass. Drew did the same.

I rolled my eyes, but lifted my glass. "Means nothing," I murmured in reference to my raised glass, even while I wished like hell that she was here.

"Sure, tell yourself whatever you need to," Drew chortled after taking his sip.

We settled back into our chairs. Steph looked around at the yard, or what she could see in the shadow. Chief came in and out, going wherever his nose led him.

Finally, Steph looked back over to us. "Has Ivy seen your backyard?"

Her comment took me off guard. I mean, what? "Um, I mean, she's been in my house. The kitchen windows look out on it. Why?"

Steph's eyes twinkled in the light. "Just saying, this place is barren. Maybe a green witch would relish the chance to get their hands on it, mold it into their own."

Drew laughed. "Kind of like how Ivy could mold our boy here into the perfect guy while she's at it."

Steph nodded. "Hell yeah, one that doesn't call a father spending time with his kids babysitting."

Jesus. I tipped my head back ignoring their asses.

"So, Steph, did I text you about the moon water?" Drew asked.

I suppressed the groan that wanted to bubble out.

"No, do tell." She scooted to the edge of her chair.

Looking at the two of them, I felt both incredibly irritated by their conversation and overcome with gratitude that I had the two of them in my life.

In the morning I picked my way into the kitchen, stepping over Chief's prone body and heading to the coffee maker.

Drew and Steph had both crashed here last night. Eyeing the bottles on the counter, I was both impressed and concerned. We had luckily switched to beer after a glass of the good stuff, but I wasn't sure how either of them might be feeling this morning. We certainly didn't drink like we did ten years ago, but it still might be a bit much for them.

As I was grinding the beans, Steph walked in the kitchen and Chief poked his head up. "Chief been out yet?" she asked.

"Nah. But you can just open the door, and he'll do his thing," I said.

She moved over to the door, letting my grateful dog have access to freedom. I looked her over. I could see what I was betting Theo had recognized, she was wiped. Even so, she looked great. Her dark hair was piled on top of her head. She was wearing her glasses, so I'm betting her eyes were a bit dry this morning. Her leggings, fuzzy slippers, and long-sleeved T-shirt all stated she might be lounging most of the day. I didn't blame her. Sounded like a plan.

"What's on your schedule for the day?" she asked.

I glanced at the clock on the coffee maker in front of me. "I need to run, then head to the brewery for a bit." Bracing myself for her reaction, I said, "Then I need to pick up Addie at two until Ivy's off at five. It's my last day of watching her for Ivy. Mom and Dad thought they'd be down around six. I figured we could have dinner here or the brewery."

Steph grinned as she pulled down a few coffee mugs. "Don't think I didn't notice you slipping in the comment about Addie and Ivy. We'll get back to that. Why don't we do dinner at the brewery? I know we'll be there tomorrow already for the celebration, but maybe tonight could be more low-key?"

I nodded. That had been my instinct as well. Pushing the button for the coffee to begin brewing, I leaned back against the counter and regarded Steph. "Anything else you want to bust my chops about right now?"

She looked at me, then to the closed door to the basement. Then, taking a step closer to me, she spoke. "Drew."

My gut clenched. She sensed it too. "You think something is wrong."

"You do too?"

"I couldn't be sure, but there's something there he isn't telling us. Maybe why he's here or what brought him here. But I can't get him to share."

Steph stared out the window at Chief patrolling the yard for a moment. Then she looked back at me. "You know him, Jake. He's private. Hell, we all are to some extent, but he's more. He won't share until he's ready—"

The door to the basement door opened. Drew stepped into the kitchen in sweats and a T-shirt that advertised some Snowmass ski resort. His hair stuck up in the exact way it had when he was little. I was taken back for a moment to standing in our kitchen growing up, watching him wake up slowly just as he always had. He'd never been a morning person like Steph and I were. He stretched and looked at both of us.

"What are you two talking about?" he said, rubbing his face with a hand.

I looked at Steph and we had a silent nod of agreement to leave this topic for now. I looked at Drew. "Running. I'm going to head out to Highland Woods to hit the trails for a bit this morning. Either of you two want to join me?"

"Sure," Drew said.

"Leave in thirty?" Steph asked.

I nodded.

"And then this afternoon I get to meet Addie and Ivy? Best. Day. Ever." Steph grinned. "Think Ivy would mind if I had Theo on FaceTime when we meet? I mean, it's only fair." Steph waited a beat, looked between Drew and me, and then said, "Now, let's get down to the important question of the day. Who wants to tell me why you both have these gorgeous pink nails going on?"

Drew and I looked at each other for a second, then burst into laughter. Steph joined us, wiping away the tears streaming from her eyes. These people. God, I loved them so.

13

VETTING PROCESS

Ivy

It had been a slow day in the store, which was odd for a Friday. I stood behind the counter, mentally running through my to-do list of things needing to be checked off before the party at the brewery tomorrow.

Who was I kidding? I couldn't get Jake off my mind. That kiss last night. That. Kiss. I knew it couldn't have gone much further. Even in my addled state, I knew Addie and Drew had been there, but still.

Jake and Drew had hung around for a while afterward, which honestly surprised me. I thought for sure he'd find a reason to leave as soon as his brother interrupted our moment, but he hadn't. Drew hung out in the living room, coloring with Addie. The sight of the two of them, heads bent over their illustrations, was enough to make me melt, but then hearing Drew ask Addie questions about her drawings and solicit suggestions for his own made my mama-bear heart take a few extra beats. I didn't know Jake and Drew's parents, but clearly they did something right.

Jake stayed in the kitchen with me, and we made pizza. Not going to lie, that was almost better than the kiss. We'd talked. There wasn't our typical dance of what I'd now begun to recognize as flirting, then teasing, then flirting, then a bit of infuriating conversation, then flirting. He hadn't teased me once but instead asked questions about the bookstore, what I had done to get it off the ground, et cetera.

I'd shared more about the formal proposal I'd been sent about the purchase of the bookstore. It was a good offer, I knew. But something was keeping me from going all in on it. I told Jake I had a few weeks to decide, and he agreed that was a good call, to sleep on it some more. He also offered to look over my books with me, saying that maybe fresh eyes would help me see if I was missing anything.

While grateful for his offer of help, I felt like again I was taking from him. He'd watched my daughter this week, and now he wanted to help me figure out my business? Part of me wanted to say no, I could do this on my own.

Instead, I reminded myself that I was being stubborn and switched topics to this Reds of Christmas event. Jake had said there wasn't a ton left to do, but I wanted to contribute in some way. We'd talked about using social media to our advantage, something we both did in our own businesses but something that hadn't been capitalized on for events like this one coming up for the chamber.

Thinking over the night, once I got past my own issues, I wasn't sure what I liked more: having someone to cook with, someone to bounce business ideas off of, or someone who helped me unwind from my day. As much as my independent streak hated to admit it, it was pretty damn nice not to feel alone. The fact that I wanted to climb Jake, wrap my legs around him, and kiss him into tomorrow was simply an added bonus.

All too soon, the big boys had gone home. Addie and I completed our nighttime routine, including two stories from the Elephant & Piggie series. She dropped off quickly, and I — Well, let's just say my fantasies about one Jake Spencer were none too shabby last night.

But today? Today I couldn't focus worth a damn. I mean, darn. If the shop had been busy, maybe I would've been able to get my mind off the package that was Jake Spencer. As it was, we had a trickle of business throughout the day but not enough to keep my wandering and lustful mind occupied. The lack of customers made me stress and wonder if the increase in sales I'd seen since summer was leveling off. It was a gorgeous fall day. Maybe people had decided to spend time outside? Couldn't say I'd blamed them. I hoped business would pick up after lunch.

The bell over the door signaled that I'd finally have a customer. Thank goodness. Glancing over, I saw a tall woman with dark hair and glasses come in.

"Welcome," I called. "Please let me know if I can help you find something."

Her eyes found mine, and they crinkled at the corners with what appeared to be amusement as her mouth turned up. She headed straight for me. "Oh, I'm willing to bet you can help me."

"Oh?" I looked her over, sure I hadn't met her before, but she did seem somewhat familiar.

"Yes." She paused on the other side of my counter. "Let me introduce myself. I'm Steph, Steph Nolan. But I think you know my brothers better, Jake and Drew." She held out her hand.

I ignored the offered hand and moved around the

counter. "Of course I know them. Are you a hugger? I tend to be, but that's a bit much for some people."

Steph grabbed me, pulling me in for a tight squeeze. Yep, she was a good hugger.

I pulled back. "I didn't know you'd be down so early today. I thought Jake said you all were coming in this evening." I mentally revisited the conversation from last night while also trying not to freak out about meeting another family member of Jake's while still having no idea why our lips had fallen on each other or how I could sign up to have it happen again.

"I crashed the bro time last night as a bit of a surprise instead of waiting until today. Drew and I wanted to toast Jake with a small sibling celebration, so I came down early. My husband decided to stay up north with our girls because they had some stuff scheduled. Also"—she looked at me expectantly—"I couldn't help but get my ass down here when Drew sent me a smokin'-hot pic of you and Jake in what I assume is your kitchen yesterday afternoon." She waggled her eyebrows. "Damn, girl."

Ahhhhhhh. Was my face on fire? It felt like it was. I wanted to run from the bookstore in mortification. It was embarrassing to be caught making out like a teenager. To be caught on camera and have said picture be the way that Steph was introduced to me? Holy hell. "Um, I can explain?"

She raised a brow and gave me a wide smile. "Really? I can't wait to hear this."

Explain, explain, could I explain? If so, I'd need to start by explaining it to me. I looked at Steph and thought about Drew and Jake. The three of them were super close, it seemed. They also didn't seem to hold anything back. With that in mind, I decided to lay it all out. "Honestly, I have no idea what's going on with your brother. We annoy each other beyond what's rational, then he is the sweetest man alive and absolutely wonderful with my daughter, then we get near each other yesterday and... Bam! Kissing." I throw my hands up in the air.

"Bam?" Steph raised her eyebrows. I nodded. She looked over at the stool I had set to the side for Maggie. "May I?" she asked, gesturing toward it.

"Be my guest."

She pulled it over and sat down a bit gingerly.

I belatedly realized she was in exercise clothes. Before I could stop myself, I blurted out, "Are you okay?"

Her eyes widened. I'm guessing that wasn't what she thought I was going to say. "Yeah, I just got finished running at Highland Woods with Drew and Jake. I'm the stubborn older sister, have to keep up with those two, you know? But my typical distance is two miles on my treadmill, not seven through the trails." She shook her head. "Completely my fault, and they'll be pissed if I limp around them, so a fast recovery is needed." She gave me a mischievous grin. "They headed toward the brewery while I said I was going home to shower before joining them."

I smiled while beating back a twinge or two of jealousy. I wished I had the relationship she did with her siblings. Hell, I wish I had a sibling. Shaking my head to clear out the pointless thoughts, I addressed her comment. "So, I'm just a quick detour?"

"An absolutely necessary detour," she clarified. "As well as a moment to recover away from those two."

I smiled and nodded my understanding. "One, I'm happy to be a recovery spot for you. Two, how do you feel about essential oils? I think I have some ginger and orange oils that I massage on my muscles the rare times that I run.

It feels like it helps for me, so you're welcome to them if you'd like."

"Hell yeah, I'll take anything you've got." Steph paused, seeming to gather her thoughts. "So you're cool that I came here to check you out?"

I'd ducked down to rummage through the oils I kept on hand at the store, grabbing a rollerball to fill up for Steph. Standing up to face her, I had to laugh. She seemed so serious, a bit unsure, which didn't seem to fit the woman sitting across from me. "Of course it is. Vetting is required of anyone sucking the face of your sibling, especially one you're clearly close to."

Steph threw her head back and laughed out. "Damn, girl. I love anyone who can lay it out there like that."

I shrugged. "Well, no point in denying what Drew has already sent out into the ether, right?"

Steph watched me for a minute, which did make me wonder if she was waiting for a confession to pour fourth. But what would I be confessing? I mean, I didn't know exactly how much the picture showed, but I felt about as in the dark as you could get. I had no idea what Jake thought about what was going on. Hell, I didn't know what to think myself. As a result, I waited.

After a long bit of eye contact, Steph's face softened. "Tell me about Addie."

Holy detour, I was taken aback. Talk about my kid? Done. "What would you like to know? I can brag about Addie for hours." I pulled my cell out of my bag behind the counter. "Or I can show you ten million pictures, give or take a few hundred."

Steph nodded. "I hear you. What I really want to know more about is what power this little girl has that she got my brothers to willingly paint their nails pink."

We stared at each other for a beat, then hooted with laughter. The more I laughed, the harder it was to stop. Tears streamed from my eyes as I bent over to catch my breath.

"Yeah, I gave them a load of grief when I saw those beautiful nails last night. Did you catch the sparkles in the polish?" I wiped my eyes. "But seriously, what would you like to know?" I slid my phone over to Steph, opened to an album of pictures of Addie.

Steph flipped through them, pausing every so often. Looking from the pictures to me, she paused like she was considering her words carefully. "Well, Ivy, I can't help but notice there are a ton of pictures of Miss Addie, who is adorable, FYI, and a few of the two of you..."

Steph looked over to me with a tilt of the head, waiting. I met her stare. "And you're wondering where her dad is?"

"Or her grandparents," she replied. "I mean, you know I have two girls and Theo. No fucking way could I do this juggling act known as motherhood otherwise." She examined me carefully, and I noticed the way she studied me. I had to wonder what she was thinking. "I just wonder what your support system is like. I swear I'm not trying to be a nosy bitch."

I gave her a look with just a hint of skepticism.

She raised up her hands as she laughed. "Okay, okay, not *only* a nosy bitch, but I am wondering if you're some kind of superwoman because no fucking way could I do this gig alone. As a matter of fact, this speaks to an argument the boys and I had last night..." Steph's voice trailed off as she seemed a bit lost in thought.

One, I loved that she called Jake and Drew the boys. I could just see her as a nine-year-old, ordering those two around. Did they follow their older sister's directions, or were they annoying little brothers? Considering the two of them, I was going to go with a bit of both. At any rate, I was curious. "Steph, I absolutely want to know what you all argued about. Being an only sibling, I'm going to be completely frank and say I'm a bit green with jealousy at the whole sibling dynamic you all have going on."

She laughed. "Well, I get that. As much as those two drive me nuts, I love them completely. And I'm glad to share our conversation as long as you know we're heading back to the topic you so artfully dodged. But before I get into it, do you possibly have any water here I could snag?"

"Holy crap, I'm a horrible host. My nana would be mortified if she knew I hadn't offered you anything—"

"Well, to be fair," Steph said, reaching across and squeezing my hand, "we're not in your home. I don't think beverages are expected at a bookstore, and I wouldn't ask if those damn brothers of mine hadn't worn me out completely."

I moved out from the counter to the little hall we had on the way to the back of the store. There I had a small counter complete with coffee maker, teakettle, some cups, and a small fridge and bar sink. "I have water, coffee, and tea. Pick your poison."

Steph tilted her head, considering. "What type of tea?"

I glanced over where we kept the tea bags. "We're running low, just green tea and my favorite—peach."

Steph's smile widened. "I'll absolutely take some peach, and a shot of honey with it if you have it."

"You got it, and I'll join you. Now, argument." I gestured for her to go on with my hand as I grabbed everything needed for our drinks and got the water boiling.

Steph leaned against the back counter, as she seemed to debate where to begin. "Well, you have to know that Drew,

Jake, and my relationship is built on lots of love and calling each other on our bullshit."

I nodded, flipping the switch on the kettle before moving to the mugs and dropping the tea bags in. "So last night, you called them on their bullshit?" I guessed as I finished up our drinks and we moved back to the front of the store. Steph reclaimed her spot on the stool as I slid her mug toward her.

"Thanks," she said, taking her mug. Glancing at the cup with the woman meditating and the phrase *let that shit go*, she laughed out loud and took a sip. "Um, excellent. Okay, where was I?"

"Calling them on their bullshit," I supplied.

"Yes, so when I got here last night and explained that Theo had volunteered to stay with girls at home, Drew made a comment about Theo being a saint and Jake said something about babysitting."

I raised a brow at her. "Because Theo stayed at home with his own kids?"

"Apparently."

I shook my head. "That's some borderline misogynistic bullshit, babe."

"Amen. Here's the thing. My brothers are the best. However, my parents—as well meaning as they are—have very traditional gender roles. I love them completely, but I push Jake and Drew all the time to open their eyes to what is actually around them. They aren't antifeminists as much as they are learning as they go."

I considered this, considered what I knew about Jake and Drew as well as some of the conversations Jake and I'd had. "Well, you must have been doing this work for quite a while because men steeped into traditional views aren't going to color with my daughter for hours, much less choose to babysit her for an entire week to help me out, putting their own business to the side during a busy time, much less get their nails painted. You've done good work, lady."

Steph nodded. "Don't get me wrong. My dad is amazing and a huge supporter of mine. Both my parents are, as are my brothers. It's just that my parents are a bit older, and I think he believed he contributed to the household because he earned the money to keep it running, you know? As a grandfather, he's around so much more for my kids. Jake and Drew have seen that, and they've seen Theo and the way he is with our girls. It also helps they are two big kids themselves and they love children."

"That's obvious," I said, memories of Jake with Addie from this week popped into my mind. "Well, I'm grateful that you've educated them. Keep up the good work."

Steph laughed. "Now, talk to me. You know who my support network is, tell me about yours."

I took another bit of tea as I considered where to even begin. "Short version? Heck, there isn't really a short version."

Steph snorted.

"I was twenty-four when I had Addie. Her dad was a boyfriend who I already knew wasn't sticking around. After a trip to Africa during college as part of an engineering internship, Noah had pledged to go back after graduation and help bring water to rural areas. I don't think he ever had a plan to settle down, at least not for a while. He tried to give me money for Addie's care, but I refused. I mean, look where he was going. People there needed the money far more than we did. He comes back to the states several times a year and sees Addie when he does. She knows him, knows he's her dad, but also knows our family doesn't look like most others.

"My parents should have never been parents, so they aren't around. We see them once or twice a year, talk to them around once a month. My grandmother, who I called Nana, took me in each summer as a kid. She lived over this place, owned the whole building. She left it and her nest egg to me when she passed, so we eventually made our way here. I've only been here six months, but I've made some friends that are quickly becoming my family." I took another drink, feeling a bit emotional. "I'm a big believer in the family you create versus the one you are born into."

Steph slipped her hand over mine and squeezed. "And my brother is worming his way into that found family of yours?"

That statement filled me with warmth. "Honestly? I guess? I mean, I've known Jake since I moved here. We've talked, argued, teased, but that was really it. And then he sort of rescued us in a freak storm last week, and he continued rescuing me when I hit a day care snag. It's like we went from zero to sixty in a matter of hours, and now I have no idea how I would have survived this week without him." My eyes welled up, realizing how true those words were. After not having a support network for four years, having someone have my back was huge.

Steph nodded, but then proceeded to blow my mind. "Well, you might think it's been zero to sixty, but considering Drew knew about Bookstore Ivy before that freak storm, I'd say it's likely you've been on Jake's mind more than you'd think over the past few months."

My breath caught. "Really?"

She laughed. "Yeah. And I'm sorry as shit that you don't have Addie's dad or your parents to lean on. Safe to say, after hearing Jake talk about Miss Addie for the past few days, no matter what happens to the two of you, you will have him."

Goddess, that was a great notion. I wanted to trust it, but that scared me more than a little. "I hope so, Steph. As confused as I am about what's going on with your brother, I know Addie loves him. I need to make sure that she comes first."

"As any good mama bear should." Steph raised her hand for a high five, which I gladly gave her.

The bell over the door called to both of us, and we turned to face it. I laughed as I saw Drew poke his head in. "Knew it!" he said to us, before turning and calling down the street. "I was right, Jakey boy. Big sis is introducing herself to Bookstore Ivy." He ended with a bit of a cackle.

Steph grinned at me as Drew, then Jake, entered the bookstore. Oh boy.

14

BOHEMIAN PRINCESS

Jake

"Well, think we're ready?" Sully asked as we looked over the brewery where appetizers were set out, scattered on tables throughout the place. There were a few beer stations around the dining room, one for each of our signature beers. At the counter near the hostess station we had our normal merch, as well as canned beer to go. Everyone who worked for the brewery was scheduled tonight, not because we expected giant crowds, but because we'd given everyone an hour shift at some point in the night, asking them to stay and celebrate with us for the rest of the evening. This place was what it was because of the loyalty of our staff, and both Sully and I recognized it.

"As ready as we can be," I said, moving behind the beer. Looking over the beers we had on tap, I grabbed two glasses and poured a Black Hole Sun IPA for Sully, then one for me. It had been our first beer that hit with the public as well as the beer competitions we'd entered. "Toast?" I raised a glass to Sully.

Sully smiled an easy grin, one that I'd seen more and

more on his face this year. Since he and Maggie got together, the man was happier than I'd ever seen him. Sully had always been a great guy, loyal friend, bullshitter extraordinaire, and a terrific businessman. But with Maggie, he was all that and more. He seemed settled in a way I couldn't explain. I was waiting anxiously for the next seven weeks or so to move on by so I could get a glimpse of him as a dad. I was pretty certain that he'd be an overprotective one but also would love their kid beyond belief.

"Hell yeah. And this toast is just for us, man." Sully raised his glass to mine. "So damn glad you worked two jobs all those years ago, Jake. Glad we met at that bar, that you got drunk enough after work to dream a dream with me. And I'm sure as hell glad that your parents raised you to know your way around a kitchen so you could think up some kick-ass recipes when we opened this place. Wouldn't have been the same without you. Shit, that doesn't even touch your construction knowledge when we rehabbed this place."

We clinked glasses and took a sip.

I glanced around. This place was a far cry from the building we found seven years ago, that was for sure. Looking back at Sully, I grinned. "Yeah, this is not the life in construction that I thought was ahead of me. Not that I'm complaining. It's better than anything I imagined."

"Shit yeah," Sully replied. We sank down onto some bar stools, spinning so that our backs were on the bar, the brewery laid out in front of us. I watched some of the folks who worked for us congregating in small groups, having a beer, a few appetizers. Everyone else would be coming shortly. I couldn't wait.

My parents had arrived in Highland last night. The five us came to the brewery for dinner and some beer. It'd been amazing, as it always was, to have them see what this place had become. My dad had visited with strangers at the bar, delighting in telling them that he was the father of one of the owners. He'd come back from the bar to our table, regaling myself, then Sully when he stopped by, with the stories of the people he met. He was proud of the fact that some folks had driven an hour or more to come here for dinner. "This place is a destination," he'd crowed.

The pride in his voice had been a balm to my soul. My parents had always supported me—hell, they'd supported all of us. Steph and Drew had gone more of the traditional college route, though Drew's job was anything but traditional. I remember telling my mom and dad my senior year in high school that four more years in a classroom might kill me. I worried like hell I'd be letting them down, and I'd do anything I could to avoid disappointing them. But my dad had just nodded and said he could see that, then asked me what I saw myself doing. They wanted the best for us, always, and they wanted us to work like hell. Work ethic was something drummed into us early. But wanting to go the unconventional route in life was fine with them. Find what you love and find a way to get paid for doing it was my dad's advice to me all those years ago. Looking around now, I can honestly say I'd done just that.

Sully's voice brought me back to the present. "Maggie says you had Ivy's daughter with you all week."

I bit back a grin. "What are you asking, man?" He was going to have to work a little harder if he wanted to gossip like school girls.

"Just saying two weeks ago I would have thought the sexual chemistry around you two could burn the place down around us if we weren't careful. How'd you handle being in her presence every day for the past seven? Walk around with a fire extinguisher?"

"Fucking hilarious, man."

"But not denying the chemistry, I see. Interesting."

I shook my head at him, then took another drink before scanning the bar with more than a bit of excitement for the night ahead. I chose to ignore that I was looking for Ivy. Damn. Seemed like two girls had taken up residence in my brain and I was no longer in control. Ivy should be there anytime, but I knew Addie was hanging at home tonight with a babysitter. I'd miss her but understood this wouldn't be an exciting gathering for a kid. Still wished she'd be there as well.

I'd picked up Addie from school yesterday with Drew. After finding Steph at the bookstore, we'd left Ivy to work as we went off to grab some lunch. Steph finally said she needed to get home, shower, and check in with Theo before dinner. Drew and I headed to grab Addie.

Damn, that girl. We waited for her on the playground at her school. When she'd come out in a line with her class, I heard her call to some of her friends, that her boys were there. Then she came flying across the playground toward us. She ran full tilt until she was a few feet from me, upon which she launched herself through the air and I grabbed her. My heart melted, knowing she felt secure enough that I'd never let her fall. Damn.

Clearing the emotion that was clogging up my throat, I tried to answer Sully. "Not sure what's going on, man. And no fucking idea how to explain it."

Sully nodded like he was considering my words carefully. "Well, at least you aren't feeding me some line of bullshit like there's nothing going on there."

"You mean like you did before you knocked up Maggie?"

Sully looked at me, puzzled. "What are you talking about?"

I snorted. "If you think that it wasn't obvious you were gone for that girl far before you put any bun in her oven, you're a blind man."

Sully ran a hand over his face, chuckling. "Yeah, you could say that, I guess."

"So what made you finally go for it?" I asked, thinking back over the journey he and Maggie had been on this year. When we began the brewery together, he treated her as a good friend, one he had years of history with. At some point during the past five years running this place with him, I'd noticed the looks he gave Maggie switched from a friendly glance to one of need. It was a trip to sit back and watch them do that dance.

Sully gave me a shrewd glance. "Just curious or doing some research for yourself?"

I didn't even know what to say to that, so I took another sip of beer as I watched the first of our guests begin to arrive. Max Harp walked in with his fiancée and Sully's sister, Emma. They paused at the counter, looking at some of the canned beers before Emma wrapped her arms around the giant that was Harp. He grabbed her chin and pressed a kiss on her that raised the temperature of this place significantly. I glanced at Sully and found him watching the same show.

"You've certainly evolved from this spring when a kiss between those two had you doing some deep breathing," I noted. It had been a shit ton of fun, giving Sully grief about his younger sister and his best friend. He had been a bit grumpy about their relationship at the start, but that had been short-lived.

Sully shook his head. "Yeah, I had some growing up to do there, as many of you pointed out to me." He took another drink before setting down his beer and standing up. "Max is great for Emma…"

I looked back to the door to see why he didn't finish his thought and saw Maggie walk in. Sully watched her like she was the oasis and he'd been lost in the desert for days. Although, in his defense, she had a black long-sleeved fitted T-shirt dress on that hugged every one of her curves, including the giant basketball that was her very pregnant belly.

"I need to go see my wife," he growled.

I began to laugh, wondering if he was just going to drag her to the nearest closet when I saw Ivy walk in behind Maggie. She was laughing at something Maggie said as she made it past the hostess stand, and her eyes swept the room until they locked on mine.

Damn.

I moved without a word, without even realizing I was doing so. My eyes scanned Ivy. I couldn't look away. Typically she wore her flowy dresses and skirts that did nothing to show off her amazing body. Thus my love of her leggings at home. Tonight she was in a dress again, but this one had a deep *V* that ended at her belt. Not long, the dress hit her midthigh. I groaned as I saw a flash of her legs and noted the knee-high leather boots she had on that laced up the back.

We continued to move toward each other until we were close enough to touch. Finally. I adjusted my pants in a way I hoped like hell was subtle. Ivy's eyes crinkled as she grinned and raised her eyebrows at me, so I'm guessing she noticed.

"Hey, Jake," she said as she leaned in and a kiss brushed my cheek. There was a smell that I associated with Ivy and couldn't place. Lavender? Something floral? All I knew was that it meant she was near and didn't help my pants situation one bit.

"Hi, babe," I said, trying to get my bearings. Looking over her dress up close, I inched to run my fingers over some gold embroidery on the navy material. "Are these suns?"

"Addie thought so. She was a fan, so I went with it."

I nodded absentmindedly. Addie loved all things related to the solar system, so that tracked. That being said, I wanted to send Addie a card of thanks. The deep *V* meant that the swells of Ivy's breasts were visible. Holy God, how would I make it through this night? I wondered what closet Sully had dragged Maggie to. Was there another one open?

"Jake?" Ivy snapped her fingers. "Eyes up, bud."

My eyes shot to her blue-green ones that looked more blue than green tonight. She looked like she might burst out laughing. And while I was a fan of the dress—hell, of the entire thing she had going on here—her relaxed and happy smile did it for me. My heartbeat sped up, and I reached forward to link my hand with hers. I had to touch her.

"What?" she began to say, but then looked at where our hands joined. I brushed my thumb over hers, soaking in the sensation of touching her. It was overwhelming, and I needed more at the same time. I wanted to drown in her. It was like seeing her daily over the week had woken up something inside that was screaming that this person was what I needed. What I had been waiting for.

"You look incredible, Ivy."

"Thanks." She looked down at her dress and back to me. "Addie good?"

Her face lightened, and she visibly relaxed. "Oh yes. She's overjoyed to have a teen over to show her all her treasures."

I chuckled, thinking of the fairy garden she had outside. Even in the rapidly approaching winter, she had little secret spots in the landscaping around the house. I'd put money on her giving the sitter a quick tour before a night of coloring and cartoons.

I tugged her closer to me so I could lower my lips to her ear, hoping to keep our conversation between the two of us. "Have you given more thought to the proposal to purchase Pages?"

I stepped back a breath and watched Ivy's smile quirk. "Lots of alliteration there, Jake."

"Avoiding the topic, Ivy?"

Her face drew serious as she lowered her voice. "No. I mean, I have thought about it. I wondered if you could look over some stuff with me after this weekend was over. Maybe see something I'm missing?"

She looked so vulnerable. I knew it took a lot for her to ask for help, and I didn't take that lightly. "I'd be glad to."

She exhaled, seeming to relieve a weight she was carrying. Her blond waves cascaded over her shoulders as she took in the brewery before meeting my gaze again. "Jake, look at what you and Sully have brought together tonight."

I felt a lightness, a joy, that was almost foreign to me. "Yeah." I glanced around. "This came together better than I anticipated."

Ivy watched me. "It feels magical here."

I tucked a lock of hair behind her ear as her eyes widened, then warmed. "I think you're magical, Ivy."

Her lips opened as she tugged the lower one in and bit it. Holy hell. What was the protocol? Could I kiss her here? What were we doing?

"So." She gave me a mischievous smile as she changed the subject. "I'm taking it that you like the dress."

I shook my head at her, grateful for the reprieve. "Damn, babe. It's incredible. You're incredible." I looked back to my hand, still joined with hers, when I heard a throat being cleared.

I looked over my shoulder to where my parents and siblings stood, watching with wide grins on their faces. Because of course they did.

Mom spoke first. "So, I'm guessing you're Ivy?"

I groaned, turning to drop my head on top of Ivy's as she peeked over my shoulder and whispered, "Is that your parents?"

Shit.

15

———————————

QUIET APPROVAL

Ivy

Over Jake's shoulder I saw Drew and Steph, both laughing and not even remotely trying to hide it. Between the two of them stood an older couple. The man was easily six foot two, and while not as trim and muscular as his sons, the resemblance was uncanny. Jake's dad wore jeans with a button-down shirt and sport coat. Next to him, wearing a ginormous grin and a kick-ass navy wrap dress, stood his mom. Margot had a cropped haircut that was somewhere between gray and blond. Her eyes were the same as Jake's, ice blue. And if I wasn't mistaken, they were dancing with amusement.

Margot moved in our direction, grabbed Jake by the biceps, and shoved him out of the way. Drew pretended to wipe away tears of laughter as Margot held her arms out to me. "Come here, dear girl. We were hoping to meet you at dinner last night."

Margot pulled me toward her, and I looked at Jake in confusion. Was I supposed to have gone to dinner? Jake shook his head. Glancing at Steph, I couldn't help but notice that she was now bent at the waist, hooting with laughter. Clearly Drew and Steph were all in for my introduction to the family. Margot pulled back and looked me up and down.

"Your dress is positively darling, Ivy. Now, is Addie here?" She looked around like Addie would be appearing from behind me or something.

Talk, Ivy. Open mouth, form words. Good gracious, Nana would have a field day if she'd been here. "Um, hi? And no, Addie has a sitter tonight. I thought this would go later than her bedtime. Also, not sure if a four-year-old would find a lot of entertainment in a night like this." I stood still in front of Margot as she continued to study me for Goddess knows what.

"Jesus, Mom, let her go." Jake took my arm and tugged me back by him, my hand clasped in his. My head spun with the amount of questions I had for him, such as when did we become friends who held hands in public? And how about a repeat of that kiss the other night? I'll take more please.

Margot shook her head at Jake. "Mind your manners, son. I was just being friendly with your lady friend here. And Ivy, I agree, not exactly a kid-friendly evening. Steph said the same thing. Now, Sam? Sam?" She turned, calling to Jake's dad behind her. With a knowing grin, he shook his head at her as he stepped to her side. She looked over at him, lightly slapping his arm as she did. "Knock it off, you."

"Just following orders, ma'am," he said. Dang, his smile was Drew's smile. I loved how I could see so much of the three siblings by looking at their parents, even the easy way they teased one another.

"Quiet, you," she said. "I want to introduce you to Ivy James. Be on your best behavior, mister."

"Always, my dear." Sam shook his head before taking my offered hand that I tugged away from Jake, but Sam leaned in to kiss me on my cheek. "It's lovely to meet you, Ivy."

Stepping back, I slid next to Jake and replied, "It's nice to meet you both, Mr. and Mrs. Spencer."

"Oh hush," Margot replied. "It's Sam and Margot. No formality here. So are you and Addie available for brunch tomorrow? I'd love to meet this beautiful girl that I've heard so much about before we head back home."

I looked up at Jake curiously to see what he had to say.

Jake was looking at his mom with love and more than a smidge of exasperation. "Mom, I haven't told you all about Addie." He glanced over to me. "But of course you guys are welcome to come to brunch."

"I know you didn't," Margot replied. "Drew and Steph did."

"Jesus." He dropped his head to my shoulder as he fake whispered to me. "You sure you really missed out on having siblings? I can give you mine."

I laughed. "It's fine, really." Looking over at Sam and Margot, I said, "Brunch would be great. Would you like to see pictures of Addie?" I unzipped my clutch and pulled out my phone.

Margot reached over, hooking her arm through mine. "Yes. But let's head to the bar. I think I can get Sam to order us a beer, unless you'd rather drink something else."

Sam fell into step with the two of us as I replied. "Beer sounds great. I love the Black Hole Sun as well as the Barn Owl Stout."

"You've got great taste," Sam replied.

"Bring her back soon," Jake called out to us. I looked

over my shoulder as he shook his head at me. Drew and Steph waved goodbye with big smiles.

"Now, before we do a deep dive into the pictures"—Margot leaned against my arm as we moved toward the bar—"what does your Addie love to eat for breakfast?"

"Donuts?" Sam spoke up. "I'm a fan of donuts, and I'd be glad to pick some up in the morning."

"Sam!" Margot chastised. "Donuts do not make for a nutritious homemade breakfast."

"No, but they make a delicious one," he quipped.

"We are trying to make a good impression on Ivy here and we can't do that with donuts." Margot was leaning around me as we finally reached the bar.

"Of course we can." Sam looked at me. "What are your thoughts on donuts, Ivy?"

I held back my laughter that wanted to bubble out. Margot was watching me nervously, which was a hoot. "Addie and I are fans of breakfast in all forms. So donuts, pancakes, eggs, we will eat it all and be grateful for it."

Max Harp leaned over from his spot with Emma at the bar. "Hey, Sam and Margot, didn't mean to eavesdrop, but if you want an inside tip with Little Miss Addie, she loves it when Jake makes her hot chocolate with mellows."

I shook my head at him as Margot nodded hers.

"Yes, I remember that from our phone call. Great idea, Max. Did you hear that Sam? We'll have pancakes *and* donuts *and* hot chocolate with marshmallows."

"And we'll get our sugar levels checked after that?" he asked.

"Oh, hush up and order us some beers," she said. Then she looked at me. "Now, Ivy, let's see some pictures of your precious daughter."

Man, I loved this family.

~

The night flew by in no time at all. I couldn't remember the last time I'd been able to dress up and go out with friends. It was pre-Addie, for certain. Maggie had given me the names of several former students, and one of them was watching Ads tonight. Addie had been ecstatic to meet her new best friend. I glanced at my phone and saw that it was only a bit after nine, and I didn't turn in a pumpkin until eleven.

Looking around, I saw that Sully and Jake were getting up on the makeshift stage they had near the hallway to the tank room. Jake nodded at Steph, and she let out a whistle like a New Yorker hailing a cab. Impressive.

The music stopped as Sully stepped forward. "Can I get everyone's attention?" he shouted.

I drifted with everyone else toward them, intending to hang out at the back. That lasted for about a minute before Margot materialized at my side and shook her head with a look of displeasure. Sliding her hand into mine, she began to work her way through the crowd, not slowing down until we were right in front of Jake. He looked down and winked.

Goose bumps rose on my arms. Dang.

Steph leaned over and whispered in my ear, "Mom is not letting you hang back, Ivy. I hope you're ready for the full-force approval of Margot Spencer. It might make your head spin."

I laughed and returned my gaze to Sully and Jake, but part of me thought about how nice it would be to have the approval and support of someone like Margot.

Sully looked to Jake, and Jake nodded back to him. They shared a smile, then Sully looked out at the crowd. "I want to take a moment to thank all of you for coming out tonight to celebrate our fifth anniversary of this place." He paused while a cheer went up. "I know how busy this time of year can be, so we really do appreciate you taking the time to be here."

"I'll go anywhere for free beer," Drew called out to the laughter of the group.

"Shut it, you," Jake said with a grin.

Sully looked from Jake back to the crowd. "But that beer is why we're all here, right? When Jake and I were working together at a college bar ten years ago, I'm sure we never dreamed this was what we would one day create."

Jake slowly shook his head with a small smile. "Hell, no."

"But here we are with a ton of hard work, beer recipes, Mama Spencer recipes in the kitchen—"

Margot waved to the crowd as someone from the back yelled out, "Love those nachos!"

"Amen," Sully continued. "At any rate, we wanted to thank you all for your support. From our families helping finance this place, to all of you who joined us for free hours of labor as we restored it, to those of you who come in to eat and drink each week, to the amazing folks who work with us, to those we love who keep us sane, we send out sincere thanks to you all."

Hoots, hollers, and cheers rose up.

Sully looked over at Jake. "Want to say a few?"

Jake shrugged, then moved up toward the crowd. "I'm not much for public speaking. I'd much rather belly up to the bar with you all, but I would like to echo Sully here and give my thanks. Small businesses are a risky enterprise." He gave me a nod, and a feeling of warmth flowed through me at the acknowledgment. "We're grateful for your support— from when we opened and you all came in to our new venture into canning our beer."

Cheers again.

"Yes, and thanks going out to my baby brother for helping to make that dream come true for us," Jake said, looking for Drew.

"No problem, Jake the Snake!" Drew shouted out.

"Jesus, quiet. I also wanted to send out a special thanks to you Highland Falls folks. Unlike Cole Sullivan here, I'm not a hometown boy. You all made me feel like a part of this community from the start, and I'm damn grateful for it." Jake looked down and met my eyes. "I've met some great people here over the past few years, and it just keeps getting better."

Wow. Okay, that was something, right?

Steph leaned over. "Well, that wasn't very subtle, was it?"

"Our boy is talking to you, Bookstore Ivy," Drew said over my shoulder.

I ignored them both and kept my eyes locked on Jake.

Jake grabbed his glass of beer from the stool he'd set it on, nodded at Sully to grab his own, and they held them up. Jake called out, "Thanks for a great five years, and here's to many, many more. To the Homestead!"

He and Sully raised their glasses up, clinked them together as the rest of us raised ours and shouted out our own cheers of support.

I clinked my glass with Jake's family. We all laughed and took a drink. Drew whipped out his phone and pulled Steph and me into a few selfies. After a few minutes, I looked over as Margot was wiping away a stray tear.

Extracting myself from Drew and Steph, I moved closer to Margot. Reaching out, I squeezed her hand. "You okay?"

She looked over and smiled. "Oh yes." Looking over to where Jake and Sully were now standing, surrounded by well-wishers, she looked back to me. "I'm sure you've had moments with your Addie where you watch her work hard at something and find her own version of success, right?"

I nodded, then looked over at Jake as she continued. "It's a great feeling, and it gets even better as they get older. Watching your children come into the men and women they're supposed to be, loving those people they become, well, it's just the best." She put her arm around me and squeezed, then moved back to Sam's waiting embrace.

I smiled watching Sam wrap his arms around Margot as he began swaying to the music that was now playing. I paused, listening closer, and realized that they were playing the Chris Stapleton album I'd been playing on constant repeat lately. Jake looked over to me and pointed to a speaker, smiling.

For you, he mouthed.

Oh boy, this guy was taking my heart. What the hell was I going to do with him? Keeping my eyes locked on him, I watched as he began working his way toward our group, having to stop every few feet to accept the kind words of another person or the hug from another happy customer or staff member.

I turned and looked over my shoulder at Drew and Steph who were still taking crazy selfies with what looked like some social media filter, then sending them to what I assumed were Steph's daughters. Over their shoulders I could see Margot and Sam on the makeshift dance floor. Max and Emma were out there too, and it looked like Sully had snagged Maggie and was cajoling her into a song while she pointed at her belly, I'm sure telling him that their bean didn't want to dance. To be honest, I wouldn't be surprised if she got him to head home shortly. She was a big fan of their couch right now, and who could blame her?

Turning in a circle, I let the feelings of the night wash over me. This feeling of togetherness, community, building something great. That was what I was after, what I felt like I'd begun at Pages. I knew the fear of providing for Addie on my own was what was weighing on me, and that was real. I just hoped Jake could help me find a way forward.

My eyes scanned the room until I found him again. He was headed my way with what my romance books would describe as a smoldering look in his eyes. Yum. Maybe we could talk business plans later. I was feeling the desire to climb that man like a tree wash over me. Now how could I sign up for that?

THOSE KINDS OF FRIENDS

Jake

The night had been even better than we'd anticipated. A crowd of locals, many of them people that had been integral to the success of the brewery, had all shown up. Standing with Sully, listening to him give our thanks back to this community, I'd been overcome. Looking out into the crowd, I'd seen Sully's family, our friends, the staff that we would be lost without, folks like Lou and Verdell who came in weekly and kept us afloat, and my family, my parents simply beaming. Right up front, next to my mom and Steph, was Ivy.

When Sully asked me to say something, I didn't even know what words flowed out, just that Ivy kept her eyes on me the whole time. I felt like there was a current running through me, connected to her. It was the damnedest feeling, but I knew I needed to talk to her, to touch her. It was like I was missing something without her. Jesus, if I said that to any of the guys, I'd never hear the end of it. My brain had suddenly decided I was living out a Hallmark movie, apparently.

Hopping down from the table we'd used as some type of stage, I tried to make my way to Ivy, but there'd been so many people right there, ready to congratulate us. I got caught up talking to Finn, our manager. We were debating what time we wanted to wrap everything up tonight so people could get home at a decent hour.

"Sully." I tried to catch his attention. The man had his hand on Maggie's belly, a wide grin on his face. "Can we borrow you for a sec?"

Maggie laughed as she held Sully's hand in place. "Give me your hand, Jake," she called over.

"Why?"

"You got to feel this kid. She must be practicing ballet or something in there. She's all over the place tonight." Maggie ignored the fact I did not give her my hand and grabbed it anyway, placing it on her stomach.

I stood there for a few seconds, waiting for the small movements I remember feeling when Steph was pregnant and would insist I check out her belly. I let out a snort of laughter as I felt a slight kick. Then another and another, and within a second, Maggie's entire belly seemed to shift so that now she looked lopsided.

"Holy shit, Maggie!" I stood back, looking at her in a bit of horror. She was still upright, so I assumed she wasn't in too much pain. "What the hell was that?"

Maggie leaned back, her long strawberry blonde hair lying in waves down her back, and hooted with laughter as her hands held her belly. "Damn, Jake, you should see your face."

I watched her, then glanced at Sully. He didn't seem alarmed or ready to call the doc, so I took a deep breath and assumed the baby wasn't trying to find the nearest exit quite yet. "Sorry. I mean, is that normal? My older sis was pregnant years ago, and I remember taps that I could feel, but not seismic shifts in her belly."

Maggie wiped away a tear or two. "Sorry." She caught her breath. "Yes, to answer your question. I'm told it's completely normal, especially as the baby begins to run out of room toward the end."

I shook my head.

"What?" Maggie tilted her head as she looked over my face.

I glanced at Sully who stood there looking ridiculously proud of his budding gymnast. "Man," I said to him, "we're damn lucky women are the ones that carry the babies or none of us would be here."

Sully nodded. "Damn right."

I glanced at Finn, who was standing there, watching us all with a smirk on his face. I'm sure he thought we were a bunch of lunatics. "At any rate, Sully, Finn and I were talking about what time we wanted to wrap this shindig up."

Sully glanced at his watch, then at his wife. He brushed her hair off her cheek and leaned over to kiss her. I heard him whisper to her, "Babe, how are you doing?"

The wave of longing that hit me as I watched them rocked me. I hadn't thought about marriage, babies, for years. Hell, since Rachel when the vision I'd had for my life went up in smoke. I mean, as I'd told Drew, I'd assumed one day it would happen for me, but that day was so far from now it wasn't even a dot on the horizon. So why watching my friend with his wife and their unborn baby suddenly felt like a gut punch was unexplainable.

I glanced around the place as Sully and Maggie conferred with Finn. I saw my parents slip into an embrace and begin dancing, which made me lock eyes with my siblings and share a grin. Warmth flooded through me as I thought back to the times growing up that we'd walk into the kitchen to see a similar sight. We'd always groan that they were beyond embarrassing, but in all honesty, we'd loved it. They'd always been the model for me of what to look for in a partner.

Watching them sway, I paid attention to the music for the first time and smiled. I'd told Finn to put the Stapleton album that Ivy was obsessed with on our playlist for the night, and it was up. I began to look for her and found her warm eyes immediately, locked on me. I smiled, pointed to the speaker, and mouthed, *For you.*

Looking over my shoulder at Sully and crew, I said, "Let's begin wrapping this up."

Sully glanced past me and saw Ivy watching us. Giving me a knowing look, he nodded and started talking to Finn again.

"Go get her, tiger," Maggie called. I ignored her and began making my way to Ivy, never losing her eyes as I did.

Laughter from the dance floor caught my attention as Max worked to spin Emma, her head thrown back. Sully was leading Maggie to the floor as she rubbed her belly and clearly told him he got one dance and only one.

I looked back to Ivy, watching as her smile grew the closer I got to her. I tried to tell my body to calm down, that nothing would be happening once I reached her side.

Reaching Ivy, finally, I stopped a breath away. I fisted my hands, trying to hold back from running my fingers through her hair. She had felt like she was just out of reach all night. I wanted to crush her to me, let my lips meet hers again, but I wasn't sure if that was what she wanted. And I sure as hell didn't want to fuck up whatever this was between us. A large part of me prayed it was the start of something more, but it had been so long I didn't even know how to get us on that path. Were we already on it? Did that require some type of discussion or declaration? Jesus, it felt like middle school. Maybe I needed to ask Sully to have Maggie ask her if we could go steady.

"Thanks for playing this," Ivy said, ignorant of my mental struggle.

I cleared my throat as I reached for her hand. Thankfully, she reached out, joining us together.

"Dance?" I croaked.

"Smooth, bro," Drew said from somewhere behind me. "Sorry, Bookstore, we did the best we could with this one."

I used my other hand to give him a one-finger salute as I brought my hand to my hair.

"Subtle." Ivy laughed and moved a step closer to me, our chests brushing up against each other.

"You sure you missed out on having siblings?" I asked, keeping one hand clasped with mine, wrapping my other arm around her. A groan threatened to escape, she felt so damn good. Maybe I could get Sully just to kick everyone out. Now would be preferable.

Ivy snorted, then rested her head on my chest. Before I could relax into our embrace, she popped up to lock eyes with me. "I'm sorry. Is it okay to put my head there?"

I moved my hand up to lightly push her head back down. "I know you're big on consent, Ivy, but I guarantee I'm going to say yes to anything you ask."

"Promises, promises."

We swayed as the music changed from one Stapleton song to the next. Ivy moved her hand from mine to my chest, which again didn't suck. As we swayed like teens at a high school dance, her voice rose just enough that I could hear her.

"Why aren't you with someone, Jake?"

I closed my eyes, debating how to go from here. I wasn't sure on all of Ivy's history, though she'd shared some over the past week. I was doing this, right?

Right.

I debated tipping her chin up to look her in the eyes, but somehow this was easier. Instead, I curled around her even more, lowering my lips to her ears.

"Ten years ago I was engaged to my high school girlfriend."

Her body went rigid, but she didn't speak.

Like a Band-Aid, I ripped it off. "Her name was Rachel. We dated my senior year. I followed her to college and worked while she got her degree." I swallowed, pushing down the feelings of that time. Looking back, there were so many signs that Rachel and I weren't right for each other. But young love. All I could see was the future. I was ready for it until I wasn't. "In her last year of college, a month before the wedding, she called it off."

Ivy pulled back, her eyes seeking out mine. There were tears swimming in them. But she didn't speak, which I was glad for. I needed to finish this.

"There was someone else."

"Bitch," Ivy breathed out. That made me smile; she didn't swear often.

"It's fine, Ivy. I'm better off without her."

"Damn right you are, Jake. But I'm so sorry." She bit her bottom lip and looked up at me with some trepidation. "And since then?"

I tucked a long curl behind her ear. "No one serious."

Part of me wanted to add *yet* to that sentence, but I figured that was pushing it. Maybe?

Maggie and Sully swayed by, Maggie's eyes closed with her head resting on Sully's chest, their lower bodies separated by her basketball belly. Apparently she'd gotten a second wind for at least a few songs.

Looking back to Ivy, I pulled her flush against me again. If we were doing this, I figured we might as well get it all out.

"You've told me before that you and Addie's dad never married. Do you want to share more?"

Ivy pulled back again to meet my eyes. Hers were dancing. "So we're the type of friends that kiss on kitchen counters, hold hands in public, and now talk about lost loves."

My heart sank at the term lost love, which was ridiculous. I mean, she had Addie. Of course there was a serious relationship in her past.

Steph and Drew slid up next to us, doing a spin and swaying to our side. Drew raised his eyebrows at me, then looked to Ivy. "Bookstore, why does Jake here have the lost-puppy-dog face? Did you finally share that you were more interested in the better of the Spencer siblings?"

Steph smacked his head. "Sorry, you two. Can't take this one anywhere." She led them away. I owed her one.

I moved us as we danced toward the tank-area part of the dance space. It was less populated by nosy family members. Looking down at Ivy, I ran my finger along her jaw, tilting her chin up to meet my eyes. "Yes, Ivy. I'd like to be that type of friends, and more." I fought the urge to devour her with my mouth, settling for a kiss to her forehead before pulling her tight to sway to the music once again.

Ivy's head rested on my chest in silence for a beat before

she cleared her throat. "Okay, in that case, I've had one serious relationship. Addie's dad, Noah."

I steeled myself, praying I would be strong enough not to be eaten up my jealousy after whatever it was that Ivy was going to share. He wasn't here now. I was clinging to that.

Ivy squeezed my torso with her arms like she knew I was struggling, which said a lot. Then she continued. "Noah and I dated at the end of college and for about a year after. I don't know if I ever saw us together for good, but he was a good guy. He is idealistic, lots of service trips during college. He and I came from the same area growing up. Our families are similar—lots of means, not a lot of love. I had my nana, but Noah didn't have anything like that. His coping mechanism was to pour love into the world instead. I knew he was headed to Africa after college to help bring water to rural villages as soon as he saved up enough money—"

"I thought you said his family had money?"

Ivy laughed, but it was without humor. "Our parents don't believe in that kind of work. There isn't enough status in it."

I looked to my mom and dad who were now doing some weird group huddle dance with Steph and Drew. It seems even at my age, I found more and more reasons to appreciate my childhood.

I squeezed Ivy to tell her to continue.

"So, when I found out I was pregnant, I let him know. It was right before he left, and we had, for all purposes, broken up. Noah and I were friends, but more than that wasn't in the cards. He offered to give me money for Addie, for her care, but as I told your sister the other day, how could I take his money when I knew what good he was trying to do with it?"

I looked to Steph. "My sister?"

I felt Ivy look up at me. "Yeah, she asked me about my support system the other day. I'm guessing she didn't share with you?"

I shook my head, grateful Ivy had that with Steph, but wishing I'd had some intel.

"Hmm," she murmured. "Anyway, I told Noah we'd be fine, and we have been, though times were tight. He comes back to the states a few times every year and sees Addie when he can. He's her dad, but he and I are friends."

I looked down at Ivy to find her watching me. "Are you telling me I don't need to be jealous?"

She licked her lips, which made me want to groan. "Are you saying you would be jealous?"

I pulled her closer so she could feel my arousal. Her eyes widened.

"I'm saying I'm feeling a whole lot about you, Ivy. And I don't know what to do about that."

A flush worked its way up her chest to her neck. She rose on her toes to whisper in my ear. "I'm thinking we both just shared that there is nothing standing in the way of me helping you with that *condition*, Jake."

I dipped my mouth down, pressing a kiss to her neck, and then pulled back to whisper in her ear. "You're killing me, Ivy. Can I toss you over my shoulder and head to your place right now?"

"Your family...," she whispered.

"Closing time," Sully called out, interrupting our conversation. "Time to go home, you all. You don't have to go home, but you can't stay here. Thanks for celebrating with us!"

I sank into Ivy's arms as she squeezed me, relaying that

she was ready to get out of here. I fought to calm myself. We swayed back and forth, barely moving.

My dad cleared his throat. "Son, we're heading home, and we'll take care of Chief."

I pulled back and looked at my dad who stood there with a shit-eating grin while my mom looked like she'd won the lottery. Hmm. Maybe our drawn-out dance had been seen by more than a few? Glancing at Ivy with a look of regret, I said to my dad, "No, you all are my guests. We can head out in just a moment."

Drew stepped forward and slapped my back. "You see Bookstore home, Jake. Steph and I will visit with the parental units before we all crash in preparation of what Mom assures me will be a hell of a brunch tomorrow."

Mom stepped up, giving me a kiss on the cheek before she patted it, then gave Ivy a kiss too. "I know I raised you better than to think Ivy should see herself home." Moving back, she gave me one of her famous mom looks. "Now, it's getting late," she said before looking back at Ivy. "It was lovely meeting you, dear. Looking forward to brunch tomorrow with Addie."

With that, Mom corralled the crew and we were left alone in the rapidly emptying brewery.

I tugged Ivy to face me as I heard the music for the final song on the Stapleton album begin. Wrapping my arms around her, I began swaying to the beat of the music. She immediately joined in, letting her head drop to my chest.

"Thanks again for playing this," she whispered.

"Of course." My eyes closed as I tried to sort out everything racing through my brain. Where did we even go from here? What did Ivy want? What did I want? Hell.

I opened my eyes, looking at the staff members around us quickly putting the place back to rights. No one seemed to care that Ivy and I were a dance floor of our own, and they all gave us a wide berth. I made a mental note to show my appreciation this week.

We swayed until the song finished and the brewery was nearly empty.

"Well." Ivy met my eyes. "That was quite an evening."

I leaned down, placing a light kiss on her forehead before straightening back up. "It's not over yet." With that, I grabbed her hand and headed for the door.

17

YOU SHOULD PROBABLY LEAVE

Ivy

My brain whirled as I let Jake lead me out of the brewery and down the street. My place was about four blocks from the downtown, and he headed straight for it. We'd shared a lot over the past week and a great deal more as we danced tonight. Where was Jake's mind at? Mine was full of the way his chest had felt under my hand, how safe I'd felt in his arms. It was lovely, but then a large part of my brain, or maybe my heart, warned me not to get used to this. I needed to think about the bookstore, to continue to plan for Addie and my future. But maybe not now. Maybe now I could simply follow Jake, noting the beautiful evening surrounding us on our walk home.

The neighborhoods off the downtown were quiet streets with quaint homes, each near a hundred years old. I loved the history, the uniqueness of the area. The newer subdivisions on the outskirts of town boasted larger houses, likely much more luxurious than my cottage, but I'd take these sweet homes any day of the week.

Before I knew it, we headed up the brick sidewalk of my

place onto the porch and into my home. My babysitter was camped out on the couch, scanning her phone. Jake picked up a throw from the floor, folding it as I grabbed cash out of my purse to pay her.

"Hey Sara, everything go okay?" I handed over the cash while she slid her phone and a book into her purse.

"Sure did, Ivy. Addie was a dream. She went down a bit after eight and was out quickly." She moved toward the door with a glance at Jake and a wide grin at me. Super. "Thanks for having me, Ivy. Call anytime."

"I will. Thanks again." Her ponytail swished as she headed out the porch and to her car. Closing the door, I briefly wondered if teens gossiped about adults. I mean, would Sara be sharing with the town that Jake came home with me? Did that even mean anything? More importantly, did she know Lou? That could be interesting.

"Talk to me," Jake said.

I turned from my spot at the door to look at him. Dang, he was gorgeous. Tonight he'd dressed up in a fitted white button-down and gray dress pants. I was torn between wanting to run my lips along the scruff at his jaw or unbuttoning that shirt. It was a win either way, right?

I shook my head, trying to clear out my thoughts. "What?"

He moved the two steps required to stand in front of me. "Hey," he said, tilting my chin up to meet his gaze. "You okay?" His thumb brushed along my jaw line and I fought a shiver.

I watched his expression soften. My emotions were all over the place with regard to Jake. He'd done more for me this week than anyone had since my grandmother years ago. It felt unbelievable to be taken care of, but I knew I couldn't get used to it because it would kill when he eventually moved on. My brain kept replaying the kiss from the last time he was here. I vacillated between wanting a repeat performance and wondering if we should slow down and figure this out.

"I'm okay," I whispered. "Just wondering where we go from here."

Jake tucked some of my hair behind my ear, and I melted. "I'm trying to tell myself that I need to leave."

I nodded absentmindedly. "Yeah, you should probably leave."

He ran his thumb over my lip. "Yeah, I probably should." His thumb trailed over my jaw and down my neck. "Right?" He arched an eyebrow and met my eyes.

I bit my lip. My heart was threatening to beat right out of my chest.

My gaze locked on his. I noted that he didn't look away as his hands found my hips and pulled me flush against him to let me feel just how conflicted he was. "Ivy," he whispered as he lowered his mouth to the crook of my neck. Pressing a kiss there, he continued. "I'm trying to do the right thing here, but it's killing me. Tell me to go."

Goose bumps raced up my arms as tingles intensified throughout my body. Without a doubt, I wanted him to stay. We needed to figure out what this was between us. I knew I had my own issues, and from what Jake said tonight about his ex, he probably did too. And I also knew I didn't give a flying fuck right now. Yes, it was absolutely worthy of the f-word. I needed this.

"I don't want you to go." Damn, my voice was husky, filled with all the emotions swirling through me. I sounded like Stevie Nicks, which normally would thrill me to the point that I'd want to test it out with a song. Right now I just wanted to drag Jake to my room and jump him.

"But Addie..."

Damn Jake, trying to be responsible here. I'd been living like a nun for far too long and needed to get the show on the road.

"She won't know a thing." I tried to rationalize. That would work, right? There was no reason a four-year-old had to know anything about what was happening here. She was asleep, for Pete's sake, and tended to sleep hard once she was down.

Jake gave me a skeptical look. "So we won't tell her anything has changed?"

"Why would anything change? It's just sex—" I got out before reflecting on how that sounded. "I mean—" I began again.

Jake shook his head. "No, you're right. It's just tonight. Nothing needs to change with Addie."

"Jake, that's not what I meant," I began again but was quickly silenced when Jake slammed his mouth down on mine. Holy moly. Who cares about conversations? I lost myself in his mouth. Our last kiss had been amazing, sweet. Now I felt like I was being worshipped, devoured. His tongue slid against mine as our bodies collided. He moved, leading me to take a few steps. My back hit the wall and I wrapped a leg around his, pulling us together as I lost myself in the moment.

Jake's mouth trailed down to my neck again as he dipped a finger under my dress at my shoulder and traced the neckline down over my breasts until it ended at my waist. "I've been wanting to do that all night. This dress was driving me crazy."

I let my head tip back against the wall as his lips and tongue continued their assault on my neck and the edges of my breasts. His fingers found a nipple and squeezed. "And no bra, Ivy? What are you trying to do to me?"

I gasped out my answer. "Get you to do this?"

"Mission accomplished," he murmured before letting his mouth drop to mine once again.

Minutes, hours—who knows, maybe days later—Jake pulled back and looked down at me, blue eyes crinkling in amusement as I fought to catch my breath. "Are we doing this here or in your room?"

My mind was an empty vessel.

"Doing this?"

"Sex, babe. I'm assuming that's—"

Get with the program, Ivy. "Hell, yes, we're having all the sex." What did I just say? More importantly, what was the question he'd asked?

He pressed a kiss to the tip of my nose. "Okay, so we're on board with where this is going to lead. So, couch? Kitchen counter? Dining room table? Bedroom?"

"Bedroom." I grabbed his hand and took off through the living room and up the stairs. On the landing, I looked to the left and saw Addie's door cracked, and I paused. "I should turn off her lamp and close her door," I whispered.

"Got it," Jake whispered back. "Go ahead and do anything you need in there." He nodded to my room as he turned toward Addie's.

I stood frozen as I watched his giant form move quietly into my daughter's room. He leaned down, picking up her stuffed penguin from by her bed. Tucking it into her arm, he pulled the blanket up around her shoulders and leaned down, pressing a kiss to her head. As he moved to turn off her light, I fled to my room, racing to my closet.

Standing there, I pressed a hand to my chest as tears swam

in my vision. No, this was not happening. I was not falling for this man. Sex. This was just sex. Yeah, he was unbelievably gorgeous. And had an amazing family. And was awesome with Addie. All that was bound to confuse everything. But this? This was sex. Sex that I needed. Nothing else, nothing more.

I yanked off one boot, then the other. Do I go ahead and just take all my clothes off? Do I put on pajamas? What was the protocol here?

"Ivy," Jake called out in a hush tone as he walked in.

I poked my head out of the closet. "I'm just changing," I said. Even in the darkness, I could feel his eyes on me.

"I'd say that shouldn't take too long with what you were wearing. There wasn't a lot to it." In the moonlight I could see that he was beginning to unbutton his shirt.

"I was trying to decide if I should put on pajamas," I explained as he came to a stop in front of me.

His smile was deep as he reached for me, then ran his hands up my arms to pull me in for a full body hug. Damn that was nice.

"Absolutely your call on the pajamas, babe, but from my standpoint, they'd just be a waste of time," he said. Looking down at me, he ran his hands over my back, caressing it. "And I know we kind of made a mad dash up here, but if you've changed your mind..."

Smiling up at him, I relaxed. The man was far more kind than I originally gave him credit for. And heck no, we weren't going back. I ran my hands up his now-bare chest, shoving his shirt off his shoulders. "So, no pajamas it is."

Jake shrugged his shirt off before running his hands over my dress, his gaze locked on mine. "Does this thing have a zipper?"

I smirked. "Nope, I just pulled it on."

Nodding, he reached for the hem and pulled it up and

off. Within seconds I was standing in front of Jake Spencer in a small scrap of underwear. I would say that I felt self-conscious, but that would be a lie. His eyes raked over me from head to toe, then back. "Damn, Ivy. You're gorgeous." In my twenty-eight years on this planet, I'd never felt so wanted, desired.

"So we're doing this," I whispered, running my fingers over his stomach muscles, lightly tracing the line moving from them to his waistband. I itched to unbutton his pants, slide them down. My eyes rose up to his, and I found him watching me.

Brushing my hair back and tucking it behind my ear, he kissed the top of my head. "We're doing this, Ivy." He paused then, seemingly lost in thought. "I think we've been moving toward this for months."

"Meaning we were always going to end up here?" I whispered, pressing light kisses to his chest, paying close attention to his nipples. I lightly bit one and was rewarded with a moan. Nice.

"Always," he said as he picked me up and moved toward my bed. Lowering me to the bed, his eyes raked over me. I felt wanted, desired. Jake quickly unbuttoned and dropped his pants and underwear in one fell swoop. I leaned up so I could get a good visual, but Jake's hand landed on my stomach as he pushed me back. "Give me a minute, babe. Need to make sure you're ready for this round."

I let myself flop back on the bed while my mind replayed the *this round* comment. That worked for me. Just as my brain adjusted to our extended plans, his mouth lowered, and I felt his tongue at my collarbone. I dropped my head back to the bed, arching up my breasts toward him. Oh Goddess, it had been a while. Jake proceeded to nip, caress, and kiss around my neck, driving me crazy with want.

"Jake," I croaked. He slid a hand over my breast, thumbing my nipple as he continued my undoing. I felt lost in a wave of desire, needing contact at my core to finally climax, but he was keeping all touch above my waist. It was maddening.

"Jake." I was more insistent.

His eyes came up to meet mine, and there was a twinkle of humor there. The man knew what he was doing to me. "Yeah, Ivy? I'm kind of busy here."

"I need you," I breathed out, no longer caring what that sounded like.

Jake pressed a long kiss to my lower stomach, then looked back to me. "I'm here, Ivy."

I narrowed my eyes at him, my thighs rubbing together, trying to find some type of contact. "Not there," I growled.

Jake bit his lower lip, clearly fighting a smile. "Maybe you need to be more descriptive."

I rolled my eyes at him. "Fine, I can just take care—" And I started to skate my hand down to the promise land.

Jake immediately batted my hand away, and his mouth was at my core. Oh. My. Goddess. His tongue made slow laps around my clit, then slowly moved down to my entrance, then back up.

He paused and looked at me. "That what you were looking for, babe?"

"Mrmph," I groaned.

As the sensations intensified running through my body, he slowed down, building the anticipation, moving to kiss my inner thighs before pressing a kiss to my happy place. And wowza, was it happy. I let out a long, low moan, keeping it as quiet as possible.

"Damn, Ivy. I think you're close already," he murmured, continuing to give some well-placed suction to my clit that made me want to come out of my skin.

Clearly, I'd lost the ability to form a coherent thought. What I wanted to say was, *Yes, there, right there. Never leave this spot.* Instead? I opened my mouth and "Gahhh" came out.

I heard Jake chuckle, but he resumed—thank you, Goddess—and I wondered if I might black out. My orgasm continued to build, I felt it coiling tighter and tighter in my belly until Jake tilted my hips and slid one finger in.

"Ohmygoddess" came out in one breath. A wave crashed over me as I felt my body trying to clench Jake's finger. I both wanted to pull his mouth to me more fully and felt too sensitive at the same time. Jake's mouth continued more gentle kisses until I came down from that incredible high and found him hovering over me in a plank position.

"You good, Ivy?" He kissed my nose and pulled back to take me in.

"Good? I don't know if I have words to describe that," I murmured.

"Yeah," he chuckled. He leaned down on one side of me so he could run a hand over my belly. Tracing the underside of my breast, he continued, "I don't have words to describe that either."

I turned on my side and ran a hand over his hip and down until I found his cock. It was clearly ready to continue. "What about you?" I gave him a light squeeze.

"Damn, woman. You're killing me." He pushed me off him and rolled to the side, reaching down for his pants, and grabbed his wallet. Coming back onto the bed, he tore open the wrapper and slid the condom on.

"You do that pretty easily, mister."

"What are you asking, babe?" he asked, moving toward me. "I'm no virgin, sweetheart. But there also hasn't been anyone for months."

"Months?" I raised my eyebrow in surprise, my breath catching as he came over me, letting his cock slide back and forth through my wet folds.

"Months, Ivy. Over seven to be precise."

"Mine has been a bit longer, Jake," I whispered, as he continued to glide.

"How long, baby?" He leaned down to nip at my ear.

My eyes fluttered. God, he felt incredible. "Um, four and a half years plus around forty weeks?"

Movement stopped and Jake looked down at me. "Wait, since Addie?"

I wrapped my legs around him, pulling him down as I tried to move on my own. I needed the friction back. "Yes, since Addie. It's not exactly easy to date and have a toddler, Jake. Now"—I wiggled against him—"get moving."

Jake dropped to his elbows on either side of me. His hands tilted my head as he pressed a kiss to my lips, then pulled up. "Your wish is my command."

With that, he began moving again, entering me in one glorious thrust. I wrapped myself around him and held on, meeting him thrust for thrust as sensations began racing through me. Hmm. Apparently one orgasm was just the beginning.

Jake leaned down, capturing my lips with his before whispering in my ear, "Oh, babe, we're just getting started."

I prayed his words were correct.

18

SNACK TRAYS AND CARTOONS

Jake

I awoke to a mouthful of hair trailing across my face. Brushing it aside, I replayed last night in my mind. I was both grateful that we'd finally given in to temptation while being shocked as shit that it happened. I wondered if we could have a repeat performance before I had to get out of there. I hadn't planned on staying, but I'd crashed somewhere after round two and thought I'd rest for just a moment.

Turning to reach for my phone and check the time, I was met a pair of blue-green eyes watching me from where they peaked over the edge of the bed. Shit. Addie. I held back a groan, not wanting to wake Ivy to deal with the fallout that would be Addie finding us. I said a momentary prayer of thanks that I'd pulled on my boxer briefs, and Ivy a T-shirt, after round two.

"Pssstttt," she whispered. "Jakey."

I tried not to laugh at her super-serious expression. "Yeah, Ads?" I whispered back.

She pushed herself up on the bed closer to my ear. "Mustn't wake Momma. Can you make me pancakes?"

I glanced over at Ivy. I guessed we'd deal with this later. Addie didn't seem to fazed to find me in her momma's bed, though from what Ivy said last night, this would be a first. I still couldn't believe she'd been celibate since having Addie. Made me all the more grateful that she gave me a shot, though it also made me a bit nervous about where we'd be going from here. I was shocked as shit to realize that a relationship didn't make me want to head for the hills. More than that, I realized how nice it was to wake up here with Ivy and Addie.

Knowing I'd need to work through that thought process later, possibly with some Irish whiskey and Drew, I put my finger to my lips and nodded at Addie. Her little hands shot up in what I now knew was her patented cheer complete with jazz hands as she raced from the room on silent feet. Shaking my head as I watched her, I slid out of the bed and pulled on my dress pants and dress shirt. I didn't know if Addie would have any comments about what I was wearing, but likely not. She typically marched to her own drummer in terms of wardrobe anyway. I glanced at Ivy to see that she hadn't moved a muscle. Phone in hand, I followed Ms. Addie down the stairs to the kitchen.

As I hit the door to the kitchen, I tapped my phone to check on the time. I noted the early hour, a little before seven, while also seeing a text thread from my siblings. Super. I should probably deal with that chaos before breakfast. A glance at Addie found her doing her twirls in the kitchen. She wore a pajama shirt and leggings, but a blue sparkly tutu completed this morning's ensemble. Glad to know that she dressed for breakfast.

"Ads, I need to message my brother, Drew. Can I give you some chocolate milk to start?"

"Yeah, Jakey. Can I have strawberries too? And some dance music?" She continued twirling, focused on her skirt.

"Sure, babe. We just need to keep the music quiet." I grabbed the milk and berries from the fridge. Ivy already had a bunch of them cut up, so I stuck them on a plate for her and poured her half a glass of milk. Drew found out the hard way this week that it wasn't always a great choice to give a four-year-old a full glass.

I began playing Fleetwood Mac's Greatest Hits from my phone on low, enough that she could hear it and keep twirling but hopefully low enough that Ivy could continue to rest. Finally, I opened my messaging app and prepared to get a load of shit.

Drew: *I'm guessing we've seen the last of you for the night. Steph and I have polished off your whiskey with Dad. Mom crashed. Chief has been walked. And I'm guessing you've gotten laid. All's right in your world, but my hand is tired.*

Steph: *Crass. I don't need to know about your hand. And why don't you go wash it, bleach it, something.*

Drew: *You're sitting across the living room from me. You could just say it instead of texting.*

Steph: *Dad is between us. I'd rather he doesn't know how disgusting you are.*

God, these two. I had to laugh. They drove me crazy, but I couldn't imagine my life without them. I checked out Addie. Still doing some type of interpretive dance. Excellent.

Steph: *And Jake, I'm assuming from your lack of texts*

that the Neanderthal that we call our baby bro is correct and you and Ivy have done the deed.

Drew: *I'll give Bookstore a high five at brunch. I like her. Let's keep her. Don't fuck this up, bro.*

Fuck, brunch. I forgot about that. I didn't want to make Addie pancakes and ruin her appetite. I'd figure something out.

Steph: *Not to agree with the fool, but I hope you know what you're doing here, Jake. Ivy's great and she has a kid. This isn't something to play with.*

Drew: *Not that we don't have faith in you, but you know. Love you and want you to keep your head out of your ass.*

Steph: *I'll just echo the caveman above. Love you, bro. See you in the morning. Drew and I are crashing at your place with Mom and Dad. I'm taking your bed because I'm assuming you won't be returning to use it tonight.*

Drew: *Well, at least you'll know if he comes home tonight.*

Steph: *Exactly.*

I laid my phone down as I dropped my elbows to the counter and let my head rest in my hands. Rubbing my temples, I had so many competing thoughts. One, what to tell Addie about breakfast. Two, the notion that I was playing with Ivy. I mean, I didn't know what the hell we were doing, but I certainly wasn't trying to hurt her. And I'd never do anything to hurt Addie. I hadn't drunk that much last night, but I felt a headache looming.

Addie tugged on my pants. "Jakey, are we having pancakes?"

I opened my eyes and peered down at her. My heart

skipped a beat. What the hell was that? "Sorry, peanut. I forgot that we're having brunch at my place."

"What's brunch?" She wrinkled her nose.

I stood, picking her up to place her on the counter closer to my own height. I placed a hand on either side of her, then tweaked her nose. "Brunch is a grown-up term for lots of breakfast food but a bit later than normal breakfast time. My mom and dad are in town, and my mom wants to make you pancakes."

"Your momma and daddy are here?" She began doing that thing where she rocked back and forth when she was sitting. It's like she had too much excitement to contain in her little body, and it threatened to overflow. My parents were going to eat her up.

"Yeah, peanut, they're here. My mom wants to make you pancakes, and my dad wanted to get donuts."

Her eyes widened. In a whisper voice, she said, "Pancakes and donuts? For the same breakfast?"

I heard laughter over my shoulder as I turned to find Ivy leaning on the doorjamb to the kitchen, watching us. "I think they've won her over before they even met her," she said with a soft smile.

Holy hell, she was gorgeous. I mean, she always is, but wow. Her blond waves that I'd woken up with in my face tumbled all over. She wore leggings and a worn T-shirt with some feminist saying because of course she did. However, the T-shirt did not disguise the lack of bra, so I was immediately a fan.

She gave me a soft smile as she moved to join us at the counter. Turning to Addie, she leaned in and gave her a kiss on her temple. "Hey, Sunshine. You have fun with Sara last night?"

Addie nodded, looking very serious. "Yeah, Momma. I

want her to come over again to play. But pancakes and donuts?"

Ivy gave Addie a soft smile as she moved over to the cabinets. I was delighted to see her pull down coffee beans. Thank God.

"Yes, Addie, pancakes and donuts. But Jake's momma and daddy don't get up as early as you did today, so we need to let them sleep some more. How about a snack tray while you watch cartoons?"

"Yahoo!" Addie's arms shot up again. "Best day ever." She looked over at me. "Down please," she asked with her arms out.

I leaned forward to grab her, and she wrapped her little arms around my neck. With a squeeze, she whispered in my ear, "Thanks, Jakey." I slid her to the floor, and she took off to the living room.

The emotion I felt for that little girl was not something I wanted to sort out right now, so I picked an easier topic. "Snack tray? Sounds like it's something special."

Ivy laughed as she twisted her hair into some type of knot on her head, securing with an elastic from around her wrist. "Not sure it's that special, but it's something she loves." She leaned over and pulled out a cupcake pan. "I just fill up each cup with a different type of snack."

I nodded, seeing the appeal in the eyes of a kid. "Do we get to snack with her?"

Ivy gave me a mock glare. "Are you trying to steal my child's food?"

I laughed, enjoying the easy feeling of this morning. "Ivy, your kid can't weigh more than forty pounds soaking wet. There's no way she needs twelve full cups of snacks." I gestured to the cupcake pan.

"Fair point. And I typically only fill each cup up a

quarter of the way. But sure, we can snack with her. Want to help?"

"I can do the snacks if you want to tackle the coffee."

"Need coffee that bad, do you?" she asked as she filled the pot with water.

"You have no idea." I shook my head.

I opened the cabinets and fridge to grab what, after a week with Addie, I knew were the hits in terms of snacks in this house. Nothing too exciting, I filled up the cups with fruit, some veggies, cut-up cheese, and dry cereal. Ivy glanced over as she poured the coffee. She moved to hand me a mug and paused, considering the tin.

"You've got all her favorites," she said. She sounded different. I looked up and saw some moisture in her eyes.

"Hey, babe." I pulled her toward me, taking the coffee mugs and setting them on the counter. "You okay?" I wiped below her eyes where a few tears had spilled over. What the hell had happened? Cradling her jaw in my hand, I let my lips brush hers.

"Sorry," she whispered.

"No need to be sorry, just wondering what's going through that mind of yours." I leaned back and handed her a coffee mug before taking the other for me.

Ivy put her coffee down and hopped up to sit on the counter before picking it up again with both hands. She inhaled the coffee with a deep sigh and looked content once again, not sad. I was going to go with that, not sure what had come over her a moment ago.

I glanced at her mug, then mine, and laughed as I read my mug. "You bought this one with me in mind, didn't you?" I asked as I held up my mug toward her with the WOKE UP SEXY AS HELL AGAIN message facing her way.

She winked. "It might fit you, I suppose."

"Where'd you get this?"

"Maggie got it for me last month when I was lamenting the lack of guys in my life. I was just being generally whiney and feeling blah about myself."

I felt my brows draw together. When I thought of Ivy, I thought of a confident, sexy-as-hell woman. Though it made sense. All people had low moments. And when I thought about her doing all this—parenting, running a new business, moving to a new town—on her own, well, that would be a difficult time.

"One, Ivy"—I moved into her space and leaned down to kiss her neck—"you'd be sexy as hell anytime, day or night."

She groaned, letting her head drop back. "Jake." Her voice trailed off.

"Nope, shush." I whispered, my mouth against her neck. God, she smelled incredible. "Two," I licked her collarbone, then nipped it. She jumped, then groaned again as I kissed the same spot. "I'd love to know where your head was a few minutes ago. I hate seeing you sad." That was an understatement. She made me want to slay dragons. I had no idea what to do with these feelings, but again, I was dealing with that later.

Her head dropped to my shoulder. I placed my coffee back on the counter and grabbed hers to do the same. Sliding her off the counter and pulling her to me, I began to sway to the music still pouring out of my phone. She wrapped her arms around my shoulders and let her head slide to my chest. It felt just as good as last night, but more intimate somehow.

"It's nothing, Jake," she whispered.

"I want to know, Ivy," I whispered back, running a hand through her hair.

She swayed with me for a few minutes without talking.

Often with women I'd tried to date, I felt the need to fill the silences. Not with Ivy. Silences felt as comfortable and easy as conversations. Finally, she met my eyes.

"You knew her favorite snacks."

I let that statement roll around for a minute, then looked over at the cupcake pan, then back at Ivy. "You mean the snack-tray stuff?"

She nodded.

"Ivy, I've been with her for five days after school. Your kid likes to eat, so we have snacks. Not shockingly, you've raised her to speak her mind. She has zero issue extolling the merits of certain foods over others." I pressed a kiss to her head. "And in case I'm not clear here, I think that's a good thing."

Tears began forming again in her beautiful eyes that were looking more blue than green today. I kissed one tear as it slipped over her lower lid. "Babe, why the waterworks over her snacks?"

"Her dad doesn't know what snacks she likes, Jake. Noah's a great guy and he does her best, but sometimes I get a sense of what Addie has missed out on. I can't be every-thing for her, as much as I want to. And now we're going to brunch with your parents and siblings, when my parents have seen her a grand total of four times in her life." She pressed her face to my chest and continued, though her voice was a bit muffled. "It's just a lot." With that, she let out a sigh so large it seemed too big to have kept in for so long.

"Babe." I kissed her head again as we swayed around the kitchen. "I'm so sorry your parents are dicks."

She snorted. "Jake..."

"No other word for it, Ivy. Their loss, clearly—"

She interrupted. "They're not dicks, exactly. They're

just emotionally closed off. They're not cruel, but in their brain a visit once a year is plenty."

I shook my head. "Not going to debate their obvious dickheadedness right now, babe. But I want to say I'm sorry you don't have more of a support system. I'm sorry Addie's dad has missed out. And I wish like hell that your nana was still around for you."

She squeezed me tight and pressed her face to my chest. I could feel moisture gathering, so I'm guessing some tears were flowing. "I do miss her so."

"Not sure how much it helps, but you're welcome to my family. They're a lot to take at times." I smiled thinking of their texts last night.

She laughed. "I love your family. And while I'd be glad to borrow them, I'm not sure how smart that would be."

I stopped swaying and pulled back, looking down into her face. She was a bit blotchy from the tears that seemed to have stopped. "Why wouldn't that be smart?"

A crease formed between her brows. "I don't know. Because we don't know where this is going?" She gestured between the two of us.

My stomach dropped with the thought of trying to define whatever the fuck we were doing while another part of me wanted to ask why she wouldn't assume we were building something together. Not at all confusing. Sure.

Pounding feet pulled me out of my internal tug-of-war. "Momma, Jakey, where's my snack tray?" Addie appeared at the door and placed her hands on her hips in a Wonder Woman pose. This kid.

"Miss Addie, is that how you ask for something?" Ivy faced Addie, mirroring her stance. Damn, she looked hot. *Not the time, man.*

Addie immediately looked chagrined. "Sorry, Momma. Is my snack tray ready please?"

Ivy nodded, apparently pleased with the change of tune. "It is, babe. Do you want to watch cartoons or play games while we snack?"

Addie did a little shimmy dance as she turned to race back to the living room. "Cartoons! Let's go!"

Ivy grabbed her coffee and mine. "Can you get the tray?"

"Sure," I said as I turned to grab it and then followed my girls to the living room for a morning of snacks and cartoons. Sounded surprisingly like a good time.

PANCAKES AND SLEEPOVERS

Ivy

Jake and I headed down the sidewalk toward his house behind a twirling Addie. As she went, she talked to the leaves underfoot, bare trees soaring overhead. We passed houses with dogs barking from inside, to which she answered each in a singsong voice. To say she was excited about pancakes *and* donuts would be an understatement, but that wasn't the only reason for her unbridled joy. She was just a happy kid.

I didn't know what to think about the fact that she hadn't reacted at all to waking up to find Jake in my room. Part of me felt the need to explain it, to see if she was okay. Another part of me felt that I wanted her to grow up with positive feelings about what sex was and to never feel shame toward it. My parents were closed off in regard to conversations about sex, to say the least. There was zero discussion about it other than good girls weren't doing that. Fortunately for me, Nana did not subscribe to that philosophy. Chalk one more reason to miss her. She wouldn't have felt I was living in sin by having sex, much less a child, out of wedlock. She would have just celebrated along with me.

All that was to say I missed the heck out of her, and I needed to figure out what, if anything, to say to Addie. So far, my parenting conversations had been guided by her inquisitive nature. We talked about all the parts of our bodies without shame. I told her about penises and vulvas when they came up.

Before we moved, her gymnastics teacher had told the kids he was having a surgery. He left it up to the parents to elaborate if we felt like our children were ready for it. I'd explained to Addie that some folks were born in bodies that didn't fit who they were and that Cody had been born with breasts, but that he was a boy and he was having surgery to have them removed. Addie had rolled with it, wanting to make a card for Cody after his top surgery and bring him some cookies and dinner, so we did.

We'd talked about sex when she asked where babies came from, but I hadn't thought about how to teach about sex for pleasure. She was so young, but when do you have that conversation? What if I waited until it was too late? How did you know when it was right?

This was when being a single parent sucked. And to be honest, I didn't know how to talk to her about Jake and what was happening with us. I was certain he wouldn't want anything long-term. Jake was great with kids, but would he want an already-formed family? I doubted it. In all likelihood, we just needed to get it out of our systems. He said it had been a while, and goddess knew it had been for me. We could go back to being friends if that was what he wanted. Addie already understood that friendship. It'd be fine.

"I'd give a million bucks to know what's going through

your head," Jake said as we followed Addie down the sidewalk, his dress shoes crushing the fall leaves underfoot.

I glanced over at him. Stubble stood out over his face and jaw, making me really wish we could have spent the day in bed. His button-down and dress pants were rumpled from the night on my floor as well as the morning on the couch watching cartoons with Addie. He carried my cake container. The idea of going to brunch at his place with his family empty-handed was a no go, so I'd whipped up Granny Hill's coffee cake. Granny Hill was one of my nana's closest friends, and I had begged for this coffee cake every time I visited as a kid.

Debating if I wanted to share with Jake that I was trying to decide what to tell my daughter about the two of us, I decided I hadn't had enough coffee for that conversation.

"Are you sure your parents are going to be okay with the two of us coming back to your house like this?" I gave a gesture to encompass his rumbled outfit. I mean, it was clear he hadn't changed since last night, and since they'd stayed in his house, there really was no question as to what happened.

Crapola.

Jake shifted the cake carrier to his opposite hand. "Slow down, Ads," he called up.

Addie turned to look back at us.

"Take a left, babe." He jerked his head in that direction.

"Okey dokey, Jakey!" Addie sang and then began twirling down the sidewalk to the left, taking us the rest of the way to Jake's.

Jake glanced at me, raising his eyebrow. "Okey dokey?" His hand reached out, nabbing mine as he laced our fingers together.

Yep. Heart skipping a few beats. No biggie, we were

just holding hands. Ignoring all the questions that were whirling in my brain, I closed my eyes for a step and took a cleansing breath. Opening them back up, I stared down the sidewalk at Addie, who was now bent over, talking to a statute of a frog. "She likes rhyming words."

Jake squeezed my hand. "Gotcha. And to answer your earlier comment. Yes, I'm sure my parents will be fine. Whether we will be when they get through with us, that's another story."

I stopped, frozen to the sidewalk. Jake turned to look at me, his face showing his confusion.

"What do you mean?" I asked, needing to understand what I was heading for.

Jake shook his head. "You've already met my mom. What I'm saying is I know you said last night was a onetime thing, and I get that. With being a mom, starting a business, all of it, it's a lot. I really do get it."

I wondered if Jake knew CPR because sure to goddess a heart rate pounding like this couldn't be healthy. "I'd like to state for the record that you were the one who said it was just for the night."

Jake's eyes narrowed. "That's right. You said it was just sex."

"We never clarified what I meant," I started. I mentally beat myself up for saying anything. But really, that's all that I thought Jake wanted, no strings, just sex. And yeah, maybe only once. Clearly I was right since he hadn't exactly fought that line of thinking, except... "Um, you're holding my hand," I pointed out helpfully.

Jake gave me a slow smile. A smile I wanted to tackle him to the ground and kiss off his face. "You saying friends can't hold hands, Bookstore Ivy?"

I laughed out loud at Drew's name for me. "Hmm, some friends can, I suppose. Are we that type of friends, *Jakey?*"

We started down the sidewalk again, drawing closer to Addie's spot talking to the stone frog. I could hear her conversation. She was asking it where Toad was. Apparently, she'd decided it was Frog from her Frog and Toad books. Of course, makes complete sense.

"Let's go, Ads. Jake's house is just up ahead," I said as we reached her.

She beamed up at us and shouted a rallying cry of *donuts* as she ran toward Jake's house, fist raised, blue tutu bouncing from underneath her jacket.

As she moved up the drive to the back door, Jake squeezed my hand again. "Ivy, I think we can absolutely be friends who hold hands." He tugged me, and I turned and looked at him. My breath caught as I watched his eyes heat and rake over me from my messy hair in a knot over my fitted shirt under my wrap from Athleta. I had on a pair of yoga pants because Jake had assured me brunch would be super casual and that Drew would likely still be in lounge pants if he could manage it. His gaze spoke volumes, but his words took my breath away. "And, if you want, I think we can be friends who spend the night together when they want."

I didn't realize it was possible for your heart to break *and* soar at the same time. "Oh?" I tried to ask super casually as I watched Addie go up the back steps and into the kitchen.

He nodded. "You said that's what you're ready for right now, and as I mentioned, I totally get it. So, just saying, there's no need for you to wait another five years or whatever. I'm here for you, when you need a sitter, a friend, or more."

Oh. Did I want that? Part of me wanted to scream, to tell him heck no, I wanted more than friends who hop into bed when they feel like it. But then, if I was honest, this was likely perfect. Because in all reality, we weren't ending up together, so if I entered this friendship with added benefits with my eyes wide open, I wouldn't get hurt. Right?

Fudgesicles. I had a feeling I'd get hurt. But maybe have a lot of sex on the way. And then Jake would find the perfect girlfriend, and I'd buy a new Lelo vibrator. Whatever. He *was* a good friend. He was great with Addie. If I could just keep this casual, we could always have that. And if for a few days, weeks, months, that came with the added bonus of hot sex, who was I to complain?

"Sounds great," I muttered.

Jake gave another light tug to my hand, and I moved to him. He pulled my hand up so ours were sandwiched just to the side of our chests. He looked down and lightly kissed the tip of my nose. "You good, Ivy?" he asked, his blue eyes skating over my face.

"Peachy," I said on a sigh. My breath had disappeared. Poof.

His smile widened, creases appearing in the stubble on his face. "Peachy?" he paused. "I'll take it," he whispered, then lowered his mouth to mine. When he was just a breath away, he stopped. "Is this okay?" he asked, his lips moving over mine.

"Heck yes," I said, rolling up on my toes to close the distance between our mouths. All common sense and any debate about the type of friends we were had left the building. My entire being, my focus, was on having his lips meet mine. We met, lips parted, and his tongue immediately slid in to meet mine. It was heavenly for all of a few seconds until I heard the catcalls begin.

Pulling back on a breath, I looked to Jake's back porch where Drew and Steph stood waving at us. "Nice lip lock, Jakey!" Drew called. "Now get in here with what Addie tells me is a killer Granny Hill coffee cake because clearly we need more sugar and carbs at this brunch." With that, he and Steph stepped back into the kitchen.

I laughed, my cheeks heating up, but also somewhat excited to spend more time with this family. Looking up at Jake, I shrugged. What else was there to do? "Let's go."

Jake and I walked into his kitchen to what can only be described as controlled chaos. Addie was chasing Chief around the kitchen to the living room calling out, "Chief, it's time for a dannnncccceee partyyyyyy!" Music was flowing out of the speakers, but I couldn't place the band, though it sounded familiar. Sam and Margot were loudly debating how many pancakes to make from the stove. There were donuts spread across the counter on platters—clearly the entire neighborhood should be arriving imminently, there was that much food. And Steph was pouring what appeared to be mimosas. It was loud, somewhat boisterous, and felt like a welcoming hug.

Drew came over and gave Jake a pounding embrace. Pulling back, he made an obvious production of looking over Jake and myself. My brows drew together as I watched. Finally, curiosity got the better of me.

"What are you doing?" I asked in a low voice.

Drew was clearly waiting for that question as he pulled back with a wide smile. "Just checking to make sure there are no visible love bites. No need for the parental units to see that shit, am I right?"

Jake mumbled something about his brother being all kinds of an idiot before saying he was going to change. As he walked by Addie, he rubbed her head. Then he moved to his parents, gave his mom a kiss on the cheek. My heart melted. Jake placed the cake carrier on the counter, then headed toward his room.

Here we go. I faced the kitchen, wondering what to say. I mean, *Hi, Mr. and Mrs. Spencer. Thanks for creating a man who can give a girl a hell of an orgasm* didn't seem to strike the right note.

Steph moved to my side, handing me a mimosa. "Here you go, girl. I find a little champagne before talking to the family of the guy you had hot sex with the night before seems to take the edge off."

Considering I'd just been taking a sip of said beverage, I spit it back into the glass and gave her a small glare. "Jesus, Steph. You don't hold back."

She laughed. "I said it before, I'll say it again. Two younger brothers. *Two*. Really, it's the only comment necessary. I mean, they're great guys, but the topics they think are appropriate are ridiculous. I've learned just to roll with it." She glanced behind me, then her eyes twinkled. "Incoming," she whispered.

What? Before I could process that comment, I felt a hand on my shoulder. "Ivy, dear." I turned to see Margot standing there. As soon as I turned a bit more, she pulled me into a heck of a hug. "We're so happy to have you and your daughter." Pulling back, she looked to the living room where Addie could be heard directing Chief. "Do you mind introducing us? Sam and I were having a bit of a discussion about pancakes when she came in and found Chief, so we haven't said hello yet."

I pulled back to see that Margot actually appeared nervous. That was unbelievably sweet, but also unnecessary. "Sure, hold on." I stepped back to call Addie from the living room. "Ads, come here please."

I watched Addie race in from the living room, followed close behind by Chief. "Yeah, Momma?" Her blond waves were already a complete mess, likely due to a good case of bedhead tousled even more from twirls and the wind on the way over. Her outfit, of course selected by her, included a pink long-sleeved T-shirt with a unicorn in sequins. It was multicolor or gold, depending on which way you flipped said sequins. She, of course, had it on multicolor. Her blue tutu was flowing around her. She had on polka-dot leggings that also had rainbows interspersed among the dots. Somewhere in Jake's house was her coat and shoes, because she was already down to her socks, one striped, one purple. I hoped she never lost the joy she had in expressing herself through her clothes. Addie gave zero *f*'s about what people thought you should wear. She wore whatever made her happy, and I was here for it.

"I wanted to introduce you to Jake's parents." I looked to see that Sam had joined Margot and Steph and Drew were standing nearby. Shaking my head with a smile, I looked to Addie. She was grinning at the assembled crowd while also trying to check out the spread of donuts behind them. "Okay, babe, this is Mr. and Mrs. Spencer." I gestured at Sam and Margot.

"Oh no, Sam and Margot please," Margot added, bending down and offering Addie her hand.

Addie grabbed her hand and shook it. "Hi Margot," she sang. Looking up at Sam, she said, "Did you bring the donuts?"

Sam's smile widened. "Yep. I'm Sam."

Addie's eyes looked up with a whole lot of joy. "I love donuts." Her voice trailed off. Obviously she was angling for some prebreakfast snack.

Sam gave me a look, and I nodded. He grabbed the

platter and offered it to Addie. "Would you like one before breakfast?"

Addie glanced my way. I replied to her unasked question, "You can have one after meeting Jake's sister and brother."

Addie looked over at Drew. "I already know Drew, silly. I painted his nails with Jakey."

Steph coughed, trying to cover up her laugh.

I didn't even try. Laughing, I said, "That's right, baby. But this is Steph, Jakey's big sister."

Addie smiled, then said, "Steph, do you want a donut?"

Steph smiled. "No, sweetheart. I'll get one later. Did you have any breakfast yet or are you ready to eat?"

Jake came back into the kitchen and leaned against the wall, watching our group standing around Addie as she analyzed the platter of donuts, making her big decision. He wore some black lounge pants that were molded to his ass and hung loose on his legs. His mauve thermal stretched across his chest. I felt drool pool in my mouth.

Addie finally picked a chocolate-glazed long john. Looking up at Steph, she said, "I had a snack tray. I woke Jakey up in Momma's bed. They were real tired. He said he was going to make me pancakes, but then he remembered we were coming here." She took a big bite and chewed, not noticing the smiles and looks that Drew, Steph, or Jake's parents were exchanging. As for me, I wanted to disappear. Could the floor just swallow me up whole right now? That'd work for me. Swallowing, Addie caught sight of Jake. "Can you make pancakes after your next sleepover, Jakey? Maybe with chocolate chips?"

"Yeah, Jakey," Drew called over. "When is that next sleepover?"

"Can I come?" Steph asked, wiping away a tear or two

of laughter as she looked at Jake. Addie had moved over and stood in front of him. I'm sure she was giving him her pleading eyes.

Jake leaned down and picked her up, swinging her to his hip. "Sure, peanut. Now, how about some cartoons?"

He headed down the hall with her to his den, a raised middle finger behind his back to his siblings. While I knew it was for them, I wondered what his parents would think? Watching them all burst out laughing, I knew this was a group I felt at home in. There was a lot of teasing, but so much love weaving through it all. What would that be like to be able to depend on that around you, always? I wish I knew.

20

POP-POP

Jake

Jesus, I wondered if I was pitting out my thermal. This brunch was beginning to feel like an interrogation. We were all gathered around the farm table in my dining room. Addie was at the end near my dad on the other side of Ivy. Ads sat on her knees, occasionally dropping food to my ever-present dog. My dad had decided to be her partner in crime and was adding more food to her plate when needed. Judging by the conspiring looks she was giving him, they were becoming fast friends.

Clearly Dad had been won over by this pint-sized dynamo. However that left my mom free to grill Ivy and me to her heart's desire. Steph and Drew weren't helping matters, oh no. They were joining in, asking as many questions as they could. Ivy looked like she was minutes from bolting, and I didn't blame her. Hell, I might beat her out the door.

"So, Ivy, tell me about Addie's dad. Is he in the picture?" my mom asked from the head of the table to my left, taking a sip of her orange juice.

I nearly spit out my coffee. "Mom, that's none of our business."

My mom looked offended, like I'd been the one asking her personal questions. "What? I'm sorry. I was just making conversation. Addie is just delightful, and I wondered what family the two of them had around."

I turned to Ivy to my right and whispered, "Sorry, Ivy. You don't need to—"

She placed a hand on my forearm and squeezed. "It's fine." Looking past me to my mom, she said, "Addie's dad is Noah. We were in college together and dated through our time at school and for some time after." She took a drink of her coffee, and it appeared to fortify her. "He's a great guy, a friend from childhood. Being a father wasn't in his plan. He was always headed to somewhere else after graduation. He's doing a lot of good in the world, but as a result, he's not in Addie's life as much as he would like."

She sat back and took a bite of her pancakes, but I could see that her hand was shaking. I slid my hand to her thigh and squeezed, wanting her to understand that she wasn't alone.

She glanced at my mom, and I saw that Ivy was fighting more than a few tears. "Noah offered to change his plans when I shared I was pregnant, but I turned him down. The two of us both come from families with means, but without a lot of affection. Noah has a good heart and wanted to give to the world, and I didn't want to stand in his way. Addie knows who he is and sees him when he visits. She also knows he is helping to change the world. I'm not keeping her from him but also not making him change who he is or asking him to give up something that means so much to him. That wouldn't be fair to any of us." She took a deep breath and looked past my mom and toward the living room, her gaze on the front window. "Noah's a good guy, just not one ready to be here, to settle down. Even if he did, we're friends. We parent together when he's around, but nothing more." She turned back to the table and shrugged.

I noted that she had no issue having this conversation in front of Addie, though she wasn't trying to pull her into it. That told me that she looked at this in a matter-of-fact way and tried not to make it a big deal to Addie, more that it was the way things were. How in the hell had she figured this all out on her own?

My eyes met Drew and Steph's across the table. They both looked like they'd like to have a few words with Noah, more like with Ivy's parents, but shockingly for them, they were quiet. Turning my head, I looked at my mom. Her mouth had fallen open, though I don't think she realized it. Closing it, she swallowed, then whispered, "Might I say, Ivy, that you are wise beyond your years and have done an amazing job with your daughter."

"Chief!" Addie squealed as Chief licked her fingers. I caught my dad's eye, and he winked. I guessed he was working on entertainment at that end of the table.

My mom shook her head at my dad, then she looked back to Ivy. "Tell me more about your parents. Or do you have siblings? Do they all live close?"

I squeezed Ivy's leg again. I'd tell my mom to cut the questions again, but Ivy appeared to be okay. Ivy took another bite of pancakes and then put her fork down. Seemed this answer was going to take a minute or two, or she was done. Part of me was eager to hear if she'd share more about her family than I already knew.

"Well, Margot, I'm going to start by saying that I love my parents, but what my family looks like is pretty much the opposite of what you all have shown me today."

My mom sat back, I'm sure not knowing if that was a good or bad thing.

Ivy didn't let her wonder for long. "I'm an only child, so my house was pretty quiet."

"Yep, opposite for sure," Drew muttered.

Steph snorted.

I looked at Ivy to see that she was giving those two a tolerant smile. She continued. "We're from Madison. My dad is a banker. My mom stayed at home and met friends for lunch at the country club. Honestly?" She looked across the table at Steph who nodded at her. Ivy had mentioned they talked about her family when Steph stopped by the bookstore. I was grateful that it seemed Ivy was pulling some strength from her.

Ivy continued. "I'm honestly surprised, knowing my parents for all these years, that they became parents in the first place. I often wonder if I was unplanned or if they just felt like it was something they were supposed to do. The next part of being an adult or something." She looked down at her lap where she was twisting a cloth napkin back and forth. I'm guessing she realized what she was doing because she dropped it and smoothed it out, then looked back at my mom, sitting up straight as she continued.

"But it is fine. They're good people, just not terrific parents. I had my nana who lived here in Highland. I came down and visited her at some point for most summers from fifth grade on. Nana was the opposite of my parents but so similar to me. She made me feel loved, whole, and left me the building the bookstore is in for me to begin my own life when I was ready."

Ivy seemed to nod to herself but then glanced to Addie, who was now thumb wrestling my dad; to Steph and Drew, who were looking at her like they wanted to tackle her until she had no doubt of their already growing affection for her; to my mom, who sat dumbfounded; to me.

I squeezed her leg again and whispered, "Ivy, you are rather impressive."

Her eyebrows went up. "Impressive? Why?"

I leaned forward to lightly kiss her forehead. Totally a friend move, right? Was now. Pulling back, I looked at her watery eyes. "Because you just sat there, explaining how the people that should be there for you, the people that utterly failed at being there for you, are fine people; it's just not in them to parent. Whether it's Addie's dad or your own parents, you acknowledged their complete lack of that caring gene, but then soldiered on yourself and don't appear to resent them for it."

She laughed. "Oh, Jake, I do resent them at times, at least my parents. Noah is just Noah. He cares; he's just not here. When Addie is sick in the middle of the night and I have to figure out how to rejuggle my entire schedule the next day, or when she was small and I didn't know what the heck I was doing, there were plenty of times I wished I wasn't alone. But the fact is, I was. And there's no use bemoaning it. It is what it is. My only regret, as you already know, is that Nana didn't get to meet Addie. I try to tell her stories about her, but it's not enough." She shrugged again like it wasn't that big of a deal, but I knew that it was.

Mom cleared her throat. I glanced over and realized she was pissed. Like the mom level of pissed that usually had Steph, Drew, and me hightailing it to our rooms to stay the heck out of her way as kids. She spoke with a quiet, controlled voice. "Ivy, suffice to say, I don't really have words to express what I'm feeling right now."

She caught my dad's eyes, and I noted that he nodded at

her, his jaw ticking as he helped Addie down to play with Chief.

Mom looked back to Ivy. "And I'm not sure what's going on with you and Jake here." She nodded at me. Thanks for that, Mom. "But you should know that no matter if you two date, are serious, or simply stay good friends, I think I can speak for my entire family when I tell you that we are all here for you anytime you need it."

"But, I can't ask—" Ivy began, but Mom cut her off.

Placing a hand up, Mom spoke. "No, I can see that you are independent and have done a brilliant job with your daughter, but I have no idea how you do that alone. My parents, Sam's parents, were there for us. We've been there for Steph and Theo—"

"And thank God they were. I have no idea how we would have showered that first week. I couldn't keep anything straight on that little sleep," Steph said from across the table, reaching to squeeze Mom's hand.

Ivy gave a small laugh. "Yeah, showering was tricky. When Addie was super tiny, I just put her on a towel outside the shower and went quick. As she got older, I put her in a water sling and brought her in with me." She gave us a quick smile as she looked over in the living room to see Addie talking to Chief. "You adapt, and it gets easier." Her warm smile found me, then Steph. "It's worth it."

"Bookstore Ivy, you're showing me again why men are the weaker sex, as Steph frequently reminds us," Drew said with a smile. "You need to let us tell you how damn impressive you are and listen as Margot here tells you we are your backup. You need anything, you tell us."

Ivy raised a brow with a wicked grin. "Now Drew, am I calling you up at the base in Colorado to come watch my daughter and get your nails painted? Because if you think there are other hotshots that are willing to come with you, we could get a babysitting pool set up in town. I'm sure there are many single moms that would take you up on it."

I began to growl at the thought of Drew's colleagues coming to Ivy's when I realized Drew hadn't had a quick retort.

Drew cleared his throat. "Well, I guess that's my opening." He looked around the table. "There's something I wanted to talk to you all about. I've decided to leave the hotshots and am moving here."

The table erupted. Steph socked his arm since she was closest. My mom cried out about how glad she was for her baby to be coming home. I said something about how he wasn't moving in, and my dad sat in silence.

Drew held up his hand. "I don't really want to talk about it now, but off-season is a good time to make a change. So I let them know before I came out this way." He looked across the table at me. "Hoping you and Sully weren't bull-shitting when you said I always had a job at the brewery."

"Drew, language," my mom admonished.

"Of course, man. And if you want to move in here, that's actually fine," I said, raking my memories for anything he might have mentioned in the past year to indicate he was thinking of this switch.

"Nah, I've talked to the guys I'm renting the Airbnb from. We're working something out on the cheap while I look for a spot to land," he said. Looking down the table, he took in our dad. "Dad?"

Dad sat back in the chair, nodding. Finally, he met Drew's eyes. "Son, you know we've been proud of the work you've done out West." He sat for a moment as Drew nodded, then continued. "But I'm happy as hell to have you back, even if you'll be downstate." He let that sit, then on a whisper, he finished, his voice full of emotion. "Welcome home."

Drew stood and moved to the end of the table. Dad stood too and fell into a tight hug that said more than my dad was capable of expressing.

"How do you expect us to listen to this with dry eyes?" Steph wailed dramatically, hopping up to rush them both. Mom moved to join, grabbing my hand as she went by, and we created a family hug.

We stood there in our huddle, soaking in this news. I looked up, finding Ivy's eyes, and she shot me a wink. Taking in a deep breath, I let out an exhale that I think I'd been holding in since Drew joined the hotshots.

Drew cleared his throat from his spot in the group. "Just saying, I had a lot of coffee cake, pancakes, and donuts. I'm not responsible for my lower intestines if you squeeze too hard."

Steph backed away immediately groaning. "Good Lord, you need to grow up."

I stepped back and moved to Ivy who'd been watching with Addie on her hip.

Steph came to join us and moved to fake whisper to Ads. "Boys can be stinky, Addie. Beware."

Addie nodded seriously. "I know. They sometimes do at school."

Everyone laughed, and the mood lightened. Steph gave me a glance that said we'd be returning to Drew's decision later.

Dad put a hand over his heart. "Addie, we've bonded today, haven't we? Not all boys are stinky."

Addie squirmed to get down and raced over to my dad, holding her arms out to get picked up. He immediately complied. I guess they really had bonded, likely over how to feed Chief from the table.

"We're friends, Sam. Do you want to have a dance party?" She threw up her jazz hands to show her excitement.

"Dance party, huh?" Dad asked.

"Yep, we can do that while we clean up," she said.

Dad looked to me, then to Mom. "We're cleaning up?"

Addie looked at him very seriously, taking her hands and putting them on either side of his face, some truly serious eye contact. "*Sam*, we all have to clean up. Many hands make light work, ya know. And then, we can sing the cleanup song."

Ivy leaned over to me. "It's from Teri's and also preschool."

Steph leaned in to both of us. "I don't care where it's from. I just want to see if she gets him to clean up *and* have a dance party."

"If she does, she's a miracle worker," Drew muttered.

Dad looked over to all of us. "I'm standing right here. You know that, right?"

We chuckled, but Addie was still waiting for an answer.

Dad looked back to Addie and said, "Sure, princess. We can have a dance party while we clean up."

Addie raised her hands up. "Woo-hoo!"

Mom came up to Addie and Dad. "What music do you like to listen to, Addie?"

"Whatever is on Jakey's phone. He has Fleeing Max," Addie said, bouncing in my dad's arms.

Dad looked back to me, and I called, "Fleetwood Mac."

The three of them turned to head toward the kitchen. Drew, Steph, Ivy, and I fell into step behind them with the dishes from the table.

Addie's hand was twirling some of my dad's hair as she spoke in a soft voice. "You guys are lots of fun. I wish you were my nana and pop-pop."

Ivy's head spun to catch my eyes and Steph sputtered.

Mom didn't falter. "Is that what you call your mom's parents?"

Addie shook her head. "No. They are Grandmother and Grandfather." We made it to the kitchen, and my dad moved to the counter, lowering Addie to sit on it. "Mom says they're nice, but they aren't a lot of fun." Her little legs swung back and forth off the counter. "My friend Trevor in class calls his grandparents Nana and Pop-Pop. He says they're nice and fun. I'd like that."

Steph moved to squeeze Addie's knee. "My girls call them Nana and Pop. It's pretty cool that your names are so close."

Addie nodded thoughtfully, then looked at my dad. "If you were my grandad, I'd still call you Pop-Pop."

Dad kissed her on the nose, then met my eyes as he whispered his reply, "Deal."

Drew laughed behind me.

Well, shit.

21

INTO THE MYSTIC

Ivy

The brunch had done a number on Addie. She had a blast, to be sure, but ate loads of sugar and didn't get her typical nap because we'd still been hanging out with Jake's family. Maybe some kids actually went to sleep easier if the nap was missed, but not Addie. That just meant you could possibly add an hour to bedtime, sometimes more.

Tonight her excuses had been included that she needed a drink, then another, then she had to go to the bathroom. She wanted an extra story, so I read one of her favorites, *Jabari Jumps*. Not the greatest of choices. Her sleepy voice immediately became more alert, and she began talking about going to the pool.

"Momma, when can I go off the high dive like Jabari?" she said, trying to keep her eyes open. In the glow of the night-light, her long lashes stood out against her cheeks as she gave up the battle of keeping those eyes open. Her blond hair flowed out over her pillow. She had her blanket pulled up to her chin and was surrounded by her stuffed animals, most importantly her stuffed penguin. Sometimes I looked at her and couldn't believe she was mine.

I leaned over to her side table to turn on her sound machine. Ocean waves filled the room. "Not till summer, baby. Now I will sit here while you go to bed." I put my hand on top of hers, waiting until she stilled. "I'm here. I'm here. Rest."

I slowly moved to my typical spot if she was having a hard time, on her rug where I could steal some minutes to meditate while she drifted off for the night. Sinking down, I folded into a cross-legged position and worked to find my center. Where usually I could clear my mind easily, chasing away errant thoughts when they appeared, tonight was a trip on the struggle bus.

I took some centering breaths. On my exhale, Jake's face appeared in my mind. Nope. Not now. I told myself it wasn't a big deal. I just needed to chase away distracting thoughts.

Inhale, exhale.

Anxiety popped up as my mind raced to the bookstore proposal. I needed to make a decision and soon. I had no answers. Still.

Inhale, exhale.

Flashes from last night in my room popped right into that cleared-out space in my brain. Shoot. I shook my head and let out a forced exhale, trying again.

Inhale, exhale.

Jake's mouth trailing down my stomach filled my subconscious.

Inhale, exhale.

I threw in the towel after my happy place refused to stop sending shivers over my core.

A glance at Addie showed that she appeared to be in a

solid sleep zone. Crossing my fingers, I said a quick prayer to the goddess above and snuck out of Addie's room, backing out as I watched her to make sure she didn't wake. Again.

Out in the hall, I grabbed my phone off the railing outside her room where I'd left it and trotted down the stairs to the kitchen. Once at the fridge, I considered the choices of wine or beer before the unpleasant task of the night.

Jake's face popped up in my memories again. Argh! Beer it was. I grabbed some of the Black Hole Sun cans he'd brought me on his last visit. I poured it into a glass and headed back to the living room.

I had the overhead lights turned off, and the room was softly lit with some lamps. I placed my beer on the coffee table before heading to my record player to pick an album. Flipping back and forth through my collection of vinyl, I finally settled on *Moondance*. The album was one of Nana's favorites, and I needed her with me tonight.

Curling up in the corner of my turquoise sectional, I took comfort in my space. It was eclectic. I had what was likely far too many throw pillows and blankets on here, but it worked for Addie and me. We curled up here to listen to music while we read or colored. Often we had movie night at this spot. Here, surrounded by my plants, my girl, and cozy fabrics, I felt centered and relaxed.

I leaned forward to take another swig of my beer for a moment of bravery. I had this. I did. My parents were expecting my call. With a glance to the time, I winced. In actuality, I was running a bit behind. Usually I called on the second Sunday of every month at nine p.m. Why nine p.m.? Because they knew that was when Addie was asleep. They preferred to talk to her over video chat and only for about ten minutes. *That* call was every other month because, and I quote, *that's plenty of time for a four-year-old, Ivy*. They were certain Addie would have nothing to say monthly, and goddess forbid we combine our chats into one. Whatever. They would be upset that I was late tonight, I knew. They could call me to check in, but that wouldn't happen. I had to be the one who called, or no call would happen.

I gave a brief thought to how much time would go by without us talking if I refused to be the one who called but immediately dismissed that idea. That was childish. And while they frustrated me to no end at times, they were my parents. I did love them. They were who they were, and I'd stopped wishing for them to be different some time ago.

Shaking my head, I stopped procrastinating and tapped the phone to call them. After two rings, my mom answered.

"Hello, my dear. You're late." My mom's voice flowed out with a bit of irritation mixed in. "Your father is here too."

"Hello, Ivy," my dad's deep voice called.

"Hey guys. Sorry I'm late," I said, taking comfort in the title track to the album that was now filling the room. I tapped my foot on the couch to the beat. "We went to a brunch with friends today, and Ads was a bear to get down."

My mom couldn't hold back a *tsk* sound over the phone. Not surprising. "Now, Ivy, that girl is four years old. You don't want her to be in college relying on you for comfort. You do what we did, march her in her room and tell her it's bedtime. Shut the door behind you and don't go back in. She'll figure it out in no time."

I rolled my eyes. I mean, it wasn't like she could see me. "Sure, Mom. Then, soon enough, she'll know not to come to me when she needs anything."

"Exactly," she replied.

Clearly nothing was going to change here. Moving on. "Christmas is coming up. I'm assuming nothing has changed for our plans. Dinner at the club on Christmas Eve, your place Christmas Day?"

Dad cleared his throat. "Actually, your mother and I wanted to talk about the holiday."

My heart skipped a beat. Every year I've asked them to come to us for Christmas. That way Addie could wake up at home and see that Santa came. But they'd insisted our yearly visit be at their house on Christmas, so I'd relented. Maybe this was the year we'd finally be at my place.

"Your mother and I have decided to take a trip to France for the holidays this year. Steve and Diane from the club are going with us. We're leaving at the start of December and will get back after the New Year. We'll catch up with you and Addie sometime this spring or summer," he said, sounding like he was bored and needed to get on to the next part of his evening.

"Oh? So we won't see you for the holidays?" While part of me wanted to dance at the idea of staying at home for Christmas, part of me was heartbroken that they cared so little if they saw Addie or me.

"No, dear. Your father just said we'd see you sometime this spring or summer." Mom sounded impatient.

Okay. I had no idea what to say to them. Then I caught on the names of the couple they were going with. "Steve and Diane. Noah's parents?"

My mom sounded almost bored with our conversation as she let out a huge sigh. "Yes, of course, the Lawsons."

"Sorry, Mom. Just wanted to be sure."

Dad joined in the conversation. "Well, Steve is thrilled that Noah is finally leaving that godforsaken country and coming back to the states even though he still refuses a job at his father's firm. Always has been an ungrateful kid…"

Dad continued on his rant, sure in his own misguided

sense of what was right while I was fixated on one bit of information.

"Um, excuse me. Noah is coming back? For good?"

"That's what Diane says, not that he gave them much notice." My mom's voice was ice-queen worthy. "Now, because you were late, our schedule is off. We need to get going. We'll send you some money to buy a gift for Addie for Christmas. Something of quality, of course."

"Of course." I mused.

"Love to you all," she said, hanging up before I got a chance to reply.

I looked at my phone for a moment before dropping my head to look up at my ceiling. Parents of the year, they were. Jeez. "Into the Mystic" was flowing out of my speakers now. I closed my eyes and let the music roll over me as I sank back into my couch.

Noah was coming back. I wondered where he planned to settle. And why hadn't he let me know? I hoped everything had gone well with the program. I knew he was proud of what they were accomplishing.

Vibrations from my phone pulled me from my thoughts. For a moment I wondered if my parents were calling back. Looking down, I saw that I had a text from Jake.

Jake: *How you doing, babe?*

Me: *Funny, I was rocking my gypsy soul.*

Jake: *Just like way back in the days of old?*

Me: *Just like.*

Jake: *So you and Van Morrison. You good? And who will tell him about the ethnic slur he has committed on Moondance?*

Dang, this guy. At least he was learning. Right? I debated what to tell him about my night, but I went with the idea that no matter what, he was becoming an important friend. And whatever else was going on, I needed friends.

Me: *Been better. Just talked to my parents. Let's just say your parents would not have approved of the conversation.*

Jake: *You're referring to Nana and Pop-Pop of course.*

Groan. It had been a day.

Me: *Of course. Have I apologized enough yet for my daughter claiming your parents in her own way?*

Jake: *Already told you, Ivy. My parents are in love with her. They might disown me to adopt her. You should be on the lookout.*

Me: *Well, then at least Addie would have family that would want to spend time with her for Christmas, so she will come out ahead in that deal.*

I waited, assuming I'd see the three dots telling me a text was imminent. Instead, an announcement of a Face-Time call coming from Jake appeared on my phone. My heart kicked into gear. Shit.

I tapped my screen and Jake's face filled it. He didn't look happy.

"Ivy, you're going to need to explain that last text," he said, wasting no time on small talk.

Yep. Not happy. Borderline pissed.

"Um, well, hello, Jake. I mean, it isn't anything shocking for them, really." I debated how to break this news without sounding like I had the worst parents in the world. "It's just that I call my parents on the second Sunday of the month for our monthly talk. I just got off with them—"

Jake interrupted. "But isn't Addie in bed? Or did she stay up later since she didn't have her nap?"

My heart melted on the simple fact that Jake knew my daughter even while I told myself to keep my distance.

"Well, they prefer to talk to only me on our Sunday chats. They feel like they can talk to Addie every other month for a quick chat during the day..." I trailed off, not sure what to say about that because it pissed me off.

Jake seemed to growl. "And..."

Deep breaths, get it out. "And tonight they told me that they were headed to France for a month-long trip with friends—actually they're Noah's parents—and would be gone over the holiday. Apparently, Noah's coming back, which I didn't know, and his dad is irritated that he won't come to work for him. Whatever." I hurried on. "But this works out, Jake, because I really have always wanted Addie to wake up at her own house for Christmas, and now she can."

I looked at the screen to see Jake staring up at the ceiling. "Jake?" I whispered.

A voice off-screen spoke. "You're going to have to give him a minute, Bookstore. He's trying not to lose it in front of his lady."

Drew. Super. We had an audience.

More importantly, I was his lady?

Jake looked to his side and growled. I heard Steph's laughter from the other side.

Jake looked back at me. "Ivy, I hate that you were on your own tonight when your parents put something else in front of you *again* in terms of importance. This is just complete bullshit. But know this, on Christmas Day you and Addie are invited to my place."

I sat back in surprise. "Oh no, Jake. We're not there. I mean, we don't know if—"

"Babe," he said in a gravelly voice that really made me wish his siblings weren't around. That, or that he was issuing this comment from a spot next to me on my couch.

"Whatever we are on Christmas Day, we will be friends. And my friends don't spend the holidays alone. My parents were already planning to be down here. Steph and Theo are with his family this year. They alternate. So on the years they go to his folks, mine come down." He jerked his head toward the side where Drew was sitting. "And apparently this guy will be here. So you two are more than welcome. Or we can come to you. We'll work it out, but you are not going to be alone."

Warmth filled me up. I felt wanted, but not the way Jake made me feel the night before. Not to say that I hadn't enjoyed that, because I absolutely had. But this sensation, this was the feeling my nana gave me. One of belonging. Of having a person who wanted to spend time with you, to be with you, because they cared about you. The idea that Jake and his family were becoming that both terrified me and filled me up at the same time.

Goddess, I was in trouble.

22

CRANK THE MUSIC IF NEEDED

Jake

I worked to school my expression so that Ivy wouldn't fear that I was imminently going to look up her parents online, find their address, and then Cousin Eddie kidnap them so they could get their collective heads out of their asses and see what they were missing.

Jesus. She was just lucky that Mom and Dad had already headed off to bed because if Margot had heard the gist of this call, she'd already be marching down the block to find Ivy and give her a mother's hug. Wouldn't matter that she didn't know the address, she'd knock on every door until she found her so that she wasn't alone. My mom was a lot, but you never wondered where you stood with her. This would cut her, deep into her soul.

"Bookstore," Drew called over to my phone, and I tipped the screen so she could see him. "You're damn lucky Margot wasn't around to hear that your parents are bailing on Christmas. Because I'm telling you now, she'd be rearranging the holiday to get Steph's clan down here as well so you'd be surrounded by the entirety of the

Spencers. And, quite frankly, Theo's mom would have none of that."

"True, true," Steph said, raising her glass to Drew.

"Hold on, I need to do something," Ivy called. I watched as she got up from her couch and took us with her to her shelves on the side of her living room. She sat her phone down, but propped up so that she could still see me and I could see her. I could tell she was flipping the record over. Sure enough, Van Morrison's "Come Running" began pouring out of her speakers after a minute. She picked up her phone to head back to her couch. As she sat down, she found another spot to prop us up and grabbed a glass of what looked like beer. She scooted back into the corner of her couch with a shitload of pillows all around her and smiled.

"Now, that's sorted," she said. "And heck no, Margot can't go rearranging plans for you all. Truly, we will be fine. As I told Jake, I've always wanted Addie to be able to wake up in her own house for Christmas. Now she gets that chance, so I'm choosing to look at this as a blessing."

I wondered briefly if Ivy ever let herself just get pissed at her parents. I mean, I was angry enough on her behalf, but she seemed to try to cushion all their actions in excuses. What was that about?

Steph snorted, and I moved the phone so that Ivy could see her. "That's good because Theo's mom will lose her shit if I said we're switching it up and coming down here."

Ivy wrinkled her nose. It was adorable, which meant I'd clearly had too many beverages.

Steph continued. "Though I totally get you, chickie. I want my kids to wake up in their own beds at Christmas. There's something kind of wonderful about that, right? It's magical."

Ivy nodded thoughtfully, and I detected a trace of moisture in her eyes.

"Ivy...," I began.

"Holy hell." Drew groaned. I looked over to see him waving his hand in the hair. "Your dog is ripping them over here."

Chief lifted his head to look in Drew's direction, then laid it back down, unimpressed by Drew's dislike of the gas coming out of him.

Steph choked back her laughter, rocking back into the couch, until the smell reached us. "Ugh!" she groaned, burying her face into some cushions.

I laughed since I was practically immune to Chief's nightly emissions, being around them as often as I was. They certainly didn't smell great but were a regular occurrence as long as the hackberry trees lining our street were dropping their berries and he was gobbling them up.

I looked from Steph back to the phone and saw Ivy's expression. She didn't look like herself.

Ivy shook her head, almost to herself, looking toward her ceiling, then looked back at the phone. "It's getting late, guys. I need to go. Thanks again for today. Talk soon." She quickly hung up, and I sat looking at a black screen.

Fuck.

"Do you want to go to her?" Steph said with a concerned look on her face.

I debated it. Yeah, of course I wanted to go to her. But I had a feeling she was needing some alone time to sort out some shit in her head. And I needed to respect that.

I looked to Drew, then Steph. "Not sure. I think, from what I've gathered over the past few weeks, that Ivy would likely want to be alone right now." I hesitated, not wanting her to feel like I was one more person who would abandon her. Hell, she'd probably make excuses for me too.

Steph scooted back into the corner of my couch. "I hear that. Maybe text her?"

Wise one, my sis. I set my beer down so I could thumb out a text. Steph began talking to Drew about the White Sox and whether he'd actually be up for a game this year if he truly was moving here. Drew stood and whistled to Chief, who followed him and Steph out of the den.

"Come on, stinky ass. Let's get you outside," Drew muttered at my dog. Chief didn't care at all that Drew had insulted him but began to wag his ass in excitement when he heard that magical word, *outside*.

I sat with my phone in hand as I briefly debated what to say. Ultimately, I decided to keep it light.

Me: *Babe, what's with the mad dash to leave? Could you smell Chief through the phone? He means no harm.*

My concern grew as the three dots didn't immediately appear. Maybe Chief and I should take a late-night walk and just happen to head down by Ivy's house. No, that was a bit stalker-like. Right? Right.

To stop myself from heading out into the night, I moved over to my own record collection, thumbing through to find something to listen to. With Ivy on my mind, I pulled out some Bob Dylan. Somehow, I think she'd be a fan.

Soon enough, the notes to "Hurricane" poured out of my speakers, quiet enough not to wake the parental units if they were already out, but loud enough to fill the room, cutting the silence. Moving back, I settled and glanced at my phone, relieved to see a text was waiting for me.

Ivy: *I'm good, promise.*

Me: *Lies. I saw your face. Spill or I'm coming to check on you with my stinky-ass pup.*

Ivy: *Poor Chief, no respect.*

I waited, wanting to give her a chance to share. A minute went by, nothing. Not even the dots.

Me: *Babe...*

Ivy: *...*

I felt a bit of relief, even without seeing a message. For a moment, I let the fact that I wanted her to confide in me, to share her concerns, wash over me. That hadn't happened since, well, quite frankly, ever. Looking back, Rachel and I hadn't had that. Was it because we were too young? Was I too self-centered? Or she was? Quickly, I dismissed that line of thinking. Now wasn't the time.

Finally, her text came through.

Ivy: *It's really nothing, Jake. Just a pity party of one over here.*

That wasn't that long of a text. I wondered if she'd typed something else and deleted it. Hmm. How could I get Ivy uncensored? After sex, sure. My dick perked up at that thought. Down, boy. Not now.

Me: *Talk to me about this pity party.*

Ivy: *Jake, it's nothing. Truly. It's just that for a person who has lived her life as an only child in a pretty quiet house, I hope you appreciate what you've got.*

Ahh. I thought back over our day. I woke that morning with Ivy's body curled to mine. Addie and I'd dealt with breakfast and Ivy joined us. Then it was off to my place with my loud, in-your-face family. Ivy and Addie had stayed into the afternoon, playing card games, having a dance party, before they finally left. She'd gone home to dinner with Addie at her quiet house, only to call the people that are supposed to be her support system, to find them lacking. Again. Then had a video call with me and my siblings, where privacy was never respected and they were their typical opinionated selves.

I guessed it would be a lot. But, just guessing here, it would also feel a lot like love. And, I assumed, if you had never had it, you might not realize how much you were missing until you saw it.

Damn. How did I navigate this one? Thinking of Ivy, I knew what I needed was the truth. Unvarnished.

Me: *I'm sorry, Ivy. I wish I was with you. I hate that you're alone right now. To answer your comment, yes, I appreciate them. Parents, siblings, I know I'm lucky. Even when I want to toss them in the nearest canyon.*

Me: *How else can I help? What else is on your mind?*

Ivy: *How much time you got?*

Me: *All the time in the world.*

Ivy: *I've been thinking more about the store. About the offer.*

I sat up, looking at the phone. Ivy and I'd talked a bit about the offer on the store this week. I'd looked over some of her financials, and we'd talked about her options. She could sell, clearly, and stay on to manage. She could sell and find another job. Or she could find a way to bring in some extra income, just to help her feel comfortable. That could be through an increase in revenue, so a focused effort to bring in more business. Or, it could also be what I suggested...

Me: *Did you make a decision?*

Ivy: *I'm still undecided on selling, but you're right. I need to rent out Nana's apartment. The income from the* *apartments really helped when we had our dip in sales this summer. Another tenant is only going to help.*

Ivy: *I also found a tenant for the business space next to mine. Kristine, the yoga instructor, texted me after I got back here tonight that she's interested. We're meeting Monday to go over the contract.*

I wanted to cheer as she paved the way for more income each month. That could give her a nice cushion. I couldn't imagine running the brewery and having every decision rest solely on my shoulders. It would be hard to run anything without someone else to help. I only hoped I worked as a sounding board for Ivy.

Me: *All this points to good things, Ivy. The money coming in from the business as well as the apartments all should be more than enough to keep you afloat.*

Ivy: *Wow, Ivy? This must be a serious conversation if you're using my name.*

Ivy: *But seriously, I don't know why I'm still considering the offer. I just got, I don't know, worried this summer when I watched a few weeks dip into the red. It reminded me too much of the days after I had Addie when times were lean.*

Me: *I get that. When Sully and I were supposed to start canning, he got cold feet because he was nervous about us overextending ourselves. He had some lean times as a kid and they made an impression. I didn't get it at first, but he explained. You do whatever you're comfortable with.*

Me: *Are you okay with renting out your nana's place? I mean, you hadn't, so I wondered.*

Ivy: *I just haven't been ready to face going through her stuff.*

Me: *You know I'll come help if you want.*

Ivy: *No, I've got this. But thanks. It's helped to talk to you about it. It's nice to have someone to listen.*

I sat for a moment, wondering how to help her feel less alone. I wondered when she felt surrounded by love of family. Ever? Ahh... got it.

Me: *What would your nana do for you in a time like this? Family stress, business stress?*

I waited, wondering if that was too much. I mean, we'd had sex, I'd helped her out with Addie for the past week, she met my family, but somehow, I felt like we were just getting to know each other. Was I here for that? Interestingly, I thought I was. Another topic to examine later.

Finally, her text came through.

Ivy: *Nana would tell me to crank the music, dance with abandon, have sex, and smoke some pot if the mood struck.*

I needed to come back to the sex comment later because I wanted to rush her house and volunteer to help out. However, circling back. Did Ivy partake? Seems like something I should know. It was legal in Illinois, and I couldn't deny that I'd smoked once or twice, but it wasn't typically my scene. I didn't want to sit in judgment of someone else though. I debated how to communicate that in a text, but not come across as an ass.

Me: *And does the mood strike?*

Ivy texted back immediately. I had a feeling she was laughing at me. I'd take it.

Ivy: *A mood for sex?*

Ivy: *Kidding, kidding. Ask what you want to ask, Jake. No, I don't smoke, though I will say that I have been known to enjoy an edible, but that's pretty rare too.*

Ivy: *As for the rest of Nana's advice, my album is over.*

I'm going to pick another and then dance up a storm. Thanks for asking, I think it's the perfect way to spend my evening.

Damn if I didn't wish I was there. I felt a need to connect in some way. I needed to flip Dylan's album to side two. Thinking of Ivy, I texted her first.

Me: *Thoughts on Bob Dylan?*

Ivy: *All good thoughts. Why?*

Me: *Wishing I was with you. Figured we could listen to the same album. I've got Desire on here right now.*

I immediately wished I could take the text back. It seemed vulnerable, but she'd put herself out there tonight too. I sat on it, but didn't have to wait for long.

Ivy: *Excellent. One, I have that one on vinyl. Two, I love the opening track. Off to play it and dance up a storm. Get your siblings and do the same. Thanks for everything today, Jake.*

I read it over. Sounded like our conversation was done for the night, which was fine. As long as she was in a better place than she'd been earlier, that worked for me.

Me: *You bet, babe. Go dance. The three of us are here if you need anything. I can be to your place in minutes if you decide you need company.*

Ivy: *Sounds good. Thanks.*

I tossed my phone on the coffee table, then rose up to move to my record player. Instead of flipping to side two, I started it over so we were at the same spot as she would be. Yeah, I realize that said a lot about where I was with this woman.

Drew picked that moment to stroll back in the den.

"Dylan?" he said as he sank down into the couch a cushion away. Stretching out, his feet hit the coffee table.

I nodded. What more needed to be said?

"How's Bookstore?" he asked.

"Better," I replied. "She thinks we need to dance."

"Pass, for now."

We sat there, heads nodding, as Dylan told us the story of Hurricane. After a few minutes, Drew spoke. "Steph went up. She was checking in with Theo and then getting to bed. Plans on getting up to run, then hit the road by eight."

I nodded. "You running with her?"

"Thought I would. You?"

I quickly thought of my schedule for the week. I realized I assumed that Ivy's babysitter was back on for Monday. I made a quick mental note to text her in the morning to be certain. Other than that, I needed to meet with Pete to go over the planned specials, check that our scheduling was set with Finn, and talk to Sully about the current beer we were brewing. It should be ready in time for the Reds of Christmas.

Hell, that reminded me that Lou had bailed and Ivy and I were on for the finalization of the event and it was quickly approaching. I penciled in a longer text to Ivy.

"Yeah, a run would be great."

Dylan continued to croon out the lyrics about the boxer who was the victim of systemic racism in our country. Wish it could be said that we were doing better as a country, but clearly, we still had work to do.

Turning to Drew, I broached the topic that had laid dormant all afternoon and evening. "Want to talk about it?"

Drew looked at me and, fortunately, didn't play ignorant. "Moving back?"

I nodded. Drew closed his eyes and nodded along with the violin solo. Finally he opened his eyes and met my gaze. My stomach sank as I took in the pained expression.

"Can't yet, man." He looked away from me, tapping his

knee along to the beat as the record moved on to the second song.

Drew might be my baby brother, but the man was almost thirty. I needed to respect his choices, as hard as that might be. I followed his gaze to the window. "Respect that. Can you promise me that if you aren't okay, you'll talk to someone about it? Me, Steph, Mom and Dad, someone professional? I don't give a fuck who, just someone."

"You got it, bro."

I leaned back, my legs stretched out on the other part of the sectional, and I leaned my head back on the cushion, looking toward the ceiling. Dylan's words filled the room as Drew and I saw there in companionship. As "Mozambique" began, I held my beer out to him. "Good to have you home, baby bro."

Drew tapped his beer against mine. "Thanks for giving me a spot to land, Jake."

Yep. Something was going on. Fuck. Quietly, I replied, "Always."

23

HORIZONTAL DANCING

Ivy

A feeling of being in over my head washed over me as I sat in the midst of my grandmother's apartment. She'd lived over the space I used as a bookstore for her entire time in Highland Falls. When I'd visit over the years she'd say that one day, when the stairs became too much for her, she'd move to the retirement community in town. Apparently the goddess had different plans.

After she'd passed five years ago, I'd had a local manage the property. At the time, the space the bookstore currently occupied had been a resale shop. The business next door was a real estate agent. And the two other apartments above had all been occupied.

In the past five years, both businesses and rentals had changed hands, but there was enough income from both to allow me to leave Nana's apartment as is. I'd come in after the funeral and cleaned out anything that needed to be pitched, but otherwise, I'd left it until I decided what to do with it. Coming to Highland this past spring, I'd briefly thought about moving in but quickly decided against it. Addie needed space to run and her own bedroom.

Now, I really needed to deal with it. As Jake pointed out, the income from the rentals up here helped the bookstore make it through the lean months, and one more tenant would be even better. Ditto to finding a tenant for next door, which I thought I secured earlier this week. That agreement led to finding someone for Nana's place. I'd planned on having a few weeks to clean it out, but it turned out the new tenant could take it as soon as possible.

"Ivy?" A voice called from the front door.

"Come in," I called, looking toward the door from my spot on the floor in the living room.

Maggie and her pregnant belly led the way, followed quickly by Emma. They both glanced around the space and then gave me big eyes. Yep, you could say it was a lot to take in all at once.

Nana had been in her midseventies when she passed. She was firmly of the generation that celebrated love, peace, and Woodstock. The white walls of her place highlighted the vibrant colors of the tapestry on one wall, her basket collection hanging on another. When she was alive, there were plants all over the apartment, music pouring out of her record player and filling the space with warmth. When she passed, I'd taken both with me. Many of those plants were still around my place, and of course her record collection was too.

And on any flat surface in the apartment, you could find pictures framed. Her life was documented—friends, concerts, and me, from when I was small to the awkward middle school years to high school to college. My grandmother had more pictures of my childhood in this small space than my parents did in their entire enormous house.

"Holy hell, Ivy," Maggie said, clearly trying to take it all in. "What are you going to do with all this?"

I glanced around the living room and into the dining area and kitchen. It was all one big space with a short hall that had a bathroom and her bedroom. "It really isn't as bad as it looks. I donated her clothing years ago. I just need to go through her personal stuff and decide what I'm keeping. The new tenant is renting it furnished, so I'm good there."

Emma lowered onto Nana's love seat and let out a small moan as she sank in. "This is pretty comfy. Are you sure you want to let it go?"

I looked up from the papers in my hands and smiled. Nana's love seat was a harvest gold velvet, appropriate for the decade she bought it in, but also still fit the vibe of this place and some current trends. "Yeah, the new tenant up here is Kristine's new partner in the yoga studio that's moving in next door. She is coming here and traveling pretty light. Right now she's crashing on Kristine's couch. I think Nana would be thrilled that someone else can use all her stuff."

Maggie slowly lowered herself onto the couch next to Emma. "Are we surprised that Kristine is opening a studio instead of sticking with the nomadic nature of her class?"

I shook my head as I got back to sorting the papers into piles of keep, shred, and trash. Quite frankly, most of this box was trash. I had no idea why Nana had kept half this stuff.

Without looking up, I answered Maggie. "No, not surprised. When the space opened up last month, Kristine came to talk to me about rental, utilities, et cetera, but she was still unsure. I think she will continue to do some stuff out at the park in summer, maybe some pop-up classes here and there, but to build a bigger client list, she needs to be in one place and had been looking for the right location."

"That makes sense," Emma said as she helped to put a throw pillow behind Maggie's back. "So what do you know about your renter who will be working with Kristine?"

"Partnering with," I murmured as I scanned the document in my hand. It looked like a trash bill from 1990. Why on earth would she have saved this? Shaking my head, I moved it to the trash pile.

"Partnering?" Maggie's voice rose in surprise. I put the papers down and looked up.

"Um, yeah?" I shrugged, trying to remember my conversation with Kate and Kristine. "I think Kate, that's the new tenant, knew Kristine from school or something. She's partnering with her in the studio. That's what made the decision for Kristine. She didn't have to carry the load alone, and the space next door will be perfect for the studio they envision. There only needs to be minimal changes."

"Well, I think I'll have to take your word for it until sometime this spring. If I tried to do any yoga right now, I'd never get back up." Maggie rested her hand on her large belly that looked like a basketball under her T-shirt advertising for Sully's brewery.

Emma snorted. "Yeah, yoga would probably be good for you, but I think it would require a lot of modifications right now."

"You think?" Maggie raised an eyebrow. Looking at me, she asked, "Are the other apartments up here rented out?"

I grabbed the papers in the trash stack and moved to dump them in the garbage bag by the coffee table. "Yeah. Nicole, or Nic, is the tenant that's been here the longest. She moved in last year, at least six months before I came to town—"

"Do I know Nic?" Emma asked.

I nodded, still sorting through more paperwork. "Yeah, she works for me, remember? She just started taking over more hours in the past few weeks. She's also going to school part-time online to finish her degree. She was working at Starbucks to make some extra money, but I lured her away with the super-short commute and competitive wages."

Maggie snorted. "And no Starbucks coffee, but there is as much hot tea as she'd like."

I took the shred pile to the dining room table. I'd brought the shredder my parents had insisted on purchasing for me here today. Looks like one of their gifts was actually going to come in handy. While I shredded the pile, I raised my voice to be heard over the noise. "Yeah, so Nic's up here and Elle."

Emma's eyes met mine. "Elle?"

I nodded. "Elle's new to the area. This fall has been a whirlwind. She moved in at the start of the month. Her sister is a teacher at the high school. Elle works from home, super nice. Quiet. Loves to read romance books, so she's a great customer."

"I wondered if there was more than one Elle in town," Emma said. "She's a frequent patron at the library, and I'd agree, seems great. Shy, but nice."

"So were you before I corrupted you," Maggie said, elbowing her.

Emma gave her a look. "Corrupted? In second grade?"

Maggie shrugged. "You needed it."

I finished the last papers and dumped the shredded mess into the trash bag and tied it off. I'd pitch it in the dumpster on my way out of here later. "I don't have much up here to offer you guys. I think." I stepped into the kitchen and scanned the cabinets. I'd brought a few things to have on hand while I sorted through this place over the next week. "I have tea, soda, water, and some crackers."

"What kind of crackers?" Maggie perked up.

"The best kind. Triscuits," I replied. It was the only logical answer.

"Lies." Maggie replied. "A sleeve of Ritz is the perfect snack."

"Nope." Emma disagreed. "Club crackers are where it's at."

I glanced back to their perch on the sofa. "Girls, we're working with limited supply here. Triscuits or nothing."

"Triscuits," they chorused.

I brought the box. We weren't operating on formality here.

I lowered to sit on the rug by the coffee table and placed the box on it after taking a few crackers for myself.

"Your dad and Irene good?" I asked, munching on a cracker. Maggie's dad was a long-haul trucker. He and his girlfriend partnered up to drive routes together. They had recently announced they were getting married, and I knew Maggie was beyond excited for them.

"They're great. I think they're headed to the Carolinas this week." Maggie had swung her feet up, plopping them on Emma's lap.

Emma shook her head but quickly moved to remove Maggie's shoes and started a foot massage.

"This is why we are friends." Maggie said as she dropped her head back to rest it on a pillow, getting as comfortable as she could.

Emma laughed at Maggie but then focused her stare on me. "How are you doing with all this?" She tilted her head, indicating the apartment.

"You mean with renting out Nana's place?"

Emma dug into the arch of Maggie's foot, and Maggie positively groaned. Looking back to me, she continued. "Renting this place out, running a business on your own, whatever you have going on with Jake, pick your topic."

"Jake, let's start with Jake." Maggie spoke from her spot of relaxation.

I tried for an innocent look. "What do you mean?"

Emma hooted with laughter. "Oh, Ivy. You need to do better than that. We were at the brewery celebration, and you two had so much heat coming off you as you circled each other you threatened to combust."

"Yep, and Sully says Jake has been in a really *good mood* since this weekend. So, chickie, spill." Maggie sat up to get some crackers, but her belly was in the way. "Before you spill, Emma, cracker me."

Emma grabbed the box and held it out toward Maggie. She got what she needed, and they both turned to me, clearly ready for the details.

I looked at my phone at the time, wondering if I needed to get Addie yet. Nope. Hours to go. I loved these girls. They'd become good friends in my time in Highland Falls. "Are you two sure you don't want to call Lou to come over? Or are you the next generation of Highland's gossip leaders?"

"Those are big shoes to fill," Maggie said.

"And Miss Lou is on a Christmas shopping trip with her friends to Indy," Emma replied. "We're here for her too."

"Course you are." I shook my head. "Well, let's just dive in and lay it down. I have no idea what's up with Jake and myself."

Maggie was lacking any form of patience today. "Any horizontal dancing?"

Emma slapped her arm.

"Yep," I replied, my cheeks heating a bit, but staying the course. "And brunch with his family on Sunday, calls and texts since then." I looked around Nana's place. "And he's been helping me with some business decisions, like renting out this place." I looked down at her crazy patterned rug, running my hands over the softness.

Emma leaned across the low table to squeeze my shoulder. "You okay with letting this place go? Well, kind of."

I looked around, soaking it in for a moment. It was time. "Yeah, I am. I mean, I feel Nana here, you know? But I feel her with me in a lot of places. It's time, and Kate will do well up here."

Emma settled back, watching me. "I'm glad Jake has talked to you a little about business. I know Sully says often that it would be too hard to run the brewery on his own."

Meeting their eyes, I worked to ignore the way my stomach was twisting. "I still don't know if I'm going to sell. I wouldn't even consider it if it wasn't to another independent bookstore. But it is, and well, things were tight this summer. I'm just not sure—"

"You don't need to explain to us," Emma interrupted.

Maggie bulldozed over Emma's words. "I wish I'd known that things were so tight last summer. Why didn't you say anything? You didn't need to pay me."

My heart lightened. It was hard to trust that people would stick by you sometimes. But these two? I think Nana would have approved.

"It's fine, Mags. We just had a dip. I think I'm a little more sensitive to that because things were tight when I first had Ads. I don't want to ever go back to those days."

"But sell Pages?" Maggie's brows were drawn together. "You love this place. The vibe is so you, and it's your dream. Are you really considering it?"

I studied my hands, at a loss for what to say or, truly, what to do.

"Ivy," Emma called.

I glanced to see her watching me, kindness pouring off her.

"We support you with whatever you decide. And I hope it goes without saying we're here if you want to talk." She slid back into the couch as she tugged Maggie's feet back into her lap. "Now, let's talk about happier things, shall we?"

I smiled at her gratefully.

"So you're together." Maggie pulled us back to the topic of Jake.

"Not sure," I said, figuring we might not be on that much happier of a topic. I picked at my flowy skirt, twisting it. "I had a thing with my parents the other night. Jake was upset by it. I can't stop thinking about Lou saying Jake's a born nurturer. Maybe that's what he's doing?"

"While getting some?" Emma asked.

Maggie looked at her. "Proud of you. That sounds like something I'd say."

"You must be rubbing off on me," Emma grinned. Looking at me, she asked. "What happened with your parents?"

I shrugged, knowing this was going to sound worse than it was. "They called Sunday night to let me know they wouldn't be around for Christmas. Addie and I usually visit them once a year, but they'll be on a trip with their friends to France this year."

"Cuntbagwhorefuckerbitch," Maggie muttered, sitting up again.

"What the heck is that?" I asked.

"Whoa." Emma gave Maggie a look. "That's Maggie's

middle school word for when she would be really mad. All the bad words she loved in one, but I haven't heard it for years."

Surprisingly, I noticed that Maggie's eyes were welling with tears. At the beginning of her pregnancy she'd cried easily, but that let up since she got in her second trimester. "Mags? You okay?"

Maggie wiped her eyes. "Sorry, babe. I just admire you so much. You are a hell of a mom to that little girl of yours, and you've done an unbelievable job raising her. I just hate that you have had to do that on your own. The people that should be there for you seem to be letting you down over and over. I hate that." She took a stuttering breath. "And now you are on your own for Christmas? Not happening." She placed a hand on her stomach. "No idea if this kid will be in utero or out by the time the holiday hits, but you're welcome to celebrate with us."

Emma leaned over to place her hand on mine on the coffee table. "Yes, Ivy. Please come celebrate at my parents."

Warmth flooded me. These women were certainly becoming my own version of my family, and it was not one that was going to let me down. "Thanks, ladies, but Jake has already insisted that Ads and I join the Spencers."

Maggie and Emma glanced at each other, then back to me with wide smiles stretching on both their faces.

"Did he now?" Maggie asked, wagging her eyebrows up and down. "Maybe we should go back to that quick list of what all has been happening between you too. Horizontal dancing? Was it all you hoped for?"

I looked to Emma, then Maggie, then my own Cheshire cat grin appeared. "And more."

We all hooted with laughter. That was better, lighter.

I looked around, feeling the warmth of Nana everywhere. She approved.

24

FIRE AND RAIN

Jake

Laurie and I looked over the reservations book for tonight. Not crazy for a Thursday, but it certainly wouldn't be quiet. The first reservations would begin rolling closer to six, so we still had some time. Right now was the calm before the storm as the staff prepared stations and familiarized themselves with the specials for the night.

"Anything we need to be ready for tonight?" I asked, scanning the reservation list.

Laurie looked over her notes. "Severe nut allergy coming in at six thirty. They've been in before. Mom is cautious, and rightly so. Any cross contamination for her kid and they're headed to the ER."

"Yikes," I muttered, thinking through our menu. "And we can assure them that it will be safe?"

Laurie nodded. "Yep. That's why she gives us a heads-up. I let Pete know in advance, and he ensures that everything is good on our end."

"Okay," I looked over at the windows to the tank room

and saw Sully pulling some beer out to sample. "Let me know if you need anything else from us."

"Will do," Laurie said, reaching for the phone. "Homestead Brewery..."

I weaved through the empty tables, noting the quiet hum of the servers talking. Typically, the brewery would be filled with a background of music, but several employees were gathered in the bar area, watching the preshow for tonight's game. The Bears were on Thursday night football, and there were some questions about who was going to be able to play. I called over to Adam and Dan who were watching. "Sound off, captions and music on, in the next fifteen." I got a chin lift from Adam, so I knew they'd get on it and then get back to work shortly.

Reaching the tank room, I saw that Sully had poured out two small glasses of one of our current beers we were brewing. Our goal was to have it out for the Reds of Christmas event next month, if not before. It was a West Coast IPA. We figured the pine flavor would tie it to the holiday.

"You try it yet?" I asked, looking Sully over. The man looked exhausted, and the baby wasn't even here yet. "Sully, you okay? Looking like you've pulled an all-nighter."

Sully tossed the towel he was holding over his shoulder. "No, haven't tried it yet. Waiting on you." Running a hand through his hair, he muttered, "And I'm fucking exhausted. There's just so much I want to get done before the baby comes, and Maggie won't sit around with her feet up. I feel like half my time is following her around to make sure she relaxes a bit."

I snorted before picking up the glass. "Maggie? Sit around and put her feet up? I think you forget who you married."

"Tell me about it."

"Sully, people have been having babies since the beginning of time. You need to relax. Everything doesn't need to be perfect before this kid comes. You can do plenty of stuff on your to-do list once the baby is here too."

"Yeah, I know." He stared off through the windows and into the brewery. Shaking his head, he grabbed a beer. "Let's try this and see what we think."

We each took a sip and sat with it. Putting my glass down, I looked at Sully. "Fucking perfect, man."

Sully's smile made the exhausted look he had moments ago fade away. "It is. Now, let's get down to it. Name?"

I groaned, looking up to the ceiling. I was shit with names, no matter how often we did this.

"Come on, it isn't that hard." Sully laughed. "Think. We typically go with a song, album, band, or something to do with this place." He waved his arm around the brewery, housed in the old barn. "Let's think what we've got to work with. Pine flavor, West Coast, winter, Reds of Christmas event..."

"Good Lord, I have no idea." I thought of the holiday. What did I listen to? Watch? "Something from *Christmas Vacation*? Um... It's All Part of the Experience? Her Eyelids Are Frozen?"

"That scene rocks. What about Tree Through the Forest?"

"For when they cut down the tree?"

"Well, and the taste of pine. Or we could do something about fire." He mused.

"Fire?"

"Yeah, we talked about dedicating this one to Drew. Stepping in and partnering with us on the canning, it's been huge. We could do something about Colorado, firefighting."

He looked out the windows that looked into the brewery, seemingly lost in thought.

An album from childhood came to mine immediately. My parents loved James Taylor. His greatest hits record was on constant rotation in our house, and one of my mom's favorite songs would fit the bill. Looking to Sully, I asked, "What about Fire and Rain?"

He tilted his head for a moment, then nodded. "James Taylor?"

Taking another sip, he looked back to me and raised his glass. I tapped my glass to his.

Savoring his beer, he knocked on the table and looked back at me. "Fire and Rain. I think it will be a hit."

"Me too."

I finished off my beer and held my hand out for his glass. We had a small sink area set up for when we had tastings back here.

Moving over there, I washed the glasses and raised my voice to be heard over the water. "So you're really okay with Drew coming here to work?"

Sully walked over to the beers we had on tap at the wall. Pulling a pint of Barn Owl Stout, he turned to me. "Of course I am. Want anything?"

I rinsed the glasses. "Evolution," I replied as I moved the glasses to the drying area.

Sully brought the beer over to a high-top. I looked out on the brewery, Adam did a chin lift and I noted the music filling the brewery. I nodded back my thanks.

"'Hurricane'?" Sully asked, listening to the music. "Damn, haven't heard any Bob Dylan for some time."

"Hell, none of us were even born when this came out," I said. "Listened to it this weekend and told Adam about it. Working on his music education."

"Hell of a song, or album for that matter," he said. We sat, letting the music wash over as the first customers of the night began to fill some tables. Sully looked over at me. "Drew say any more about why he's leaving the hotshots?"

"Nope," I replied, thinking over the attempts I'd made to get him to open up before he headed out. "He took off Monday around the same time Steph did. I'm not thinking good things." My gut clenched, wondering what could have caused the change in direction for him. "Said he was headed back to pack up, wrap up everything with his boss. Since it's the off-season, they weren't requiring notice, just that he's able to talk to his replacement when they're hired. Then he was going to come back here."

Sully mulled that over. "Margot must be over the moon."

"Understatement. Both my parents are relieved, I imagine, that he's out of the line of fire, no pun intended. But I think they're worried too." I thought of the looks they exchanged after Drew shared his news. They knew—we all knew—there was more to it, but didn't want to push.

I looked over to Sully to see him watching me.

"It'll be fine," he said. "Might be that he just needs to be around some people he's comfortable with. We've got this, Jake."

I raised my glass. "And the single women in town can rejoice."

"Well, especially since the possibility of the older Spencer seems to have dried up," he noted with a smirk.

"What? I mean...," I stammered.

"Man, no bullshit. The sparks shooting off you and Ivy were enough to send this place up in flames on Saturday." He raised a brow and gave me a look. "You two serious?"

I looked down at the reclaimed wood table, smoothing

my hand over the surface before taking another drink. "I think I'd like to be."

"Well, that's progress."

Sully did not mince words. But he'd known me back when I was devastated by Rachel.

I met his eyes. "You know I've had zero desire to get back into anything serious for a while."

"That would be an understatement. But I'm damn glad to see that the green witch is working some magic on you. I know your ex did a number, but that doesn't mean you ignore any chance for happiness again." Sully tipped back his head and took a long drink. Placing his glass on the table, he glanced out the window into the brewery. "And speak of the devil."

I followed his gaze to see Ivy walking in with Addie's hand clasped in hers. Without a word to Sully, I headed toward the door.

"No worries, I'll take care of the glasses," Sully called out, chuckling.

I ignored him and headed toward the hostess stand. Ivy's name hadn't been on the list for tonight. It had been four days since I'd seen her or Addie since the sitter had been back this week. I talked to Ivy each day through random texts, but it wasn't enough. I was worried about her. She was cleaning out her nana's place, and I'd assume that would bring up some memories.

"Jakey," Addie called, catching sight of me. She dropped Ivy's hand and sprinted in my direction. I stopped moving because I knew what was coming. Sure enough, a few feet from me, Ads sprang up and her arms reached out. The trust that I would catch her, that she was safe with me, got me every single time.

"Hey, Jakey, Momma said we can eat in your beerary."

Her arms went up for her jazz hands as she shimmied as well as she could while sitting on my hip.

I laughed. "Brewery, Ads. And yeah, you are always welcome here." I looked over to Ivy and Laurie, who had now reached us.

"Hey, Ivy." I said, taking in her T-shirt with some type of constellations on it. It was knotted at her waist, and she had a flowy kimono as well as jeans that hugged every curve and some more of her boots that she loved. Her hair was down, and I longed to run my hands through it, tug out the headband she wore, and toss it to the side.

Ivy was clearly oblivious to my one-track mind. She looked worn out.

"Hey, Jake." She gave me a tired smile. "Sorry I didn't let you know ahead of time. It was a long day, and someone else cooking sounded like the way to go."

I glanced to Laurie and nodded to a leather sofa and armchairs in one corner. "That open?"

Laurie nodded, moving to lead us that way. I followed, carrying Addie, who was bouncing and telling me all about school today and the glitter she got to use for art. *Brave teacher*, was all I could think. Looking at Ivy, who sank onto the couch, I asked, "Mind if I join you guys?"

Ivy's face registered some surprise and, I was happy to note, a smile. "Of course not," she said.

"Woo-hoo!" Addie said as she squirmed to get down and proceeded to spin, making her dress billow out.

"Ads, you need to sit down." Ivy said quietly. "We're in a restaurant."

"Momma." Addie put her little hands on her hips. Throwing those arms up, she cried, "There's music. It's time to dance!"

I heard Laurie snort a laugh as she placed the menus

and silverware on the low table. "I'll be back with another set," she said.

I smiled and sat down next to Ivy on the couch. Leaning over, I murmured, "Absolutely your call, but I had Laurie put us here because Ads can dance in the corner to her heart's content and not be in anyone's way. She can also spread out down there and color if she wants."

Her expression immediately relaxed. "Smart man. You sure you aren't keeping some kids of yours secret somewhere?"

"Nieces, babe, nieces. This isn't my first rodeo or my first time eating out with a four-year-old."

She nodded. "Ads, Jake says you can dance in the corner or color back here."

"Dance party!" Addie skipped over and immediately began spinning.

Ivy leaned forward and grabbed her menu. Adam dropped off the set of silverware we needed and quickly took drink orders. Ivy asked for a plate of cut-up fruit for Addie to eat until we could get our entrées while I ordered some mac and cheese bites. We placed our entrée orders and sat back with our drinks.

I glanced over at Addie, who had now moved on to coloring. She had a sketchbook on the low table and was kneeling as she worked, many crayons in reach in a small zippered bag.

"So, how did today go?" I asked Ivy.

She groaned. "I mean, good?"

"Not sure?"

Ivy's head dropped back on the couch as her body seemed to relax into it. "Good, I suppose. It was harder than I anticipated, but it also felt very much like it was time."

"I hate that you worked through that stuff by yourself."

She rolled her head toward me, meeting my eyes. "That's sweet, Jake. But Emma and Maggie came for a bit to keep me company. After they left, I really got through a lot. And while it was sad, in some ways like another goodbye, it also reminded me that Nana wouldn't have wanted that place to go unused. She's not there, she's with me." Her eyes were a bit wet.

I slid my hand to her thigh and squeezed.

Ivy's gaze met mine as she brought her beer up and took a sip. Watching me, she darted her tongue out to lick her lips, and I held back my own groan.

She smirked.

Adam came over with the appetizers, much to Addie's delight. She snacked on some apple slices as Ivy put a few bites on a small plate and scooted back in the couch again, folding her legs up under her. "So, should we talk about whatever this is that Lou has roped me into?"

I grabbed some bites for myself and nodded. "Reds of Christmas." I said, popping a bite into my mouth. Damn, the hit of cheese was unreal. I needed to commend Pete on this one. I held one up to Ivy. "Think Addie would like this?"

"It might be too hot."

"Got it," I said, breaking one open to let the steam escape. "Here, Ads. Let this cool, but I think you'll like it."

"Thanks, Jakey," she said, before resuming her coloring.

Looking back to Ivy, I saw her watching me with an odd expression on her face. "You okay?" I asked.

She nodded.

No idea what that was about, so I continued. "So, Reds of Christmas. We're honestly mostly done. We need to go over how many reservations we have, make sure the tickets have been sent out, and confirm with local businesses that had indicated they wanted to be involved that they are set for the night. We also give them the number of folks attending so they can have enough of the food or drink they're serving."

"Okay, that isn't too bad," Ivy said. "The bookstore is serving red velvet mini cupcakes."

"Perfect. We used to have only red wine served, but people prefer variety. Now each stop has something, but it isn't even only red. Hell, we'll have a beer here, but it's a West Coast IPA. We'd thought of a Christmas Ale."

Ivy wrinkled her nose. "Ugh, I hate those."

I laughed. "So does Sully. Thus the switch to the IPA."

Ivy pulled up her phone, appearing to look over her calendar app. "Want to do dinner this week? Maybe we could go over anything we need to get knocked off for the event."

I pulled up my calendar, looking it over. "How about Monday? Too late?"

"Perfect," she said, tapping her phone and putting in the info. "How about—"

"Ivy?" a voice from my right interrupted her. I glanced over to see a guy about our age standing there. His clothes were a bit rumpled, and he looked beyond tired. His dark hair was disheveled, but his blue eyes were locked on Ivy.

The hairs on the back of my neck prickled. Who the hell was this guy, and why did I want to deck him on sight? Jesus, I was a mess.

Turning to Ivy, my heart sank when I saw her expression, which was blinding happiness.

"Noah?" She popped up, all exhaustion completely wiped away. She rushed over and fell into his open arms.

I'm not sure when I had gotten up, but now I was frozen in place. If I had any lasting questions to his identity, however, they were gone the moment Addie's head shot up from her coloring spot on the floor. My brain was now racing back to the conversation with Ivy on Sunday night. Clearly, I should have clarified her comment about Noah returning to the states.

"Daddy?" Addie hopped up, doing her shimmy, and raced for Noah.

He swung her up into his arms and then turned to say something to Ivy as he pulled Addie in for a hug.

A voice next to me pulled me out of the pit of despair I was wallowing in.

"Well, what is this little cozy picture I'm looking at?"

I glanced to see Drew standing by my side.

I let out a deep breath as I glanced back to my nightmare. Addie was now telling a story with lots of gestures as Noah laughed as he looked between Addie and Ivy.

"Well, apparently that's Noah. Addie's dad."

"Excellent. Caught up, then." Drew muttered.

"When did you get back?"

"Five minutes ago? Threw my stuff at your place. Airbnb isn't open until next week."

"You know you're welcome. Period."

Ivy looked over, seemingly just remembering that I was there. "Jake— Oh hey, Drew! Come over here, guys."

"Dad, these are my big boys," Addie said with a wide grin.

Jesus. I'd entered hell. Good to know.

Drew and I moved to join them. I wanted to run out of the brewery and never look back, but one look at Ads kept me there.

"Noah, this is Jake Spencer. He owns this place with Cole Sullivan. Jake's a good friend of ours. And this is his brother, Drew, who just moved to the area." She beamed up at me, then looked to Noah. "And guys, this is Noah Lawson, Addie's dad."

Noah adjusted Addie to get a hand free and reached out to shake ours. I noted his measuring glance and gave him one in return.

Addie pipped up. "Mom, are Dad and Drew joining our dinner party at the beerary?"

Ivy looked to Noah, Drew, then me. "Sound good?"

No, it sounds like a damn nightmare. With a sigh, I gestured for them to join us and bit back a comment as Drew slapped my back, letting out a laugh of his own.

Terrific.

25

WELL, THAT WAS AWKWARD

Ivy

I looked around our little group. Drew and Noah had taken the armchairs. Jake and I were still on the couch. After her initial excitement over more guests, Addie had gone back to her coloring. Adam had come over to take orders from our new arrivals, and now we sat in what could only be described as awkward silence.

Drew broke it because *of course he did.*

"So, Noah, you just happen on the brewery here randomly? Saw the five-star rating on Yelp and wanted to try it out?"

I watched him give Jake a glance. I wondered what that was about. Jake was emanating irritated vibes. No idea what was going through his mind. I'd told him about Noah already. And Goddess knows I didn't realize he was coming to town today.

Adam reappeared, handing beers to Drew and Noah. Noah took it with a thanks, then looked to Drew.

"Well, actually, I came down hoping to find Ivy." He

glanced my way. "I texted you a few times tonight, but hadn't heard back."

I sat up, grabbing my purse from the floor and digging through the giant bag for my phone. Coming up with it, I saw the series of missed texts. "I'm sorry! I turned it to silent when we got here. You know I hate when other people's phones are blaring for everyone else to hear."

He shook his head at me with a look that spoke to all the conversations we'd had about technology and my strong belief that people were missing out on life if they didn't look up from their phones. "I figured as much. You'd mentioned this place, so I thought I'd get a bite to eat before trying to get ahold of you again."

"You mentioned the brewery?" Jake looked surprised.

Noah looked from me to Jake. "Well, sure. Ivy and I don't talk weekly, but we've talked since she's moved here. We haven't spoken for a few weeks, but she's told me about you before and how comfortable she's been in this town since arriving. That you and your friends were so welcoming."

I could tell Noah knew something was off with the vibe in our group, and he was trying to set Jake at ease. I wanted to tell him not to waste the effort. We'd done nothing wrong. I wasn't sure what was going on with Jake, but I wasn't sparing it another thought. I was more interested in finding out why Noah was here.

"So," I began, "it's a surprise to see you here. Mom mentioned the other day that she heard you were heading back, but I didn't think that meant you were coming to visit us. Or did I forget that we had something planned?"

Noah put his beer on the low table in front of him, running his hands down his thighs like he was nervous. He cleared his throat. "I hadn't wanted to say anything unless it came through. You know I love the work we've done in Africa getting water to populations that haven't had regular access. There was a chance for me to move back and work out of the office here, doing fundraising and planning. I'd still head over to do work on the ground, but it would be less regularly, maybe once every year."

My eyes widened. Noah would be in the states? "Where's the office here?"

Noah gave me a shy smile. "Well, it's located in the state capitol, but I can work from home a lot too."

"Springfield? That's only an hour away from here. Where were you thinking of stationing yourself?"

He looked around to Drew and Jake like he was a bit uncomfortable. "Well, I thought if it was okay with you and Addie, I'd move to Highland."

"To Ivy's?" Jake practically growled.

Noah put his hands up, laughing. "Oh no. I'll get my own place."

I needed a minute. Possibly more than one. But I soldiered on. "Noah, when did you decide to come back? I had no idea you didn't want to stay in Africa. I thought you loved it there."

Noah grabbed his beer and settled back in the armchair, seeming to relax a bit with the familiar topic of his work. "I do love it; the work is important, and the people are wonderful. But recently I got my quarterly statement for Addie's college fund—"

I put my hand up. "I'm sorry, what?"

He tilted his head, looking at me. "You know, when you didn't want money to support Ads, I began that college fund for her."

"You started... but all this time... a college fund?" My brain was reeling.

"You haven't been getting child support all this time?" Jake looked at me, horrified.

I swore we already went over this, but now was not the time.

I looked to Noah who was watching me with a crease between his brows. "I told you this when you had Addie."

I glanced at our beautiful girl. Another kid around her age had joined her dance party at some point, and they were spinning each other, lost in the music. Had Noah mentioned a college fund? Heck, I could barely remember to shower when I had Addie. He could have told me he'd signed up to travel to the moon, and I wouldn't have remembered.

I looked back to him. "I'm sorry. I don't remember you ever telling me that. So you've been putting money into a fund for her ever since she was born?"

Noah looked affronted. "Of course I have. I wanted to give you something, but since you wouldn't take it, I figured this would work."

Jake's voice was rather gruff. "Just saying, if you'd taken his offer to help, those early days wouldn't have been so lean."

Noah's expression darkened. "Times were lean? What is he talking about?"

I sighed, wanting to get the heck out of here and avoid all conversations. "Jake is being dramatic. I told him how I struggled a bit to make ends meet when Addie was a baby, but it was fine."

"If it was so fine, why are you thinking of selling your bookstore so you don't experience those times again?" My former friend asked.

I narrowed my eyes at him. "Not. The. Time."

Noah moved to the edge of his chair to get closer to me.

I noted that Jake moved to the edge of the couch at the same time.

"She's thinking of selling Pages?" Noah asked Jake, then looked to me. "But that's your dream."

"I know, man," Jake said. "Some indie from up north offered to buy the store and let her run it."

Noah's face spun from Jake to me. "If times were that tough when Addie was small, I'm assuming that meant your parents didn't help?"

I gave him a look that conveyed exactly how stupid I thought that question was.

He nodded, realizing it as soon as he'd asked.

"Smile for Steph, kids." Drew had stepped back from our group, phone raised to take a picture.

"Sit the fu— fudge down," Jake growled, with a glance at Addie, then Drew.

"Have to commemorate this meeting of the minds here for Steph. She'd never forgive me otherwise." Drew sat, fingers flying. "Give me a minute to get the text out."

Jake dropped his head to his hands.

"Noah, do you spell your last name L-a-w-s-o-n?" Drew asked, not looking up.

Jesus take the wheel.

"Yes," Noah said. He looked to me. "Who's Steph?"

I was suddenly very tired. "Their sister." I sighed, then looked at Noah. "So, you're back?"

Noah nodded. "As I was saying before we went down the path of savings accounts and all the ways our parents suck, I realized all that I was missing with Addie. I want to be here."

I nodded, mulling that over. This would mean a lot of change. Just the sheer number of questions I had threatened to overwhelm me.

"You're back," I whispered again.

"I'm back," Noah said in a quiet voice.

The chime from Jake's phone and the screen lighting up showed Steph's texts starting to come in.

"Fuck," he muttered.

My sentiments exactly.

26

ADDRESSING THE ELEPHANT

Jake

Another glance at my watch reinforced what I already knew. Ivy was late. Not extremely late, but over five minutes. Basically, enough to get me wondering if she was canceling. I tried to relax. I told myself that Drew had gone over there to watch Addie. If she wasn't coming, surely he would have come back. Right?

Hell, as my luck would have it, he could have decided to stay there and have dinner with Addie *and* Ivy, just to screw with me. It wouldn't be shocking in the slightest. Drew had a front-row seat to the implosion that was my reaction to Noah Thursday night. He knew I'd tried to talk to Ivy since then, but she'd been pretty closed off, and it was making me crazy.

I needed to distract myself. Waiting for her was like watching paint dry. I moved to the oven to finish browning the turkey sausage. Dinner tonight was a pasta recipe my dad had put together after we ate at a place in downtown Chicago years ago. It was nothing fancy, but it was easy and

I could cook while I overanalyzed everything about Ivy. Well, that was if she actually came.

Just as I was getting ready to search for my phone to text Drew and ask him what was going on, there was a knock at the door. I let out the breath I didn't know I'd been holding. I turned, sliding the skillet to another burner and then flipped the front one off before I moved to the door.

She was at the front door instead of the back, which seemed to say something to me, and it didn't feel great. Like she was intentionally putting distance between us. Opening the door, I took her in. Ivy stood there, her back to me as she waved at one of my neighbors and his ironically named enormous dog, Tiny. Hearing the door open, she turned to me, an unsure expression on her gorgeous face.

"Hey, Jake," she whispered.

Did I just say hey back? Kiss her? Pull her in and go for it on the floor just beyond the front door? Probably not.

"Hi," I said, stepping back to let her pass. It felt wrong, all wrong. A little over a week ago we'd jumped each other in her bedroom and it was the best sex of my life. Now? I didn't know what this was, what to call it, but we were far from where I wanted to be. Noah wasn't here, but he was metaphorically between us. Or my reaction to him was. Damn, this was terrible.

"Come on back," I said, leading her to the kitchen. As we walked in, Chief made his presence on the back porch known at the door, hopping like a kangaroo to hit the door handle.

I glanced back at Ivy. She was grinning at Chief as he bounced in the windows because of course she was. For him, she had a smile.

"Beer and wine in the fridge. Help yourself while I let him in."

Ivy nodded and headed toward the fridge.

As I opened the door for Chief, I quickly grabbed his collar so I could wipe off his paws before letting him loose in the house. He tolerated it, but barely.

I let him go, and he headed straight for his water bowl. Water sprayed everywhere as he gulped some down, then plopped to the floor in exhaustion. His tongue lazed out of his mouth, and he looked at me as if to tell me he thought I was incredibly lazy not to run laps in the yard with him. I shook my head.

"Can I get you a beer?" Ivy asked from her spot at the door of my fridge.

"Sure, want to pull out that growler?" I asked, grabbing two glasses.

"What beer is this?" She moved to the counter with the growler.

I placed the glasses on the counter, filling each only a third of the way. I picked one up and gave it to her. "This is the beer I told you we're brewing for the Reds event. Really, it's just one we wanted to try out and thought it would be a good beer to have at Christmas due to the pine flavor of a West Coast IPA."

She picked it up and took a whiff, holding the glass close to her nose and closing her eyes. Her long blond hair fell in waves over her shoulders and down her back. She'd already tossed her coat over one of the stools at the counter and was wearing leggings and a long-sleeved deep purple shirt with a hood. Her clothes skated over her curves, hugging and highlighting them to a maddening degree.

She opened her eyes, and they locked on mine, taking my breath away. Clearing her throat, her voice was gravely. "Smells good." Her eyes didn't leave mine as she lifted the glass to take a sip, then let her tongue catch the beer on her lip. "Mmm," she said, her eyes widening as she looked back at the glass. "I like that." She drank the little beer that was left in her glass before holding it out to me for more. "You have a name yet?"

I finally took a drink and looked away from Ivy. I needed to gain some control, but I worried that was a lost cause. Refocusing, I grabbed the growler. "Want a full glass?"

"Yes please," she said, holding out her glass.

I filled us both up and then gestured at the stove. "Pasta with red sauce, sausage, and peas. Sound okay?"

Ivy glanced at the items I had out on the counter. "Sure, what can I do?"

I nodded at the stool. "Sit and relax. This is easy and I've got it." I said as I moved to assemble the sauce.

The pasta would be done in a minute. I'd already added the frozen peas to boil with it. Then it was just a matter of adding tomato sauce, cream, and parmesan.

Pasta sorted, salad was already made in the fridge. I quickly worked as I looked over my shoulder at Ivy. "So, the beer. We're naming it after a James Taylor song, 'Fire and Rain.' Know it?"

She smiled. "I absolutely know it, but that surprises me. It's not exactly Disturbed or Soundgarden. I'm assuming there's a story there?"

I nodded, straining the pasta and returning it to the pot. As I made the sauce, I filled her in. "Yeah, I can't remember if I've told you this or not, but Drew invested in the brewery this summer. Well, specifically, he invested in the canning."

Ivy laughed lightly, which made me look back at her. She raised her hands. "Sorry, I'm not laughing at you. Promise. And no, you haven't told me about Drew investing, but Maggie worked with me all summer and this fall. I know all about Sully's response to impending fatherhood. I mean, I learned about it after it was all sorted, but Maggie did share."

I shook my head as I returned to stirring the pasta. Looking at the sauce, I assessed it as my dad had taught me. It needed a little more parmesan, then to cook on low for just a few minutes to come together. Looking back, Sully's response to fatherhood and wanting to play it safe wasn't unlike Ivy's current response to the sales slump this summer. Hmm.

I moved to grab two plates and looked to Ivy. "Can you grab the salad from the fridge?" She moved, and I continued as I plated up our pasta and passed her bowls for our salad. "So, yeah, Drew invested. Sully and I talked about finding a beer to dedicate to him—"

Ivy looked to me as she picked up our salads. "Got it, firefighting, 'Fire and Rain.' That's awesome. Does he know yet?" She asked, then turned. "Where did you want to eat?"

I picked up our pasta. I nodded back to my dining room table. "I have some papers for the Reds of Christmas in there."

Ivy nodded and led the way. Reaching the table, she let out a whistle. "Wow, Jake. This is..."

I shook my head. This was a lot, that's what it was. Drew had set out crystal candlesticks my mom had pawned off on me sometime that she was purging her house. There were wineglasses, and the table was set, my papers nicely piled to the side. I knew he'd put some stuff out, but I hadn't seen quite how much he'd done. This was like some romantic setup. Fuck. Now what would she think I was trying to do?

"Um, this is Drew," I muttered. Because of course it was.

Ivy snorted, and we settled down in our seats. I looked at the wine sitting on the table. "Did you want wine?"

"Oh." She started to stand. "No, I'd rather finish my beer, but—"

I stood. "Got it." I moved back to the kitchen and prayed for some deliverance. This felt awkward, and no time I'd spent with Ivy since I'd met her felt like that. How did I get past it? How would we?

After handing off a bone to Chief so he'd stay occupied, I headed back to the table with our beers.

Ivy took one and looked at me, a bit unsure as she wiped her mouth with a napkin. "Sorry, I meant to wait, but I had to take a bite because it smells amazing. And wow, I should know by now, but you can cook."

I relaxed a bit at that and sat down across from her. "Yeah, Ivy. My dad taught me to cook. Both my parents are good, but my dad loves to make pasta." I looked at her as she watched me. "Eat, eat."

She dug into her salad, then looked up. "You didn't say. Does Drew know about the beer?"

I nodded, swallowing a bite of salad before continuing. "Yeah, Sully and I toasted with him at the brewery on Saturday night."

She nodded. "And was he good with it? More to the point, has he shared why he decided to move back yet?"

I sighed. Steph and I had just talked about this yesterday but decided it was more important to give him space than to figure out what was going on. "He loved the name, but no, no idea why he's back. Trying just to enjoy time with him."

We sat for a few moments, eating in silence. At first, it was relaxing. Gradually I realized that Ivy was on edge. I had to do something.

"I'm thinking we need to address the elephant in the room," I said, taking a drink of my beer.

"Not cool to call Noah an elephant, Jake." Ivy gave me a small grin, and my heart unclenched.

I chuckled and shook my head at Ivy. "Babe." I swallowed and prepared to lay it out. "I don't know where to start." I looked down to the table and thought about everything I'd wanted to say since Thursday. Was she getting together with Noah? Would they be a family? Were we done? I had no idea where to begin.

Looking back at her, I started. "So, Noah's back."

Ivy's eyes met mine. She waited long enough that I felt my resolve and hope begin to crumble. I wished we were sitting on the couch, that I could touch her, but she didn't move toward me. Maybe she needed distance? If so, that didn't bode good things.

"Noah's back. Well, I mean right now he's in Springfield, squaring some things away. But he'll be back this week."

I braced as I nodded for her to continue. Nope. Couldn't do it. I stood up, grabbing her hand and pulling her up too. "Sorry, Ivy. I tried to give you space for this conversation, but that's not going to work." I tugged her to follow me to the leather couch in the living room, just steps away. I sat down and tugged so that she was pressed right next to me.

Ivy looked at me with wide eyes. After a moment, she seemed to gather some resolve. "Jake, you need to talk to me about why you pulled away at the brewery."

I closed my eyes, dropping my forehead to hers. I couldn't lose her. I knew Steph would tell me that honesty was not only the best policy here, but the only policy.

"I was jealous."

"Why? You knew about Noah. You know we are friends."

How did I explain this to her? My heart clenched. It was like I'd seen everything I'd dreamed of. It was just in reach but then was torn right from me just when it was finally mine.

"I don't know how to explain it, Ivy. I don't understand it myself. I just saw Noah and wanted to beat my chest and claim you and Addie as mine—"

"Jake, that's..."

"I know. Horrible. Sexist. A true example about what the patriarchy has done to our society."

"I'm so proud of you." She wiped away a fake tear. "I feel like I should call Steph and tell her how her boy is growing."

"Ivy..."

Just as she started to speak, my phone lit up on the coffee table. I'd left it on the table when I'd been sitting here after work. A glance at the display said it was Drew FaceTiming.

"Drew," I said, grabbing it.

Her eyes shot to mine, and she slid off to sit by my side, and I connected the call. When Addie's face filled the screen, I relaxed. No emergency, Addie was positively beaming with joy.

"Hi Jakey!" Addie called out. "Hi Momma!"

"Ads," Ivy said. "Why are you calling on Drew's phone? Is everything okay?"

Addie appeared to shimmy in place. "Yeah, Momma. I wanted you and Jakey to see how pretty Drew is."

Oh yes, I thought, my mood lifting. This was going to be glorious. I had no idea what Addie was up to, but this would be worth it, I was certain.

Ivy was laughing. "Okay, Ads. Let us see how pretty Drew is."

"'Kay, Momma." Addie panned to the spot next to her, and I couldn't help it. I fell over on the couch, laughing. Drew sat next to her, enough eyeshadow on that you wondered if he'd been punched. Red cheeks that made him look like he might have a fever. And bright, *bright*, pink lipstick.

"Oh, Addie..." Ivy seemed to be at a loss for words.

"I'm gorgeous. You can just say it," Drew said with an exaggerated wink and a lip pout.

I sat up, wiping the tears away that were streaming down, and grabbed my phone to take a screenshot to save Drew's look for posterity. "You're something." I said. Looking at Addie, I asked, "You having fun, peanut?"

"Yep!" She bounced up and down.

Drew shook his head at Addie. "Now Ads, we've got stuff to do. Tell them goodbye. And don't think I'm unaware of that photo, *Jakey*."

"Worth it," I called, sure I'd hear about that more later.

"Bye," Addie called and immediately disconnected.

Ivy looked to me. "Not sure if I should call him back to thank him or if we should message Steph."

"Steph needs to witness his beauty."

"That sounds like a good idea." Ivy nodded to my phone.

I quickly sent the screenshot of Drew in our group text so that Steph could check it out. Setting my phone aside, I looked to Ivy.

I tucked a strand of hair behind her ear. "So we covered that I was jealous."

"And that you are really working on your personal growth," she whispered.

"So we're okay?" My heart was beating out a rapid beat to the point where I wondered if I might need a cardiologist.

Ivy's beautiful blue-green eyes that were more blue than green tonight looked up at me. She blinked, clearly trying to stop the tears that were forming and spilling over her lower lids.

Shit.

"I think I need some time, Jake."

Shit. Shit.

"How much time?" I croaked. Yes, my voice croaked. I was living my worst nightmare.

Tears were now streaming down her face. "I don't know."

"Is it Noah?" I hated to ask, but I had to know. All I could see, all I could feel, was Rachel telling me there was someone else, ten years ago. Was I losing everything again?

"No!" Ivy pulled back, hand to my chest, her eyes narrowing on mine. "Hear me now, Jake. Noah is my friend. He is Addie's dad. I need some space because as much as I am attracted to you, I need to get my mind straight. I need to understand what you and I are working for, if anything beyond hopping into bed. And I likely need to wrap my brain around where I want my business to go, if anywhere. I can't do all this right now. I'm feeling overwhelmed, anxious, and stressed. It's not healthy." She took a breath and met my gaze, looking as lost as I'd ever seen her. "Can you understand that?"

My heart broke as I took her in. I hated this. Absolutely hated it. And I would give it to her because there was nothing else I could do.

"Ivy, you're protecting your heart, so of course I get it." I tucked a lock of her hair behind her ear and leaned forward, brushing my lips across hers. I took a deep breath and continued. "I'll be here. Take the time you need."

Ivy laid her head on my chest and let out a huge breath as I wrapped my arms around her. Resting my chin on her head, I wondered how I could protect my own heart when I suspected I'd already lost it to her.

27

SEEMS WE'VE BEEN HERE BEFORE

Ivy

I woke long before Addie, emotion flowing through my veins. I gave myself a brief moment to fantasize what it would be like to wake up next to Jake Spencer, set my mind back to a better place by kissing him and letting nature take its course.

It was a glorious fantasy, but that was all it was.

Jake had honored my request Monday night to give me some time and space, and I hated it.

There was a part of me that wanted him to tell me that I couldn't get rid of him that easy. What on earth was that about? I mean, I'd hate to be with someone who wouldn't honor my words, but there was this small part of me that said if he was willing to leave, that was because it was already on his mind.

It was childish thinking, and I knew it.

It was also my reality.

All day Tuesday and Wednesday, I'd watched the door to the bookstore, hoping he'd come through.

Nope.

I simply got a text each morning from him wishing me a good day.

And a detailed email sharing what I needed to do for the Reds event.

And I hadn't responded.

Because that's who I'd become. Though I had finished my part of the Reds by scheduling social media posts from now until then and finalizing the head count.

Ugh. I rolled to my back, looking at my ceiling. The creamy white was just starting to warm up with the rising sun. Another hour or so and Ads would be up and I'd have to lock these feelings down. I knew I wasn't being fair. That was a no-brainer. And yet I couldn't shut it off.

Watching Jake shut down when Noah joined us had made my walls go up. I didn't know—I hadn't known—what we were doing, what we were working toward. For whatever reason, watching him pull away made fear course through me in a way I was unprepared for.

My instinct was to pull back. To protect Addie and me from someone walking away. Again.

Or let's be real, to protect myself.

This was ridiculous. I was better than this. I couldn't imagine what my nana would say if she saw me wallowing here like this.

But I would give anything for that conversation.

Sometimes when I allowed myself to feel all the feelings I pushed away, I wondered how I existed in a world void of my nana's presence.

I told myself she was still here, she was alive in me and in the lessons she left.

But that didn't help.

I got to keep my parents but lose her.

It seemed like a cruel joke.

Not that I wished them ill will.

But still.

With a huff, I pushed myself out of bed. Nana would have said that was enough, time to hit the mat and get my mind right for the day.

I headed downstairs, avoiding the center of the second step from the top. The creak would certainly wake Addie. With every step, memories of Nana were all around me. It'd been that way for the past week, since I went through her place.

She'd been gone for years. When did it get easier?

I slid the coffee table back to open up some floor space and rolled out my mat. Closing my eyes, I took a centering breath. And another.

It began to work.

I moved through a sun flow, concentrating on my breathing. As Nana taught me, I let thoughts come and go, trying not to concentrate on any one thought but let myself feel.

Memories of being with her at the pool, walking through Highland Woods, sitting on the benches downtown and eating ice cream before it melted, they all flashed through my mind.

If I didn't know better, I'd say she was here. I felt her, more than ever.

Goddess, it hurt.

I took another breath and turned my thoughts to Jake.

That hurt too.

I knew I was scared.

If I was being honest, I was looking for a reason to push him back.

I was getting too close; my feelings were stronger than I'd anticipated.

He had a power over me, and I didn't know what to do with that.

"Oh, Nana," I whispered. "I'm such a mess."

I lowered to child's pose and dropped my head to the mat, finally letting the tears spill over without trying to hold any back.

Thanksgiving day and I'd never felt so alone.

Glancing at the cinnamon rolls in the oven, I debated how much longer they needed. At least five minutes, I decided as I shut the door. The caramel sauce was just beginning to bubble, and the dough was a light brown. The smell, however, rocked my world.

It was a happy memory.

It was just Ads and me today. Noah was up in Chicago, preparing for his move down here. He'd met with the office in Springfield early in the week, then headed back north. He still had some stuff in storage up there and more items packed away at his parents' place. He was going through it all and then moving down any day.

We'd had some conversations since he left about how we'd co-parent with him back in this country. Part of me seized up, having no desire to have any time without Addie, but that wasn't fair. He was her dad.

For his part, Noah was not ready to come in and split time. He said it wasn't fair to Addie or me. Once he got settled, he said he could pick Addie up a few times a week, maybe come over here for dinner once a week. He wanted to ease his transition into our lives as much as possible.

I'm here to make your life easier, Ivy, not harder.

He said that in our last conversation, and I'd been

thinking about it since then. What would it be like to have someone else to make parenting decisions with? It could be good. He told me to think of what I saw for us in the future, was it where he'd have Addie every other weekend? Weekly dinners together? He was open to any scenario.

All of it made my heart hurt.

Addie was skipping around the living room, singing something of her own creation. A quick scan of the kitchen counters told me that I had clearly taken on too much. There was the detritus from the final steps of the cinnamon roll recipe. Papers from my checklists for the Reds of Christmas coming up a week from tomorrow. And my recipe cards for dinner tonight. Even though it was just the two of us, Addie had requested her favorites: spiral ham, mac and cheese, Brussel sprouts, and some rolls. We'd be eating leftovers all week.

I'd thought maybe we should just have eggs this morning, save some belly space for the feast that was to come, but Miss Addie had stomped her tiny feet at the idea we weren't having my caramel cinnamon rolls this morning because *it's tradition, Momma!*

This child. You had to plan carefully because if you made it once, it was happening for the rest of eternity. Luckily, she'd laid down the law last night while we were having dinner at the brewery, giving me the time after she went to bed to get them set up.

I thought dinner might have been awkward, but for better or worse, Jake hadn't been there. Drew had, and he'd joined us for a drink before taking Addie around to show her the giant tanks. The two of them had been like long-lost friends, even though he'd just babysat her on Monday. I don't know who had a harder time getting a word in. They both talked nonstop.

The pounding of Addie's feet brought me out of my thoughts as she raced into the kitchen. Today's outfit was her pink tutu, striped leggings, and a flippy sequin T-shirt that had a rainbow on it. Her bare feet showed off her nail polish, with a different color on each toe. If my parents were here, they'd admonish me for those bare feet. Lord knows they wouldn't think that was appropriate dress, much less in the winter, but fortunately for all of us, they weren't here.

"Moooommmmmaaaaaa," her singsong voice called as she spun in circles around me.

Holding back a laugh, I looked down. "Yes, baby?"

"My rolls smell sooooooo good," she said again as she spun.

I held back an eye roll as I reach into a low cupboard to grab the grater to start prepping for the mac and cheese. "Is that what you wanted to share?" I asked. We had the Macy's parade on in the living room. Addie loved watching the balloons, so I was honestly surprised she wasn't glued to the set.

"No," she said. "I wanted to bring my big boys back."

At that, I stood up so quickly that I forgot to move back and hit my head on the inside top of the cabinet.

"Sugar cookie," I muttered, rubbing my head as I finally stood and then turned toward the opening to the kitchen. Yep, sure enough, Drew and Jake both stood there, watching me. Drew looked amused, Jake concerned as he crossed to where I was.

"Ivy," he murmured, lightly sliding my hair around, I'd assume to check and see if I broke the skin. "You need to be more careful, babe."

I took a step back, wanting to put a breath of distance between us.

Looking from Drew to Jake to Addie, I asked the only question I could think of. "Did I miss something?"

Jake looked confused as he glanced to Addie and Drew, who immediately laughed. Oh boy. Now I knew why she insisted on a double batch of cinnamon rolls.

"Ads, did you invite the big boys over for breakfast?" I asked.

"I invited them for Thanksgiving." She put her hands together under her chin, trying to look angelic. "But Momma, they haven't had your rolls, and you said it's nice to share. They *had* to come this morning."

Drew muttered, "I think Jake has tried her rolls."

Jake leaned over and slapped his arm. "Knock it off."

Addie looked from the two of them to me with confusion. "Momma? You made rolls for Jakey and didn't give me any? Did he like them?"

Drew choked out a laugh and had the decency to mouth *sorry* in my direction. "Princess, was that the parade on in the other room? Want to watch with me?"

Addie's jazz hands shot up as she raced back to the front of the house shouting, "Parade!" as she went.

Jake looked over to me. "I'm sorry. I thought you *and* Addie had talked to Drew last night to invite us here today. I'd apologize for Drew, but really, at this point, I think you know what to expect."

I snorted, nodding my head, and turned back to the oven. Checking the rolls, I saw they were ready. I slid them out and turned back to Jake as I tossed the pot holders on the counter.

"Sorry, I just wasn't expecting you guys." I gestured at my outfit. "Clearly." I mean, I loved my pajamas. I'd bought them as a gift to myself last Christmas with my parents' check that was supposed to be for something appropriate for me. I figured a pajama set from Anthropologie that I'd never spend the money on was perfectly appropriate, as was the pink bralette I wore with it. I often left off the button-down top and just wore the bralette and the pants, like during my yoga practice. Thankfully, I'd pulled the top back on this morning after I stretched. Looking down, I'd wished I'd buttoned it before seeing Drew.

Meeting Jake's eyes, I was taken aback by the heat simmering there. Holy moly. Jake took a step toward me, then another. "Babe, these pajamas..." His voice trailed off as his hand came out and then dropped, as if he couldn't decide what to do. "Jesus. I could get a headache from looking at this print."

I took a step toward Jake, but then paused. I felt like there was so much to say, but I didn't know where to begin. I went with the topic at hand. "So you don't like them?"

He ran a hand over his face. "Nope, not saying that." His gaze found mine. "You haven't messaged me back."

I gulped. "I didn't know what to say."

"And now? Do you still need space?"

My heart pounded. Did I? I still had no idea where we were headed. I was still overwhelmed with all that lay ahead for me with Noah, with the bookstore. But I also knew the only times I hadn't felt completely alone lately were when I was with Jake.

That had been nice. With him, I felt more like me than I had in years.

I looked at him. "I don't know." His gaze dropped. Shoot, not what I meant. I reached out and touched his chest, and his eyes shot back up to find mine. "I mean, I'm a mess, Jake. I have so much going on in my head right now. But I want to see you. I want to be near you." Drat, I felt emotion welling up. I was officially cried out.

Jake stepped up, pulling me against him, and he pressed a kiss to my temple. "That's all I need to hear, babe. The rest we can sort out later. As long as you don't need space, I'm here."

"You're here for me even when I'm wearing crazy pajamas?"

His laugh reverberated through his chest as I rested my head against it. "I am here for these pajamas. To be honest, all I can think of is how much I want to see them on your bedroom floor," he whispered, his mouth coming to my collarbone. Tracing it with his mouth, he then moved up and whispered in my ear, "And this bra." His finger came to lightly trail under the band of the bralette around my back, across my ribs, and then under the swells of my breasts. My nipples hardened in response, and my happy place reminded me that my rationale was simply bullshit. Whatever.

"This print is gorgeous," I said breathlessly because of course I did.

"Baby, there're stripes *and* florals," he said as his mouth worked down my neck again.

"So?" I asked as my voice hitched.

Jake stopped his downward descent and lifted his head to meet my eyes, crinkles forming at the corner of his as he leaned forward and lightly brushed my lips. "Just saying, I think we've found Addie's style influence."

"Hey," I began, but then thought of what I really wanted to know. "So, we're good?"

"We're good."

"And we can go slow while I sort my life out?" I asked, holding my breath.

"How slow, Ivy?" Another brush of his lips scrambled my brain.

I let my eyes close as his lips hovered over my collarbone. "Not too slow," I said in his ear.

"Good. Though I won't complain if you button up," he said pressing a kiss on the upper swell of each breast, then leaning over to put one on my stomach that made everything quiver and goose bumps race over my arms. "You are gorgeous, but Drew doesn't need to see all this goodness."

My cheeks heated. I mean, part of the feminist in me wanted to argue that I had less on display than the average swimmer at the public pool. However, the woman who'd given birth to a child five years ago and was conscious of, but always working to accept, the stretch marks and extra weight that I couldn't seem to shed was fine with buttoning the shirt.

I looked up at Jake, suddenly ready to ask Drew to take Addie to a park and not come back for hours. Pressing my mouth to his neck, I whispered, "But you're good with seeing me again?"

He groaned, his hands finding my waist and quickly helping me to hop up on the counter. Within seconds, my legs parted and his hard ridge met my core. I then knew exactly how okay he was with seeing me. "Mmmm, seems someone is happy to see me," I said with a small laugh.

"Babe," he said, meeting my eyes. "It's been three days since I've spent any time with you and far too many days since my mouth has worshipped your body. I'm dying."

"Dying," I looked up at him. "Can't have that, Jake."

He nodded with mock seriousness. "Because you care about me."

I tilted my head as I looked at him. "No, because I need the Homestead to keep me supplied in that buffalo chicken sandwich. I worry that with you dead and gone, I might have to go without." I replied with a shrug.

He tipped his head back and let out a deep laugh. Looking at me, he kissed my nose. "At least I know where I stand." Keeping his arms wrapped around my waist, he looked to the side. "So, babe, what do we have to do to have those rolls? Because damn, they smell amazing."

"They taste even better," I said. Because truth.

"So do you," he said with a raised brow.

"Maybe you should taste me," I said and immediately gasped as I clasped a hand over my mouth. I mean, who was I?

He nodded, apparently not fazed by my brazenness. "I guess I'll have to settle for your mouth. For now," he said as his lips crashed to mine. He nibbled at my lower lip until I opened and his tongue slid in.

I knew Addie was in the living room. I just hoped she'd do her typical pounding run if she was coming back to us. Because, for the life of me, I couldn't pull away.

I hooked my leg around Jake's hips, pulling his core even closer to mine. I could feel the outline of him against me, and it felt delicious. *Just another minute,* I told myself.

Before I could find the willpower to stop, I heard a slow clap from the kitchen door. Jake pulled up and met my eyes, refusing to look behind him. "I'm guessing Drew couldn't help himself."

I glanced from Jake to Drew, who now had his phone out, back to Jake. "Um, yep?"

"Seems we've been here before," Drew said, leaning against the wall.

"Out," Jake muttered, not turning around as he looked down. I had a guess as to why he didn't want to face his brother quite yet. I bit my lip to keep from laughing.

Drew did not hold back. Through his laughter, he said, "One, I'm glad to see that Addie and my evil plan has worked. She'll be delighted. Two, feel free to get the mast situation in your pants taken care of before joining us for what has been a riveting Macy's parade. Three, what's the ETA on those rolls, Bookstore?"

"Shoot, I need to flip them." I pushed Jake back and got to work, noting Jake's raised middle finger in Drew's direction while he leaned over, elbows to the counter, and did some deep breathing.

I slid the foil-lined cookie sheet on top of the baking dish before grabbing some pot holders. I flipped the whole thing over and sat it upside down so that the rolls could drop and the sauce could drip over the whole shebang. "I'll bring some in soon, Drew," I said over my shoulder.

He gave me one of those chin lifts and headed out, saying, "I'll let the princess know. Carry on, you two. I think I feel a group text coming on."

I laughed, coming behind Jake at the counter and wrapping my arms around him, then was suddenly hit by a wall of emotion.

"What are you laughing at, Ivy?" He asked, placing a hand over mine, not realizing the warring feelings I had at work inside.

I leaned my forehead against his back, thinking of how to express what was filling me up.

"Ivy?" he asked, standing and tugging on my arm until I came in front of him. He placed a finger under my chin and gently lifted it until our eyes met. "Fuck, babe, what is it?" he asked, likely noting the tears that had welled up.

I blinked furiously, willing them to not slip over, to no avail. "Sorry, Jake. It's just, I was, I mean..."

He lifted me to the counter again, legs wrapped around his torso, his arms around my waist. Pressing a kiss to my nose, he said, "Let's try that again."

I was positively cocooned in his warmth, and it was glorious. Looking at his torso instead of his clear blue eyes, I found I was able to organize my thoughts. I dropped my head to his shoulder, and the words spilled out. "Sorry. I was just so happy. You and Drew, you fill up this place. It was a rough morning, or has been a rough week. I was going to say this felt like being home, but then I realized I was far happier right now than I'd ever been at home. It was actually like being with my nana, and that threw me for a loop."

Jake smoothed down my hair and pressed a kiss to my temple. "Glad to hear that you feel that way, babe. Now, do we want to make some eggs to go with these rolls? Or bacon?"

"Well, I was making a Thanksgiving meal for Addie and me today, and now I know why she had me making so much. We were planning on having that around two p.m., with snacks before and after. So maybe eggs and bacon now would be good. Does that sound okay?" I glanced down at my lap. "Heck, maybe I should go put something else on first."

Jake's arms around my torso tightened. "Fuck no, babe. I don't know what Thanksgiving was like for you as a kid, but ours were about comfort, food, and being with those you loved. So stay in your pj's all day if you'd like because I'd really like the chance to take them off you myself later."

My cheeks heated up at the thought. Could we make that work? Possibly. But I was trying to ignore the comment from Jake about spending the day with those you loved. Surely, he was talking about previous holidays, right?

I got a squeeze around my waist as Jake spoke in my ear. "Ivy? Are the pj's staying, or are you changing?"

I met his stare. "Staying and bacon. We should always have bacon."

"Sounds like a good rule to live by," he whispered, brushing his mouth over mine. "Happy Thanksgiving, my green witch."

"Happy Thanksgiving, Just Jake," I said with a grin, telling myself not to get too wrapped up in this man and knowing that I was failing at that mission miserably.

28

I DON'T WANT TO FALL IN LOVE AGAIN

Jake

Drew pushed back from the table, groaning. He waved the floral cloth napkin in the air toward Ivy. "I surrender, Bookstore. You could work in a restaurant. This was delicious."

Addie looked up from her spot next to him where she was coloring. "Why do you give up?"

Drew looked down and grinned. "Your mom's cooking is so good I ate too much. I feel like a balloon that's going to pop!"

Addie's eyes widened, and she dropped her crayons to place her hands on Drew's stomach. "Oh no," she whispered.

Ivy glanced my way with a grin. The literalness of kids was something I tended to forget with my nieces at times.

Drew leaned over to Addie as he gave Ivy and me a conspiratorial, and blatant, wink. "You know what would help, Ads?"

She leaned closer and asked in a hushed tone. "What?"

"Taking Chief for a walk," Drew replied, looking from Addie to Ivy and me with a wicked grin.

But hell if I was complaining. My dog absolutely did need a walk. I had planned on bringing him down here after the big lunch. Ivy's backyard wasn't fenced in yet, so I hadn't wanted to deal with keeping him away from the food. But while we watched the game? Chief would be cool.

Drew *and* Addie vacating this place for a walk? I hoped like hell it was going to more than around the block.

Addie spun to Ivy. "Please Momma? Please can I go with Drew and walk Chief? And then can we bring him back here?" She batted her cat/Shrek eyes at Ivy. I briefly wondered how Ivy said no to Addie for anything.

Ivy laughed and looked to Drew. "Ads is welcome to go with you, of course, if you're sure you want the company." She glanced my way. "And Chief is welcome here anytime."

I smoothed a hand over her thigh under the table. "No worries, babe. I always planned on going back for him after we ate. Just easier that way." I looked to Drew and tried to be casual. "So, how long of a walk do you plan on taking Chief on?"

Drew's grin proved that he was completely aware of what I was really asking. Instead of giving me shit, he looked to Addie. "Think Chief would want to go to the dog park for a bit? It isn't too far, right?"

Ivy piped up. "Nope, it's just down by the ball fields, maybe a half a mile?"

Drew nodded and looked at Addie, but glanced up to us as he talked to her. "Okay, Princess. So we'll go get Chief, walk him to the dog park, play there for a bit, then come back here to watch some football. I'm guessing we'd be gone for over an hour or so. Sound good?"

Addie bounced up and down. "Yes, yes, yes!" She

hopped down and took off with a pounding run up the stairs to her room. I could only guess she was headed for socks and shoes.

Drew looked across the table at us. "And what about you two, an hour alone sound like a decent plan?"

"Knock it off, man." I growled, not wanting Ivy to feel put on the spot or pressured in any way. To my surprise, she was neither.

"An hour sounds great," she said, squeezing my leg like I had hers just a moment ago. She looked up at me with a wide-open expression. "Do you think an hour is enough?"

Drew groaned. "No, Bookstore. Just, no. Don't let this asshole corrupt you."

She looked over to Drew with an innocent gaze. "Why Drew, I don't know what you mean."

I laughed as Drew stood. Before looking back to Ivy, he asked. "Maybe Steph influenced you?"

Ivy nodded slowly, like she was processing. "Yes, I do think hanging around you all, not just your sister, is rubbing off on me."

"God forbid Steph ever adds you to our group text," Drew said. I shuddered. Ivy didn't need to see that mayhem, no way.

She tilted her head and looked from Drew to me. "Is Theo in the group?"

Drew laughed as I had the decency to look embarrassed. "Well, he was, briefly. But then he asked to be removed."

Ivy nodded as she pushed back from the table. "You all are a lot to handle, I'm sure." She grabbed some plates and walked to the kitchen as she called back to Drew, "Text when you're on the way back. Don't want to interrupt anything, you know."

Drew looked at me as we heard Addie's footsteps

coming toward the stairs. "You are a damn fool if you let her slip by. Figure out how to hold on, Jake, because this is not someone to lose."

"No shit, Drew. What do you think I'm trying to do?"

He shrugged. "Didn't know if you still had the mindset of *I've been hurt by love and can't risk it* bullshit that you'd been living with for years."

I glared at him. "No, I'm not there. I'm all in. I just have to tread lightly here."

Any other conversation had to wait as Addie chose to fly down the stairs and rush in at that moment.

"Drew, I'm ready!"

I looked over her outfit. Her original color explosion was now complemented by a fuzzy pink jacket with a hood that had a unicorn horn coming out by her forehead. She wore purple glitter high-tops, which were untied.

Addie plopped down by Drew's feet and thrust a foot in the air. "Tie please!"

Drew clearly knew what he was working with because he immediately tied, double knotting, before saying, "Next!" and repeated the same on her other shoe.

Shoes tied, Addie hopped back up calling, "Momma! We're leaving!"

Ivy came back in, wiping her hands on a towel. "Come here, you."

Addie wrapped her arms around Ivy as Ivy pressed her lips to Addie's forehead. "Stay with Drew, Ads. And watch out for Chief." She glanced at Drew, who for once in his life looked serious.

"I've got her, Bookstore." Then the seriousness disappeared as he gave us a wicked grin. "And I'll text."

And with that, Addie grabbed his hand and they headed out the door.

I looked to Ivy and began, "So, did you want to,"—before she jumped on me. "Ooof!" I said as I wrapped my arms around her, not sure whether to thank God for divine intervention or just to go with the flow.

"Sorry," she said, pulling back and looking up. "It's just, I've missed you. I know I asked for space, but I'm here. You're here. And I'm so glad you're okay with moving forward. I feel like we need to take advantage of this."

I looked down at her in her maddening pajamas, knowing she wore that sweet pink bra below this buttoned-down shirt. Her hair was still up in a messy bundle on top of her head, strands escaping all over. Her blue-green eyes were staring up at me, framed by her lashes as she watched. I could sense she was nervous, like maybe she thought I was going to say no. Like hell. I couldn't wait to get her to her bedroom.

I pressed a kiss to her lips and pulled back. "Bedroom, Ivy. Now."

"Roger that," she replied with something that I think was supposed to resemble a salute.

Shaking my head, I grabbed her hand and we raced for the stairs.

As soon as we hit her room, I immediately spun her around and pressed her body against the door. I reached around her to lock it. I knew Drew said he'd text when they were headed back, but I thought extra insurance was key.

"Where's your phone?" I asked. I'd left mine downstairs, but I thought Drew would text Ivy anyway. If I had to make a dash for a phone, now was the time.

Ivy's hands skated under my T-shirt before pushing it up so I'd take over and take it off. "Bedside table, charging," she said before pressing her mouth to my chest.

I dropped my T-shirt to the floor as I groaned. Three

weeks. Three weeks since I'd been in this room with her. Since then, there hadn't been a moment we were alone. Then the awkward dinner where she'd asked for space and I, like an idiot, gave it to her. However, my dick didn't give a damn about any of this. He was firmly in the *more of that, now* camp.

I unbuttoned a few of Ivy's top buttons on her shirt, just enough to loosen it, then up and off, it joined my shirt on the floor. I lowered my head to her collarbone as I licked and nipped my way across. "Fuck, this bra is amazing." I murmured, feeling her nipples harden under my touch. "You should wear it daily."

"Bralette," she whispered. "And I often do." Her head dropped against the door as I dropped my mouth to bite her nipples through the material. She moaned, and I felt it in my core. I could stay here for hours, worshipping her body. I was so damn glad we were here, but it also felt like there was a ticking clock.

As I took a step behind me toward the bed, Ivy stopped me and locked her eyes on mine. Her hands came to the waistband of my lounge pants I'd worn over here and she tugged, bringing my boxer briefs with them as she pushed them to the floor.

I smiled at her. "Okay, Ivy. Your turn." I reached for her to push her pants down, or pull this bra thing off, but she stepped back and then sank down on her knees before me. Oh *fuck*. Her gaze locked on mine, she moved forward and brought her mouth to the tip of my cock. With a sigh, she enveloped as much as she could, and my mind immediately short-circuited. Holy God, I needed a wall, the bed, anything. How was I going to remain standing?

Ivy's hands came to my thighs as she continued to move, alternating from paying attention to the crown to hollowing out her cheeks and going to town. I gathered her hair and held it in one hand so I could get a good visual. As soon as I did, her gaze found mine again, and I knew all was going to be lost in a matter of moments.

Quickly I pulled back and Ivy popped off.

"Hey," she said, looking grumpy.

I leaned down and scooped her up, turning and taking a few steps before dropping her on the bed. I yanked her pants and underwear off, then pulled the bra up and off as well, tossing it all behind me. "Condoms?"

She glanced at the side table where her phone was charging. "Drawer," she muttered. "But—"

I didn't pause, but pulled the drawer open. Grabbing a foil packet, I paused and looked back to Ivy. "This is quite a collection of vibrators, babe."

Her cheeks heated up, but she didn't shy away from looking at me. "Five. Years."

"Enough said." I nodded and shut the drawer. I quickly rolled on the condom as Ivy reached up and pulled me to her.

"I liked what I was doing," she whispered in my ear.

I smiled down at her pouting mouth. "Babe, I did too. And if you kept going, I was going to come in your mouth."

"Oh."

Her mouth formed an O, and I kissed it as my cock notched at her entrance.

"Well, I've never done that, but maybe?"

Damn, this woman. "Another time. Okay, Ivy? Because I really wanted to you to get off too, and we're in a bit of a time crunch."

To that she simply nodded, then wrapped her legs around me, pulling me toward her, welcoming me inside.

We groaned in unison.

I wasn't a terribly spiritual person, but this felt like coming home, finding my place, all that bullshit. I hadn't been lying the last time we'd had sex. It had been a while. But that didn't mean Ivy was my first. There had been plenty before her, including Rachel. Ivy was the only one I'd had this feeling with.

I didn't want to examine it too carefully.

I pulled out slowly, dragging my cock against Ivy's pulsing center, and angled again, wanting to hit her g-spot. She clenched more, but not enough. I looked up, grabbed a pillow, and pulled her against me, sliding the pillow under her ass.

Pulling out and entering again at this angle, her breath caught. "Fuck," she whispered.

I grinned. Getting Ivy to curse was like winning the lottery. We were on our way. My mouth crashed to hers, and her tongue immediately slid into my mouth. I sped up my thrusts, working to build her climax while beating mine back. I'd had a head start thanks to her mouth, but I couldn't go before she did.

I pulled back on a gasp. "Babe, need you to get there," I said, trying to hold back, tingles racing up my spine. My balls were tightening. Dammit.

She arched up, grinding her pelvis against me. "I'm close, Jake."

"Touch yourself, babe. Get there," I murmured, placing my mouth on her breast and waiting to see if she would. Her eyes shot to mine, uncertain at first, but then her hand snaked between us, and I felt it between our pelvises. Her fingers began to swirl, and I felt her channel tighten around me. I worked to hold back as I continued to thrust.

Within a minute, her breathing changed. "Jake," she gasped. "I'm there."

"Let go, baby," I said as I bit down on her nipple. At that, she arched up and gasped my name as her body rippled with her climax. *Thank fuck.*

Ivy's hand dropped off to the bed behind her, and I thrust through her orgasm a few more times before following her over into bliss. My body shuddered into hers, and sweet relief swept over me. I watched her as I climaxed, her eyes locked on mine. I felt bare in front of her, every-thing heightened. I dropped my head to hers, pulling her into an embrace.

I rested for a moment before realizing I was likely crushing her, and I rolled to the side, bringing her with me.

After a moment, her eyes fluttered open and met mine. "Wow," she whispered.

I laughed and kissed her nose. "Yeah, wow about covers it, Ivy."

She looked away for a moment, vulnerability clearly written all over her face.

"Ivy," I said, getting her attention. "What's going through that gorgeous mind of yours?"

She took a breath, and I could almost see her steeling herself for whatever she was going to say. "Um, I mean, I clearly don't have tons of experience, but is it that way every time for you?" The flush lit over her cheeks and down her chest.

Rolling her to her back, her hair flowed out in waves over her yellow-and-white floral bedding. I pressed a kiss to her chest and met her eyes. "No. I'm not bullshitting in the slightest when I tell you that it has only been this good with you. And I'm not even going to try to figure that out right now. I'm just going to enjoy it."

With that, I pulled away and stood, moving to the hallway bathroom to ditch the condom.

Coming back in the room, Ivy was sitting up against her headboard, her gray duvet pulled up to her chest. She watched me cross to the bed and climb in.

"What are you doing?" she whispered.

I looked at her, trying to puzzle out where she was now. "Well, by my calculations, we have somewhere between ten to twenty minutes before they come back. So I figured we could talk about the toy box you have in the drawer over here."

Her cheeks flushed.

I leaned over, pressing a kiss to her mouth. "Babe, I'm teasing. Just saying, I have no issue with any toys you have in there. I'm just wondering if we can pull one out next time and use it too."

Her shocked eyes found mine. "Really?"

I laughed. "Fuck yes, that would be hot."

She leaned over, snuggling into my arm, and slid her head to my chest. "Thanks for a great Thanksgiving, Jake."

I kissed the top of her head. "Back at you, babe."

I sat there, Ivy's head on my chest as my fingers ran through her hair. I alternated with wanting to stay here forever and the desire to tell my panicked heart that we were good. When I looked down at Ivy, the lines we'd drawn for this relationship were so blurred I couldn't see them if I tried.

Friends that had sex. Yeah, great idea. My heart felt like it was standing outside my chest, preparing to get stomped on again. When Noah had appeared at dinner, I'd wanted to dash off to a jewelry store, buy a ring, and stick it on her finger. Or pee in a circle around her. The desire to say that she was *mine* was overwhelming. And I was certain that line of thinking would make her kick me to the curb so fast my head would spin.

I thought back to Rachel. I'd thought I loved her, and I did, in my teenage and early-twenties way. But from where I was sitting, it seemed like that hadn't been love because if it had, what the hell was this? It felt stronger and a whole lot scarier. I didn't want to fall in love again. I wouldn't survive it when she left, and then I'd lose Ivy and Addie. I couldn't do it.

Joke was on me, I guessed, because I knew the jig was up. I was gone for this woman.

"You okay?" she whispered, looking up.

I brushed her hair back from her face, ignoring my gut that was churning. "Yeah, babe." I said.

Before I could continue, her phone vibrated. I grabbed it from the charger and passed it to her. She looked at the text and laughed, holding it out to me.

Drew: *Tony Stark said it best, part of the journey is the end. The end of our dog park trip is here, sadly I'm sure for you. The princess and I will be arriving with Chief in ten minutes. Get dressed and be presentable.*

I looked up at Ivy who was grinning.

"Your brother is wacky."

"That he is, babe. We better get presentable."

I pressed a kiss to her lips and moved to get dressed, turning from her while I did so. I felt like everything I was thinking was out and readable to anyone who looked. Vulnerability wasn't my thing, but I had somehow landed here. Now what did I do?

29

―――――――――――

CHRISTMAS LIGHTS

Ivy

The bell rang behind my customer, and I put my head down on the counter. Deep breaths. It was only a little after lunch, and we'd been slammed the entire day. I shouldn't complain after my concerns about our sales this summer. I wasn't complaining, but wow. Christmas shopping was the real deal.

A bell interrupted my brief break. Digging deep, I sat up with a smile on my face. "Welcome to Pages," I called before focusing on who was coming in. Realizing it was Kristine and Kate, I hopped up to come around the counter toward them. "Hey, you two, come out of the weather," I said, arms out for a hug as I glanced over them at the snow that was drifting down outside. I looked over my two new neighbors. "Is the studio all set?"

Kristine leaned against the counter and wiped a hand theatrically across her brow. "Finally. I feel like Kate and I have been living, breathing, that place for the past two weeks. Our goal had been to be open for the Reds event, and here we are, five days ahead of schedule."

"And everything is all set?" I asked. "Nothing more you need?"

"Nope," Kate replied. "As a matter of fact, we're holding a soft opening tonight for our friends at five. Just want to have a quick class to get the feel for the space, give back to some folks that have helped make this dream a reality. We wanted to come invite you in person."

A warm feeling washed over me. Kate and Kristine had been in a lot in the past two weeks as they finalized the studio and Kate moved in upstairs. Between these two, Maggie and Emma, Jake and Drew, I was beginning to feel like I was part of the fabric of this town. Maybe I couldn't give Addie a big family or, heck, any family, but I could show her what friends that you chose to be your family were like.

"I need to figure out Addie, but if I can, I'll be there. I'm beyond excited for you. Now"—I gestured to the shelf by the coffee maker and teakettle—"tea?"

"Yes please," Kristine called while Kate just replied, "Peach."

I headed over and kept talking. "How many are you having tonight?"

Kate thought about it, then replied. "I think, including Kristine and me, we've invited around ten. We have the library crew, including Emma. We asked Maggie, but told her she could just come for company if she didn't feel like doing any poses. Then there's you, and I invited Nic and Elle."

I smiled, thinking of the three of them in the apartments upstairs. "Have you gotten to know Nic and Elle in the past week?"

Kate let out a light laugh. "You could say that. They're fabulous. We're going to do a weekly dinner where we rotate apartments depending on who hosts. Elle was up first. She's sweet."

I thought of the quiet woman who'd moved to town to be closer to her sister. Elle had been here several weeks, and I felt like I was finally getting to know her. With her working from home, I was grateful that Kate and Nic had struck up a friendship with her. The three of them could have a lot of fun together.

"That's awesome," I told Kate. "I expect to be invited to one of these dinners." My phone vibrated from the drawer. I slid it out and glanced down.

Jake: *I have the afternoon off because Sully wanted to switch schedules. Would Addie be up for hanging out? I can get her from school.*

A whoosh sensation rolled through me. *Jake.* Thanksgiving had been unreal. Drew and Addie had come back from the dog park with Chief. Addie and Chief were glued at the hip. Drew had given us a knowing look, which made me laugh. The guys had hung out, watching football, Addie and Chief having a dance party, until we had to haul out the leftovers for sandwiches for dinner.

Jake and Drew shared that in their family, Thanksgiving Eve was for watching Christmas movies. Addie immediately pleaded for our favorite, *Christmas Eve on Sesame Street.* I'd watched it as a kid, and Nana bought me my own copy years later. Now I just streamed it for us anytime we wanted to see it, Christmas or not.

While I am certain that wasn't the movie the guys had planned on, they still sat and watched it with Addie, discussing how Santa could get down that skinny little chimney. Then the guys had gone home, and it was just Addie and me.

To be honest, the house had felt empty.

For the past three days, Jake, and by extension, Drew, had been in and out of our house. Stopping by when they could, asking if we wanted to walk Chief, checking to see if we wanted to get together for a meal. I felt at once grateful and worried. They were weaving their way into the fibers of our lives, and I felt like we were a house of cards. One false move, and it would all come tumbling down. I couldn't, shouldn't, rely on Jake. And yet I was, more and more.

Goddess, I was in love with the man.

I felt like Nana should be there, slapping me teasingly on the side of the head, and saying, *Finally*. Jesus, how'd I get here?

I looked at his text again. *Focus, Ivy*. Addie would be over the moon to get picked up by Jake. And looking at the time, there was plenty of time to let Teri know as well as the school.

"Earth to Ivy," called Kate.

I glanced up to see Kate and Kristine watching me with twin grins on their faces.

"Thinking about someone special?" Kristine asked.

My cheeks heated up. Darn fair skin. Well, heck, why not bounce this off of them? "Well, Jake texted—"

"Um-hm," Kate said, nodding. "I've heard about Jake, and I've only been here for a few weeks."

Raising a brow, I considered Kate. "Really?"

Kristine laughed. "Miss Lou came in last week before the holiday to see what our schedule of classes looked like. She was hoping for some pole dancing classes."

I let out a sharp laugh. "I mean, pole classes are cool, but she does realize you're a yoga studio, right?"

Kristine shook her head. "I think she mainly wanted to get our reaction. At any rate, she proceeded to fill Kate here in on all the gossip in Highland, including you and Jake."

"Gracious," I said. "Well, Jake texted to see if he could pick up my daughter from school today to hang out." I gestured at my phone.

"Heck yes," Kate said. "Tell him to keep her for an early dinner and your childcare during class is solved."

"Great idea," I murmured as I pulled up Jake's text on my phone.

Me: *Sure. I'll call the school and Teri to let them know. Any chance you could have dinner with her as well? The yoga studio is doing a soft opening at five p.m. and invited me to class.*

Jake: *You bet. Do you want to pick her up at my place or me take her to yours?*

I thought about it. Either would work, but if they were at my place Addie could get ready for bed after they ate and I'd be home early anyway.

Me: *My place, if that's okay. Key is still under the pot.*
Jake: *Got it.*

Is this what it felt like to have a partner? To be able to say yes to things you were invited to because someone else had your back? I craved and feared it at the same time.

Looking up at Kate and Kristine, I smiled. "Looks like I'm in."

Hours later, I walked home, enjoying the brisk air. The downtown was decked out, ready for Christmas. Each of the acorn streetlights had greenery wrapped around the pole. White lights were strung over the courthouse square. And the dusting of snow earlier clung to the grass and plants on the courthouse lawn. Magic was in the air.

My house was maybe a five-minute walk from the bookstore. As I walked home, my breath a cloud of air in the cold evening sky, I marveled at the transformation in the space next door into the new studio.

It was in the corner location with windows from floor to ceiling from the front door to the corner, then wrapped around the side for about twenty feet. They'd put some type of vinyl over the lower three-quarters of the windows, allowing light in, but giving the yogis some privacy from folks passing by.

Some of the walls were exposed brick. Other walls had mirrors for you to watch your form in. Kristine and Kate had cleared out the space, pulling up the old carpet to find beautiful pine floors below. The lights had been low and the scent of sandalwood had come from a diffuser. It was a perfect space for them.

Maggie had bailed, making a joke about being a beached whale, but I'd been joined by Emma, Grace, Gabby from the library, Elle, and Nic. Kate and Kristine led us through a slow class, but it had been exactly what I needed. They were all headed to the brewery for dinner, but I'd declined. Sure, Jake would have likely said it was fine; however, I was ready to get home.

I thought about the sales numbers Nic and I had looked over for the past week. According to other local businesses, Thanksgiving was the start of the holiday shopping, but things really got flowing this weekend. That boded good things for us, which made me feel good. Between my new income from the apartments and the retail space, as well as the increased traffic from holiday shopping and the push I'd been doing on social media, my anxiety was easing.

Turning on to my street, I glanced at the homes lining it. In warmer weather, people often would be on their porches in the evening, calling to me as I passed. The turn in the weather put a stop to that, but the warmth coming from the lit windows filled me with peace. It was like the houses were alive with the families within.

Soon enough, I reached my block. It was strange to come home to a house that was lit up. It was silly how that made my step quicken, and a lightness filled me up. I reached the porch, then the door, opening it as I called out, "Anyone home?"

"Momma! Surprise!" Addie called, the thunder of her bare feet racing from the back of the house.

"Surprise?" I asked, coming in and kicking off my shoes. Unwinding my scarf, I hung it and my coat on the hooks by the door. "What surprise, baby?"

Jake appeared behind Addie, whose hair looked like it had been in a variety of styles today and never settled on one.

Jake looked sheepish. "Hope I'm not overstepping here, Ivy."

I looked at him, trying to figure out what he could possibly be talking about. He gave me a nod in the direction of the dining room over his shoulder.

Addie had reached me and grabbed my hand, dragging me in that direction. "See, Momma?"

Our dining room was on the long side of the house with a huge window that faced the street. In front of that window was an absolutely gorgeous Christmas tree that certainly hadn't been there this morning.

"Oh," I whispered, gazing at it. "When did you, where did you..."

"Isn't it beau-ti-ful, Momma?" Addie whispered in a reverent voice. I glanced down to see her wide eyes taking in the tree, then looking to me.

Magic.

I took it all in, a tree in my dining room, Addie to my

side, Jake standing behind me, the smell of, if I wasn't mistaken, some type of roasted meat coming from the kitchen. Was this real? Could this be my life?

Looking to Jake, I whispered, "How?"

His blue eyes softened as they met mine. "Well, I picked up Miss Addie from school today, and she was lamenting the fact that other kids were drawing their houses with Christmas trees in them, and she couldn't yet because the bookstore was exploding with people."

I smiled. "That makes it sound interesting. In other words, we've been busy."

Jake shook his head. "Figured that, Ivy. So I asked if she wanted to go get a tree. We headed out to see Max at Highland Woods and pick one out. It was only when Drew found out what we were doing that he pointed out you might have wanted to pick up your own tree." He looked to the tree, then back to me, giving a small shrug. "Addie said you had your decorations and lights in the basement. I was going at least get the lights on there. My mom hates doing those, but I figured if you didn't want this, I could put it at my place. So..."

"So you got us a tree?"

"I got you a tree."

I didn't want to speak. It was like there was a spell woven over my house, and if I moved, if I uttered another word, everything would disappear. Addie clearly hadn't gotten the memo.

"A tree, Momma! *A tree!* Can we decorate it? Can we?" She spun around the dining room table, effortlessly avoiding the tree as she spun. At the end of the table she stopped to shimmy, then continued around the other side and toward the living room.

I stopped watching her and looked to Jake, taking a step

toward him. Then another. And another. Coming to a stop in front of him, I place my hands on his chest. Tonight he wore a forest-green thermal with his jeans and wool socks. His hair had grown a little long on top, his ever-present stubble on his jawline.

"You okay, Ivy?" he asked, placing his hands lightly on my hips.

I tipped my head back. "You got me a tree."

He stared at me, his hand coming up to brush a tear that spilled out before I even recognized it was there. "Sensing this is bigger than I realized, babe. But yeah, I bought you a tree. Is that okay?"

The truth came unbidden. "Besides my nana, no one has taken care of me, Jake. Not really."

He gave me a slow nod. "Catching on to that," he whispered.

"But you do," I said, almost to myself.

He looked at me, almost with a pained expression.

"What? Are you okay?" I asked.

"Really want to kiss you, baby. Trying to respect you and not devour you in front of your kid, but that urge is there." His voice had taken on a gravely quality that I was here for.

I smiled up at him. "I'm thinking Addie's seen us kiss before."

He leaned in. "You saying I can kiss you, babe?"

I looked up. "I'm saying maybe you could tell Drew to bring Chief here for the night, if you'd like, but you better kiss me. Soon."

Jake's eyes crinkled at the corner as he leaned down and caressed his mouth against mine. Tilting his head, he parted his lips, and he deepened the kiss as I pressed myself against him. My brain short-circuited as I fell into the sensations racing through me. Before I could suggest we find something for Addie to watch and nominate myself for the parent of the year, he pulled back.

"That good?" he asked with a wink.

"It'll do." I smiled.

Even better than the kiss, he pulled me to him, wrapping his arms around and resting his chin on my head. We stood there for a moment, me listening to Addie singing to herself in the other room, Lord knew what Jake's was thinking.

Looking at the tree, I knew what I needed to say.

"Jake?" I whispered.

"Yeah, Ivy?"

"I hate doing the Christmas lights."

His laugh was glorious. It reverberated through his chest as his arms tightened around me. Pulling back, he looked down at me. "You want me to get the lights?"

"In the basement in the Christmas tubs."

He leaned forward, pressing a kiss to my forehead. "On it."

30

PUNCH TO THE GUT

Jake

I whistled to myself on the way to the grocery store. Last night had been better than I could have planned for or predicted. When I'd called Drew to help me set up the tree, he'd come quickly, but gave me a look that let me know he thought I was a fool. Then he'd pointed out that Ivy might have a whole tradition around setting up the tree, which hadn't even occurred to me.

I'd worried, thinking maybe I should just take it home before she saw it. However, there was the small matter of Addie, who'd not only picked it out, but named it Bob of all bizarre names. So I'd waited and worried, only to have her show her gratitude for the tree by asking me to spend the night.

Yeah, last night was better than I'd planned.

This morning I'd rushed out to meet Sully for an early-morning run, then a meeting at work. I had just enough time to run a few errands before we needed to prepare for dinner at the brewery. We were anticipating a busier night than usual. With the Reds of Christmas chamber event tomorrow night, some folks would get their celebration on by going out tonight too. We added staff for this evening as well as Sully and I both planning on being there tonight and tomorrow night. I was looking forward to a great weekend.

Pulling in the parking spot at the grocery store, I went over my list in my head. I only needed a few things, namely dog food and bread for sandwiches. I typically did one shopping trip every two weeks, but a few things got missed last time and I wouldn't make it until the next week.

The store wasn't packed but had an early-afternoon crowd. I grabbed a small cart and nodded at a few folks I recognized from the brewery. As I walked up the first aisle, I pulled the list I'd found on Ivy's fridge out of my pocket. She had a list started too, and I figured two birds, one stone and all. Glancing down, I took in her list.

Green seedless
Fruit Snacks
Triscuits
Tampons

Not much there, but I wondered how particular Addie was about her fruit snacks. My nieces refused to eat certain brands when they were her age. And did Ivy go with Tampax? I know Steph had opinions about pads and tampons, and she had educated Drew and me well. The only pads in her world were the ones with wings. Otherwise, back to the store you go. Oh well, better to be safe. I grabbed my phone and typed out a text.

Me: *Preferences on fruit snacks and tampons?*

Sliding my phone back in my pocket, I headed into the produce section to grab some fruit. I tossed the bag of grapes in the cart and headed toward the fruit snacks as my phone vibrated. Finding a spot that was out of the way, I pulled out my phone and looked at the text from Ivy.

Ivy: *Congratulations for sending me the strangest text I've ever received.*

Me: *Got your list off the fridge, Ivy, since I was going to the store. Wanted to make sure I got the right shit.*

Ivy: *And you're going to buy tampons for me?*

Me: *Well, you have them on your list. Don't you need them? Though, not to be selfish, but I hope you don't need them soon.*

Ivy: *You've got a week before I need them, Jake. FYI— Never could have predicted that you'd not only pick up tampons without being asked or that you'd be discussing periods with me in a text.*

Me: *Babe, you've met Steph. Periods are a part of life, a fact she drilled into us, often. So, brands? Absorbency? Is Tampax the only brand?*

Ivy: *Nope, not the only brand, buy I do use Tampax Pearl, regular absorbency. And Annie's Fruit Snacks.*

Me: *On it.*

I swung into the fruit snack aisle, then through the rest of the store, motoring through in record time. My phone didn't vibrate again until I was getting into the truck. Looking down, I shook my head. This woman was killing me.

Ivy: *Thanks, Jake. Sometimes you feel too good to be true.*

I wanted to find her parents and throttle them for making her grow up in a world where she wasn't taken care of. Always. I also wanted to go back in time and meet her nana and thank her for being the one decent family member in her life.

Me: *Get used to it, Ivy. I've got you.*

Before I tossed my phone to the seat, I checked out the

time. Addie would just be getting out of school in fifteen minutes or so. I was about a block from her preschool, so I turned in that direction and found a spot to park and fired off another text.

Me: *I'm in the neighborhood for Addie's school. Cool if I swing by and say hi to her and Teri?*

I figured I could swing by the school and say hello to her before heading to the brewery for the night. It was crazy to realize that just a few weeks back I had never met the little girl. Now the idea that I wouldn't see her until Saturday at the earliest seemed wrong. I'd met Teri last week when Ivy and Addie brought her into the brewery for dinner. Nice lady. I could visit with her for a few, see the kid, then hit the road to play with Chief a bit before work.

Leaving the truck, I followed a few other adults who all seemed to be heading toward Addie's school, but no sign of Teri. I nodded to a few parents I'd stood by last month when I'd picked Addie up for Ivy. It was pretty cool out. I was grateful I'd actually pulled a jacket on this morning instead of just a heavy flannel. The snow that fell yesterday had all melted off in the afternoon sun, but the temp had to be just a bit above freezing. I glanced at the brick building, but there was no sign of the kids yet. Glancing at my phone, I noted that we still had a few minutes until dismissal and that I'd missed a text from Drew.

Drew: *Sully called, I'm coming in to the brewery tonight in case you all need backup.*

I thumbed out a message back as I felt the gratitude that was getting to spend time with my brother regularly after all these years.

Me: *Works for me.*

Drew: *Where are you at?*

I glanced around, no sign of any students yet. Damn, it was cold.

Me: *Freezing my ass off outside Addie's school.*

Drew: *What? You're watching Ads for Bookstore? How did I miss this?*

Me: *I'm not. Just wanted to say hi before the busy weekend starts. Not sure when I'll see her again.*

Drew: *I'm wondering…*

Me: *Pins and needles.*

Drew: *Just wondering what it feels like to be whipped.*

Me: *Fuck off.*

I glanced around again for Teri, but didn't see her. My phone vibrated, and I looked down to see a text from Ivy. Drew would have a shit ton of comments about the lightness I felt just from seeing her name.

Maybe he had a point. I opened the text.

Ivy: *You're welcome to swing by the school and say hi to Ads, but Teri won't be there. Remember, Noah is back in town as of today. He's picking her up so they can hang out. I'm sure you can join them if you want.*

My stomach ached. I'd forgotten about Noah coming back today. As I'd told Drew, the guy seemed nice and was trying to do right by his kid, but part of me hated it and I didn't know why.

Before I could psychoanalyze myself too much, the doors were thrown open, and kids and teachers began streaming out.

"Here they come," I muttered. I should have immediately left, but I didn't. Apparently I wasn't in the mood to be kind to myself.

I looked up to see Noah was indeed there and talking to a teacher. She looked at her clipboard and nodded, pointing at the class coming out of the doors. Noah signed the clip-board and began scanning the kids as they came out. When I looked back to the school door, I saw Addie's friend, Trevor, exit. Coming behind him was Addie. I saw Noah step toward her. Her head turned toward him, and a smile lit up her face. I heard her shout, "Daddy!" as she ran toward him at a sprint. He knelt down, holding out his arms as she barreled toward him, wrapping herself around him.

I took a step back, feeling like I'd been punched in the gut. It wasn't rational. With one look at the two of them, I knew I was in trouble. I loved Ivy and Addie. I wanted the dream with them. No part of my dream had Noah in it. And how long till Ivy decided her dream didn't include me? I took one last look at Addie in Noah's arms as he picked her up, and I hightailed it back to my truck.

31

THE WORLD IMPLODED

Ivy

I glanced down at my phone lying on the counter at the bookstore again. I'd texted Jake a few times in the past hour to arrange a time to see him tonight before his shift. He'd picked up some stuff at the store for me, and I didn't want him to go out of his way to get it to me. He had enough going on.

Weird, still no reply.

I couldn't believe that he was cool with picking up tampons. It my somewhat limited experience with guys, they preferred to pretend that periods didn't exist, which was patently ridiculous. I mean, bodily function and all. When I was in middle school, I had mortified my parents by petitioning my principal to get sanitary supplies place in the bathrooms at school for free for anyone who needed them. In our meeting he'd explained that I didn't understand there was a cost involved and were the females in the student body okay with helping shoulder that cost? I acknowledge there was a cost, but asked where the females and males were shouldering the price tag for toilet paper, which was also used for a bodily function.

We got pads and tampons.

I thought back to Jake and my conversations on feminism over the past six months. I had assumed he had some misguided misogynist beliefs, but now I wished that I had a record of those conversations because his actions over the past few months were showing me I might be mistaken.

But I knew who I could ask. I grabbed my phone again.

Me: *Hey Steph, fun question for you. Where would you say your brother falls on the scale from feminist to misogynist?*

I mean, I knew when Steph and I talked she'd explained that their parents were pretty old school and she was constantly educating her brothers. Did it matter, really? I had to say it did, deep down. I needed Addie surrounded by people who would fight right beside her to make sure she had all options open to her.

My phone vibrated.

Steph: *Which Neanderthal are we talking about right now?*

Steph: *Though, honestly, the answer is the same. Jake and Drew are a work in progress. Deep down, they believe women are equal and should have every opportunity they do. Do they always recognize the opportunities they are simply given for being white, cis-gendered males gracing this earth? Nope. Are they open to realizing that they've been given certain privileges and advocating for others? Yep.*

Steph: *Why? Do I need to kick Jake's ass?*

I laughed as I watched one text roll in after another. Her big-sister tendencies were pretty amazing. Once again, as often happened in the presence of any of the Spencer siblings, I wished I'd had one of my own. I prayed to the goddess above that Addie didn't end up being an only child.

Me: *Well, Jake and I disagreed a lot when we first met. He tended to push back during conversations when we were debating what I considered to be a feminist topic. He even referred to me as Steinem.*

Steph: *What a dork. Sooooooo not an insult. Gloria broke so many barriers down. And honestly, doesn't surprise me. The way the three of us have discussed issues for as long as I can remember is to push each other. So, in his weird way, he was likely treating you like he'd treat me.*

That made me smile, and after being around Jake's family, I had to acknowledge that Steph could be on to something.

Steph: *And I'm no unbiased party here, but Ivy, I think you go with your gut here. If Jake doesn't treat you well, as much as I'd hate it, he's not the one for you. What does your gut say about him and the patriarchy?*

My grin widened. Damn, I loved Steph.

Me: *That he'd help me burn it to the ground while not understanding completely why he was doing it.*

Steph: *I just snorted. Sounds about right.*

Me: *I'm giving you the credit for getting him there. That and the fact that he bought me tampons today.*

Steph: *Good boy. Did he buy the right ones?*

Me: *Not sure, I haven't seen him yet, but he did ask.*

Steph: *Then I've done my job. You would not believe the shit he and Drew used to try to bring home for me. It was like they grabbed whatever was the closest to the door. No go. So, spill, how goes life?*

Ivy: *Bonkers, actually. The Reds event is tomorrow night. I need to make a decision on the bookstore. And*

Addie's dad, Noah, is back in town.

My phone immediately began to vibrate with an incoming call. Steph.

I tapped to answer, laughing. "So this warranted an immediate call versus text?" I tapped speaker so that I could continue to organize some of our pickup orders while we talked.

"Thought you had a lot on your plate, chickie, and this is faster. Which part of the list you just texted is weighing the heaviest?"

"I'm actually feeling better than I was the last time we talked." I bagged another pickup order. "I've meditated, switched up some oils, and bought a few new houseplants."

Steph chuckled. "I'm guessing my bro might have something to do with that as well."

Ha. "He really does." I looked around the store, and my heart settled. "I think I'm going to tell the indie no," I whispered.

"The bookstore up here that made you the offer?" Steph asked.

My heart rate sped up, but this felt right. I'd been wavering over the past two weeks, but I'd been closer and closer to this decision. Jake had said I'd know what to do and Goddess, he was right.

"Yeah. I can do this on my own. I want to do it on my own." I spun around, taking in the space. Tilting my head back, I closed my eyes and soaked in the feeling of being home, of Nana.

"That's awesome, babe. Have you told Jake?"

I came back to the present. "No, I literally just made the decision when we were talking. I texted him a bit ago. He asked if he could see Addie, and I told him Noah was picking her up from school, but I haven't heard from him since."

Steph's laughter caught me unaware.

"What's so funny?"

"Oh, Ivy. You texted him that Noah was picking up your precious daughter, who Jake absolutely adores, and you haven't heard from him since? I think the man has likely turned a violent shade of green, tucked tail, and is hiding and nursing his wounds."

I took that in. Paused. Thought about it again. "You mean, you think Jake is jealous of *Noah*? I mean, he absolutely was at first, but he's past that."

Steph's laughter was louder.

"Steph—"

"Oh, Ivy, sorry. I just wish I was there. Think I can get Drew to follow him around with his phone to get it all on video?"

"To get what on video?"

"My poor brother, realizing he's fallen in love."

I sputtered. "What? Jake doesn't love me."

Steph's laughter stopped and her tone of voice told me to pay attention. "Ivy, Jake Spencer is head over ass for you. For you *and* Addie. I hope you know that. Now, the only question is, how do you feel about him?"

I sank down onto the stool by the counter. "I love him," I whispered. "But I haven't told him that yet."

"Maybe you should?" Steph asked.

A few hours later, Noah, Addie, and I were walking home from the bookstore. I'd texted Jake a few more times and finally heard back from him. He said he was busy getting ready for tonight but would catch up with me soon. I couldn't help but worry that all was not okay with him, but I'd have to wait until I saw him to figure that out for certain. I didn't think my stomach would settle until we talked.

Noah had picked Ads up from school, and the two of them had gone to play at the park before meeting me at the bookstore to go home together. Addie was dancing up the sidewalks ahead of us, twirling as she moved and singing to herself.

"She's gotten so big, Ivy," Noah said as we walked. "Thanks for letting me pick her up."

I watched as Addie stopped from her spot on the sidewalk and looked up to talk to a squirrel clinging to one of the tall trees that lined the right-of-way. Her mittened hands found her hips as she looked back at him. Her stocking cap had slipped low over her head again as she tried to peer up at the squirrel from below the hat.

"Push your hat up, Ads," I called. "And turn left here." I pointed in the correct direction.

"'Kay, Momma," she called back.

I looked over to Noah who was watching her with what appeared to be more than a little bit of wonder. "I'm glad you wanted to spend time with her, Noah." I said as we turned to head down Jake's street, following Addie's fuzzy pink jacket as she continued her shimmy. I shook my head, wishing I could bottle her joy for the world.

"It was great," he said, continuing to watch her. "I was such an idiot, Ivy. I should have come home so much sooner. I've missed so much."

"You were doing something important. Addie knows that, so do I. No guilt, not from us."

Noah laughed. "My parents don't share your mindset, but I'd guess that wouldn't be a surprise to you. I still hate that you were alone when she was young. And that Jake said you struggled for money. I wish I had known." He stopped and looked at me, putting a hand on my arm. "Can you ever forgive me?"

I looked over to Addie. "Ads. Hold up for a minute," I called. She stopped and then crouched down, pushing something in the grass. I looked back to Noah's hand on my coat, then to him. "Noah, there is nothing to forgive." I smirked at him. "Now, when can I set you up with someone? Because I have several women renting apartments above the bookstore, and I'm glad to get to work. Just say the word."

Noah laughed and pulled me in for a hug. "Steady, matchmaker. Give me a week or so to get settled at least. However, while we're on the subject, want to share what's going on with you and a certain brewery owner?"

I rolled my eyes. "Cole Sullivan is a happily married man and preparing to have a baby."

"*Ivy...*"

I put up a hand. "I know, I know. It's just." I got choked up unexpectedly.

"Ivy?"

"Sorry, not sure where that came from. I just..." I looked at Noah, who was watching me with a ton of worry etched all over his face. "I haven't heard from Jake much today, and I'm worried he's upset with me."

"Why would he be?"

I snorted even as a tear rolled down my face. "I think he's jealous of you, and I just realized today that I love him."

Noah smiled. "Well, you've had a big day."

I laughed.

"For what it's worth, I like him." He reached over to brush a tear from my cheek.

I looked away and noticed that someone was on the

sidewalk across the street, just a bit up from us. I locked eyes with a furious-looking Jake Spencer.

Shit.

As I started to take a step toward him, the world imploded.

Addie saw Jake with Chief at the same time. She hopped up, yelling, "Chief!" as she darted off the sidewalk.

Noah and I both saw her go as a car turned the corner.

"Addie!" I screamed.

Noah began running.

Jake looked to Addie.

Addie ran into the street.

Chief tore off the curb, running straight at Addie, and hit her square in the chest, causing her to ricochet back to the right-of-way, right as he got clipped by the car, which slammed to a stop.

And Chief lay on the road.

Time stood still.

32

MAN'S BEST FRIEND

Jake

Time stood still for a moment as the horror unfolded in front of me. All I could see was Chief and Addie, the two of them prone, but also what could have been running through my mind.

I raced across the street to them, the breath only coming easier when Addie sat up and cried out when she saw Chief lying on the road. The driver came tearing out of the car, a young mom who was in tears, but she'd done nothing wrong. It was just bad luck, and I knew that, but knowing Addie was okay, my gaze fell to my dog.

Chief was awake and his eyes met mine, then looked for Addie. That fucking dog, he loved her so. I had no idea how the brain of an animal worked, but I knew what we'd just witnessed. Somehow he'd known what was happening and saved Addie. I didn't know what the cost was, but I was grateful.

Ivy sobbed as she scooped up Addie, kissing her all over as she checked her out.

Noah looked from Addie, to me, to Chief. "Hey, Jake."

He quickly knelt down on the road next to me, hesitating to touch Chief but his gaze searching his body.

I'd looked back to Ivy whose eyes were swimming with tears as she held Addie like she would never let her go.

Noah looked from Ivy to me. "Do you have a vet in town, or do we need to take him somewhere else?"

I wanted to hate this fucker, but damn if he wasn't considerate at every damn turn. I worked to compartmentalize my feelings and focused on Chief. "We have a vet. I'll get him there. You guys take Addie home and check her out."

Ivy was talking to the driver now, who seemed to be on the phone with the police, seeing what kind of report they needed filed, if any.

I nodded at my truck in my driveway to Noah. "That's my truck. Could you get the tailgate so I can slide Chief in?"

Noah looked over to the truck, then back to Chief, whose tail beat out a slow rhythm, but he still hadn't budged. "You have a blanket? Might make it easier to carry him if something's broken."

I looked at Chief. He was right. "Under the bench seat," I said, running a hand over Chief's hip as he whimpered. Fuck. But he was with us, that had to be something. Cling to that.

Noah ran over to my truck and lowered the back tailgate. Moving to the passenger door on the front part of the cab, he leaned in to grab the blanket, then came back over to our little group.

He went to Ivy first, running a hand over Addie's head as he spoke to Ivy. Ivy held Addie on her hip as Addie's big eyes watched Chief. Noah nodded at Ivy, then came back to me, handing me the blanket.

"I think we can slide this under him, then you hold one side and I'll hold the other and we can carry him over," Noah said with a jerk to my truck. "I can ride in the back with him to get to the vet."

My eyes met his with confusion. "But you don't need to stay with me."

Noah shook his head. "Ivy said it's just a half mile or so from here. She's calling the vet to give them a heads-up we're en route, then calling the doc to make sure Addie doesn't need to come in. She doesn't think so—Addie wasn't knocked out and doesn't have a mark on her. But I'll let her do that while I ride with you. Then I'll come back and check in with her."

"Hold on a second," I said. "Can you hang with Chief for a minute?"

"Sure," Noah said, smoothing a hand down Chief's head.

I stood, moving to Ivy and Addie. I didn't focus on Ivy right now. I couldn't. I looked at Addie. "You okay, peanut?"

Addie's lower lip trembled. "Chief."

I glanced quickly at Ivy. "Can I take her for a second to see Chief?"

Addie's arms came out before Ivy even nodded. Ivy's face was a mess of tears, but I couldn't think about it. Instead, I let myself feel the comfort of Addie's solid weight as she curled into me.

Addie's arms went around my neck, and she whispered in my ear. "Jakey." Her breath broke. "I'm sorry I ran into the street."

I looked at her face, which matched her mother's for the devastation I found there. "Peanut, you're right. We don't run into the street. But we also all make mistakes. And I'm betting Chief is going to be just fine. I'm going to take him to the doc to get checked out. You know what would make him feel better though?"

"What?" she whispered.

"If he could see you."

She nodded and I moved next to Noah, bending down so she could put her small hand on Chief's side. His eyes found hers, and his tail thumped out a faster beat.

"Thank you, Chief," she whispered. I loosened my grip so she could kneel down and press a kiss to his head.

Damn. My own eyes were fighting back tears.

Ivy appeared by our side as she bent down to Chief and whispered in his ear before pressing a kiss to his head before she stood up.

Working quickly, I passed Addie back to Ivy so that Noah and I could get Chief in the truck before I completely broke down. Within ten minutes, we were at the vet's and they were taking him back for X-rays as Noah jogged back to Ivy and Addie.

And my thoughts spiraled.

I paced a lap around the waiting room for at least the millionth time. Dean McCallister, a friend of Max's and Sully's from school, was a vet here and had taken Chief back as soon as we arrived, telling me to wait out here.

My heart couldn't seem to slow down and find a normal rhythm. The past hour seemed to be on some kind of horror repeat in my brain. I needed to stop seeing Addie running into the street, my dog racing to rescue her somehow, and the vehicle clipping Chief's hip as he crumpled to the road and Addie to the curb.

It was the stuff of my nightmares.

And let's not forget Ivy hugging Noah.

Fuck.

I moved to the window, letting my gaze lose focus as I

looked outside. I didn't see the snowflakes that had begun to fall as the sun went down. Instead, I focused on the old Bronco pulling into the parking lot.

Drew.

I watched him park, hop down from his vehicle, and stride into the clinic, clearly looking for me.

"Hey," I called from my spot at the window.

The tension on his face lessened. "Hey," he said, moving to me. "How's Chief?"

"X-rays," I said, nodding to the doors that led to the back. "How'd you know?"

"Bookstore called," he said. "She thought you could use company."

My heart clenched. Of course she did. Damn, I didn't know what to think.

"Want to talk to me about it?" Drew asked.

I turned to the window, resuming my position. "How much did Ivy tell you?"

He moved so that we were shoulder to shoulder, both our gazes directed out the window. "She said Chief is a fucking superhero and pushed Addie out of the way of a car. She said Addie is completely fine." I exhaled, grateful to hear that. "And she said Noah was there too." I felt Drew's face turn to watch me.

Super.

"Think that about covers it," I muttered.

He nodded. "So you more fucked up over your dog getting hurt or some guy coming around Bookstore when all you want to do is piss around her, marking your territory?"

I turned to glare at him. "It's not like that." It was totally like that.

"So why isn't she here? Why did she send me?" Drew raised an eyebrow, daring me to try to bullshit him.

I looked away, not wanting to see the pity in his expression as I spilled my guts. "You know I was headed to see Addie at school today. Before I got there, Ivy texted to say Noah was picking her up, but I could join him and Addie."

"Horrors," he muttered. "Up-front, honest. Clearly this bodes for terrible things."

I rubbed my nose with my middle finger to his chuckles. "I know, I know. But still, watching Ads come out of school, run to him shouting, *Daddy*..."

"Oof," Drew said. "Punch to the gut."

I nodded. "It's ridiculous. I'm being ridiculous."

"Look at you, owning your actions and everything," Drew said sarcastically. "What are you worried about? Ivy told you he was there. You've met Noah. You know nothing is going on with them." He raised his eyebrow, clearly questioning my sanity.

It was fine. Sanity had fled long ago. "I don't know. Maybe she's getting back with him and they're going to have their perfect family," I growled, looking at him. "Maybe that's what's going on."

Drew put both his hands on his hips as he watched me with a look of disbelief traveling over his face. "Good Lord, abandonment issues much?" He shook his head at me. "What in anything Ivy has said over the past—what's it been since you met, eight months?— What has she ever said that told you she was hung up on that guy and wanted to get back together with him?"

I looked at him in confusion. "Well, nothing, but if he's back here..."

"Jesus, Jake, not everyone is Rachel." Drew shook his head like he couldn't believe my stupidity. He then studied my face and spoke gently. "So, have you told Bookstore that you love her yet?"

I started to deny it, but Drew just glared in my direction. "No," I said.

"But you do."

"Yep." I looked at the snow that was starting accumulate.

"Maybe you should tell her," Drew said, bumping my shoulder.

I swallowed around the lump in my throat. "And what if she still leaves? Or doesn't want this?"

Drew watched the snow with me in silence while my emotions swirled inside. Finally, he spoke. "She's not Rachel, Jake. I don't think she's going anywhere. But more to the point, you love her whether or not she wants more with you. Yes, she could tell you this isn't what she's ready for. But what if she doesn't? What if you could have Ivy and Addie in your life just the way you want them? And all you have to do is ask?"

The feeling of the nerves in my body threatening to explode overwhelmed me. Just as I was getting ready to say something, the door opened and Dean stepped out, looking at a chart in his hand.

"Jake?" he called, looking up.

33

BEYOND BLESSED

Ivy

Noah came into the kitchen as I hung up with the doctor's office. I smiled as I put my phone on the counter, even if my body still felt like I was waiting for the other shoe to drop.

"That was the doctor," I told him. "They said to call back if we saw any issues, but since Ads appears to be fine and doesn't even have a scratch on her, there was no need to come in."

He nodded, moving to pull out a chair at my kitchen table. Nodding at one across from him, he said, "Want to sit for a minute?"

I crossed and sank into the seat gratefully. My legs were practically trembly. I felt like I'd been holding everything together and the slightest of breezes would blow it apart. "How's Chief?"

Noah watched me for a moment, then nodded like he was confirming something. "Not sure. The vet and vet tech met us when we arrived and took him back for X-rays immediately. He was still alert, so I'm thinking that's good, but honestly, I have no idea."

I nodded, glancing down at my phone even though I knew Jake hadn't texted. I'd sent Drew to him, but I wished I'd gone in his place.

Shaking my head, I moved to stand. "Let me go check on Addie," I said.

Noah waved a hand. "She's good. She's watching some cartoon and said she'd like a snack soon. I told her we'd bring her one. But before that, I want to talk to you."

I looked at him, puzzled. What did we have to talk about?

"Jake's the guy. Correct?" he asked.

I raised my eyebrows in surprise. "The guy?"

"*The* guy," Noah said gently. "The one who I need to get to know because we'll all be co-parenting that amazing little girl in there together. Right?"

With a shaky breath, I nodded. "If he'll have me, yes."

Noah's face grew even more serious. "He seems great, Ivy, but he sure as hell better realize how amazing you are. I know I didn't—"

"Noah," I interrupted. "You know we were better as friends."

"Doesn't mean I wasn't a fool. I'm just saying he better work his ass off to deserve you." He leaned over, pressing a kiss to my cheek.

Tears hit me so suddenly they threatened to take my breath away. Through the waterworks, I could see the alarm on Noah's face.

"I'm sorry, Ivy." He placed a hand on my arm. "I wasn't trying to make you cry."

"No, it's just..." I tried to get it out. "I mean, I hope he's the guy. I think he's the guy. But I might be too late. I don't know."

Noah squeezed my arm and got up to grab some tissues from a box on the counter. Handing them to me, he said, "Take a breath and I'll get Addie a snack, then we can talk. What does she like?"

The tears increased because it made me think of Jake and the fact that he knew Addie, knew what she liked, and now he might be gone. Somehow, I got it together enough to list out a few snacks to Noah, and he brought them to her, then came back and settled in so that I could spill to him.

What the heck? At this point, it couldn't hurt.

After trying to explain all that had been Jake and me over the past month, but really going back to April, I wrapped it up. "...and then he wanted to pick up Ads at school today, and I let him know you were going to be there. And now he probably thinks I'm dropping him like a hot potato like Rachel, and his dog is at the vet, and it's just a lot." I dropped my head onto my arms on the table.

A beat or two went by, then I felt Noah's hand on my head. I left my head down. I was about out of any energy to deal with my life, and this was comfortable. "I can honestly say giving you advice on a guy was not how I saw today going." I heard Noah's chuckle, and my heart gave a hopeful beat. "But Ivy, I think it's going to be okay."

I chanced a look up at Noah. "Really?"

He nodded. "Sounds like this Rachel put him through the wringer. My guess is if you can show him you're not exchanging him for another guy"—he gave me a wry smile—"including me, well, I think you'll be on the path to happily-ever-afters and all."

I felt lighter. I could do that. I could.

"Does he know you love him?" he asked.

My gaze found Noah's as my eyes welled up once again. Super. "Um, no. Honestly, I just figured that out in the past day or so."

Noah squeezed my hand. "Well, it's not like either of us had excellent parental role models of healthy relationships."

I snorted. "That's an understatement."

"Give yourself a break. At least you figured it out. And you know that's not changing, right?" Noah gave me a serious look. "No miracle is at work. Neither set of Addie's grandparents are becoming decent human beings. I hate that for her," he whispered.

I squeezed his hand back. "I know, Noah. And thanks for the reminder. I'm trying to focus on the fact that I had one person I could count on growing up. My nana. I turned out okay. I think Addie will too. We're surrounded by some pretty great people down here. My parents will be what they will be, but I'm not trying to change them. That's not on me."

Noah stood, tugging me to stand as well. Looking down, he smiled. "I think you're in a good place, with or without this guy."

I grinned up at him. "I'm really hoping it's with, but time will tell."

He tapped my nose. "You have hugs available for an old friend?"

"Only ones I had a child with."

His eyes danced with amusement. "Then it's my lucky day." He reached out and we hugged. I felt part of me regain strength I didn't know I'd lost.

Stepping back, he squeezed my waist. "So, I know we aren't sure exactly what our new schedule will look like, but I was thinking at the bare minimum we could do a weekly dinner."

I smiled at him. "That sounds great."

"And if a certain brewery owner wanted to join us, I wouldn't say no."

"Noted."

"And if he wanted to provide the beer each week, I also wouldn't turn that down."

I laughed. "Well, if he's still speaking to me, I'm sure that could be arranged."

At that, the pounding of her feet announced her immediate presence. "Dadddddd," she called, coming to the kitchen doorway. "Did you meet Bob?"

Noah looked to me with a puzzled expression. "Bob?" he asked.

I shook my head and grinned. "The Christmas tree."

Several hours later Ads and I were cuddled together on the couch, discussing what bedtime stories were on the itinerary for tonight, when there was a knock at the front door. I looked up to see Jake's face in the window, and butterflies took up residence in my stomach, beating their wings like crazy.

"Jakey!" Addie got up and ran for the door, opening it to let him come in.

"Hey, peanut." He bent down, getting to her height. "I just wanted to check in and see how you were."

"I'm good. How's Chief," Ads asked, and I came to stand by her, needing to hear that Jake's dog was okay. I'd been tempted to text him a million times since Noah left, but I willed myself to stay strong and simply be here, praying eventually he would come.

I was trying not to read too much into the fact that he was here now.

"Chief's good." Jake looked from me, to Addie, then back to me. "The vet had to give him some drugs for the X-rays. He fractured his hip, but he doesn't need surgery. Just to take it easy while it heals. They're keeping him overnight, but he'll be home tomorrow."

"And he'll be fine?" I asked softly.

"He'll be fine, babe," Jake said.

I exhaled all my anxieties with that one word. Surely if he was calling me *babe*, we were on the right path, correct?

"Peanut, want me to tell you a story before bed?" Jake asked, eyes still locked on mine.

"Little People?" Addie asked.

"Yep," he replied, still watching me. "Go get ready for bed, and I'll be right there."

Addie took off running as I kept my eyes on Jake, waiting.

"Babe," he said, taking a step closer to me.

"Yeah?" I asked, stepping closer to me.

"You okay?"

I nodded.

"What's going on through that brain of yours?"

Goddess, where did I start. "Um, I turned down the proposal on the bookstore today."

Jake's smile grew. "Good. You don't need anyone else. You've got this, Ivy, and your store is going to rock."

I might need someone, I thought.

"Where's Noah?"

"Airbnb." I replied.

His hands came to my hips. "Good."

At that, my heartbeat sped up. Might as well get it all out. "Jake, Noah is moving here. He's going to be part of our life."

"He wants to be with Addie," Jake said, his heated gaze finding mine. "What about you?"

"What about me?" I asked, nervous that we weren't where I thought we were.

"What do you want with Noah?"

I moved closer until I was flush against Jake and tightened my arms around him. I wanted him to feel secure. "What I want is Addie to have her dad in her life if he's open to it."

"And how do you want Noah in your life?"

"As a friend."

"That's it?" I could tell he was bracing. Screw Rachel for making this glorious man doubt that people would stay, that people would love him.

"That's it."

Jake cleared his throat. "Does Noah know that?"

"Yep. I asked him if I could set him up. He's considering it. He wants weekly dinners with Addie, me, and you."

The ghost of a smile emerged on his face. "Drew might ask to be invited."

"Done. He also said you needed to provide the beer."

"Done. Anything else?"

I looked up at him, taking strength from his gaze that was locked on me. "Well, I told him that I was in love with someone else."

Jake's breath caught as his eyes narrowed. "In love?"

My heart was pitter-pattering so loud I wondered if he could hear it. "Yep. In love. You might know him. He's a surly brewery owner who, I hear, will buy Christmas trees and tampons. Though I haven't seen evidence of the tampons yet."

Jake's body relaxed, and a grin spread across his face. "Sounds like a hell of a guy, though not sure how trees and tampons go together, Ivy."

I felt like my body was beaming, the joy couldn't be contained.

"You know he loves you too, right?" He dipped down to press a kiss to my forehead.

Holy moly.

"I do now," I whispered.

"Jaaaaakkeeeeeeeyyyyyy," Addie bellowed from upstairs. "It's time for the Little People!"

"You're being summoned," I said with a laugh.

He brushed his lips across mine. "Ivy?"

"Yeah?"

"Is it okay if I stay tonight?" He asked as he moved toward the staircase.

"Counting on it," I said. "Meet me in my room when story time is over?" I asked, pulling him back to me and planting a wet kiss on his lips.

Taking a step back, he groaned. "What's the likelihood that I can get Addie to sleep after a five-minute story?"

I pretended to shake something in both hands. "Hmm, my Magic 8 Ball says outlook not so good."

I moved ahead to go up the stairs ahead of him. He squeezed my butt as we got to the top and whispered in my ear. "We'll see about that."

An hour later I was leaning against Addie's door, watching Jake as he lay next to her in her small bed, his head against the headboard. I could barely hear his voice as he wrapped up what had to be the fifth Little People story of the night.

"And they were snug, cozy, and safe in their tiny beds behind the brick in the wall of their home..." He looked at Addie's eyes, which remained closed as he leaned down and pressed a light kiss to her temple as he smoothed her blond curls. Even quieter, I heard him whisper, "Thank the goddess you are safe, peanut."

And the tears began flowing. This man.

All I'd wanted since the moment I knew I was going to have a baby was to have a child who was healthy and knew she was loved. For so long, I'd felt like it was Addie and me on our own, adrift in this world. Now, the people of Highland Falls had taken us in first. Then Jake and his crazy family. Now Noah was waking up and realizing what he'd been missing. There were so many people who loved us it felt like the goddess was giving with both hands.

We were beyond blessed.

I moved back into my bedroom, sliding between the covers in my tank and underwear. I could just shed them both, but I didn't want to be presumptuous.

Minutes later, the door creaked open and Jake stuck his head in the room, his eyes finding mine. "Mind if I come in?" he asked with a wink.

"Waiting for you." I made a show of checking my phone on the bedside table. "Looks like your five minutes was more like sixty."

He laughed as he kicked off his shoes and dropped his jeans and flannel on the floor, sliding between the covers in a T-shirt and boxer briefs. "Yeah, Addie had lots of questions about Chief. She's decided she needs to visit each day to walk with him around the yard and keep him company until he can run again."

My eyes teared up. Dang, my girl had a good heart.

Jake brushed away a tear that spilled over. "Ivy, you okay?"

I rolled to my side to take him in. "Are we really okay, Jake? I mean, I'm so sorry I hadn't texted you a heads-up that Noah was picking Addie up ahead of time. I just thought you knew they were hanging out when he could. I'd never mean to hurt you."

He slid down in the bed until we were front to front. "We're okay, babe." His arm snaked out to grab my hip, pulling it to him. "I'm sorry I was so afraid, waiting for you to leave me like Rachel did."

"I won't," I whispered against his mouth.

His lips brush mine. "Ever?"

I pulled back, scanning his face. His blue eyes stared into mine. His hair was curling a bit over his ears. The part that stuck up in front was a little long. I could see that there was a hint of a shadow under his eyes, like he was tired. But the lines in his face that I saw earlier today were smoothed out.

I felt like he was asking something big here. "Do you mean will I stay with you forever?" I asked, my heart suddenly taking up residence in my throat.

The corner of his mouth turned up. "I'm not proposing now, Ivy. I won't do that until I have a ring. But fair warning, it will be soon."

Yep. Going to have a heart attack. I guess tonight was the night to lay it all on the table.

"Really?" I asked, breathlessly.

"If that sounds good to you," he said, his lips descending to blaze a trail down my neck.

I arched into his mouth. "I agree on one condition," I said on a gasp.

"What's that? Daily orgasms?"

"Two conditions then," I said with a moan as his mouth found my nipple over my tank. I pulled back, pulling my tank up and over my head, tossing it to the floor. I pushed my underwear down and kicked them off as well.

Jake leaned back, watching the show. "Suppose I should

shed my clothes too," he said as he did just that. "Okay, daily orgasms and what's the other condition?" Naked, he pulled me against him. His hard cock told me he was ready to get this party started.

I made myself meet his eyes. If he wasn't okay with this, I needed to know now so I could decide if it was a deal breaker. "Well, it's just, I mean I love Drew and Steph—"

"Jesus, babe, I mean I love them too, but they are not what I want to talk about when I have you naked," he said with a laugh, trailing a finger up my side and thumbing my nipple.

I gasped, then rushed it. "I want to have more babies," I got out, pulling Jake's mouth to my breast.

Jake pulled back to meet my eyes, his suddenly serious. "Babe, you want kids with me?"

My body cried out for his mouth, but I could see from his gaze that he was serious. "Of course I do," I said. "You're wonderful with Addie, and I don't want her to be an only child. Plus, if we're getting married one day, I absolutely want babies with you."

It was Jake's turn to get misty-eyed. "When can you go off the pill? I'm good with you being pregnant tomorrow."

This man. I pressed a kiss to his mouth. "I can stop the pills, but it will take a while for us to be able to get pregnant."

"Then..." Jake lowered his mouth again, his tongue circling my nipple. Sucking it in, he bit it lightly. "I think we better practice."

He continued his path down my body, his mouth worshipping my breasts, then my stomach, the baby belly that hadn't completely left after I had Addie. He slid my legs apart as he settled in, dragging his tongue through my wet folds, then circling my clit before pulsing it in his mouth, taking only seconds before the sensations built to a crescendo that screamed through my body as I arched from the bed, stars in my eyes.

Jake's mouth gentled as he let my body come down from my climax. Coming up to press a kiss to my lips, he reached into the drawer for a condom. Sliding it on, he kissed my nose. "Ready, Ivy?"

"Always," I whispered.

Jake slid in with one thrust until I was filled with him. As he began to move, the sensations in my core began to build again from the slight tingle to a pulse as my clit brushed his base. But more than that, I was overwhelmed with the feeling of completeness, like I was exactly where I was meant to be. I had no idea what was visible on my face, but there was something because Jake looked down at me and his eyes widened as he slowed down.

"You okay?"

I studied him, not even sure how to express what I was feeling. Hell yes, I was okay. I was more okay than I'd ever been. Pulling his head to mine, I whispered. "I love you, Jacob Spencer. And I'm so damn glad you're not a misogynist."

He blinked, blinked again, and then threw his head back and laughed. Leaning down, he spoke to me against my lips. "I love you too, Ivy Jameson. And I can't wait to love on you for the rest of our lives."

I wrapped my arms around him and let him bring me to another orgasm.

Yeah, daily orgasms. I could live with that.

34

REDS OF CHRISTMAS

Jake

The brewery was hopping. Laurie was stationed at the far corner of the bar, getting the complementary Fire and Rain for the Reds of Christmas guests. We'd had a steady stream of people from the event as they visited the local businesses, showing their red bands around their wrists that entitled them to different items at each location. We'd gotten great feedback from not only the Reds folks but also our normal Friday crowd. Sully smiled from his spot at the taps, wiping a hand across his forehead in mock exhaustion.

"Lots of new-to-the-brewery people tonight," he said with a head nod to the stream coming in. We'd participated in the Reds each year that we'd been open, but since it was only celebrating its sixth year, the event had grown as we had. Looking over the reservations with Ivy over the past few weeks, I'd been floored by the numbers. We were easily over double the participants from last year. We also were bringing in people from larger towns nearby, which was great for our business community. Hopefully they'd visit tonight and then remember us in the future and come back.

Ivy's social media campaign had really knocked this event out of the park. I was so damn proud of her and thrilled she decided to stay on as the owner of Pages. I saw a great future for her in that bookstore.

I hung a towel off my shoulder and cleared some glassware from the bar before running it through our sanitizing station. "Yep, numbers are great. Lou did a lot of work for this one."

Sully turned and leaned a hip against the bar to watch me. "You and Ivy did more than a little, Jake."

My gaze immediately searched the bar, looking for her. The bookstore was open tonight, of course, but she was taking the early shift and then Nic was taking over with a high school worker for the second half of the evening. She should be here anytime, and I was getting impatient.

"Lou truly did the bulk of the work," I replied to Sully while I searched the crowd. "Ivy and I just confirmed numbers, and she hit the cesspool known as social media."

Sully chuckled. "Yeah, but that cesspool brings in new customers. See the evidence in front of us." He glanced around. "Where's Ivy? Mags said she was coming here tonight."

I wiped down a glass, then another, fighting the urge to pull out my phone to check and see if Ivy had texted yet. "Coming when Nic relieves her. Mags staying home?"

"Yep." Sully didn't resist the urge and pulled out his phone, clearly looking for a message from Maggie. "Says she is officially exhausted."

"Her school's on break in what, two weeks? Think she'll make it?" I began to ask when I heard Max's voice.

"Beer me," he said from across the bar where he stood with Emma and another guy I knew I'd met before but struggled to place. Sully moved around the bar to greet the group.

"Harp," I nodded in his direction. Looking to Emma who was pulling back from a hug from her brother, I teased. "You couldn't convince Mags tonight?" Emma had been working on what she called Maggie's hermit-like ways as the pregnancy went on and Maggie's belly grew.

Emma laughed. "I gave her a rest tonight. The end of the week makes her want to crash in a normal year. Cooking this baby is a lot of work." Glancing at the guy next to her, she waved in my direction. "Nate, do you know Jake Spencer? He and Sully are partners here at the brewery."

I glanced to Emma's side and saw Nate Roberts, the librarian that had joined her at the Ryan Library this fall. "Hey, Nate."

Nate greeted me then nodded as Sully offered to get him the new IPA that he'd just passed to Max.

Nate had joined us for drinks once or twice over the past month as we got to know him better. Good guy. His grandparents had lived in Highland, but he'd moved to Chicago for a bit, just coming back this fall when he'd inherited their place.

"You feeling more settled here? Still haven't seen you in the brewery much over the past few weeks."

Nate grinned. "Promise I will be one of your loyal customers. Still getting my feet under me at the library and some work on my place, but now that winter's hit, I'll be slowing down and coming in. We'll have to do wings again soon..." His voice trailed off as he lost focus.

I followed Nate's gaze, and at first, I thought he and I were going to need to have a discussion. He was looking at Ivy as she made her way to us through the main room. I mean, I'd give him that she was a vision. Then I noticed that his gaze was actually on the women Ivy was dragging with her toward us. I'd allow that.

Without giving the group another thought, I moved around the bar and toward Ivy. We'd stayed up for hours last night, talking, laughing, planning, kissing. Waking up with her naked body in my arms, I felt more settled than I ever remembered feeling. That feeling only increased when I stopped at the vet and picked up Chief. They said it would take weeks for his hip to heal, but reducing his activity, keeping him calm, and some medication to start would all help. Drew had stayed home with him tonight to make sure he got the rest he needed.

Life was pretty damn good.

Reaching Ivy, I stopped when she was flush against me. "Babe, you're killing me."

Her grin widened as her eyes blinked up in some fake innocent look. "Jake, I'm sure I don't know what you mean."

I ran a finger in the neckline of the forest-green sweater she wore that dipped off a bare shoulder. Her blond curls were a loose and messy, like we'd just spent the day in bed. The sweater was over some short cream slip dress, and she had her suede boots on that went over her knees and drove me fucking crazy. I wanted the entire outfit on the floor of her bedroom twenty minutes ago. Unfortunately, that wouldn't be happening for hours, but it would be happening.

I kissed her neck and then whispered in her ear. "You'll pay later, babe."

She wrinkled her nose at me. "Counting on it, caveman."

"My parents settled?" I asked. I'd texted my mom and dad this morning to tell them about the accident yesterday. Their response had been to hop in the car and drive for three hours, insisting that Addie needed them more than a babysitter tonight.

Ivy had kept Addie home from school today just to watch her, making sure all was still well. I'd been there at lunch since I brought Chief to see Addie so she'd know he was fine. The two of them had been curled up on the floor, Addie reading stories to him while Ivy and I cooked. My mom had charged into the kitchen, and Ivy took one look at Margot in mama-bear mode and had burst into tears.

Mom took it in stride, turning to Ivy and pulling her in. Eventually I'd left them there for the afternoon, knowing there was no way my mom or dad would be moving from Addie's side.

Ivy's eyes immediately welled up. "I still can't believe they're here, Jake."

I kissed her nose. "Believe it, Ivy."

Her eyes widened. "Oh no, where are my manners?" She turned and found the woman she walked in with talking to someone at a nearby table. "Elle?" The brunette looked at Ivy, then gave the woman she was talking with a hug, crossing to us. "Jake, Elle's one of my tenants above the bookstore. Elle, this is Jake. My boyfriend." I noted Ivy's cheeks heated up at that label.

I slid an arm around Ivy's waist, squeezing her to me. I offered Elle my hand. "Hey, Elle. Ivy's talked about you a lot. Sounds like you and the other women living above the store have really gotten to know each other."

Elle shook my head, her cheeks pink as well. Her voice was softer, so I moved us closer to hear her over the loud crowd of customers. "Yeah, Kate and Nic are amazing."

"Let's get you a drink," I said to them both. Taking Ivy's hand, I began to snake our way back to the bar area where Max, Emma, Sully, and Nate were gathered.

"Want our new IPA?" I asked Ivy. She nodded. I glanced to Elle and tilted my head toward the bar.

"I'll take an IPA too," she called.

Daryl was behind the bar now, so I held up three fingers and pointed at the tap for Fire and Rain. Daryl nodded.

I looked to Ivy to see that she and Elle had greeted Emma. It seemed that Elle already knew her. I brought them their beers and then grabbed my own. Joining the circle, I watched as Max wrapped his arm around Emma. I'd watched these two over the past eight months. They'd fallen in love and now were engaged to get married next summer. Looking to Sully, I realized that in the same time he and Maggie had gotten together, married, and would be having a baby in less than a month. Hell, Ivy and my relationship had been on its own version of warp speed. We were all damn lucky.

Nate returned to the group and raised his beer to Sully and me. "Great beer, guys. You canning this one?"

Sully moved in Nate's direction while I noted Elle's response to Nate joining our group. Her cheeks had flamed up, and she whispered to Emma and Ivy something, taking off toward the bathroom.

I leaned over. "Everything okay?"

Ivy turned from Emma to me, her eyes twinkling. "Yep. Emma was just telling me that Elle is a regular at the library since she moved in. And it seems her gaze is often drawn to Nate."

I shook my head at the two of them. "You don't have to take Lou's matchmaking role, ladies."

"Who's taking my role?" I heard behind me. We turned and saw Lou dragging Verdell to our group. Lou looked to where Ivy and I were practically joined at the hip and turned, whacking Verdell on his arm. "See, I was right. They just needed a push!"

Verdell shook his head and kissed Lou on the temple, then moved on to the bar, catching Daryl's attention.

Lou looked back to Ivy. "Great turnout. It's packed all around town."

"You did good work, Lou," Ivy said, squeezing the older woman before moving back to my side.

"You do good work too, big bro," I heard. Looking back to the group, I noted that Drew stood next to Max.

I looked at him in confusion. "Thought you were staying on dog duty tonight."

He grinned. "And miss the big night? Hell no. Steph wants us to FaceTime her later from here. Addie insisted on sleeping on the floor with Chief, so Mom and Dad brought her to your place. They said they're having a campout in your den." Drew gave Ivy a wry expression. "And Dad might have promised Addie donuts tomorrow."

Ivy laughed. "Might have?"

Drew shrugged. "Might have, or might have already called in an order to be ready at seven. You know how it goes."

Sully looked to me. "Time for a toast."

I glanced around, making sure everyone had a beer. Ivy's arm slid around my waist too, squeezing as she raised her beer.

"To the Reds of Christmas; to Ivy, Jake, and Lou for this amazing event; to Jake for being a kick-ass partner, and to Drew for the inspiration for our newest beer." Sully raised his glass.

"To friends, family, and Highland," I said in response. Looking at Ivy: "And to you." I tapped my glass to hers.

"To Highland." Everyone raised their glasses.

"I'll drink to that," Lou crowed.

"Of course you will," said Verdell, smiling at her.

"Think that will be us in fifty years?" Ivy whispered.

"If so, we'd be beyond blessed," I replied, lowering my mouth to hers. She tasted of Ivy and pine. In other words, perfection.

Ivy

I woke up to an empty bed on Christmas morning. We were at my place because I wanted Addie to wake up to Christmas at our house. My parents had already called yesterday during the morning because, as they said, they couldn't possibly predict what Christmas Day would bring and didn't want to be confined to a time to call us. Addie hadn't cared, and I found that I really didn't either. Our lives were blessed without them.

Chief was getting around pretty well, so Jake had brought him to stay here last night so he'd be part of our morning activities. His parents were at his house with Drew. We were all gathering there for lunch and dinner, but the morning was just for us.

I wondered how long we'd do this dance between two houses. I'd say it was rushing things to think in terms of the future like that already, but Jake had gleefully—with my okay—thrown away my birth control pills after the Reds of Christmas, so I'd say our living arrangements would likely need to be figured out sooner rather than later. I'm sure to some it would make no sense. The typical order of dating, engagement, marriage, baby was not something I was too concerned with. Did I want to one day be married to Jake? Absolutely. Did I need it to happen before a baby? I think I'd already proven that it didn't need to.

Speaking of, Noah had proven he truly had turned over a new leaf. Since he had visited a few weeks ago, he'd called and texted Addie at least once a week. He'd officially moved to Highland, we were all excited about it. Well, Jake was getting there.

It helped that Noah was reaching out to him too, even sending a care package for Chief in his recovery. He was coming over tomorrow for Christmas with Addie, saying he didn't want to interfere with Jake's family's time with us today. Maybe one day we could all celebrate together, but these were good baby steps.

I rolled over onto my back and stretched. Sun streamed through the windows, so I knew I needed to get moving. Addie was a sleepyhead, but even she would want to be up early today to see what Santa brought. Just as I had that thought, the door creaked open. I looked over to it, expecting to see Addie's tousled head, but Jake's dark hair popped in, his eyes finding mine.

"There you are, sleepyhead. It's all I've been able to do to keep Ms. Addie entertained. Shake a leg," he said, coming to press a kiss to my lips.

I groaned. "Five more minutes."

"Up, babe," he said as he pulled me out of bed and slapped my butt.

"Promises, promises," I grumbled, pulling on my robe, but then I turned to shoot him a grin to let him know I was kidding.

He shook his head at me.

Leaving my room, I looked and saw Addie sitting on the top of the stairs, talking. Glancing down, I noted that she held Jake's phone in her hand, and she was clearly Face-Timing Drew. Sure. Makes sense.

"Hey Drew," I said because what else do you say to this crazy family. Honestly, I was surprised we'd convinced Margot and Sam to wait for us all to gather at lunch. It was a Christmas miracle.

"'Bout time, Bookstore," Drew called. "It's Christmas. There's no sleeping."

"Clearly," I replied.

"Let's go, Momma!" Addie exclaimed, standing up and dancing in her Christmas pj's.

"Hold on, hold on." I slid by her on the stairs. "Let me get to the bottom of the stairs and take a picture of you coming down," I said. I'd always wanted to do that traditional picture of kids waiting to come down the stairs, but that wasn't the way Christmas at my parents' place rolled. Well, it was time for new traditions.

Addie was practically dancing in place. I got to the bottom, and Jake was still at the top, running his fingers through her hair. His eyes locked on mine. "Ready?"

I smiled. Our first Christmas. Heck yeah, I was ready.

"Ready."

"Now?" Addie said, looking at me.

"Now, baby," I said, phone at the ready.

Addie ran down, jazz hands flying. She tore into the dining room, running to Bob the tree as Chief came from the living room. I'd bought him a crate so he had a quiet spot at our place, and he liked crashing in it when we weren't around.

Addie stood in front of the tree, hands clasped. The lights were twinkling, and I noted that Jake must have gotten up to turn music on earlier because Christmas music was coming from a portable speaker on the dining room table. "Oh, Momma. Bob is so beautiful," she said in a reverent voice. Looking around the tree out the window, she exclaimed, "And it snowed!"

I looked past her, and sure enough, several inches had piled up outside. I hadn't realized that was in the forecast, but it seemed pretty perfect.

I pulled out a dining room chair to settle in and watch Addie open her presents. She talked to Drew as she propped up Jake's phone a bit away from her so Drew could participate. I noticed that Sam and Margot were in the background, coming over and talking to Addie as she opened, then puttering around Jake's house in the lull between gifts.

Addie's gifts from Jake's family would be opened at his place later. Here we just had the gifts from Santa and us. Even so, she squealed with joy at more tutus, rain boots with ladybugs all over them, books, and art supplies. As she opened, Jake brought me coffee and sat down beside me, an arm resting on the chair behind me. Finally, she finished.

Addie ran around, picking up her trash and putting it in the bag Jake had brought in to go out later. When she was done, she picked up the phone and gave Drew a big wink. Well, that was adorable. I hadn't seen her wink before. Must be a new trick. Knowing Drew, he taught her.

Addie crawled up on Jake's lap as he whistled to Chief. I noted that his lumbering walk was getting faster each week. I hoped the vet was correct that he'd be feeling like himself in no time. I felt horrible at the beginning when I'd watch him walk and he was clearly in pain. I'd already loved this dog, but I was now devoted to him.

Chief came straight to me and did what was now our

greeting after the accident. He'd plop his head in my lap, and I'd say the words I said every single day as I rubbed him down. Kissing the top of his head, I placed my hands on either side of his head. "I've never known a better dog, Chief Spencer, and I never will." Rubbing his head back and forth, I felt something stuck to his collar. Twisting it, I found a ribbon tied to a ring.

"What?" I looked at it, then felt movement.

Looking to my left, I saw that Jake and Addie had slid off their seat and now were both kneeling in front of me, Addie holding up Jake's phone with Drew, Sam, and Margot on it. Sam was holding up his phone where, I was guessing, Steph and Theo were watching. This family.

Tears. There was no stopping them.

I looked to Jake.

"Ivy, I know this might seem fast, but Addie and I had a talk."

I looked to Addie who nodded solemnly at me. I couldn't stop myself and kissed her head, then Jake's for good measure. Hell with it, I kissed Chief again too.

Jake leaned over, tugging the ribbon loose that was on Chief's collar. Holding the ring out to me, I gasped as I got my first look. It was a pink sapphire with diamonds on the side. Oh my goddess. I had no idea what the ring of my dreams was, but it looked like Jake did.

"As I said, Addie and I had a talk. And, it seems, she has some conditions for the two of us." He looked to Addie, and she nodded.

"You do, do you?" I asked my daughter through a wave of tears. Not shocked at all, but I couldn't wait to hear this.

Jake nodded. "Yep. I asked her after I found this picture that she'd colored and left on my fridge when you all were over a few weeks ago." He pulled out a picture from behind his back and I looked at it. There was clearly Jake's house. In front of it was three stick figures, one tall with black hair, one in the middle that was short with blond hair, and one last one at a medium height with blond hair. They were all holding hands. To the side was a brown dog. But that wasn't what caught my eyes. There was writing, which she'd been working on at Teri's. She had Teri spell things for her all the time so she could add to her illustrations. This one had our names: Chief, Momma, Addie, and Daddy 2. At the top of it, she'd written *my family*.

Oh my goodness.

I wiped away a tear, then another. "Daddy 2?"

Addie nodded very seriously. "I decided that was Jakey's name. I asked Daddy and he said that sounded good. Jakey said he loved it."

I met Jake's eyes, which were watering as well. "Did you?"

He nodded. "Pretty big fan of it, actually. So, what I was wondering was if you and Addie would be up for a name change too?"

Hell with this. I knelt down in front of him and Ads. "Hmm, a name change? I kind of like Ivy, though."

Addie spoke up. "No, silly. He means our last name. We can change it to Spencer."

"Just like that?" I tilted my head, looking at Addie. "We change our name?"

"Momma." She let out an exasperated breath. "If you marry Jakey and make him Daddy 2."

"Oh." I looked from Addie to Jake with a smile that hurt, it was so wide. "Is that what you want?"

His hands came to my hips, and he pulled me to him. "You know it is, babe. Will you marry me?"

I placed my hands on his shoulders. "What's in it for

me, caveman?"

He pretended to think about it for a minute. "Well, I'll be happy to debate the feminist movement with you anytime. I have a great yard for collecting moon water. You can plant as much as you want out there, my beautiful green witch. We can listen to Stapleton on repeat. And I'll buy you tampons anytime you need them, though I hope that isn't for a while."

I nodded at him, pretending to consider his offer when really, my heart was ready to burst. Finally, I pulled him to me. "You make a compelling argument, Jake Spencer. I'd love to marry you."

His mouth crashed to mine as I fell into his kiss. I could hear Addie cheering, and more cheering from the phone. It sounded like Margot might be crying, which would surprise no one.

Addie's voice pulled me out of the kiss. "Did you hear that Nana and Pop-Pop? We're going to be a family!"

Margot's cries were more audible as I looked over to the phone's screen to see Sam giving Addie a thumbs-up. "You bet we are, sweetheart. Donuts tomorrow for breakfast sound good?"

Addie began her shimmy as Drew laughed. "Dance party!" she cried.

Pulling back to scan my face, Jake's blue eyes twinkled. "So, we're getting married?"

I sighed, resting my head on his chest. "You're stuck with me, caveman."

His hand smoothed down my hair. "No place I'd rather be."

Addie wrapped her arms around us as Chief tried to nose in from the side. Yep, we were blessed beyond my wildest dreams.

ACKNOWLEDGMENTS

I've now written more books than I have children. Interesting. This book was easier and harder than the previous two. Jake and his siblings were easy to write. I got their relationship immediately because it reminded me like mine with my brother and sister - they give each other a whole lot of shit, but love each other unconditionally.

However, from the moment Addie met Chief, I could see a scene unfold in my head, but wasn't sure what the outcome would be. I'm being purposefully vague here incase you're a person who hasn't finished the book and I abhor spoilers. I finally wrote that scene sitting in a Panera during a pandemic while my youngest took the ACT at an unfamiliar high school down the street.

I sobbed. People stared. It was awkward. By the end of writing it, I knew I loved this book.

Thanks to the people who love me that have sent out support as I travel these unfamiliar roads. Thanks to readers who have flooded my inboxes and messages to tell me they love my characters and the small town I've created. And thanks to my students who can't read my books, but tell me each day they want to be writers too. That makes it all worth it.

All my love,

Kat

ABOUT THE AUTHOR

Kat Ryan is a middle school teacher by day and a budding romance author in the free time she steals for herself. She loves to write about small towns, found families, strong women, and cinnamon roll heroes that love them. She's a sucker for a HEA and more than a bit of steam in the stories she writes.

Kat lives in the Midwest with her husband and her two teenage sons where she consumes a steady diet of coffee, chocolate, and romance books. And while her students and sons plan to never read the books she writes, her husband has and continues to cheer her on.

Want more from Jake and Ivy? Subscribe to Kat's newsletter on her website, https://katryanwrites.com. All "extras" for each of Kat's book are linked in the newsletter that comes out every month.

Coming Home

Finding Beauty